NANO

THE GIFT
BOOK 1

MARC STAPLETON

Copyright © 2023 by Marc Stapleton

All rights reserved.

No part of this book may be reproduced in any form or by any electronic or mechanical means, including information storage and retrieval systems, without written permission from the author, except for the use of brief quotations in a book review.

Cover designed by Deranged Doctor Design

For my Wife

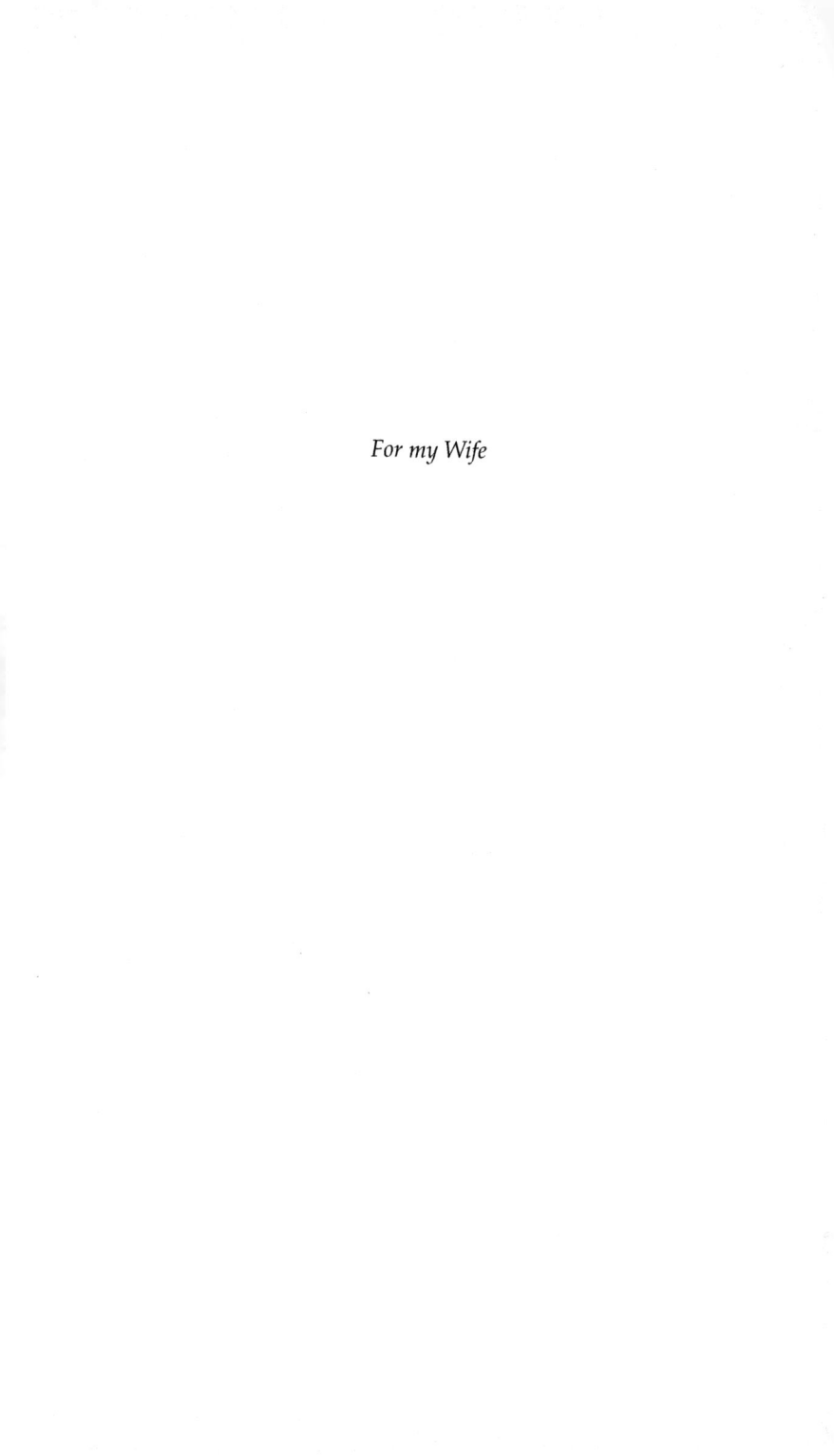

"The cemeteries of the world are full of indispensable men."

CHARLES DE GAULLE

CHAPTER 1

"God," I mumble under my breath, hopefully quietly enough that no-one heard me. It's 3:00 AM, the second of my three weekly shifts at the sandwich packing plant. A very careful process of taking sandwiches off a conveyor belt and placing them into plastic packaging, and then sealing the packaging.

At least careful would be the idea but in practice no one cares.

My manager shuffles along the conveyor belt, eyeing us tiredly. He's a 36-year-veteran of the conveyer belt and looks like a man weary of carrying the industry of sandwich packaging on his shoulders. He makes eye contact for a second before dragging his eyes away from mine.

Then I feel a chunk of something wet and slimy hit me on the cheek. I look across the belt to see one of my esteemed colleagues – Dave, or Carl, or Charlie, or whoever's name I never bothered to memorize in my two months here – grinning at me inanely. I look down to see a wet trail of egg-mayonnaise sitting on the belt. Great, now I'm getting food catapulted at me.

Another hour passes. I've almost forgotten about the egg

assault when a chunk of processed chicken lands on the lapel of my coat. I look up and there's that grin again. At least he's managed to figure out that the chicken will travel easier than the egg-mayo. Learning on the job.

"Hey, Pedro," I call to my manager. "Have you seen this?"

He looks over with those sunken, tired eyes and sees me brushing food from my lapel. He looks over at Dave or Carl or Charlie, and then shrugs at me before continuing his languid walk along the line. There he goes, another weak, beaten man. Too weary and tired to stand up for the very workers he's paid to manage. I shouldn't be surprised.

And yet I know I'm the weakest of the three of us. Why couldn't I reach across, grab the guy by his lapel, jam it into the conveyer belt, and watch him beg for his life? Because I don't dare. Because I need this job. Because I need any job. Because I have a heart condition. But mostly? Because it just isn't me.

And that's how I passed the remaining five hours of work: quietly seething and yet paralyzed by my own inability to do anything. And now, some 3000 sandwich packages later, it's time to go home.

The bus home is a numbing experience. The sun is just peeking out above the towers and apartment buildings on the horizon, blinding me with golden rays every couple of yards. It's the start of another beautiful day, and yet my own day is just ending. I like to think if I were lucky enough to have another job – one with sociable hours – I wouldn't wake up at 3:00 PM and stumble into bed at 7:00 AM; hell, I might even have a social life. But deep down, I know I'm kidding myself.

I unlock the door to our apartment, and like every morning my Dad is sitting there, hastily stubbing out a cigarette by the open window. He nods to me and goes back to the television in the corner of the room, burying himself in whatever sports show happens to be on. I used to get a welcome. Then I got a word. Now I just get a nod.

I don't dislike him, even though we're worlds apart. He's a lot like me. He was a steelworker for 20 years until an accident took away his ability to walk without a limp. Now he shambles around the apartment, smoking, and speaking Bible verses. When I can finally get him to speak, we do one of two things: pick a takeout or argue.

I leave him to ignite another cigarette and go to my room. I put some wildlife documentary on the lowest volume, wrap my head around a pillow, and fall asleep.

You know the immense powers bestowed on us by Jesus, the Lord, our Savior...

He plays this stuff way too loud. The tinny sound of my Dad's radio fills the air. Once, after my mother died, Dad fell into a deep depression. Then, he fell into what he considers a deep embrace from God. But in my eyes? He just plain fell.

I shake my head, rub my eyes, and look at my cellphone. My lockscreen still hasn't changed. It's been one month, but I still haven't changed the picture. Maybe it's laziness; maybe I've been too busy. Or maybe there's something else rattling around in my subconscious.

Jessica. Her face stares at me. I thumb it away and spend some time absent-mindedly browsing social media, trying to force her from my mind. And then I remember something that makes me bite my tongue in frustration. My stuff is still at hers and has been for the better part of a month. Why haven't I been and picked it up yet? Laziness, boredom, forgetfulness, etc.

I decide: I'll do it today.

"Uhh, yeah, it's me," I croak down the line to her voicemail inbox. "I'll be over later today to pick up my stuff. Let me know if that makes sense."

I sound stupid.

Waiting for me in the living room is Dad along with the sound of today's flavor of mega-preacher from who the hell knows where. I shamble over to the radio, turn it down, and earn a look of something between annoyance and surprise from him.

I try to time my run to the refrigerator so that I can grab something to eat and pace back to my room, but it's too late. He's already put his cigarette out and cleared his throat with a hacking cough.

"You know," he says, turning to face me. "I'm walking past the college today, why don't I pick up a brochure?"

"Sure," I reply, in the dullest tone I can muster before making my escape. I've just woken up and I don't want to fight. He's still on his Christian education kick – harboring ambitions that I'm going to find the light and become some mega-preacher – and I've just got to wait it out.

It's not that I don't believe in God. It's just the performance that I can't stand. The grasping and the flailing and the undying need to figure it all out. The need to absolve himself of guilt somehow or show me that he isn't just stumbling around in the dark; that he can guide my path too. But it's hopeless. He won't ever make sense of what happened to Mom. Neither of us will.

Anyway.

I spend some time wasting time. Videogames, TV, whatever. Really I'm just wiling away the hours until Jessica replies. Of course, an hour passes and she doesn't. So I decide to just go down there.

It's a brisk October afternoon; the sun has disappeared, the sky is a blank white coat above, and my skin breaks out in goosebumps. At the bus stop there's me, what I can only describe as a generic old man, and a skinny younger guy, shivering from the cold. Or just another dope fiend waiting for his next fix.

He turns to look around, and when I lock eyes with him, I

instinctively look away. Why do I do that? He's got a scar on the back of his shaven head. A bottle broken over his head in a fight? A scar from the surgery they forced him through to enable his release from the sanatorium for the criminally insane? I'm kidding. I think.

After 10 minutes an old lady joins the queue. And then another generic old man, this time bald. He's reading a newspaper, holding it high in the air with his arms splayed wide. You don't see that much. I can see the headlines and practically smell the black ink drifting off them:

BOMBING CAMPAIGN INJURES ANOTHER

Some lunatic with too much free time and no streaming TV subscription, renovating the city one bomb at a time. I don't even pay attention to that sort of thing anymore. Unless this guy had a traumatic run-in with a packaged sandwich, what do I have to fear?

The skinny guy turns around and looks at me again. What's his problem? I look down and feel his eyes burning a hole in the side of my head. I begin to feel something – a slow bubbling of panic deep within beneath my sternum. Is he eyeing me up? His next victim? He looks like he weighs 100 pounds soaking wet. But I don't like this. I don't like it at all.

The bus turns up at last and I watch as everyone gets on. Old man, old man, old woman, skinny guy. And then, without another thought, I bail. I walk, briskly at first, and then when I see the bus pass me I slow down. I feel a wave of something like embarrassment and relief pass through me. It's a regular occurrence.

At least I have an excuse. When I was a baby, I caught a virus. I forgot its name. I wasn't close to dying or anything, but they found something – a heart defect. A hole between the chambers of my heart. It was serious enough for my Dad to say he wouldn't have another child. And for my mother to let every PE teacher, summer camp instructor, best friend's parent, and scruffy-looking kid around the block to know I was a fragile little boy.

I spent my whole 24 years living like this: under the shadow of a heart attack that I may or may not have, that may or may not kill me.

And how does that play out? By me avoiding every provocation, confrontation, or conversation that begins to make me feel *the fear*. And today, that's me running from the skinny guy on the bus, and instead walking the three or four miles to Jessica's apartment.

You know, now that I consider it out-loud, I guess I over-reacted.

I cross the road, looking up and down the road for traffic, and then up and down the gutter for needles or broken glass. Any bit of trash that could rise up out of the skeleton of this city and stab me.

I'm so preoccupied I barely notice the giant billboard above me: the perfect family – mom, dad, brother, and sister, all smiling, perfectly wholesome – holding a can of soft drink, or soup, something else I clearly paid no attention to.

Dad's attitude – his advice to me and my fragile heart – was always *live every day like it'll be your last*, and then when my mother passed, it became *live every day for Jesus Christ*. I don't feel capable of doing either. *Some things are out of your control*, he'd say. And still says.

I'm about a mile into my walk when I succeed in getting that billboard out of my head, then someone passing me on the sidewalk breathes a lungful of smoke into my face and makes my mind instantly zero in on Dad again.

I take a turn off the road and head down an alley. I make it a few steps before I even realize that this probably isn't the safest of paths. I've walked it a hundred times before, but something's already caught my eye.

A strange, fleshy colored mound lying next to a dumpster below a fire escape staircase. The buildings around are derelict offices some five stories high, with broken windows and the occasional flicker of a bulb. There's no natural light here.

I take another two steps before I see red marks on the pavement beside him, and a mass of brown that I quickly worry is hair. Then I pause in my tracks. I feel that deep welling of trepidation again rising in the pit of my stomach. *The fear.*

I should turn back. Whatever *this* is, I want no part of it. Nine times out of 10 it'll be a shirtless drunk, passed out. I'll walk over there, call out to them, and they'll turn and slur obscenities at me, and I'll turn and get out of there. The circle of city life.

But, then...

What if I'm wrong?

With my near fatal encounter at the bus stop fresh in my mind – and the hot rush of embarrassment that brings – something stops me from my usual halt, turn, and run routine. This could be someone hurt. Someone in need of help. Any normal member of society would rush to their aid. Why the hell can't I?

I take a couple of tentative steps forward, and then a couple more. Already I can see red stains on the skin and rusty, dark brown puddles around them. They're facing the wall, curled up in the fetal position with their hands sat politely by his sides. I see he's male. His face is tucked up besides the wall, but I can see that his eyes are closed. My heart's beating. I call out:

"Hey, buddy."

But he doesn't move. There's no sound from him and no smell; just a motionless, completely conspicuous body lying in the alley. He almost looks like he fell from the fire escape above and landed neatly in the alleyway's embrace.

I take another couple of steps and think to take out my cellphone to call an ambulance. There's something else though. I feel an overwhelming urge to touch him – to rock him forward and back, and see if he really is sleeping or if he's, you know, *dead*.

I bend down at the waist and reach out. He's cold. But not just cold. He feels like he never ever had a degree of warmth in his body. I pull my hand away; my fingertip instinctively curls back to my palm, like I just touched a cube of ice. I hesitate for a moment, thinking what to do. This man is dead. Clearly. He's not moving and he's stone cold. He's *dead*.

I swallow and look around. The street seems so far away, and the windows around are broken, dark, and empty.

I make myself look at the body again and take a deep breath. Then, I fumble around in my pocket for my cellphone and get as far as the lockscreen – *that* lockscreen – before I feel the strangest sensation. Almost like a tickling feeling at the side of my right eye, then my left.

I wonder if this man is wearing some extravagant aftershave I'm allergic to before the real fun starts: a high-pitched tone, small in volume but increasing every moment.

Louder now.

Deafening.

I drop my cellphone and clasp my ears, and then…

Nothing.

CHAPTER 2

And then, light. Blinding light.

And the strange dances of darker shapes behind it and a voice accompanying them.

"Hello, Mr. Chambers? Hello?"

There's a hand raking itself across my face. It takes me a moment to realize that it's mine. I blink a couple more times, and then I finally regain that sense of self-consciousness I've been missing.

"Huh?" is all I can say.

"You're in the hospital Mr. Chambers."

I pull my fingers across my face again, and slowly start to discern the nurse's face in front of me. She's pretty, if a little tired. Her eyes are small and buffeted by deep purple circles.

"Why am I…" I trail off as I start to recall the bus, the walk, the alley, and the…

"You were found with another gentleman, and uhm, you both made it here to us."

"Another gentleman," I repeated gormlessly, remembering *him*. "Is he, uhh…"

I can't find it within myself to complete the sentence.

Instead, I avert my eyes from the nurse's and go back to my memories. I passed out. I dropped my phone and passed out.

"I'm afraid the man you were brought in with is dead."

This isn't exactly news to me. Instead, I'm beset by dread. The day I've been waiting for, the day when my heart finally gives way. Is this that day?

"Did I have a heart attack?" I bark at her. She blinks, and her expression hardens. I see I took her by surprise. Maybe she expected me to display more concern for my friend in the alley. She doesn't know that we'd only just met, so to speak.

"The doctor will be here to see you in 10 minutes or so. Just try to remain calm and comfortable until then."

I feel that panic again; my heart is oddly slow. No rapid heartbeat, no palpitations. Surely these are the symptoms of the afterburn of a heart attack? Or a consequence of the massive amounts of drugs with incomprehensible names they've undoubtedly pumped me with?

I look down my arm to look for any intravenous leads but find it unexpectedly empty. And then the other arm, also empty. Strange.

The nurse leaves with a labored smile, and I spend a nerve-wracking 10 minutes alone, my thoughts rattling around inside my head. I try to imagine telling my Dad I've had *the heart attack*, and then I try to imagine the ways I can tell him I'm not interested in the word of Jesus Christ right now.

"Hello, Mr. Chambers. Kris, yes?"

The doctor has arrived. He's a small, wiry man with a smart blue dress shirt and an impeccable tie. Depressingly, he looks only five years older than me.

"Yes."

"Okay, cool." *Cool*? A strange choice of word for a doctor to say. Especially a doctor with bad news to deliver. He seems nervous, his eyes can't seem to look at me directly; they're almost looking through me.

"So I suppose you've been told already about the man we found you with." There's a strange accusatory tone in his voice, like he thinks that man and I were up to something decidedly *un*cool in the alley.

"Yes, I know," I say, and he furrows his brow. "How severe was my heart attack?"

"Pardon?" he says, and strokes his chin.

"My heart, I—" He immediately cuts me off.

"Mr. Chambers, you didn't have a heart attack."

I can't believe it; a rush of relief runs through me, followed by an inevitable rush of something like panic. If I didn't have a heart attack, then why did I pass out?

"So what happened to me?"

"Well, you were brought to us unconscious; breathing and seemingly healthy, but in a deep sleep of sorts. We had assumed you were respiratory depression due to opioids or other such drugs, but…" he fiddles with his tie a little. "The tests we ran proved that was not the case."

I sit upright in the bed. It's taken me this long to realize that I feel fine. I feel better than fine; no aches, no pains, no problems.

"In fact, we're quite happy that you've woken up as there did appear to be nothing wrong with you."

"What time is it?" I ask, looking around the room and seeing there are no windows and no clock. In fact, it's suspiciously empty in here. Blank white walls, a very dull-looking cabinet, and a bare light bulb.

"It's 9:00 PM. You've been unconscious in our care for roughly four hours."

My apparently unperturbed heart jumps again; four hours!?

"Look, I was walking in the alley and I found the man, the naked man," saying it out loud makes me appreciate how ludicrous it all sounds. "And then I just passed out. I'm just thankful I didn't have a heart attack. You see, I have a heart condition, and..."

"Mr. Chambers," He cuts me off. "We did an ECG on you when you arrived. Your heart is perfectly healthy. Like brand new."

I can't believe it. They must have missed it. I've had a consistent murmur since childhood. *I'm sure of it.* I sit there, bolt upright, in silence with my eyes darting around between the blank corners of the room and the doctor's too-perfect tie. He must sense that I'm stuck for words, because he strokes his Adam's apple and speaks:

"There are some gentlemen who wish to talk to you." The tone of his voice changes gravely. That sounded ominous. "We'll be wanting to run a couple more tests, if that's all right with you, but for now I have to let the detectives speak to you."

Detectives. I'm so caught up in my own melodrama I keep forgetting that they found me passed out next to a dead body. *Of course the detectives want to speak to me.* All of a sudden this blank, empty room looks like a prison cell. I nod to the doctor, and he smiles awkwardly before turning and leaving. Before the door can slam shut a couple of men walk in.

"Sir," the taller one says, somewhat ironically. He's 40-something with a neat shirt underneath a blue sweater. His colleague is younger with stubble. They both look annoyed to be here. The younger one immediately begins scanning the room, undoubtedly noticing the distinct lack of windows, or anything else for that matter. "I hope you're feeling better."

"Yes, uhm, I guess." I don't exactly sound convincing.

"Good." He sits at the foot of the bed, somewhat invading my personal space. If he's looking to make me feel uneasy, he's succeeding. His younger colleague stands by his side, still looking around the room. "I'm Detective Clarke, this is Detective Ramos, and I assume you've been told about the circumstances that brought you here."

Strange way to put it.

"Yes."

"Well, first of all, I'd like to offer my condolences."

"I, uhh…" I pause, trying to think of the most adequate way of saying it was my first time meeting the dead naked man. "I didn't know the man. I was walking to my, uhh…"

I trail off, unwilling to hear myself utter the *ex-g* word.

"I was walking to someone's house, and I went down the alley, and I found him there."

"Right," he says, and his colleague very quickly grabs a notepad from his pocket and begins scrawling things in it.

"And my first reaction was to help him, call an ambulance, that sort of thing." I suddenly wonder if lying to a detective is a crime. "But then I passed out, blacked out, whatever. And then I woke up here."

"Right," the elder detective repeats dispassionately. "And you didn't recognize him at all?"

"I've never met him" I reply. "I couldn't see his face too clearly, but I—"

"Right," he barks again. "Well I can see you're not drunk, and we're told you weren't suffering an overdose or on drugs or anything like that. We have no reason to disbelieve you."

"Okay," I say, somewhat nervously. His colleague reaches into his pocket again and takes out a picture. A Polaroid, probably snapped at the morgue. He holds the picture within my vision and I can finally see the man's face clearly. "No, I don't recognize him at all."

"Have you blacked out for several hours before Mr. Chambers?" I shake my head. "Do you suffer from epilepsy or any similar conditions? Fugue states? Psychological concerns? Do you or have you abused drugs or alcohol in the past?"

I've been shaking my head from side to side for this entire dialogue. Finally, after a moment of pause, he exhales deeply, and gets to his feet. Then he reaches into his own pocket and retrieves a broken, sorry-looking cellphone. My cellphone. As he does so, he snags a button and the lockscreen pops up. Jessica behind a cobweb of broken glass.

"We found this, I assume it's yours."

"Thanks," I say, timidly reaching out for it.

"Thank you for your time Kris. If you remember anything else about your afternoon, please let me know. Detective Clarke." I put down my phone so that I can shake his hand, but somewhere, somehow, a strange, disembodied voice seems to call out to me.

Kris.

"What?" I say, looking at the elder detective, and then his younger colleague. The younger one raises an eyebrow, and says:

"I didn't say anything."

With a look of confusion, the elder man smiles at me, points to the door, and turns towards it.

"We must go. Hope you feel better soon Mr. Chambers."

They both make for the exit. The elder man first, and then his younger colleague, with him taking one last opportunity to scan the room for some reason. I've one more question, something which will bug me forever until I find out for sure.

"How did he die?" I ask, my voice quivering a little.

The younger man turns around before making it out of the door, and speaks without pausing his departure:

"We were hoping you'd tell us. Get well soon Mr. Chambers"

And with that, the door shuts behind them and I'm alone in this blank, sterile room again. I feel deflated. That was my first time speaking to a real, live detective, and I feel like I flunked the test. But still, other than hiding the fact I wanted to run as soon as I saw the body, I couldn't have been any more honest.

It isn't my fault this dead, naked man means nothing more to me than a magical item that when you touch it, it transports you to the hospital. Should I have displayed more concern? I've just been reeling from the distress of thinking my heart had given way. And then reeling from the relief of being told it hadn't.

Yeah, my heart, apparently working just fine. Huh.

Kris.

There it is again! The same strange voice, emanating from somewhere in this characterless, empty room. I look behind me, I search every corner. I leap off the bed and look underneath it. There's nothing.

I walk over to the cabinet and try to open it, but it's locked. But still, there surely can't be anyone lurking inside. Can there? For the second time today I come out in goosebumps. Someone seems to be beckoning me by name, but I can't be sure it isn't just all in my head.

Uneasily, I get back into the bed, realizing only now that I'm wearing a hospital gown and my clothes are nowhere to be seen. I look around me, noting a button on the frame of the bed close to the head. I press it once, wait anxiously, and then jam it another thousand or so times.

After a couple of minutes of me nervously eyeing the cabinet, a nurse bounds in with a cheery grin and an armful of my clothes from earlier. She tells me about some more tests they want to run, and says a bunch of other small talk that I can hardly pay attention to. But there's only one thing on my mind.

"Excuse me," I say politely, lulling her into a false sense of security before I hit her with an insane line of questioning. "But is there anyone in that cabinet?"

She looks confused, dazed even, and turns around to look at the cabinet. Before turning back to me, laughing and shaking her head. Back to the cheery grin now. I feel ridiculous.

"I just, heard a voice, is all."

She's already on her way out of the room when she

answers, "This place is teeming with doctors, nurses, patients. There's a busy corridor right out here. You're lucky to have your own room!" She looks around before opening the door, taking in the sparse surroundings, and maybe regretting her enthusiasm on that last point. "See you soon."

And with that she's gone.

CHAPTER 3

The remaining tests are too dull to mention. A couple of blood tests, a concussion test, and I'm done. I'm told to wait for both the results and a giant bill, which I already know I have no way of paying. It looks like I'll be packaging sandwiches for the rest of my goddamn life. And even worse than that, no-one can tell me what the hell happened to me.

But more than anything, I'm relieved I didn't have a heart attack. Hell, maybe my heart has improved over the years? Maybe I don't have the murmur? Or the threat of dropping dead in a single moment; that one big cardiac arrest that I've always waited for, always feared. Maybe it no longer exists?

Or maybe the doctors were wrong.

I get out of the hospital – a place I know sadly too well from years of tests in my childhood – and quickly work out the best route home. It's 10:00 PM or so, but rather than subject myself to the night bus and the murderer's row of weirdos and outcasts on it, I think I'd rather walk home.

I feel good.

Hell, I feel *great*. I can feel my heart beating – pushing blood to every cell in my body – and for the first time in my life it doesn't feel like one, great mechanical liability in my chest. I've always come to dread the sound of the thumping of my heartbeat in my ears, but tonight it feels more a part of me than ever.

I accelerate my walking pace, even looking around me; I feel closer to the world than ever before. The dazzling lights of neon store signs, the ever-moving glow of car headlights in the street, and the perpetual humming of industry and engines piecing it all together. At last I feel like my eyes are open.

Before I know it I'm in the park. Uneven grass and a neatly tarmacked path lit by the occasional orange circle on the floor, with the remainder bathed in darkness. It's only a brisk 10-minute walk to get to the other side, but I soon realize I wouldn't normally dare walk this route, this late, in one of my usual moods.

I barely even notice the gang of four or five hoodlums gathered on the grass 30 meters or so ahead of me, laughing and joking, illuminated only by a couple of cellphone screens.

Kris.

When I hear it, I freeze in my tracks. I look to the sides of me and behind me.

"Who's there?"

I check my cellphone with its haunting, cobwebbed vision of *her*, just to ensure I didn't dial someone by accident. The voice is the same as before – disembodied, clear, loud. Like a broadcast, directed solely to my ears.

"What did you say?" comes a voice from ahead of me. I look forward again to see the four or five guys slowly approaching me. They're wearing hoodies and jeans slung low around their waists. One of them is grinning unnervingly. Suddenly, I feel like I'm submerged in boiling water. My heart begins to beat. I can feel the fear again.

"I, uhhh," I pause, stopping myself from telling them that

I'm hearing voices, although maybe pleading insanity would be my best way out of this mess.

"Yo man, you got a phone I can borrow?" asks the grinning one. His four buddies – I quickly count them – flank him to the left and right. Before I can work out a way to extract myself from this, the five of them are right in front of me. "I need to call someone."

"Well, I, uhh," I'm not stupid enough to think I'm ever going to get my cell back. At least it's already damaged goods. I rummage in my pocket once again and consider my options.

Do I hand it over and run the way I came? Or will they just chase me, beat the snot out of me, and take my wallet too? After hesitating, I hold it out for the grinning goon to take from me.

Fight.

The voice startles me, and I immediately, instinctively retract my hand back into my chest. What the hell is going on here?

"Hey bro, why you playin'?"

He reaches out to grab my wrist with one hand and I see him readying a punch with the other. He tugs forcefully at my wrist, but to my surprise more than anybody else's, my wrist doesn't budge. This man seems way too weak to be mugging strangers in parks.

He launches a fist at my face, and like I'm possessed by some energetic spirit I dodge it crisply, my wrist wrenching away from his grasp. All I can think of is that voice echoing in the corridors of my mind: *fight*.

I see one of his buddies swing something in the corner of my eye. I go to intercept, closing my fingers around it in mid-swing. Only after I seize it in mid-air do I see that it's a beer bottle. Huh.

Every blood vessel in my body is surging; in my stomach is a knot of pure, boundless energy, just waiting to explode if only I knew how. I look up and see the goon's face turns from that murderous grin to something like fear. He backs away, and his buddy lets go of the beer bottle before doing the same.

"Hey, fine, bro, you keep it," he says, and I'm unsure of whether he means my cell phone or his beer. With that, they carefully step past me, and walk briskly the way I came. I look backwards to see them sheepishly doing the same thing.

Here I stand, frozen in time, my cellphone in one hand, a full bottle of beer in the other, wondering what the hell just happened to me; that same, ominous word – *fight* – still ringing in my ears. I've never been in a fight before. If you can even call that a fight. I'd never in a million years expect it to be so… *easy*.

After hesitating for a moment, I say it again: "Who's there?"

I wait, not exactly anticipating a response. And then I get one:

Kris, you should find somewhere to sit and open that beer.

I swallow hard. That tight knot of energy in my stomach gives way to fear again. I do as the voice tells me, walking along the path until I find a bench, illuminated in the orange glow of a lamppost overhead. There I sit down and contemplate whether I've truly, definitively lost my damn mind.

Open it.

I look around before understanding that the voice in my head means the beer.

"How? I don't have a bottle opener."

Use your index finger and thumb.

This is absurd. I can't possibly twist the bottle cap off a bottle of beer with only two fingers. How many schizophrenic episodes start with the voices telling you to perform superhuman feats of strength?

Still though, something deep in the back of my mind –

buoyed by my beating, excited heart and the memory of that word 'fight' – compels me to try it.

I hold the bottle in one hand, and with the other grip the cap between my thumb and my index finger. Bracing myself against the pain I'm sure I'll feel, I grip it tighter and slowly twist the cap off in one movement.

The satisfying, high-pitched sound of the carbon dioxide escaping greets me, as does a rush of shock and surprise. No pain, no effort, no problem.

"Who are you?" I ask again, gripping the bottle firmly and forgetting how to drink.

You could call me a traveler, although that isn't strictly accurate. You could say I'm the consciousness of the dead man you found, although that isn't totally true either.

Dazed, I finally take a swig from the bottle.

The man you found was a traveler from a far away place. When you reached out and touched him, he gave you something. A gift, so to speak.

Somehow, sitting alone in the night, drinking from an open container of alcohol seems entirely appropriate for this kind of situation.

His body was host to a certain technology. That technology has transferred to you. I am an artificial general intelligence that governs the technology. An approximation of that man's consciousness, now severed from his mind and implanted within yours.

"I can't believe what I'm hearing", I say out loud before taking another mouthful of beer.

It is all true.

"No, I mean, I literally cannot believe it. I'm mentally ill, or I'm dreaming, or I'm stuck in some coma." The words leave me breathless.

I can assure you that you are not dreaming.

"So you can read my mind? Hear my thoughts?"

No. The nanomachines inhabit every part of your body, but they can't insert themselves into your brain's synapses. Your thoughts are your own.

"The nanomachines!?" I'd heard the term before. Something scoured from the internet, buried within my memory.

Yes. A network of trillions of tiny nanoid robots, linked by an electromagnetic field, able to communicate with each other, assume different roles, and serve different functions based on your needs. They're able to more efficiently stimulate your muscles and ligaments, augmenting your strength and speed. They're able to interpret your nerve signals, enhancing your vision and other senses, as well as your reflexes. And they're able to repair damage to your body and damage to themselves. In simple terms, you have an army of robots within you.

"Damage to my body?" I feel my heart beating again, an ever-present reminder of this day's absurdities. "So, my heart?"

Yes. When the nanomachines migrated to your body, they shut down your nervous system to an extent, resulting in your unconsciousness. It was necessary to begin the installation. At that time, they got to work repairing the instruments of your body that were deemed sub-optimal. Your heart was the first priority.

I open my mouth to speak, and yet nothing comes out. A lifetime dominated by the fear of the oncoming heart attack. And now that possibility seemingly erased, wiped clean by a dead naked man and a horde of mini-robots allegedly swarming around my body.

The nanomachines monitor every vital sign in your body. Your heartrate, your VO_2 max, your blood pressure, and countless more. The nanomachines bolster and administer the enzymes your liver produces and seek to combat and convert the unhelpful molecules within your body. For example, that beer you are drinking won't ever intoxicate you. The alcohol is quickly converted into other inert compounds.

I look at the quickly diminishing liquid sloshing around

within the brown bottle, appearing almost golden under the light. Slowly, I put the bottle down on the path.

"How can you repair my heart? I've had a condition for years."

The nanomachines are able to manipulate your organs on the cellular level. They're able to move, destroy, or recreate cells of any sort within your body. The structural problem with your heart was able to be repaired in this manner. The same goes for any other injury. Your rib had a hairline fracture, as did one of your toes. These fractures were patched up by the nanomachines. Your body is like new. It wouldn't be an exaggeration to call you the healthiest human being alive right now.

I look down at my hands, and see the same skin, fingers, and wrinkles in my palm I've looked at for 24 years.

"And you? You're part of the machines?"

Yes and no. The nanomachines share a gestalt consciousness – a shared mind – of which I am the voice, so to speak. When the previous host of this technology first used it, they worked to create a copy of his consciousness – his personality, his voice – and enlisted that copy of his consciousness to manage the nanomachines. I am that consciousness. In some small fashion, I am the man you found in the alleyway. Or at least I am an artificial intelligence-created version of his personality.

"So you know who he was?"

I know he came from a place far away here, but I have no access to his thoughts or memories. Just as I have no access to yours.

Again, I'm speechless. I think I'm out of questions, at least for now. For the briefest second, I try to picture my blood vessels – like how they were always pictured in textbooks at school – only now teeming with robots. The thought makes me shiver.

I know this is a lot to take in, Kris. The voice in my head calling me by my name is another unsettling touch. *Why don't you test yourself and see what I'm talking about. Go for a run.*

"A run? It's like 11:00 at night!" I say it and then quickly think that none of this is remotely ordinary. A run might be the sanest thing about my night. "And I was never a runner to begin with."

But you know how. I think you'll find it easier than ever before.

Compelled by sheer curiosity, I stand up and begin jogging. I've never jogged before, other than to catch a bus or train. All those gym classes spent doing track and field, or cross-country running, I'd spend on the sidelines awkwardly watching on owing to my heart defect.

Now, I'm choosing to do it, spurred on by the ghost of a man I found dead in an alley.

I slowly increase my pace until I'm at a very brisk jog, almost a run. I feel the blood coursing through my veins, my heart beating purposefully, and yet I'm far from breathless. Whereas I could barely climb four flights of stairs without doubling over to catch my breath in an earlier life, now it seems I can jog the length of the park without troubling my lungs in the slightest.

I pick it up into a run and then a sustained sprint. Soon I'm out of the park and sprinting down the street, zipping past cars stuck in traffic and bemused pedestrians. The wind is whistling through my hair and I can feel sweat beginning to form on my brow.

Every smart-ass jock at high school pointing and laughing at the kid in the stands who couldn't run. Every gym teacher who didn't bother learning my name. Every mortifying moment I had to explain I couldn't do *this* or shouldn't do *that*. I feel like I'm leaving it all behind.

All of those memories, all of that pain; it seems laughable now.

I slow myself to a stop, and for the first time, after sprinting for several blocks I need to catch my breath. I take a couple of deep breaths and wipe the sweat off my forehead with the back of my hand. My thighs and calves burn, and my chest shudders as I fill it with air and exhale deeply.

How did that feel?

"Great, that felt great!" I stand upright again, realizing my breathing has already slowed to something close to normal. My thighs and calves feel ready to go another round, and my biggest concern is where the hell I am.

You ran approximately two kilometers in five minutes.

"Two – what!?"

I look around. I'm way past the hospital. In fact, I'm closer to home than I thought. I take out my cell to take the time, and once more I see that lockscreen and that face. It's 10:30 PM and suddenly I remember the entire reason I left the house today. I need my stuff from Jessica's.

I know I should forget about it. Leave it until tomorrow. But, I feel like the fastest man on planet Earth right now. Someone needs to see me like this. Who better than my ex? Her apartment is a mile or so from here. I bet I can make that in four minutes, easy.

I turn on my heels, and with another sharp intake of breath begin to run again. Zooming past shifty-looking guys and scantily clad women selling God knows what. Yesterday I'd have been terrified to be alone in this neighborhood at this time of night. That was another day. What feels like another life.

You can keep up this level of athletic performance for an extended period of time. But you're not a perpetual motion machine. You are mostly still flesh and blood.

"Yeah, I get that," I pant, increasing my pace. I'm attracting glances and scowls from people on the streets. People wondering and worrying why a guy in a long-sleeved shirt and jeans would be full-pelt running through the streets at this time. And the best part? Even if I told them they wouldn't believe me.

Finally I reach her building and pause to regain my breath. I'm six hours or so late, but after the day I've had, I'm sure that can be excused. I look at the entrance – a drab door with a broken pane of glass. Inside there is a foyer, with an elevator that'll no doubt be out of service.

"So, can I climb?"

The nanomachines can regulate your balance and supplement the strength and grip you need to climb.

I move before the voice even finishes speaking. There's a drainpipe, looking fairly sturdy, positioned next to the building by a window and leading right up to the third floor. And I can already see the window is open.

The drainpipe? The voice inside my head asks, and for the first time I pick up on his weary tone. I ignore it. I set my foot onto a bracket affixing it to a wall, and using the window ledge shimmy up the drainpipe, one floor and then another.

By the time I reach the third floor, I let go of one of the brackets, and pull myself up one handed – an actual one handed pull-up. I can't even believe it. I feel the blood rushing to my lat muscle in my back, and then I'm perched on the window sill uneasily. With a steady hand, I pry the window open a little more and slip through.

"Why not?" I finally ask the voice in my head. "The elevator is always out. At least, it was a month ago."

Where are you? the voice asks.

"My ex-girlfriend's flat," I say, sheepishly noting how crazy I sound.

CHAPTER 4

What are you doing at your ex-girlfriend's flat? the voice asks me, completely deadpan. The wearied voice makes me question myself again. And scaling the drainpipe doesn't look entirely legitimate. So far, my relationship with this voice has been one of quaint tech support. I hadn't anticipated him to be questioning my motives.

"I just need to get my stuff. That's what I was doing today when I found the, you know..." For some reason I feel the need to moderate my language. Does an AI version of a dead man's personality grieve for the body it has lost? "It's late, but I told myself I was gonna do this."

I walk down the corridor, florescent lights flickering above. The paint is flaking off the walls and there's a certain damp smell. The building is a dump, that's for sure. But she doesn't have a Bible-obsessed elderly parent living with her, so she's already miles ahead of me in the race to have a passable home.

I make it to her door and with a moment's hesitation knock on it. After some muted shuffling from inside, a lock unlatches and the door opens.

"Kris, what the hell are you doing here? It's almost 11."

She's standing in the doorway in a T-shirt and shorts. I haven't seen her for a month or so. We didn't exactly part on glowing terms, and I can feel warmth spreading to my face.

"Sorry, I came to get my stuff. I've been in the hospital today, and…" her annoyed look turns to something between sympathy and confusion. "…and I just wanted to get my stuff. If that's okay."

I'm repeating myself, panicking. I may be able to run a sub-four-minute mile, but I still can't talk with any semblance of confidence or authority.

"Hospital? What happened?" She looks over my face and sees the sweat leaking from my forehead. "You're sweating."

"Yeah, can I come in?"

That look of sympathy and confusion turns to annoyance again.

"I'll go get your stuff. Wait here." And with that, she closes the door in my face and I hear her moving around in the apartment again. Okay, so I didn't handle that too well.

Jessica and I were a thing for five or six months. Eventually she got tired of my night shifts, my chain-smoking Bible-quoting dad, and my general lack of enthusiasm to do anything or go anywhere.

I can't say I took it too well. She was the first real girlfriend I'd had, and I didn't want to lose her. When I could tell she was acting differently – like the end was nigh – I did something stupid.

"Hey man," a nasally voice calls out. I turn my head to see her next-door neighbor – a man probably in his thirties with a thick head of hair and a prying attitude – looking at me, fiddling with his cellphone with both hands. "What's going on?"

"Sorry, I know it's late," I say to him, trying to mask my annoyance. I'd met him before; a pathetic curtain-twitcher who was always way too invested in mine and Jessica's relationship, and way too invested in her, probably. "I'm just talking to Jessica, picking up some stuff."

He doesn't respond and Jessica opens her door again with a box in both arms, and on top of that a smaller box that makes my eyes want to screw themselves shut.

Ah yes – my stupid mistake. After I got the feeling she was going to dump me I went to DEFCON 1 and got down on one knee. I proposed. Playing it out in my memory makes me feel sick with embarrassment. So stupid.

"Thanks," I say, as she hurriedly unloads the boxes into my waiting hands. "You won't believe what happened to me today…"

"What's wrong? Did you take something?" She crosses her arms, standing like a bouncer blocking a doorway.

"Take something!?" I feel a bead of sweat drip off my brow. Somewhere between sprinting around all night, climbing the drainpipe, and remembering my godawful proposal I've become flustered. Red-faced. Crazed-looking.

"Yeah, like, drugs."

If only she knew. I try to think of something to say but my jaw hangs low and my eyes narrow. Even if I wanted to tell her about the body, the voice, the nanomachines, she'd think I was crazy.

"Jessica, is he bothering you?" the neighbor asks.

That nasally voice again. I see him tentatively approaching in the corner of my eye, holding something in front of him. When I turn my head, I can see its his cellphone pointed right at me. He's recording me, no doubt.

"Look, buddy," I can't remember his name. "I'll be gone in a minute."

"Kris, you should leave, it's late. If you have anything to say to me, text me," Jessica says in an irritated tone.

That guy is still slowly walking towards me. I feel anger welling up inside me; my fingers dig into the box. I snort a lungful of breath in from my nose and out through my mouth. I hear the wooden box crack – I still don't know my own strength – and I drop it.

"You know," I reach out and grab his cell. He tries to pull it back to his body, but he's no match for me. "You don't have to record me."

I pause for a moment, thinking of all the confrontations of the previous years I'd avoided. Every street crossed to avoid someone I didn't like the look of. Every gym jock who mocked me at high school. The coworker who flung food at me yesterday. I've been backing down from a fight my entire life.

I grip the cellphone – a sleek, black, thin smartphone – and crush it within my fingers, squeezing my thumb into its middle, and letting the two fingers on each side break it in two. Then I drop it to the ground. He pulls his hand away, his eyes turning from smugness to terror.

"Kris, what the hell!" I hear her shout. "Go before I call the police!"

And with that, the door slams and she's gone. The man is stuttering something, his nasal voice breaking on each vowel as he walks backwards to his flat. I catch the words "police" and "weirdo" before he's slammed his door too. Jesus, what did I do?

I look down at the box, split, with a couple of my old clothes already spilling out. I leave it – along with the ring box – and make for the elevator. I should sell that ring, but it makes me sick to look at it. I can't bear to even be in the same room as it. One big, shiny testament to my stupidity. *My weakness.*

You appear to be leaving your belongings, the voice in my head tells me matter-of-factly.

"Yeah, I guess I am."

I take the elevator – working, unbelievably – and sullenly walk out of the building.

"Why me?" I ask out loud, arousing the glances of a

couple of homeless people. I start to walk down the block. "I mean, why did these nanomachines choose me? Why not anyone else? One of the paramedics or some genius surgeon at the hospital?"

The nanomachines were programmed to install themselves onto the first human they came into physical contact with. You were that human.

I'd never noticed before, but the voice sounds tired; world-weary almost. I've been talking to the machines for more than an hour now, and I've barely stopped to ask how they got here, or how they *feel*. I wonder if they think I'm selfish, and then I wonder if I'm deluded to assume they have feelings at all.

"And the dead man? Where did he come from?" I'm strolling down the block at night, muttering to myself. Hardly a unique occurrence around these parts, I suppose. "How did he die?"

The man – the nanomachines' previous host – was a traveler. I suppose you could call him a mercenary soldier of sorts. He came from a period of human history far more advanced than this, although I can't tell you exactly when. He died from catastrophic organ failure that even the advanced network of nanites was unable to correct in time. I do not know the exact cause of death. I can only assume he did not survive transit.

"Transit?" I say, affecting the voice's weariness. "What does that mean? You sound like you're talking about time travel."

Of sorts, yes. As I had no access to the previous host's memories, I can't tell you exactly what method of travel was undertaken, but it does seem clear to me that first he was in a world of technology far more advanced than your own, and then after a period of travel he was not.

I'm still walking, but blindly and directionless, trying to process everything I'm hearing. A mercenary? Time travel? Another world? I set out this afternoon to walk to my ex-girlfriend's flat; I didn't expect to wake up in hospital and get caught up in some live action sci-fi novel. Hell, I wasn't even interested in watching the latest *Star Wars* film.

"And why did he come here?" I finally ask; a question I should have probably asked in the first place.

I do not have access to that information. It's logical to assume that he had a mission of sorts, but that mission now seems compromised.

I finally stop walking and look around; this is close to where my mother is buried. The dilapidated church and the rail tracks suspended above the road, with the cacophonous rattle of trains every 15 minutes or so, even at this time of night. I begin walking in the direction of home, and finally ask the question that's been on my mind: "Are you sad? For your previous host, I mean. If you're a copy of his personality, then surely you miss him?"

I suppose you could say that. I didn't really know him beyond inhabiting his body. The time before the period of transit is unclear to me, perhaps because of the extreme processes necessary to travel in that manner. But, I suppose you can say I'm happy to be alive.

Here we both are – a doughy, deadbeat kid with no prospects and a super-advanced AI network of nanomachines, linked together by the dead man neither of us feel we knew. Funny old world.

"And one other thing," I say, remembering something I should have asked an hour ago. "What do I call you? If you're going to be a permanent fixture inside my head, we should probably be on first name terms."

The traveler's name was Vega. I suppose it would be logical to assume that's my name too.

Vega. The name of the network of trillions of tiny robots inhabiting my body and manipulating my ear drum to speak to me is named Vega. How about that?

I'm soon home again, pushing past the building door and waiting for the elevator.

"How about sleep, do I still need to sleep?"

The biological processes your brain undertakes during healthy sleep can't be replicated by the nanomachines. Memory processing, synaptic rejuvenation, and mood regulation are functions that sleep and sleep alone can fulfil.

I guess I'm not perfect.

It's past midnight by the time I get home. I slowly, quietly unlock the door – trying to avoid a difficult conversation with my Dad, rather than being concerned about waking him – and enter the apartment.

The smell of stale cigarettes hits me immediately. He didn't smoke his first cigarette until mother died. Now, he's speedrunning his ascent to heaven I guess.

I slip into my room, and to my surprise find myself falling into a deep sleep as soon as I hit the bed, clothes and all.

CHAPTER 5

I wake suddenly from a dream. Visions of being back at high school, knowing I should go to class, but fearing the unknown. Like I had six years of calculus to catch up on, and that I didn't remember who my Lit teacher was anymore. In the end, a wave of relief washes over me that I don't have to be there anymore.

And then I quickly remember the previous day's adventures.

"Vega," I say, slightly louder than I probably should. Is this my way of pinching myself to ensure I'm not still dreaming? To assure myself that yesterday wasn't just the fantasy of a broken mind?

Yes?

The golden light – from a sun I usually only see on my way home from work – bathes my room in its glow. It must be early in the morning. I haven't slept a regular schedule since high school. It's Monday, which means I have work later tonight. Hah, *work*.

"I don't want to go to work today," I tell Vega. A super-advanced AI consisting of trillions of tiny robots, catapulted here from wondrous unknown worlds, is having to listen to me whine about the fact I don't want to work today. Talk about slumming it.

Perhaps you can find a greater calling, Vega replies.

I sit up in my bed. The grand sum of Herculean acts I've performed since discovering I had this gift amounts to stealing a beer and breaking some creep's smartphone into two pieces, along with a dozen miles of running like a headless chicken. Surely I can do better.

I sneak out of my room, grab a shower, and get dressed quietly. If I couldn't explain what happened to me to Jessica, I stand no chance with my Dad.

I try to shuffle my way out of the apartment without arousing too much attention, but he's already sat there by the window, hastily putting out his cigarette from behind his newspaper. Too hopelessly addicted to quit; too ready to feign concern for me and my heart to smoke in front of me. That's the routine we've lived under for years now.

"You're up early," he says, looking up from his paper. I can tell this lone bomber in the news has caught his attention.

I grunt in acknowledgement and grab a bar of chocolate from the cupboard, intending to inhale the whole thing outside.

"Jessica left you a message on the answer machine," he says just as I'm about to leave, making me freeze awkwardly in my tracks. "What were you doing there last night?"

"I just went to get my things," I tell him, leaving a very conspicuous eight-hour gap in yesterday that I'm sure he can't ignore. To my surprise, he slowly retreats back behind his newspaper. "She was no good for you anyway."

Something about his tone makes me tense up with anger. My Dad – who has sat in this apartment perpetually smoking for years, not bothering to maintain a friendship with anyone but Jesus Christ – now thinks he can hand out relationship advice.

"What the hell do you know?" I say to him, barely

managing to spit the words out in the right order. "Why do you think she left me? Anything to do with the fact I'm a boring, stay-at-home, sandwich packaging monkey? With a Dad who reads the papers every day looking for the first signs of the apocalypse? She hated you just as much as she hated me you know."

He drops the newspaper into his lap. "You can't talk to me like that!" he barks back. I begin to feel bad; I shouldn't attack him like this, it's not like he's capable of changing. When my mother died he made it past the brink. No turning back for him now.

"Can't I?" I retort, defeatedly. I don't have time to get into another pointless war of attrition with him. "Well, things are different now."

And I bound out of the door, letting it slam itself shut behind me.

That's your father, Vega says, observantly. *You seem as though you have some unresolved issues.*

"Yeah, you could say that," I answer nonchalantly before realizing the absurdity of all this. "What's it to you anyway? Like, I'd never met you when I got out of bed yesterday. I still might never have met you. I mean, can you meet an AI? An AI of a dead man?"

I'm pacing down the sidewalk, muttering frankly insane things to myself. I'm getting strange glances, but truth be told I'm getting used to it.

I'm afraid I'm part of you now. Our interests are intertwined, and we will improve each other. Just as you couldn't operate the nanomachines without me, I couldn't live on without you.

"You couldn't?"

The nanomachines – and me, the AI that governs them – need a host to continue functioning. If they don't find a host within a certain period of time they're programmed to deactivate; they will become microscopic carbon dust. It's a necessary safety feature.

Nanotechnology with no central regulation and no purpose can become extremely problematic.

"Problematic?!" I cry. I'm in danger of becoming accustomed to the good times – the strength, the speed, the free beer. I hadn't thought about possible glitches in the matrix.

And that's why they're programmed to deactivate. As for whether you can meet an artificial intelligence, or an artificial intelligence of a dead man, I'm not equipped to answer that question. Although I would suspect yes.

"And the nanomachines can't leave my body?"

They can't be disconnected from your body without perishing. They can live on the surface of your body, and within your body, but as soon as they're a tiny distance from your cells they're programmed to self-destruct. Again, rogue nanomachines can do terrible things.

"So," I say, moving on from a conversation that's beginning to unnerve me. "What's my higher calling? What's my purpose? I mean, I had to meet that body, that man – sorry, Vega – for a reason, right?"

I don't know my – and my host's – purpose in coming here, to this world, to this city, to that alley. My only advice to you would be to find your own purpose. You have tremendous, potentially world-altering power. You have to find a way to use it.

I pause, standing still in the sidewalk and take a minute to watch cars buzz past impatiently and people in suits and skirts swerve to avoid each other on the curb.

"What do I know about power? I go to work and package sandwiches, I don't know anything about altering the world."

The technology that inhabits every limb, every blood vessel, every sinew of muscle in your body is advanced military-grade, not from here, but from a civilization way more advanced than your own. It works perfectly as long as you wield it responsibly. I think once you find your feet, you'll find that higher calling. Go and see what's out there.

I walk into the city and head straight for downtown.

Here's a corner of the metropolis where the factories and manufacturers were once located, but now it's home to only derelict buildings and small stores trying to get by. Whatever giants of capitalism were once here have long left this place, leaving only their towering gray houses behind.

Beyond that lie the docks, a shadow of what they were 20 years ago, or so I'm told. In this city, it shouldn't be difficult to find someone doing something they shouldn't or somebody needing a defender.

I find a bench in a dingy part of town beside a dilapidated bank I've never heard of and a liquor store and sit down. The weather's getting worse, but I hardly notice. I look around and see that the morning commute is over, other than the odd man or woman running for a train.

I can see everything you see – the nanomachines can interpret the impulses your eyes send along your optic nerves. With the full picture, I can scan your field of vision to inform you of anything important.

"Anything important?" I ask, somewhat hesitant to find out.

Threats for the most part; I can pick up on the things your somewhat more fallible human brain would miss.

If I rolled my eyes right now, would Vega pick up on that too?

But I can also detect anything you may be looking for. Faces, signals, tracks, anything that may help to accomplish whatever objective you have in mind.

"And where are you? Where in my body is the brain chip, or whatever you're living in, located?"

There is no brain chip. The artificial general intelligence is shared by the entire network of nanomachines, fluctuating between 800 billion and two trillion. Each one of them contributing a tiny proportion of processing power for the artificial intelligence.

I watch as the morning unfolds. No bank robbery, no big car chase, no deadly shooting; just the city's population trying to get on with their lives without being too bothered. What's the point of having the power to save lives if I can never be in the right place at the right time?

Eventually, the street empties for the most part. I decide to stand up and take another walk, heading in the direction of the docks. A lifetime ago I'd have avoided that place as if my life depended on it. Hell, it might have.

It doesn't take me long walking these trash-strewn streets until I hear something though. Shouting, ill-tempered, two voices, male and female.

I turn around and head towards it, jogging down the next block where I find a man, awkwardly dressed in a Hawaiian shirt in a very un-Hawaiian part of town. He's got his hands on a woman in her mid to late twenties, trying to force her into a car. They could be drunk or just sound that way when they argue.

"Hey," I say, approaching. He doesn't hear, and neither does she. "Hey!" I repeat, louder.

He turns around, looking me up and down, apparently sizing me up. I can see he hasn't shaved in a couple of days and there are dark circles around his eyes, which move excitably from side to side.

"Whut?" he slurs. "The hell you want, kid?"

"I just want to know you're both okay," I say, with an unintentional tone of self-doubt in my voice. He looks me up and down again, scoffs, and turns back to the woman. She looks at me with something like panic in her eyes; would that be panic for herself or panic for me?

"Yeah, it's just—" I manage to say before he draws back his big, dirty palm and brings it down onto her face , drawing an audible scream from her. I charge the three remaining meters to him and grab his hand.

"What are you doin'!?" he screams, letting go of her and turning to fully face me, his hand still suspended by my grip. In the briefest moment I see his wedding ring shine in the morning sun and see that they're both wearing identical rings. The woman stands frozen.

"She's my wife, buddy!"

I'm so preoccupied trying to conjure up a witty response I don't notice his other fist traveling towards me. It hits the side of my temple, knocking me off-balance and putting me into a daze. I got my bell rung all right.

Kris, pay attention, Vega says.

A moment later, I regain my senses and gladly see I haven't let go of his hand yet. He aims another punch at me, but this time I have the presence of mind to dodge it. His body, guided by its own weight, follows the trajectory of the punch until his face is six inches from mine. I look him in the eyes and squeeze his hand. Hard.

"Ahh, Argghhh!" he screams, as I feel bones and cartilage fracture and break under my fingers. He tries with his other hand to break my grip – all the while staring me increasingly desperately in the eyes – but it's no good. He finally shouts, "Help!"

"Stop it, you're hurting him!" the woman shouts. I finally let go and the two of them jump into the car – the man clutching his hand, whimpering still – and frantically try to start the engine.

There are 27 bones in the human hand. You might have broken all of them.

"He deserved it," I reply, watching the car finally to turn over the engine and speed away. "One less hand to beat her with."

That may be true, but you see that she still left with him. If your primary concern was the woman's safety while in that man's presence, your solution might not alleviate the problem.

Yeah, Vega has a point.

I don't know what I expected from that situation, but I was hardly a knight in shining armor for that woman. I could have talked to her; I could have tried to prevent her leaving with him, or I could have called the police. I'm not exactly a relationship counsellor.

Still, maybe that man would think twice before doing that again. There can be *consequences*. The feeling of his bones breaking stays with me, making me feel nauseous; I can only imagine how he feels about it.

"Vega," I say, trying to avert my mind from the memory. "How does that work exactly? I mean, how do the machines give me that sort of grip strength?"

The nanomachines specialized in muscle stimulation and maintenance are located within your muscles and ligaments. They find the substantial proportion of weaker or dead cells and replace them with better performing cells, which they create from a cached image of your stem cells. In addition, any damage that occurs doing activity – tears, strains, ruptures, etc. – is quickly repaired by the nanotechnology. The result is an upcycling of performance. A 300-400% improvement in performance over what existed before.

I jog back towards the city's downtown districts, unsure of what my next move should be. I don't get far before Vega speaks.

Kris, there's a couple of men 90 meters ahead on the right-hand side of the street. They are wearing black. One is armed.

I look over, and faintly see the silhouettes of two men, wearing all black – including two black woolly hats – standing idly in the street. It looks like they're talking, although I can see one of them is holding a shiny object.

I slowly walk closer to them. After a few paces, I can see that it appears to be a knife. They both nod to each other and pull down their hats, revealing a pair of balaclavas now obscuring their faces.

"Good catch," I tell Vega as I jump behind a dumpster. They disappear into a storefront with tacky neon lettering and I make my approach, jogging awkwardly forward.

I make it to the store and immediately hear shouting inside. It's a pawn shop by the looks of things. The men have already brought the shutters down, trapping themselves, the workers, and whoever else is unlucky enough to be in there with them. I look up and down the building and see that there's a retracted steel fire-escape staircase in the adjoining alley. No match for my one-arm pull-up.

I get over there and hoist myself up before throwing the full force of my body against the fire-escape door, smashing through it in one rapid action and hurling myself to the floor in a cloud of dust and woodchips. Perhaps I could have checked if it was locked first.

I pick myself up, dusting myself off with both hands before making my way through the room – a darkened storeroom, full of unstably stacked boxes and crates. Finally, I see another door and happily find it unlocked.

I sneak downstairs, trying not to make another sound, pausing when the shouting becomes louder. I must be close to the shop floor now. The room I'm in is dark, but I can see florescent lighting underneath another doorway. I guess that's the one. I walk up to it and with an intake of breath turn the handle.

As I slowly push the door ajar, I take a look around. There's the two men in balaclavas, one of them screaming orders and curses at a poor woman standing over a cash register, the other using a crowbar to smash open glass displays featuring watches, jewelry, and the like.

As well as the woman behind the register, there's an older man with a head wound, crouching beside a counter mopping blood off his brow, and a couple of customers I presume, forced into a corner, trying their best to look away from the robbers. Closest to me, however, is a younger woman – in her late teens, perhaps – who I guess to be another worker here given her position behind the counter.

I sneak out from behind the door, slowly making my way along the edge of the shop floor, using the counters and display cabinets to obscure my figure from the robbers. Then, closing in on the younger woman hostage, I tap her on the shoulder intending to get her to safety.

She turns quickly and anxiously, looking me in the face in a fit of panic, and then before I can put a solitary finger to my lips, she screams fearfully in my face. *Oh no...*

Both of the men in balaclavas look up from their work – one holding the knife and one the crowbar – and they freeze for a split second. One of the florescent bulbs above us flickers, and one of them yells:

"There's another guy in here!"

I suddenly feel all 14 eyeballs on me, and it dawns on me that I have to act quickly here. The man wielding the crowbar charges me down first, striding forcefully like some enraged animal. I put my body in front of the girl and put my fists out in front of me in a vague fighting stance.

This is probably the worst time to consider this, but I quickly remind myself my only hand-to-hand combat experience comes from imitating Bruce Lee movies. I see the hate in his eyes and steel myself.

He swings the crowbar and I manage to dodge it, eliciting a grunt from him. Okay, easy enough, what now?

I tighten my fist, thinking to thump him with it, but catch the other goon in the corner of my eye leaving his position at the cash register and tentatively approaching me, tossing his knife between his hands, catching the handle in one palm and then throwing it to the next. Looks like I'm not the only one who's watched too many movies.

I throw a hand at the crowbar goon; it travels quickly, but I unwittingly loosen my fist on its journey to the man's jaw, and I end up slapping him somehow, feeling the fabric of his balaclava across my fingers. He reels backwards – either from the blow or from sheer confusion as to why I'd slap him – and looks to his buddy for help.

I go back to my fighting stance and see the old man with the bleeding head fumbling around at the steel shutters blocking their exit to the street. If I keep these goons busy for long enough these people will be able to escape.

You're right!

I barely notice the knife being thrust towards me by the goon on my right. I dodge it, but throw my body directly into a blow from the crowbar, which hits me directly in the sternum with sickening force. The blow draws a gasp from the depths of my lungs and a rush of blood to my face.

At first I panic; that sort of blow could break my ribs easily, and a lifetime of cardiac anxieties – worries that I'll soon suffer the heart attack that'll end me – seem to flash before my eyes in an instant.

Kris, get in the moment, Vega says, more forcefully than before.

Then I regain my bearings. I inhale deeply, and reading the knife's trajectory towards me once more I sidestep it, quickly lift my leg, and slam the side of my foot into the knife-wielder's knee.

He yelps like a wounded dog; a shrill, high-pitched cry that I don't think I've ever heard come out of a man before. I quickly glance down to see his leg bent 90 degrees – the very, very worst angle. He drops the knife.

His buddy is spooked. I see his eyes dart from my face to my foot, to the dislocated kneecap, and back again. The hate in his eyes drains out, replaced by watery panic. He holds the crowbar above his head, but hesitates. It shakes, like a leaf in the wind.

I reach up, grabbing the crowbar with one hand, he obliges and lets go of it for me.

"Thanks," I say, bringing it down from the air and dropping it beside the knife.

The loud metallic racket of the shutters winding up fills the store. Daylight floods the room, and I see the hostages file out one by one. I grab the uninjured robber by what I think is his collar, but turns out to be his balaclava, ripping it from his head. He's young, early-20s, with a slight beard and loose, greasy hair. Hell, he looks the tiniest bit like me.

He turns on his heel and runs out of the store in the opposite direction of the hostages, leaving his stricken buddy behind. Now it's just me, a shop floor full of broken glass, and a formerly armed robber who must be wondering if he'll ever walk again. Oh, and his horrible cries and whimpers.

Hearing sirens in the distance, and looking down one final time at my adversary, I pick up the knife and pace outdoors. I suppose I don't have to worry about him escaping any time soon. I deposit the knife in the dumpster and pull up the lapels of my jacket closely around my face before running away from the scene at a healthy pace.

CHAPTER 6

"So, that wasn't so bad was it?"

I slow myself down, decelerating to a nice, unassuming, and casual walk across the block. For the first time since the crowbar hit me, I feel a sharp tinge of pain in my sternum, although nowhere near as much as I expected.

Maybe it's the adrenaline still coursing through me. Or maybe it's one of a thousand nanomachine processes I've no doubt yet to hear about.

If your mission was to disrupt the robbery and allow the hostages to escape mostly unharmed, you definitely succeeded. Well done.

'Well done' – I can't remember being congratulated by Vega before. I feel pride, or at least something very close to it. At least I don't remember feeling this way on seeing a videogame's credits roll screen.

If we were to analyze your performance moment by moment, there are certainly areas for improvement.

"Improvement?!" I cry out, incredulously. When I got out of bed yesterday, I was a sandwich packager with a heart condition. Don't I deserve some slack?

You quickly formed a plan to approach the crime scene from upstairs. However, your attempt to gain access via the door was suboptimal.

"I don't yet know my own strength. I guess I'm still getting used to that."

Your attempt to approach the scene quietly was well-executed until you engaged an innocent party without first taking steps to ensure they knew you were friendly.

"Yes, in retrospect I could have handled that better," I say, while still struggling to think how.

Your hand-to-hand combat style is... Vega pauses, *...unorthodox.*

Was that pause for dramatic effect or the result of a trillion nanomachines calculating the best possible way to describe the way I fight? I can't tell which I'd hate more.

"To say I'd never been in a fight before yesterday, and I'd never hit anybody until today, I think I did..." I pause this time, thinking exactly how to rate myself. "Seven out of 10? Yeah, a solid seven out of 10."

Yes, right, Vega says, nonchalantly. *You will improve. You will learn and get better.*

My sternum still throbs.

"I thought I handled being hit by the crowbar well, at least?" I ask, words I never thought I'd say. "It didn't hurt nearly as much as I expected."

The nanomachine network is programmed to be inherently reactive. I am programmed to be inherently reactive. If I can see an oncoming kinetic blow, and I have enough time to prepare – milliseconds for simple impacts – I can activate a layer of nanomachines on and below the skin, as well as within your bones.

The nanomachines bind to skin, muscle, and bone cells, creating a protective lattice. Millions to billions of nanomachines can be lost, but they will protect your body and are easily reproduced.

"Huh," I say, quizzical and impressed. "So I could survive a bullet?"

The process can only protect you so far. The pressure per square centimeter exerted on your skin by a bullet would far exceed the lattice's capacity. That, as well as the limited time to prepare for the speed of a bullet, makes you just as susceptible to a bullet's impact as anyone else.

"No guns, no bullets, gotcha." I'm being flippant, but hearing I have that vulnerability puts the fear of God into me once more. I ask one more question: "And the nanomachines are easily reproduced if they get battered by a crowbar?"

Yes. Millions of nanomachines are rendered inoperable every hour. Malfunction, irreparable damage, or disconnection from the electromagnetic field renders them inactive. However, a proportion of nanomachines are tasked with reproducing themselves, which they can do by manipulating carbon at the molecular level. Usually this is done by remanufacturing those dead nanomachines or by repurposing the dust and other detritus on your skin. In the event of a catastrophic loss of nanomachines, caused by, for example, a larger event, a larger source of carbon would be necessary, plus a longer time to reproduce.

"So, this entire thing is..." I try think of the words, "self-sufficient?"

Yes, if there is just a single nanomachine in your body it will eventually reproduce the entire network of nanomachines again. Albeit with the temporary loss of certain key systems, such as the artificial intelligence — me.

Finally, after walking and contemplating the previous events for a while, I find myself at the park. That same park where I first got to know Vega. It feels like an eternity ago. Strange to think it was merely last night. There's a fast-food dog stand here. I grab a hot dog and a burger, guzzling them down as quick as I've ever eaten. Nanotechnology is no remedy for good old-fashioned hunger.

"There's something I've been meaning to ask," I say out loud, finishing the last of my food, and looking out onto an eerily empty pond. "I know you said you don't know why you came here – what your previous mission or whatever was."

Yes, that's right.

"Do you think I should be wary of all this?" I ask, not expecting anything close to an answer. I guess my line of questioning is purely rhetorical. "I mean, why would that man – you, whatever – come to this city, to this time period? What's so interesting about this place that he dropped out of the ether right here?"

I'm staring into the vast expanse of empty water, a dingy dark green morass.

"Was it a mistake to travel here? A malfunction of some sort? Did he die by accident? Did someone kill him?"

I can tell you that all nanotechnology systems were functioning perfectly when you found me. I don't know anything about the journey, the departure, or the intended destination. And that he died from massive organ failure which was irreparable to the nanomachine system. He was not killed by any entity in this city or atmosphere. When he arrived, he was already dead.

I didn't expect a clear answer, but I am wary. Why would a man drop into this world – into that alley, even – with advanced military grade technology? And even if Vega is keeping a secret – if he's programmed, with his knowledge or not, to hold back something from me – there's apparently nothing I can do about it.

I move on from the park and realize I should be going home. It's been a long day.

CHAPTER 7

When I get home, Dad isn't by the window or buried in a newspaper in his usual place. This time he's on the sofa, watching some war report on TV. He is, of course, smoking nonetheless. He's already hurriedly putting the cigarette out and moving both himself and an ashtray to the window by the time I step into the room.

"You know," I say, "you don't have to do that."

"The smoke," he replies "is bad for you. Bad for your heart."

"It's bad for *you too*. It's bad for *your* heart."

He shrugs and opens the window, taking the time to light his cigarette again. There's a painful silence between us, the only sound emanating from the TV and the war report on the news.

"What is it?" I ask, pointing to the TV. He arches his eyebrows, looking at me suspiciously. He knows something is up. I never usually want to sit and chat. After an uneasy moment, he answers, "War in the Middle East. Civil war. Someone trying to overthrow their government or something, I don't know."

I look at the TV: 'PRESIDENT DARIDA PUTS DOWN POPULAR UPRISING, FACES ACCUSATIONS OF MASS MURDER.' The world is such a screwed-up place. I left the house today and rescued a bunch of people from possible injury, maybe even death. And that was just a drop in the ocean.

I see the sun beginning to set outside and see that the evening's rolling around, and thus my shift at work.

"Dad," I say, grabbing his attention once more, "I'm quitting my job."

"Oh yeah?" he says, turning to face me head on, widening his stance, readying himself for the inevitable argument. "And what are you going to do instead, huh?"

I'm loitering, moving my eyes around the room trying to avoid his cold gaze. In truth, I haven't thought one bit about what I'm going to do. Where I'm going to earn money and how. But I know I'll never package another sandwich. I exhale loudly and scratch my neck, and my eyes fall on one object in the room: Dad's newspaper from this morning And the headline: **LONE BOMBER TAUNTS COPS: YOU WON'T GET ME**

I feel like a fuse is lit. My new vocation in life. My higher calling. Maybe I can find this guy. Maybe I can use my heightened senses to piece together enough information to track him down. Maybe I can use my newfound abilities to apprehend this lone bomber. A mad terrorist, threatening the entire city? That seems a lot more than a drop in the ocean.

"Hey, I'm talking to you, son." I'm so swept up in my thoughts of justice I forget I left my Dad hanging. I finally meet his eyes. He says, "So what are you going to do?"

"I've got just the job in mind," I tell him, and walk to my room before shutting myself away in there for the foreseeable.

Your eyes focused on that headline for a long time, Vega says, *three seconds longer than I'd expect from your average baseline concentration levels.*

Baseline concentration levels? Vega has even more data on me than the social networks do. I turn the TV on, switch to a music channel, and turn up the volume loud enough to mask my conversation.

I've gathered that there's a lone terrorist currently operating in the city. I hope you appreciate this terrorist most probably represents a substantial level of danger, far exceeding any you've faced so far in the short time we have spent together.

"Yes," I reply, "but I have to use this thing – this gift – for *something*, don't I?"

I know you want to help people, Vega says, somewhat tactfully. *Altruism is a noble pursuit. However, you have to think about the most effective means of doing so.*

"What do you mean?" I ask, somewhat preoccupied by booting up my laptop.

For example, would you rather save one person from dying of starvation or save 20 from serious injury? You may be the holder of super-advanced military hardware, but you don't necessarily have to use it for fighting.

I sit back and hear Vega's case.

For simplicity's sake, let's say this technology could enable you to build farming infrastructure in an impoverished country much faster and more efficient than anyone else. Could you conceivably save more lives giving starving people food to eat than you could by chasing a dangerous terrorist around town?

"Farming?!" I ask, incredulously. I get that Vega is trying to convince me that fighting this lone bomber is not the only way I can do good in the world, but he could hardly have found a duller example. "I'm not going to spend the rest of my life planting trees and picking fruit."

I realize I'm getting carried away, but I can't help myself.

"I have a great opportunity here. I've spent my entire life hiding, sheltering, taking the easy path. I've spent my entire life being…" I hesitate to say it. "*Weak.* I've been weak my entire life. Now I have a chance to change everything. I can save one person's life; I can save a 100. I'm sure of it. I *feel* it."

My little speech has the adrenaline – and billions of nanomachines no doubt – surging through my blood. But part of it still feels bittersweet.

Am I doing this because I truly want to help people or because I want to help myself? Or do I want to right every wrong that happened to me? If it was all for me, would I ever want to admit it, even to myself?

I try to put that dissonant thought out of my mind and focus on the laptop. I look up as many information sources as I can on the lone bomber: every news story, every crime scene report, every eyewitness account of the bombings. Every word I read I try to commit to memory, and know that even if I can't Vega will be collating all the data that I set my eyes on.

The bomber was designated a codename of TECHBOMB by the police and FBI, owing to the fact his own stated intention is to send bombs to places of technology and innovation: universities, research and development departments, major tech companies, energy infrastructure, and defense contractors. However, his own preferred moniker would be 'The Quiet One,' which is how he signed a couple of letters he had sent to the police.

The bombs themselves are supposedly quite sophisticated, with a failsafe timer and proximity detectors built in to ensure the bomb goes off if someone tampers with it. Around half are mailed directly to the target and half are planted in person. The person in question is seen on CCTV as a skinny male with a black hoodie pulled over his head. There have been 13 bombs so far sent to or planted in 13 high-profile targets.

Two people died as a result of these bombs. A mail employee was killed when one exploded at a mail center. Another died at a university when a timed bomb went off next to them. So far 19 more people have been injured, some seriously. All bombings have taken place within this city.

The bomber's letters are strange. He expresses a hatred of modern technology and a belief that humanity will destroy itself if it continues along its current path. He claims his targets are justified in that they will eventually give rise to the technology that will destroy us.

Furthermore, he says his name – the Quiet One – is a hope for a quiet life we'll all live without technology. Part of me wonders if it's also picked with a sense of irony; there's nothing quiet about a bomb.

"So, a man who hates technology, huh?", I crack my knuckles.

That's right.

"I'm sure he's going to just *love* us."

I'm sure, Vega replies dryly. I'm so glad Vega understands sarcasm.

"So, what's our first move?" I ask, closing the laptop and sitting back on my computer chair.

Law enforcement undoubtedly know a lot more than we do. In addition, given that he's managed to send or plant 13 bombs to 13 targets, and hasn't yet been apprehended, it's very safe to assume this is a very intelligent perpetrator with detailed knowledge of his targets and effective delivery methods.

We of course have no chance of matching the manpower or resources of law enforcement in running our own investigation. Additionally, we have no chance of accessing the information they have unless we were to infiltrate the investigation somehow.

"Right," I say, somewhat deflated.

However, continues Vega, *we do have a number of advantages over traditional law enforcement. I would recommend we go to one of the crime scenes – one of the sites of the bombings. It's possible we can detect something that law enforcement missed.*

"Great." I can't pretend I'm not excited. I always wanted to play detective when I was a kid. In fact, I wouldn't have minded a job on the police force. Another young aspiration I tossed on the bonfire when I was old enough to understand the true extent of my heart problems. "We'll get on it first thing tomorrow."

Yes, you should rest. Like I said, this endeavor represents a high level of danger.

I move to the window, and look out onto the street, seeing only orange streetlights and the moving whites and reds of the cars outside. My eyelids are heavy but my mind is still racing. I close the blinds, turn off the solitary lightbulb in my room, and lie down on my bed.

I close my eyes and see silhouettes dancing through the day's events. It doesn't take long before I'm asleep.

CHAPTER 8

I wake up suddenly in a panic. I'm anxious about something, but whatever I was dreaming about is gone now. I don't remember. My heart beats quickly before slowing to an easier pace. I guess half-buried worries and fears still stalk my subconscious.

The radio is blaring in the front room again. More talk of the Almighty. How we are made in His image and yet here we are, stuck on this Earth awash with sinners.

I don't think my Dad will ever understand me. It was unlikely before; it's an impossibility now.

I shower, get something to eat, and find my Dad buried in the paper again. No news from the bomber. Typically there's been a week or so between each explosion. The last was six days ago, so we're almost due another one if he sticks to his modus operandi.

You know, Vega says, startling me as I pick out a pair of socks, *you should be a lot more mindful of your appearance if you're going to be investigating this spate of bombings.*

Mindful of my appearance? I'm struggling to picture myself dropping in for a haircut or swinging by the high street for some designer jeans.

"Uhh, what do you mean?" I say in a hushed tone.

You need to remain inconspicuous while being impossible to identify. You need to arouse no attention from the public or law enforcement and give away no notable features in your appearance that would aid identification.

He has a point. I don't have much: an ex-girlfriend who likely hates me and a Dad who thinks his own judgment day can't come soon enough. But even with the little I have, the cops pounding down on me – or even someone discovering that my incredible strength isn't the result of long hours at the gym – could make my life a misery.

I pick out a dark gray hoodie, combine that with some black tracksuit pants, and pick out a pair of Aviator sunglasses I was given for my birthday three or four years ago. Finally, I grab a red tartan scarf, intending to wrap it around the bottom half of my face to obscure my mouth and nose if I need it. Yes, I wish I had better than red tartan, but it's my only scarf.

"Can you see when I wear these sunglasses?" I put them on and look at myself in the mirror in the bathroom. I've got to admit I look quite ridiculous. A mixture of teenage protestor and Scottish drug dealer. "Everything working as it should?"

Your... choice of disguise is not an impediment to my functionality.

I can't tell if he's trying to mock me. My 'choice of disguise'? I hesitate for a moment and then stump up the nerve to ask.

"Vega," I say after returning to my room and the comparative safety of the noisy television. "Are you mocking me? I mean, do you have a sense of humor?"

I am a copy of the personality of the nanomachine network's previous host and user. My primary function, as hard-coded into the system, is to aid the host and user: you. However, I retain the previous host's personality traits, so yes — I do have a sense of humor.

"Why did they make you a copy of his personality? What would be the point?"

I believe within this model of nanotechnological system a newer form of artificial intelligent assistant was trialed. Soldiers, mercenaries, and infiltrators in the field would express annoyance with the bland personalities of the assistants of previous models. Hence the decision was made to clone the host's consciousness — their personality, their individual character — and use it as the assistant. I suppose you could liken it to an extension of your own mind.

"Jesus, I'd hate to be alone in my own head with a clone of my own personality. One of me is surely bad enough." I wonder why I feel that way. Perhaps I've spent too long hating myself. "Don't you feel lonely? You're a mind without a body. In fact, your body is dead. We both saw it."

I have a number of failsafe behaviors hard-coded that would prevent me from viewing this situation in an existential sense. And of course I have to run and maintain a trillion nanomachines.

I'm speechless; I'd never even asked Vega about, well, himself until now. An indentured servant, severed from his body, and condemned to administer a system of nanomachines until I presumably die. And even more than that, prevented from the luxury of feeling bad about it.

It's too much to think about right now. I should get my head back in the game. Considering the implications of having a dead man's consciousness slaving away in my body can wait; the 'Quiet One' might be out there planting a bomb as we waste time. I zip up my hoodie and try to pace past my Dad without arousing his attention. As usual, I fail.

"Kris," he calls out, and I retrace my steps back into the room after my abortive attempt to leave it without incident. "Why are you dressed like that?"

"It's getting cold," I point to the scarf.

"I imagine you look just like that mad bomber," he says, and the image of the Quiet One wearing a hoodie and sunglasses pops into my head. "You're not out to plant bombs, are you?" he says it with a bashful smile. I smile back and take my leave.

The most recent bombing was a defense contractor involved in the R&D of smart guided missile technology and autonomous drones. It's a massive high-tech facility on the outskirts of the city with its own private security to protect a huge workforce.

Despite that, the Quiet One managed to mail a bomb there.

Unfortunately, I probably don't stand a chance of getting in to view the damage.

The bombing before that was at the only big university in the city. A bomb was placed beside the entrance to a laboratory specializing in a new sort of microchip. That was a couple of weeks ago. I think it's probably my best chance of exploring a bombing scene without drawing too much attention to myself. In agreement with Vega, I ponder the logistics of getting there.

"I can't believe I'm still doing this," I say to myself, looking at the bus timetable affixed to a post. A woman at the bus stop looks over her shoulder at me before turning back to her smartphone.

The university is on the outskirts of the city some 13 miles out. I could run half a marathon in an hour or I could get the bus, and given that I'm not keen on arriving there suspiciously drenched in sweat I decide the bus is the more sensible option.

Arriving inconspicuously and on-time is important to the

mission. You should be prepared to use any transport options available to you, Vega informs me.

"There are a trillion robots inside my body," I say, turning slightly to face the noise of a car speeding past, hoping to mask the insane things coming out of my mouth. "They can't form up to create a jet pack or something? Put rockets in the soles of my shoes?"

No, they can't.

Right, that's that then. Nice and definitive. I possess a super-advanced technology from a world far, far away and light years beyond anything we currently possess on Earth. Yet I'm still taking public transport.

The bus arrives, and as me and the smartphone-attentive woman queue to get on, who do I see running to join us but the shaven-headed skinny guy with the scar; the same man who caused me to walk away from the bus in fear. The same man who led me to take the journey that ended in *that* alleyway.

I smile at him. No; grin at him. As his eyes meet mine, I nod silently at him. I can see that he's perturbed, feeling some fraction of the anxiety I felt upon encountering him just three days ago. I don't think I've ever felt as proud of myself as I do right now, nodding at a scrawny guy at a bus stop. Life is strange.

I get on the bus, pay for a ticket with what's left of the pocket change I found around the apartment, and wait the 45 minutes until my stop. I've been so wrapped up in my new crime-fighting ambitions that I hadn't even considered what I'm going to do for money now. I was supposed to be in work last night. No-one thought to call me to see where I was, but that won't last forever.

———

The bus pulls up at the university, and the pneumatic 'whoosh' noise of the door mechanism snaps me out of some daydream. I nod thanks to the driver, ensconced in a daydream of his own, and jump off. Then I tighten the tartan scarf around my neck and pull it over my mouth up to the bottom of my nose. I may not look like a superhero, but I'm dressed practically I guess.

The university campus is massive. I power-walk the distance to the science department, reaching the laboratory complex in no time. A huge, futuristic-looking building with large air vents jutting out of the sides and small windows, set in a leafy park with pleasant trees and kooky, modern-art inspired benches scattered around.

Looking at it from distance, the entire building looks like a microchip – extensions and platforms extruding at odd angles. It sticks out like a sore thumb. It is a huge testament to humanity's ingenuity and technological prowess. Perhaps that's why it caught a bomb.

And I'm struck by how busy it all is still. Students or lab techs or visitors or whoever are still filling the grassy hills and the cobbled paths of the park around it, streaming into the building. I'd expected a much more desolate scene two weeks after a bombing.

"There's a lot of people here," I say to Vega. "I expected far fewer. How am I supposed to get to the site of the bombing without being seen?"

The size of the crowd here will be an aid, not a hindrance. You can hide in a crowd. Blend in. When the time is right you can slip out of a crowd.

Vega has a point. I tighten my hood around my face and join the line of people entering the building. I look around and immediately see three or four people dressed just like me – hoodie, tracksuit pants, and sunglasses. So this is what the student life is like.

I make it inside the building's lobby. White walls, white floors, and white sterile light, with the same sort of modern art sensibilities as I came to expect from the exterior. There are queues and barriers for entry that look like they require some sort of ID to get through. After I get a closer look I can see they're switched off, and instead security guards are slowly manually checking everyone's credentials.

I pause on the periphery and watch to see if I can pick my moment.

After a minute, I get my chance. One security guard – a portly guy with sunglasses similar to mine and a permanent grimace etched on his face – pauses to look inside a young woman's rucksack.

The queue begins pushing past him and he doesn't seem to care, investing all of his attention on this poor woman's personal belongings. I join the queue, and quickly slide past him, large as he may be. I follow the crowd into the corridors and then look to consult my guide.

"Do you know exactly where the bomb went off?"

One of the news reports said it was the semi-conductor lab, second floor, room 11B.

I find the closest staircase and walk the innumerable cold, characterless corridors until I find the semi-conductor lab signposted. From there, it's easy to pick out the door with the classic yellow 'crime scene' tape haphazardly stuck across it. No security posted here. I guess they thought the tape would suffice.

I wait until the coast is clear and then duck underneath it.

There are two laboratories side by side – 11A and 11B – both intended to be hermetically sealed from the outside world judging by the amount of partitions and broken glass here, and both featuring various high-tech machinery, now lying in various exotic pieces and scarred by the blast damage.

The ceiling has panels missing and light fixtures dangling down. The rooms are lit by portable floodlights, much like you'd find on a building site. Probably placed there by the investigators. I think I can see exactly where the bomb detonated; there's a crater-like depression in the flooring and blackened scorch marks around it.

Glass crunches under my feet. I'm surprised they haven't done more to clean this place up, making me consider for the first time the possibility that I'm disturbing a crime scene. I feel that old familiar pit of anxiety in my stomach again, and the dreadful thought that I might be getting in way, way too deep here. Then Vega snaps me out of it in his usual manner-of-fact style.

I can see the bomb was placed against the wall over there, not quite within the hermetically sealed zone but close enough that it was able to wipe out both laboratories from one single, efficient location. The reinforced nature of the flooring and ceiling here seems to have ensured the structure of the room didn't collapse.

The positioning of the bomb was very well-thought out, and perhaps resulted from extensive planning. The position also suggests the bomber didn't have access to the sealed zone but did manage to bypass the security downstairs.

"You've seen how easy that is," I say. I briefly wonder why they haven't done much to beef up security since, and then remember that no-one ever believes lightning strikes twice.

Walk over to the spot where the bomb detonated, then place your palm on the floor beside it and don't move.

"What?" I ask, feeling that anxiety all over again. "Why would I want to do that?"

The nanomachines on the surface of your palm will search the area on the molecular level, and I can hopefully build a picture of what the bomb was made from.

Huh, I never knew I had that ability. I slowly walk over,

avoiding large concentrations of broken glass and other debris. I sink to my knees beside the black marks on the floor and slowly rest my palm against the debris. Then I wait, trying to keep my palm as steady as possible.

Analyzing. Please remain still.

I wait 30 seconds or so, looking around the room slowly. This particular bomb injured a couple of people – a professor and a student, who were working here at the time. It's hard to imagine the explosion and the subsequent panic and terror. But despite that, judging by the number of students still filing in and out of the building no-one seems scared. The bombing campaign isn't working.

Analysis is complete.

I raise my palms and brush them off with the cuff of my hoodie, hoping to leave no fingerprints behind. Vega lists a number of elements and compounds with long and unmemorable names, which he tells me are common ingredients in bomb-making. Then he continues…

There is one other surprising finding, however. I listen as I hop underneath the crime scene tape, put my hands in my pockets, my head down, and walk nonchalantly out of there. *The area around the blast area appears to be very lightly radioactive. Not obviously so, but above the average background level for the building.*

"Radioactive? Would that be down to the lab or the…" I hesitate to say the B word in public, "…device?"

It's impossible to know for sure.

I traverse the same corridors as before, jumping down two steps at a time and sweeping past the security barriers to get out of the building. Outside the sun is shining – it's mid-October but unseasonably warm. I look around at the masses of people, mostly my age, but some far older.

There's laughing and joking. This certainly doesn't look like the site of a terrorist bombing some two weeks earlier.

Rather than fear and uncertainty, all I see is courage and perseverance.

And then I notice something else.

"Hey Vega, what's that?" I focus my vision on a wall panel on the exterior of the building. There's a strange graffiti on the wall, something I didn't notice earlier.

Graffiti. Is that so unusual?

"Maybe, maybe not. It's the only bit of graffiti here though. It must be new."

I walk towards it and take a closer look. It's a stencil job; black spray paint over stencils of varying shapes. It depicts a man with an unnervingly blank face holding an umbrella above him.

Despite the effort, it isn't great. The stencils must have been nudged from side to side during the spraying. The blank face is the most notable feature. Did they not finish it?

I'll make a note of it. I cannot say I'm a fan of the art, though.

I cycle through the other bombing sites in my memory, planning my next excursion. All of a sudden the temperature around here seems to turn a little colder. There's a strange mood in the air; an intangible change in the wind. I pull the tartan scarf down from my mouth and look around.

Sirens blare out in the distance. More than usual. I begin walking to the bus stop, but passing a group of female students talking manically, all holding their cellphones, I slow down, and eavesdrop:

"My mom lives over there, it could have been her this time." My ears prick up; another detonation? "I just think this bombing thing is all getting out of control," one of the students protests.

"Excuse me," I say, interrupting the group's conversation and earning awkward glances in my direction. "Sorry, I overheard. Did you say there was another bombing?"

"No," she says, causing my spine to tense up for a

moment. "An attempted bombing. They got to it before it went off."

She smiles awkwardly and turns back to her friends. I turn back to my path and continue walking.

"Vega. An attempted bombing huh?"

Yes. That would be the first foiled explosion since he began his campaign. At least that we know of.

Is the Quiet One getting sloppy? Or are our incompetent, unfit, short-sighted police force finally getting their act together? I pull out my cellphone, scroll past *that* lockscreen, and search the local news sites. When my browser finally manages to pull up the front page, it's there in all caps: **CHURCH BOMBING THWARTED, BOMB FAILS TO DETONATE**

Immediately I get that sinking feeling, like I know something isn't right. A church? If it isn't a site of technological innovation – the Church of Cyberpunk Jesus – something strange is afoot.

"A church?" I get to the bus stop, my mind racing. "What do you think of this?"

It would seem to be a significant departure from the bomber's stated intent. It's possible he wants to broaden the campaign, but the fact the bomb didn't explode is another curiosity. We should go there. The law enforcement presence will be high, but we could catch something they miss.

My bus pass is good for a day's travel anywhere in the city. I look around sheepishly, seeing only students and pensioners. A veteran – 60 years old or so with a prosthetic leg – hobbles around on the spot, trying to fish some change out of his pocket.

I pull my tartan scarf back up to my nose and exhale loudly in a breathy sigh. Maybe I should learn to drive. At least that's a better prospect than the city's strongest crime-fighter - and best hope for catching the Quiet One - arriving on the Green Line number 79.

Your heart rate and blood pressure are slightly elevated, and you're taking much deeper outward breaths than usual. You're still annoyed about the bus, aren't you?

I don't answer him. Soon the bus arrives, and I take one last look at the monolithic science department building and its courageous, unflappable occupants, enjoying its shade from the sun. Whatever point the bomber was trying to make here, it looks like he convinced nobody.

CHAPTER 9

As the bus gently bobs and weaves in and out of traffic, rocking me from side to side in my seat, I read more from the news article about the failed bombing.

The device was supposedly found inside the church smoking, having failed to detonate. The police evacuated the church and surrounding area, and a bomb-disposal team was brought in who successfully destroyed it. The church itself is Methodist with a fairly low key and uncontroversial reputation. No incidents have occurred there since a small fire in the 1970s and a telethon recorded there in the 90s.

Despite searching the internet high and low, I can't find any substantive references to technology, weapons research, biomedical science, or radioactivity anywhere. It is, in the most generous terms, just a regular old church.

"So what do we think?" I whisper to Vega, hoping the scarf over my mouth muffles the sound of my voice. "He had a bone to pick with God this time?"

He never mentioned religion in either of his letters to the media, Vega says, jogging my memory. *His quarrel is with technology. If he had a religious motive I'd expect that to be mentioned in his letters. On the other hand, he could be trying to trick the authorities.*

The bus grinds to an screeching halt and it's my stop. I jump up and push gently past a couple of folks in the walkway before giving my customary nod to the driver, and I'm back in the sunlight.

This area of town is just as dull as the church. The sun reflects off a large tower in the distance, the home of some bank or insurance company or stockbroker or another one of those shirt and shoes companies.

There's a terrace of restaurants, slowly going out of business, and adjacent to them in the street a terrace of bars, kept afloat by the banker boys. The Methodist church is just beyond.

I haven't walked far when I see the police presence; 20 cars at least, some flashing their lights, some thoughtlessly blaring their sirens, and a couple doing both. The fire service is here to get in on the action too, and there's a couple of TV news crews already joining in the party. All are inside a perimeter that stretches some 20 meters away from the church in every direction.

It only takes a couple of minutes for me to walk the distance but in that time a healthy crowd has gathered to take in the sights, gotten bored, and dispersed. Twice. "Jesus, there's an army of police here, I'm getting nowhere near that church today."

I lock eyes with a disgruntled teen, evidently as frustrated that he won't get to see a disarmed bomb as I am. He flings a skateboard around in the air bizarrely, finally hanging it across his shoulders like the beginnings of a cape.

Yes, it would be foolish to attract the wrong sort of police attention here. There is something you missed, however…

I turn my head right and then left, opening my eyes wide in interest. I wait for him to tell me, and then raise my eyebrows in an expression that can only mean 'well?'

Look 30 meters to your right, 10 meters from the church, behind the police car.

There's a large LCD display with a moving image advert that's maybe six feet tall. I think the advert is about a forthcoming visit from a touring ballet company to the city. That's not what I'm looking at, though.

What I'm looking at is the spraypainted graffiti, in white this time, on top of it. You can barely see it with the advert playing in garish reds and yellows and pinks – but it's there. The same boy, the same umbrella, the same eerie blank face.

"Hah, how about that," I say.

Yes. The same graffiti. Whoever had to exhibit their wonderful art at the university bomb site did it here too.

I'm pondering the strange art it depicts when I see something else. A man ducking out of the church, coffee in one hand and a small notepad in the other.

"Hey, wait a minute," I announce, tugging up my scarf over my nose reflexively. "I know that man. He's a detective."

I forget his name; he's the younger one of the two who spoke to me in the hospital. The one who isn't Detective Clarke, I guess. He looks horrendous; purple bags under his eyes, gelled hair standing on end unnaturally, looking like he just sat down to relax in the electric chair. They must have reassigned him onto the bomber case as soon as he couldn't identify *the body*.

Yes, I recognize him too. Detective Ramos.

"Yes, Detective Ramos, that's right." Smooth. Having my own personal assistant living in my brain has its benefits.

You should talk to him, see if you can extract any information out of him.

"What!? Talk to him?" I feel that anxiety rising again. I may have strength, speed, and reflexes beyond my wildest dreams, plus a newly functioning heart, but I'm no silver-tongued charmer. I wouldn't even know how to start. "What am I supposed to say to him?"

I watch him jump the perimeter and walk down the block in the direction came from. I follow him at a distance, tracking his movements as casually as I can.

Thank him for his work for the city. Thank him for keeping the streets safe. Switch on your creative brain.

He walks wearily, dragging his heels along the floor. He puts his notepad away into his pocket and rakes his fingers through his hair before walking into one of the banker bars on the block.

This is your chance, Vega tells me. *Follow him into the bar, tell him you recognize him, and get to talking to him.*

"And what if he doesn't want to talk to some kid?" I pause outside the bar, trying to hype myself up. I breathe deeply and feel my heart pounding in my chest. I don't remember feeling like this when facing down the crowbar-wielding thug. Maybe it's because I found the one nerve-wracking experience the nanomachines can't help me with.

Buy him a drink. Make it natural.

Natural, what a joke. I push past the door, leaving the purifying sunlight outside, and plunge myself into the dingy atmosphere of the bar. The smell of stale beer hits me, and the chattering, bantering laughter of a group of men already puts me on edge.

I can count on one hand the number of bars I've willingly visited in the past. A coworker's leaving party, two dates with Jessica. I know, I'm a lot of fun.

I spy Detective Ramos propping up the bar, looking like he might pass out from exhaustion. I see him paying for a drink – whiskey, it looks like – and I swoop in as soon as he's done.

"Hey, yeah, can I get a beer?"

The woman behind the bar, with a perfectly expressionless face, picks up a bottle from behind her, prizes off the cap with a bottle opener, and plonks it onto the counter in front of me. I pick it up, take a swig, and try to think of a way to naturally get this conversation started.

I look over to my right and then my left. Then, I do an intentional double take, trying to lock eyes with Detective Ramos and tell him I recognize him. But it's no use, his eyes are practically closed. He's just staring down into his whiskey, breathing shallow. He doesn't even notice me staring at him.

"Oh, hi Detective. Detective Ramos isn't it? How's it going, buddy?" The words spill out of my mouth faster than I'd like. I especially can't make *buddy* sound convincing. He slowly looks up from his whiskey, and glances at me with narrowed eyes.

"Hello, have we met?" His eyes are bloodshot. He looks like he hasn't slept in three days. If you had to pick which one out of the two of us had been fished out of an alleyway unconscious two days ago, it'd be him. That thought gives me a small boost of confidence.

"I'm the guy in the alley." His face doesn't move. "Ya know, with the dead man? You and your detective pal spoke to me in hospital."

"Oh yeah, how you doin'?" The question surely didn't feel like a question. It felt like a polite way to fob me off. Indeed, he nods at me and turns back to his whiskey.

"Yeah, good, I uhhh…" I need to think of some way of keeping his attention. Need to make this worth his while somehow. I get an idea, but I'm not actually going to say it, am I? "I remembered some more details about that afternoon. About the body."

Oh Jesus, what am I saying? He turns to look at me, raising an eyebrow. I see him reach into his pocket for that notepad. Maybe he's actually interested in what I have to say or maybe it's just a reflex action.

"And you didn't call the department yet?" No, I was evidently trawling every bar in town to meet the detectives in their natural habitat. "I've been re-assigned to the bombing campaign. But give me what you've got."

I've got nothing. What am I going to do? Tell him the dead man was a time traveler whose ghost and personal army of robots is living within my skin?

"The details, right…" I say, trying to buy myself some time. I expected Vega to chime in with something, but I get the feeling he enjoys seeing me struggle like this.

I close my eyes, grit my teeth, and give it all I've got. "Well, I'd never believed in aliens before, but earlier that day, in the sky, I saw a…"

He immediately puts his notepad away, and turns back to his drink without an acknowledgement of my added 'details.'

This isn't your creative brain at work, Vega says drily.

There's an awkward silence between us as I panic about what to do next, and then Vega's previous advice comes back to me:

"Hah, I'm kidding of course. Let me buy you another drink; my thanks for keeping the streets safe."

He turns around again and I see a proud, expectant spark in his eyes.

"Now you're talkin'."

I order another whiskey, and Detective Ramos leads me to a booth, deeper into the murky guts of the bar. There he downs whiskeys as quickly as I can order them. One, two, three, gone.

He tells me about his newborn baby and the overtime from the bombing investigation, culminating in one hour of sleep per night. I keep up the pace with him, drinking perhaps the third, fourth, and fifth whiskeys I've ever had in my life. The taste is foul but at least I know this stuff won't get me drunk thanks to the machines in my system.

After an hour, the combination of whiskey and days of no sleep is making Detective Ramos deliriously open up to me. He tells me about his efforts to grout his bathroom before being cruelly interrupted by the bombing workload, and how his wife is spending suspiciously too much time at the tennis club.

Jesus, I didn't sign up for this. I need to get what I came here for.

"I saw the block all closed off," I say, desperately trying to prevent him going on about his home life for another half hour. "Is that what you're here for? Was there another bomb?"

He sinks back in his chair; I guess this conversation isn't as thrilling for him as the finer details of bathroom DIY.

"Yeah," he puts his whiskey to his lips and drinks the remnants. I take that as my cue to buy him another, and quickly beckon another two glasses from the bar staff. "It didn't go off this time though, thank God."

"Oh yeah, thank God." The drinks arrive and he thirstily tucks in. Strangely, he appears far more animated having drank four whiskeys than he did when he got here.

"Well, it failed. It was…" He trails off, seemingly wary of revealing too much to me. "Keep this under your hat, but the bomb was barely viable. Just complete amateur hour this time."

"Oh really?" Now he's getting interesting. "How so?"

"The previous bombs were well-designed, engineered to precision, with two timers and a short proximity sensor. This one was cobbled together from pieces of scrap; a timer consisting of an old burner cellphone and a trigger that wasn't fully connected to the explosive."

"Wow, that's got to be a relief to you guys then."

He shifts around confidently in his seat, drunk on four and a half whiskeys and his own smugness.

"The theory among the boys," he says, draining the last of his glass, "is that he's running out of steam. He's terrified by the police response, and he's blaming God for the direction his life has taken, or so we think. This thing will be wrapped up soon I reckon."

I nod along, playing the fool, but I know that makes no sense. He gets up, patting me hard on the shoulder, and slurs slightly: "Thanks for the drinks Kevin, you take care."

Kevin?

He's turned his back to me and pushed past the exit door before I can correct him, letting a ray of sun inside for the briefest of moments before it slams shut again.

I pause for a minute to collect my thoughts and then get to my feet, leaving an almost-full glass of whiskey behind. Then I dust my shoulder off and walk to the bar for the latest grueling task of the afternoon: paying the bar tab.

"Well," I say to myself, tucking up my scarf over my mouth again. "I feel like that was a waste of time."

I'm walking back to the church for one final look at that graffiti. I want to snap a picture of it before the city washes it away for besmirching their beautiful advertisement.

I don't think it was a complete waste of time, Vega chimes in. *We learned some information about the radically different engineering of this bomb and most revealingly we got a glimpse into how the police are investigating it. Or rather, how poorly they're doing.*

"And I learned a lot about grouting bathrooms," I add dispassionately. "I suppose it could come in useful one day."

Vega doesn't respond to that one.

It would be more logical to assume a bomb-maker would scale up in their sophistication as they design more devices, rather than scale down. The bomb, as the detective describes it, does not sound like one of the Quiet One's creations.

I get back to the perimeter around the church, take out my cellphone, and snap a quick picture of the sprayed graffiti when the advert cycles round to its darkest image. Then, with one final look at the church – a dull, monumental building, standing alone in a public square beside an intersection with shiny glass buildings all around – I depart.

"So what now?" I ask, distracted by the bitter taste of whiskey still lingering in my mouth.

You should seek to find out more about the graffiti. The image, the meaning behind it. Somebody might recognize it.

"Who?" I don't know anything about graffiti.

Street art tends to be an underground movement. Perhaps you could ask around the skating community, try to speak to artists at squats, or look into underground political groups.

"How do you know this?" I ask Vega. "Like, how do you even know what street art is?"

I was programmed with an encyclopedic knowledge about this era during my installation. I can't function as a general assistant without a little wisdom.

I don't even know where to start with this. Speak to the skating community? I don't exactly have experience in this field. I guess I need to go back to the drawing board on this one.

I arrive at the bus stop again, pull my ticket out of my pocket, and rack my brains about what to do next.

CHAPTER 10

By the time the bus makes its abrupt halt and the doors swing open with that familiar 'whoosh' noise, it's getting dark already. I climb the stairs in my apartment building, barely even breaking into a deep breath, and unlock the apartment door. There I find Dad sitting alone watching some tacky gameshow on TV.

"How's the job hunt?" he asks sarcastically. At least he's not smoking this time.

"Good," I say, echoing his sarcasm. "I'm getting into art."

"Art?" he turns round, fixing those big, incredulous eyes on me. His stony, pallid expression loosens into something resembling a smile. "What kind of art?"

"Street art," I say, trying hard to keep a straight face. I mean, it's not technically a lie is it? "You know, graffiti, urban expressionism."

"You're out of your darned mind," he says, with a deep, full-throated chuckle. Then he turns back to the television and duly descends into a coughing fit, before adding: "And how are you supposed to pay your share of the rent?"

"I'm still working on that," I say, selecting something out of the refrigerator. I'm starving. Somehow those glasses of whiskey didn't give the organic and robotic elements of my body the sustenance they crave.

Yeah, the rent. That and a large hospital bill I'll soon have to contend with. I wonder if there's a reward for tracking down the Quiet One.

He turns around again, searching me with those eyes. "You been palling around with those no-hope beatniks down on 45th street?"

"What?" I don't know what he's talking about. My Dad is making the fatal mistake of assuming I'm as terminally clued-up about the boring newspaper stories of this city as he is.

"The church on 45th. They took it over for some art show crap. Bunch of good-for-nothings."

Art show? I momentarily stop chewing.

"A beautiful building like that," he continues. "More than a 100 years of history. You know what they're doing to it now? They have a giant statue of a rabbit or something, strung up like a pinata. Worshipping a rabbit in the House of God! It's a travesty!"

He's veering off into ranting madness again, but I'm interested. I grab the newspaper from the table and muss his hair as I pass him, eliciting a growl. Funny, that's the closest I remember getting to him for months.

I go to my room, shut the door, and turn on the television, cranking up the volume. Then I start reading the newspaper. I thumb through the pages and stories – murders, political leaders doing things they shouldn't, idle celebrity gossip – before I'm greeted by two large black and white images.

One, the church on 45th. And two, a photograph of a large modern-art statue of a deer, crafted from what appears to be different types of metal all welded together. It's hung from the rafters by rope by the looks of it.

So this is the rabbit, Vega says.

The church lapsed into city ownership a year ago. Since then they tried to sell it off; I seem to remember my Dad blowing a gasket at the idea of it being turned into an all-you-can-eat restaurant. Now it appears they're trying to give it a second life as a cultural center. Art installations, plant-based kitchens, and a live performance venue.

"How about it?" I ask Vega. Two church visits in one day. Maybe as many as I'd visited in my entire life up to this point.

It seems as good a place as any to start.

I take off my sunglasses, leaving them on the table beside the bed. Then I turn off the television and turn out the light. That church is just a couple blocks from here, and most crucially if I'm quick I can get there before the kitchens close.

By the time I arrive, it's dark. The grassy areas around the park are populated by vaping teenagers wearing colorful hoodies and braids in their hair. Laughter fills the air. There's no fee on the door – my wallet cries out in relief – and I breeze past.

The church itself is quite impressive – a stone building with wooden rafters some 40 feet high at least. There are brightly colored streamers hanging throughout, and of course the giant deer suspended above my head.

Despite the time, there seems to be a healthy attendance. My stomach is reminding me there are more important matters at hand though. I leave the deer behind, and head to the former altar, now an open-plan kitchen, with a smirking woman standing behind a counter taking orders.

After sitting to eat some flavorless vegan popcorn 'chicken' bites, I can address the second most important task of the day: tracking down the Quiet One. I've been able to sit and watch the groups moving through the church for five minutes now.

In between the older couples standing and gawking at the Great Big Deer, and the stoned teens dragging their feet around the various exhibits, there's someone in the middle of it all: an attractive, red-headed woman wearing a lanyard. I'm guessing she works here.

When I approach she's busy talking to an elderly couple. I pass the time by looking at a couple of exhibits – an intricate model of this very church that appears to have been built with matchsticks, and a large painting of a skyscraper, appearing to have been painted with blood. Or at least blood-colored paint.

Then I circle back around and end up staring at a photograph of the sea with a blurry seagull pictured in the center. The dark blue waves, the mystery, and the darkness, plus the solitary white seagull in the middle of it all.

I'm so caught up in it I don't notice the elderly couple disappear.

"Haunting, isn't it?"

A highly-pitched, somewhat tense voice asks the question. I turn to see the red-head wearing the lanyard. She has dark brown eyes and slight freckles on her nose. I feel myself blinking repeatedly.

"Oh, this? Sure." I stammer slightly, cursing again the fact the robots can't make me talk good. "'The Seagull and the Dark Sea'," I say, reading from from the label under the image. "Erm, very nice."

I sound like an idiot, which is precisely what I am; I don't know anything about art. All I know is that it looks *nice*.

"Are you interested in photography?" she asks with a smile that makes my cheeks heat up.

"Not really, I just like the look of the water." I'm really hitting it out of the park here. She nods slightly and looks as though she's keen to part company with me. I need to get to the real subject. "My real interest is street art. You know, graffiti and such?"

"Oh yeah? You might be interested in next month's exhibit: urban culture through the ages." She lists a number of artworks, artists, and films. I nod along, feigning interest, thinking of a way to whip out my cellphone and show her the only graffiti I truly care about.

"Thanks, that sounds great," I say. She smiles again and turns to leave. I know I have to take my chance. "Actually, I wondered if you could tell me something about this."

I take my cellphone out, navigate past *that* lockscreen, and pull the photo up. I hold it up, and I can see her eyes focus on it, past the broken glass; her pupils shrinking slightly as she takes it in.

"Uhm, I've never seen it. I'm not much of a ballet fan."

"What?" I realize she thinks I'm asking about the advert. "Oh no, sorry — I mean the graffiti. Do you recognize that artwork? I'm a collector of sorts."

She giggles, putting her hand to her mouth. She focuses back on the picture again before shaking her head and looking back into my eyes.

"I'm sorry, no, I don't." I smile and put the cellphone away. I feel deflated again. To be honest, asking the guide at an art exhibition was a dumb idea. How would she be able to identify a random bit of graffiti? Then something lights up in her eyes, and she continues: "But I do know someone in the scene."

"Oh really?" I feel my eyebrows shoot up. Perhaps enduring those vegan 'chicken' bites wasn't in vain after all. She dictates an address to me, which I duly stick in a note on my cellphone. She tells me his name is 'Lion', which I have to strain hard not to laugh at, and that the address is a 'shared collective,' which I assume means a commune of some sort. No phone number, curiously. I can only assume he doesn't have one.

"But, be careful…" she tells me with some hesitation. "They open their doors to anyone. I've seen some shady characters there."

"Right, gotcha."

I thank her and leave her to the mercy of a couple of teens with camo jackets and way too many questions about the suspended deer.

I take one final look at the photograph of the gull, and thinking about *that* lockscreen again, take my cell out and take a quick snap of it. I switch it out, so that the seagull and the dark waters is the only thing peering back at me behind the broken glass. Sorry not sorry Jessica.

I leave the church with a spring in my step, filled with a confidence I haven't felt for a long time. So what if all I have is a name – a ridiculous name – and an address? Maybe it's also the fact I spoke to an attractive woman without making *too* much of a fool of myself, but I feel like I actually accomplished something here.

"So, we've got a lead," I say to Vega.

Yes. How helpful he'll be is another question entirely. Perhaps if you present yourself as a buyer of artwork he'll tell you all he knows.

I walk home, whistling a tune I don't immediately recognize, feeling one step closer to the Quiet One.

CHAPTER 11

I can see my mother. She's walking ahead of me, but I can't see her face, just the back of her head. I'm straining myself trying to keep up; my lungs are burning, my legs are hurting. She's still walking, forging her way along some unknown path. I reach out, hoping to touch her on the shoulder and turn her around, but it's no use. She's just out of reach.

I wake up. There's sweat on my brow and the dissonant chords of religious music ringing in my ears.

It's 9:00 AM or so, and I know I need to drag my jobless ass out of bed already. I check my bank balance on my cellphone: depressingly little. Plus whatever the packaging plant will decide to pay me for the last few days I deigned to work there.

In fact, I still haven't received a call from them. I wonder if I should be offended that they've forgotten I exist.

Throughout the morning I work on my cover story. I'm the son of a multi-millionaire businessman with a newly matured trust fund and a love of street art. I'm especially interested in spray-template art, and even more than that I'm interested in the mystery of the blank faced boy holding the umbrella.

I'm hoping that my privileged (although fictitious) background doesn't alienate me from the urban warriors, but assume the (again fictitious) alure of money will build bridges across the class divide.

I throw on my suit – my only suit – without a tie. I even go to the trouble of ironing a shirt. I can't even remember the last time I got the ironing board out.

"I can't even remember the last time you got that out!" my Dad barks at me in tacit agreement, stifling a cruel, deep-voiced laugh. He thinks I'm out there interviewing for a new job, despite the fact I've told him precisely nothing. He seems happy about it at least.

After making my hair look half-presentable, I put on my sunglasses, and head out.

―――

I'm daydreaming when the bus drives over a pothole in the road, jolting me upwards. I'm still stuck on that dream, chasing my mother up the hill. Strange.

I'm travelling to the outskirts of town again. I can already see the office blocks and retail lots beginning to thin out, replaced in kind by derelict buildings and liquor stores.

My new eye for graffiti is revealing a lot about this side of town, none of it pleasant. Expletives, gang tags, and strange religious messages adorns the shutters of closed-down shops and the wooden boards nailed over windows. To be fair, it's exactly the side of town I'd expect an expert on graffiti to be located.

I'm so distracted by the outside world that I don't notice the female figure pass me in the bus. Long, dark brown hair obscures her face for the most part, but then she turns and accidentally locks eyes with me… it's Jessica, waiting at the front of the bus for the next stop.

My eyes widen upon seeing her; has she been on this bus the entire time? She tears her eyes away from mine and turns her head, seemingly balanced precariously on her skinny frame, to face the door.

The bus jolts to a stop and as soon as the doors open, she's gone. I push my way past a burly guy in a sports shirt and manage to hop off just in time, completely forgetting to nod at the driver.

"Hey, Jessica!" I look around and see that I'm two stops away from my own planned disembarkation, but I feel I've got an apology to make for the other night. "Wait up, can I say something?"

All of a sudden I feel like I'm back in that dream, pursuing someone just out of reach. But then she pauses and turns around to look at me. She smiles and then grimaces.

"Kris, I'm sorry – I've got somewhere I need to be." Her work requires her to visit businesses around the city. She's something to do with the insurance industry. An adjuster or something like that. Jesus, did I forget already? "I'm working," she needlessly adds.

"Yeah, I know, I'll only take a minute." I see her expression soften and I rake my fingers through my hair, trying to conjure up the apology I know I should be making. "I'm sorry for how I was the other night. I'd had a long day, and—"

She cuts me off, taking her hand out of her pocket and anxiously jabbing it in my direction.

"You broke my neighbor's phone. You left all your crap in my hallway. I'm pawning that ring to buy him a new one, just so you know." She's angry, and now seems fine with giving me both barrels in the street. Perhaps I should have stayed on the bus. "Don't come round to my apartment again. There's nothing for you there."

"I know, I'm sorry" I repeat. "Look, something amazing has happened to me. It's like I'm a new person, honestly…"

I pause for breath, and wonder just where I'm going with this. I can't tell her about the dead body and the robot legion coursing through my body, she'd never believe me. Do I want to try and rekindle our relationship? My mouth continues talking, divorced from my brain.

"I've got an entire new outlook on life. No more fear. No more anxiety. I'm going to get a new job, move out of the apartment. Can't get a new Dad, but hey, I can change everything else!" She seems unmoved by my little joke. "I've never felt more alive, I just wish you could see me like this. That old me? The boring guy who never wanted to take you anywhere nice, never wanted to explore, never aspired to anything? He's gone for good!"

"Kris!" she shouts, shaking me out of my manic ramblings. "I didn't end it because you were boring. I ended it because you hated yourself."

I pause, feeling an icy dagger embedded in my chest. Hated myself?

"What?"

"Yes, you hate yourself. You're always telling yourself you're not happy, that you're imperfect, that you're flawed. You never wanted to be happy. You never wanted to allow yourself to be happy." She pulls an errant strand of hair away from her face, before continuing the onslaught. "It was exhausting. I couldn't deal with that, with that…"

She seems to be hesitating to find the right word to use. Perhaps she understands that she's twisting the icy dagger now.

"That negativity," she finally clarifies. "I have my own problems, my own issues, my own world. I didn't want to have to deal with the weight of your world too. And here you go again, telling me about the old you, the boring you."

I open my mouth to try to talk but find no words will

come out. Whatever demon possessed me to talk madly a minute ago has vanished without trace.

"I'm sorry Kris, I have to get to work."

And with that she turns and carries on walking. I watch her slim figure disappear into a building across the street, and she's gone.

I hate myself? I had never thought about it like that before. But of course she's right. Every social event I'd fob off, every new hobby I refused to try, every new opportunity to learn a new skill I spurned ostensibly because of my heart condition, but really? Perhaps I just wanted more time to sit and wallow.

I shake my head and straighten my shirt collar. I should get back to the job at hand.

Your ex, she's ill.

"What?" I say, wondering what the hell Vega is talking about. Right then, right there, in the arena of gladiatorial battle with Jessica, I'd forgotten he witnesses everything I witness.

I'd estimate she has a very low percentage of body fat, a percentage potentially bordering on dangerous. The pale blood vessels around her eyes would indicate anemia. In addition, her fingernails are ridged and appear brittle. These symptoms are all indicative of anorexia.

"What? Anorexia?" I'm shocked to hear the word. I know what it means, but I'd never encountered it in my life before. And then, that revelation gives way to an even more shocking one: "Does that... does that mean she was undereating the whole time and I didn't even realize?"

I wouldn't be able to answer that question.

I rub my forehead with my palm; I feel like I have a migraine. Everything except the actual pain. I wonder if I should run into that building, take her in my arms, and spirit her to a doctor's clinic or a counsellor or someone else equipped to deal with such things.

But I know that's silly. She's always been skinny. Noticeably so. But I would have never thought her life would be in danger.

I start walking – I've got two bus stops to make up. Her words are still running through my mind, though. That I hate myself. That I'm relentlessly negative. And thinking that I drearily plodded through our entire relationship without even figuring out she had her own problems to deal with.

Jesus, I feel awful. I *am* awful.

I make a mental note to text her later while having utterly no clue what I'm going to say and get back to my mission.

I'm barely round the corner before I hear the 'shared collective.' There's loud music – synthpop, vaguely European sounding – echoing out in the otherwise completely lifeless street. I take one look and know instantly I've got the right place.

A building – former offices, by the look of it – adorned with banners and streamers. Bright colors and a cloud of smoke emanating from the upper floor windows like a chimney. Reminds me of my Dad's vantage spot beside the window, funnily enough.

Every other building on this street is derelict – one burned out, another condemned and decorated with papers advertising that fact. And if there were any real business still based on this street, they surely wouldn't last long.

The banners are a hodgepodge of political expressions, clumsily written in black marker. And curiously, there's a candle lit in each window. In truth, the building brings a bit of life, color, and expression to this bland gray place.

I watch as a guy leaves the building and I look upon his appearance with horror – long hair, green hoodie, scruffy jean shorts – and I immediately get the feeling I've made a terrible mistake. I'm surely way overdressed. Way to advertise myself as an outsider.

Still, I clench my jaw and walk the remaining distance to the building. As soon as I get to the door, I can smell weed. Not a surprise, I suppose. There's a couple of people in the former reception of the office that now looks to be a meeting room of sorts with a round table and a selection of hilariously mismatched tatty seats and wobbly stools.

The girl is short, with pink and blue hair separated into pigtails. The guy is taller with sunken eyes watching me suspiciously. They're both standing awkwardly and motionless; I wonder what they were doing before I got here.

"Hey, I need to speak to someone who lives here." The girl looks at me. No, in fact, she looks just past me like she wants to avoid my eyes and stare directly into my brain. "Lion. Is he here?"

"Narc," she says to the guy, which I gather is her calling me a cop. "I don't know. I don't keep a register," she sneers.

"But he lives here, right?" I ask, before returning to right the obvious wrong. "I'm not a narc."

"You got a narc suit, you got a narc haircut, you got a smug narc look on your face. Narc shoes, narc eyes, narc vibes." She pauses, evidently trying to find another clue that suggests I'm a cop, and failing. "And I don't know anyone called Lion."

"Right, thanks." I say, moving past her and her lanky buddy.

"No problem, NARC!"

She shouts the last part, trying to clue the rest of the building into the theory that I'm an early-twenties undercover cop. I already hate this. Why couldn't that art guide give me the name of a nice librarian or a professor at the university? The guy they pay to scrub the lewd graffiti off the walls in the public toilets would have been a less painful lead than this.

I make it through the room and the building's self-appointed guardians, and find a staircase taking me up to the second floor. The music booms ever louder and the smell of incense here makes my head hurt.

The second floor looks to have once been a giant, open-plan office. Some desks are still here, in fact, with the added furnishings of sleeping bags and ratty-looking tents. There's at least a dozen folks living here: fresh-faced teens, mid-thirties new age traveler types with bloodshot eyes, all the way to professorial types in their forties.

And all of them seemingly stop their conversations to watch at me traipse through the office. Their home.

"Hi, I'm looking for someone."

"Uh-huh," one of the older guys hums, his face entirely unmoving. He's got silver hair and a thin, wispy beard. This room had floor to ceiling windows once, but some of those windows are now covered up by thin, colorful blankets. The result is a kaleidoscopic palette of colors throughout the room. A far prettier work environment than what came before, I'm sure.

"Lion, I think his name is?" The uncertainty in my voice is palpable; I sound exactly like I look: a dork, way overdressed and in way over his head. Luckily, the awkwardness apparent in me goes a long way to convincing this guy I'm not a cop. He smiles, and the rest of the dozen or so people go back to their conversations.

"He's on the fourth floor, the executive suite." He says the last words with an element of irony. I nod my thanks and turn back to the staircase.

The fourth floor is an entirely different atmosphere altogether; I hadn't even known this building had a fourth floor – it appeared to be completely boarded up from the outside. There's not a bit of natural light up here.

The entire place seems lit by candles; golden light casting wavering shadows on the walls, and completely dark corners, hiding God only knows what. I have to step over a guy sleeping on the floor, and slide past another large, tattooed man eyeing me suspiciously.

This entire floor is divided up into tiny rooms with improvised wooden partitions, like some hobbyist carpenter took a bunch of speed and went to town on it. Suddenly, just as I reach what I presume used to be the executive suite – a large room, free of the endless improvised wooden walling – the music from downstairs stops.

All of a sudden I sense eyes on me. An imperceptible feeling like I'm being watched from somewhere in the room.

"What you need, suit?" I hear a voice and see no face. I turn around to find a large, shaven-headed man, striding forward from the shadows beside the doorway, masked in darkness. Had he not spoke out, I'd never have seen him. He has a stern look on his face. At least, the parts of his face I can see in the dim light. His accent isn't American; it sounds Middle Eastern.

"I'm looking for someone: Lion." I see him smile, his features lit by flickering candlelight. But the more my eyes linger on him, the more his expression appears to be a scowl. The sunglasses may be a mistake. "Ya see, I'm a collector, and—"

"He's inside," the voice says, and his face relaxes back to that stern expressionlessness stare again.

I continue into the room, wondering what the hell that was all about. A bodyguard? A follower? This whole place has the feeling of a cult clubhouse. Looking around, there are colored blankets adorning each wall with candles and incense burning throughout.

Then I hear the footsteps behind me, and turn to see the large, shaven-headed man following me in. He steps up to me and points to a door in the corner of the wall, shrouded in darkness.

I look up at him – bridging the six or so inches in height

between us – and nod in his direction. I follow him to the door, which he duly opens for me. What I see inside shocks me far more than anything I've seen in this cult paradise so far.

Floor to ceiling windows, a desk, and a smartly dressed man behind it. He jumps out from across the desk and races to shake my hand. He's light-skinned with dreadlocks and a slight beard. His cheeks are red and his eyes are excitable, flicking side to side as he grasps my hand and shakes firmly.

"Hi, I'm Jonny, but my friends call me Lion. I gather you're a collector, yes?"

I look past him and see all the amenities and accoutrements of an office: a laptop, a printer, even one of those water coolers. And a big, homely spider plant, growing wildly out of control in the corner. I'm speechless; I forget entirely how to greet this man.

"Uhm, hi, I'm Kris." Should I really have given him my real name? It's too late now. "I hear you're the man to talk to about street art."

"You bet I am," he says, with a salesperson's panache. "Hope you weren't too perturbed by my downstairs buddies. I find keeping a certain… menagerie helps with the image, you know? I'm former entertainment lawyer by trade."

Like everything else in this city, the 'shared collective' is cheap and inauthentic. I don't know why I'm surprised. I watch Lion – Jonny, rather – duck back behind his desk.

The large man stands beside me still. In the natural light, I can see he's quite the imposing figure. Wearing a black vest with strange marijuana leaf patterns on it and camo pants. He has scars crisscrossing his left arm, and one of his eyes is noticeably lower than the other, surrounded by a deep red mark.

The more I look at this Jonny/Lion guy, the more I'm convinced I've been the mark in a fairly convincing sales operation. Suckered in by a pretty red-headed girl, forced to run the intimidating gauntlet of art students to throw me off balance, and finally given the hard sell by the salesman in charge of it all.

I watch as he unveils a series of easels showcasing what I assume are priceless examples of street art on canvas from the masters of the scene. I rush to ensure him I already have something in mind, "Sorry, I'm looking for a very specific artwork."

He stops with the easels and relaxes his posture, still wearing that broad and insincere salesman's smile.

"Sure, show me what you've got."

I sit down on the chair provided and fumble my cellphone out of my pocket, navigating to the picture of the graffiti before passing it over to him.

"Sorry about the broken glass, got a new cellphone coming in the mail" I tell him, untruthfully. I see his expression harden as he stares at the picture. "Oh, it's the art I'm interested in of course, not the ballet advert."

His eyes look up from the picture and meet mine; I can see all the love, warmth, and salesman's optimism drain from them immediately. His voice is toneless and severe: "Is this some kind of joke?"

All of a sudden, the room seems to shrink; the walls are collapsing in and that 6'6" bodyguard by the side of me seems a hell of a lot closer. I laugh out of nervousness before narrowing my eyes and trying to form a word but fail horribly. Then I feel a large, meaty paw on my shoulder, crushing the fabric of my suit jacket against my skin.

"What are you talking about?" I ask, finally composing myself and relaxing back in the chair, partly to escape the relentless pressure of that man's hand. I needn't have bothered; he quickly finds my position again and bends his posture at the waist to follow me down.

Kris, this situation appears to be getting out of hand, Vega says in a very astute observation.

"This art, this…" Jonny pauses, like the words are toxic and he's trying to spit them out as far as possible. "This man!"

All of a sudden, I feel myself getting pulled up by the clavicle. The chair is kicked out from under me and I'm pushed up against the wall by the bodyguard. I want to fight my way out of this – engage every nanomachine in my biceps and push away from him, but something tells me it'd be more in my interests to talk my way out of this rather than resorting to fists.

"What's your game here, kid?!"

Jonny/Lion is walking towards us, hiding partially behind his bodyguard, and yelling at me while still holding my cellphone in his hand. His bodyguard is unmoving, like steel, holding me in place by the shoulder.

"I need to find the man who did that graffiti," I shout back, wondering just what thread I've decided to tug on here. "I think he's involved in something. Something bad."

To my surprise, the bodyguard's grip loosens. I look at Jonny again and see that there are creases appearing around his eyes. Before long, he smiles at me incredulously and the meathead lets me go. I dust myself off slightly, straightening my suit jacket.

"I guess you know each other?" I finally ask, wondering just where this whole thing is going to take me next.

"Know each other, hmph." Jonny snorts in amusement. I feel like I'm getting somewhere at last. "My friend here is named Ahmed. He's a refugee from Aljarran. He's a freedom fighter, a former soldier."

Ahmed shows me his arm, flexing his bicep. Alongside the large, rippling muscle I can see those same sets of scarring zigzags like a brutal roadmap branded onto his arm.

"Ahmed fought wars, and yet never got a scar until he met Carver." Jonny/Lion walks back behind his desk and sits on his chair – an extravagant, throne-like seat. "You really didn't know, huh?"

"What happened?" I ask, looking at the scars again, losing myself in the patterns. It's painful to even look at.

"Bomb," Ahmed says, in that Middle Eastern accent. The word sends chills down my spine. I know what I'm searching for here. I know *who* I'm searching for. But hearing the word in this context – and seeing the scars on this man's arm – makes it all the more real to me now.

"Jesus," I say out loud. "Look, I just want to know if you can tell me anything about him. Full name, address, anything."

Jonny/Lion laughs again. He seems to have regained his salesman pep. He reaches below the table and fiddles around inside a folder before pulling out something. It's a photograph, black and white.

"Here."

I take a couple of uneasy steps to the desk, making sure not to worry anyone with my movements. I focus in on the photograph and see that it's outside the former city aquarium, long since closed.

There are a host of people in the photograph, one of them being Jonny/Lion and one of them being Ahmed. Jonny/Lion takes a pen and circles another person – an older man, perhaps in his forties, wearing a very distinctive peace symbol motif on a T-shirt.

"Carver," he says, trying to communicate a sense of steeliness but unable to hide the tone of dread in his voice. "James Carver."

I sit back down and reach across to pick up my cellphone from the desk; I hadn't noticed him place it down until now.

Jonny talks more: he tells me that Carver was a member of their 'shared collective.' A man who came from the anti-war movement before being eaten up, chewed up, and spat out by a more radical group. A couple of arrests, prison sentences, and deteriorating mental health episodes later he found his way to Jonny's zoo.

He tells me they were squatting at the aquarium, selling their art and minding their own business. Carver, on the other hand, had loftier aspirations. He wanted to mail bombs to an ever-escalating list of enemies. Churches, factories, universities. Eventually, when they confronted him and tried to remove him and his toys, one of the bombs exploded by accident, giving Ahmed his new body art.

At least, that's the story Jonny tells me.

"That image, that faceless boy with the umbrella, he's obsessed with it. He thinks he'll overturn the new world order, and, and..." Jonny seems to be getting overexcited again; his arms are flapping out by his sides. "...destroy the great lizardman hegemony, or whatever the hell he believes this week."

"You didn't report Carver to the police?" I ask, somewhat hesitantly.

"No, Ahmed here doesn't exactly have his papers in order." I look up at Ahmed, and he smiles awkwardly, raising his eyebrows in an *oops*-like expression. "And besides, how seriously do you think the cops take people like us?"

He messes with his thumbs, twiddling them together despondently. It's the first time I've seen him look remotely helpless.

"So where is he now?"

"He's still there, of course." He points to the photograph, with the boarded-up aquarium windows, and the big CITY AQUARIUM lettering behind. "You're not actually going to go there are you?"

I don't answer; I'm too busy looking at Carver's face in the photograph. Maybe it's the peace symbol, maybe it's the strange glow in his eyes. He certainly doesn't look like how I expected the city's mad bomber to look.

"He's out of his goddamn mind," Jonny says, over-enunciating each word for effect. "He's sitting in the tunnels beneath that aquarium, building weapons and bombs and God only knows what else."

And then Jonny tells me something that surprises me. "And if you're thinking he's that 'Quiet One' bomber, you'd be wrong."

"What?" I finally ask. Jonny has my full attention now. His eyes are still swimming around in their sockets, moving from side to side. For the first time, I wonder what strange substances he's taken. "The Quiet One?"

"I read those letters. The ones the bomber sent to the press. They're thoughtful, well-written, intelligent. That ain't him." Jonny turns away from me, looking up to Ahmed with another rather helpless look on his face. "That sure ain't him."

I thank him, and say my goodbyes, leaving the photograph behind.

"Sorry about the suit," Ahmed says, pointing to my jacket shoulder, now permanently misshapen.

I leave the building, my mind flooded with ideas and contradictions. The girl at reception greets me with a smile, a wink, and a "Bye, narc," for good measure.

"So I think we have our man," I say to Vega, walking back to the bus stop, bidding this gray street and its sole, colorful temple on the hill goodbye.

Well, we certainly have a suspect.

That aquarium is on the other side of town, but my heart is racing. I can hear it beating in my ears. I feel it – the mounting excitement. The thrill of the chase. Like I'm a wolf, closing in on my prey.

"I'm gonna run it," I tell Vega. "To the aquarium, I mean. I'm so close to catching this guy I can taste it."

In a suit and shirt?

"Why the hell not?"

And with that – and the crisp, cold air filling my lungs – I begin to run.

CHAPTER 12

It takes me an hour or so to get across town, even with my elevated speed. By time I get around the block from the aquarium, I'm sweating heavily. A man with a crazed look in his eye and a scuffed-up suit, running across the city. I must look insane. I love it.

My thighs are burning; my calves are tightening up and going numb but I feel fantastic.

I come to a stop and lean against a railing, taking a couple of minutes to catch my breath again. I don't even know what the distance was. 24 subway stops, a couple of fire stations, and a mall.

"So what do we know?" I ask Vega, sucking in breath through my nostrils.

We know this will be a very dangerous situation. James Carver sounds like a dangerous and highly motivated man if the entertainment lawyer is to be believed, Vega says 'the entertainment lawyer' with a hint of derision. *On the other hand, we don't know anything more about Carver than what we've been told. The lawyer seemed confident he wasn't the bomber.*

"Yeah, I feel like I need to have a chat with Mr. Carver. Get to the bottom of this."

When I've regained my breath and wiped the sweat off my brow with my shirt cuff, I feel ready to face this guy.

The aquarium closed 10 years ago or so. I remember going when I was a kid; Dad – and my mother – holding me by the hands and pointing out the different fish. I close my eyes and imagine myself being back there – majestic blue water and the silhouettes of fish dancing within.

Even that murky, dingy aquarium smell was pleasurable to me somehow. I can almost feel my mother's hand.

I'm shaken out of my reverie by drops of rain on my head. The afternoon is wearing on and the weather is turning. I make the final few steps towards the locked gates of the aquarium and try to prepare myself for everything to come.

Be careful, Vega says as I size up the imposing steel gates. *There could be traps set up. If Carver is as mentally unstable as he sounds, there's no telling what he could be capable of.*

"Yeah, I've got it."

I climb the gates and walk around the periphery of the aquarium; the main building is a dirty white paneled monolith with smiling dolphins and winking angel fish illustrated on it. But there are panels missing and moss growing from where they once stood. It's sad seeing the place like this.

The lawyer said there were tunnels beneath the aquarium. That should be our first port of call.

I look around, seeing a set of double doors chained shut. Running to hide from the rain, I grasp the chain in my hands and feel its rigidity. It's tough, but slightly rusty. The more I run the links between my fingers, the more I can smell the corrosion.

I bite my lip and pull as hard as I can on either side of the chain. I feel blood rushing to my biceps; I feel my heart beating rampantly again. Before long, I feel the chain begin to bend and curve against itself, the links deforming against my effort. And then, with an audible pop, they break. With one slightly stinging palm, I push the door open and I'm in.

Inside the building is dark; dingy, damp. But it takes my breath away instantly. Two gigantic, empty fish tanks – I remember them from visiting all those years ago – with the glass cloudy, fractured, and broken.

There's no light – I pick my cell out of my pocket and use the flashlight – but as soon as I do, I see the symptoms of a mad man.

That same graffiti, stenciled on every wall, on every surface, on every intact pane of glass. On the ceilings, on the floors, on the doors hanging off their hinges. Blacks, whites, reds, blues. The same blank face staring back at me.

"Well, I think we found our guy," I say, taking off my sunglasses and placing them in my pocket.

I light my way, finding plenty of empty corridors and ghostly fish tanks, but no signs of life just yet. Whatever Jonny/Lion and the rest of the collective were doing here, they're long gone now. Then I find a large set of red, dusty doors, rusted along the hinges, standing at the bottom of a long, gray corridor.

"You wouldn't happen to think those look like the doors to a bunch of service tunnels, would you?"

They would seem to be far from the path the public was supposed to take around the aquarium, which would support that theory. But I'm no janitor, Kris.

I chuckle to myself. I feel like I'm starting to speak Vega's language. Stupid questions get stupid answers.

I walk quietly to the doors, feeling that my sweaty shirt and suit combination may not be the best dress for sneaking around. Then, pushing the metal bar, I slowly open them.

As soon as I do so, I hear something – a voice, like a radio, droning on in the distance. I follow the noise along dark, damp-smelling corridors, finding more and more trash littering the path as I go. This place is certainly lived in.

Finally I reach a rigid cast iron staircase heading into the depths; I slowly walk down it and the noise gets ever louder –

imperceptible words spoken at a manic pace. It sounds almost like one of those audiobooks designed to teach you to speak French, cranked up to twice the speed.

Walking carefully, keeping my eyes peeled for tripwires or pits of electric eels, or anything else you could expect to kill you in a haunted aquarium, I come ever closer to the source of the noise. But the louder it becomes, the more I consider the frightening possibility that it isn't a radio.

"Cops, cops, pigs! Fighting, scheming, crying, big ones, little ones! Papists, all of them, one Pope, one world government, one plan for us all!"

That stream of insane consciousness, repeating with different words, but the same incomprehensible meaning. Echoing from wall to wall, sounding like a chorus of insane men in agreement. But I know it's just one man. It's one man, with one voice. It must be Carver.

I finally find a door ajar, and the shouting – the mad, bloodthirsty, chilling rant – is at its loudest. I peer through it to see a workshop, of sorts, lit by toxic green light. There's a diesel generator in the corner, with an exhaust pipe attached to a large hose trailing off into the darker recesses of the room.

There are dirty metal cabinets and mountains of trash lying around – everything from bin bags to car tires to rusty old springs and hub caps. The smell is palpable, filling my nostrils, making it hard for me to think of anything.

And then the centerpiece of the room: a large steel table, littered with soldering irons and saws and tubs of glue and power drills and plenty of other sorts of tools, all in varying degrees of disrepair. Sitting in the middle, the orchestrator of it all, is a gray old man with frayed hair and a navy jumper, torn in several places. The endless stream of words out of his mouth continues unabated.

Be very careful and very quiet, Vega says. *You should think about how to incapacitate him. He won't go quietly, that's for sure.*

I look around and see a couple of cable ties sticking out of a trash bag next to me. I grab them, finding them happily intact, and sneak towards him. By the time he notices me in a broken mirror, it's too late.

He turns around in panic, but I grab his head in the palm of my hand, hold onto it for the briefest of moments as I look into those scared eyes, and slam it down onto the steel workshop table. He hits it with a sickening thud and emits a low-pitched groan.

I stick the cable ties on him as quick as I can, tying both hands behind his back, before picking him up, placing him back into his swivel chair, and pushing him out into the center of the room. Mission accomplished?

Search him. He might have a weapon or a detonator.

I do as Vega asks and find nothing but a couple of screws, an old sparkplug, and the horrible, fetid smell of a man who lives in a disused aquarium. He's delirious, eyes swimming around in his head.

He had a blow to the head, but I believe he'll be fine; he didn't lose consciousness and there's no bleeding at the site of the wound.

I look around the table, seeing pans of chemicals and bits of metal bent and hammered to look exactly like how I'd expect a pipe bomb to look, albeit incredibly scrappy.

"Shame."

With my fingers, I take a feel of the pans, of the metals, of the tools. Enough for Vega to get the forensic evidence he needs, I hope. Then I'm brought back to the scene by a surprisingly cogent Carver.

He slurs, rocking from side to side in his chair, "Who are you? Police? Did they send you?"

"I'm no cop," I state, turning around to look at him head on. "Just a concerned citizen."

"I know they sent you, they always send types like you…" he begins to trail off into the same indecipherable gibberish he was saying before we properly met. I lean against the workbench and look at him closely. He's old; pathetic even. Skinny. The jumper hangs off his skeletal frame.

His eyes are zigzagging around the room and rolling back in his head from time to time. He tries to stand, but barely seems to have the energy to do so. He looks like he's been awake all week. I find myself feeling something for him I never expected. I feel *sorry* for him.

"Vega," I say, not particularly caring if Carver witnesses me talking to my imaginary friend. "I don't know about this…"

Yes, the bombs on the workbench aren't viable. They're far from it. They're entirely different in chemical make-up to the initial 13 Quiet One bombs, and there's no additional radioactivity present in any of these tools and items.

I look at the wall; the same graffiti. The blank face, the umbrella.

"There's no doubt he was at the university though, and the church."

He was definitely at the church. And I believe his bomb was found at the church. But we don't know that he set the bomb at the university. That bomb was sophisticated, functional, deadly. I don't think this man is capable.

"Right, then he was just…"

I trail off without saying the word. I'm looking at Carver again; he hasn't broken eye contact with me this entire time. He's still barking words at me, some I know, some I've heard of, and some I don't understand.

I could break out the CIA book of enhanced interrogation techniques and go to town and he'd never speak anything resembling sense.

A copycat? Perhaps.

I find some rubber tubing and take the time to tie his legs up. Now he's just a skinny, shouting skeleton, trussed up on the floor. He's going nowhere.

He could a mere admirer of the Quiet One. Perhaps he wanted to scrawl his own graffiti at the site of the Quiet One's bombs as a form of tribute, or even to take responsibility for them himself.

I try my best to rub the evidence of me being here off the few items that aren't too rusty to retain fingerprints. Then I retrace my steps without the acoustic guide of his maniacal ravings to help me this time. I pass through the red doors and take one final look at the aquarium, trying to dampen those memories of my childhood. Then I exit the same way I came in.

Outside it's absolutely pouring with rain. I rush over to the gates and quickly scale them, carefully ensuring I don't slip on the greased-up steel. Then I jog down the street to a conveniently placed payphone – probably a relic from the days when this neighborhood saw a lot more foot traffic – and call 911.

Kris, Vega says, *let me handle this.*

I'm confused; I don't know what he's talking about, but there's no time to ask.

"Hello, 911, what's your emergency?"

"Yes, hello," the words come out of my mouth, but they sound like someone else's. Deeper, scratchier than my own voice. "There's a bomb in the service tunnels underneath the aquarium. Go, quickly."

And I put the phone down.

"What was that?" I ask Vega, realizing my voice has seemingly returned to normal.

A slight manipulation of your vocal chords. I've inactivated the effect now.

"Yeah, no kidding," I say back, still slightly freaked out by the entirely different man's voice coming from my throat. "You mean I can have any voice?"

Within reason.

I'm stuck in my own thoughts, pondering the possibilities, when I get a strange feeling like there are eyes on me from behind. And not just any old eyes. Eyes that are watching me, studying me. Peering directly into me.

I turn around to find a man sheltering from the rain underneath an umbrella, his face expressionless. He's wearing a large black coat and his eyes are hidden behind two steamed up glasses' lenses. He has graying hair, and his skin is wrinkled and pale. He's standing beside a black car, motionless, other than the lit cigarette he's impatiently rolling between his fingers.

"What are you doing here?" he asks suspiciously.

"Uhh," Did he see me coming out of the aquarium? Did he hear me call the cops? "What?"

"I'm special agent Hayes with the FBI." He takes out an ID card from his back pocket with those big three letters emblazoned next to his mugshot: *FBI*. "Now, I'll ask again. What are you doing here?"

I pause in horror, unable to put the words I want to say in the correct order and get them out of my mouth. He takes a drag on his cigarette and it feels like years pass.

"I'm s-sorry," I finally stammer, realizing that I've got my own voice back. "I was just calling a friend of mine, we used to visit this aquarium together years ago, and—"

He cuts me off by waving his hand, keeping the cigarette in his mouth.

"It's pouring it down. Shouldn't you be at college or something? What's that old building there?"

He points at the aquarium.

"That's the aquarium. The one I was talking about."

He looks back at the building, and then looks back at me, finally pulling the cigarette from between his lips.

"What's your name? Have you got ID?"

I pause again; I just cracked the case of the would-be church bomber, and now I'm having to deal with the FBI derailing my efforts? A small, nagging feeling hidden away at the base of my brain stem tells me to run. I can outrun this guy and he'd never see me again. Then again, isn't it a felony to lie to the FBI? How about fleeing from them?

With an exhalation of breath, I take my ID out of my back pocket and hand it over to him.

He balances his umbrella on his head and right shoulder, rather peculiarly. He studies my ID, holding onto it with both hands for an age before looking up at me twice. It's like he's trying to memorize my face and etch my name into the stony walls of his memory.

Then, as I hear police sirens in the far distance – two and then three separate tones – I see him hand it back to me. I very quickly slide it back into my back pocket.

"Get out of here Kris."

He drops his cigarette on the sidewalk and turns his back to me, focusing all his attention on the aquarium. I take his advice and walk away as quickly as I can without looking suspicious.

"What the hell just happened?"

I think you just had your first real experience with law enforcement.

"Aren't you forgetting Detective Ramos?" I feel stupid as soon as I ask the question.

No, I'm not.

Yeah, figures.

"I didn't even know the FBI were on this case. He's the first agent assigned to this whole thing that I've seen."

I reach the bus stop five or so minutes later– something about this deluge seems unappealing for running in – and fumble around in my pockets for my bus pass. I can't seem to find it at first until I brush my fingers up against my ID, finding it stuck to the rain-moistened card.

Kris, there's something wrong with your ID.

"What?" I say loudly. Then I look around to ensure no-one heard me. Thankfully no-one is out standing in this downpour but me. "What do you mean, something wrong?"

It's radioactive. At least, more radioactive than it was earlier.

"Radio..." I pause, struggling to put two and two together. "...active?"

Radioactive. The tiniest, almost imperceptible change, but a change I can detect regardless. The duration that man was holding your ID must have been sufficient to irradiate it.

"But why the hell would he be..."

I trail off, and immediately remember Vega's pronunciation of the word *copycat*. Then, I put my bus ticket away and turn and run. I can still hear sirens in the background, although I can't be sure if they're more numerous now.

Kris, I don't know why you need to be told, but you shouldn't be seen running around the scene of a crime.

"I'll be careful," I assure him, feeling a little less confident of that myself.

I make up the distance to the aquarium in a minute or so, and from behind the faded glass of a long-abandoned shop front, I watch the front of the dilapidated building. Three cop cars are outside, and four cops are fiddling with the lock and chains on the gate. But the FBI agent appears to have vanished. Him and his car. I look around to ensure he hasn't just parked elsewhere, but see only curious onlookers sheltering from the rain.

Eventually, I watch as one of the cops climbs the gate and manages to unravel the chain, and soon all four police are out of sight. The sound of sirens still fills the air, but there's one more piece of evidence I want to recover from the scene.

I swoop in, my head low and my hands in my pockets, until I find his discarded cigarette butt on the floor. Then I stoop to pick it up – putting it in my right breast pocket – and take a look around to ensure I haven't been seen. And then I'm out of there.

CHAPTER 13

When I get home, Dad is out. Presumably he's attending one of his evening church groups, but I'm glad to have the peace and quiet. I take the damp cigarette butt out of my pocket and hold it between my fingers.

"So is this as radioactive as my ID?"

Yes. It's negligible but above the average background levels. It appears that FBI agent – Special Agent Hayes – is unusually radioactive. So radioactive, in fact, he imparts a higher reading of radioactivity to anything he touches.

I'm picking a pack of ham out of the fridge completely absent-mindedly, shoving slices into my mouth like an animal. I can't get the possibility out of my mind. Is this FBI agent handling the bombs too? Is he in league with the Quiet One? Is *he* the Quiet One?

We don't know anything about this man, Vega says, *but it does seem significant that he didn't seem to be assisting the police with their investigation at the aquarium. His car was old and beaten up – not a law enforcement agency issued car as I would expect.*

His car. I didn't even think about that. Hell, I was so creeped out by him I barely even noticed the car. I certainly didn't notice it wasn't the kind of car you'd expect Mulder and/or Scully to drive.

"So you noticed the car," I say, with a mouth full of ham. "Did you notice the numberplate?"

Yes, I did. I committed it to memory, as I do any details that may seem significant to our goals.

I feel a wave of relief wash over me, close my eyes, and emit a ham-muffled scream of joy that almost chokes me. It would seem that sometimes a trillion eyes are better than two.

Kris, your trachea was briefly blocked by partially chewed-up meat products. If I could recommend chewing more carefully, it would help us both a lot.

I ignore him and cast my mind back a couple of months ago. One of my old coworkers at the sandwich packaging factory – a real brutish, ignorant pig of a man named Lenny, or Lewis, or something or other – was bragging about intimidating his ex-girlfriend's latest date.

He would go over to her house and see whose car was parked up, note down the license plate, and go home to stew over it. Then he'd arrive at the poor guy's house to shout insults and push trash and such like through the letterbox. A gentleman, naturally.

This state allows you to look-up any license plate for a small fee and find which address that car is registered to. A horrendous lapse of privacy, exploited by domestic abusers and serial weirdos. But now? I can think of a better use for it. I'll find out whether that car is FBI or not. And if it isn't I'll get my latest lead.

I get on the laptop and have Vega tell me the license plate. I get on one of those license plate look-up websites and carefully enter the details.

"All right, let's see where our buddy the FBI agent lives." With some sense of trepidation, I click on the trackpad and wait for the page to load.

"Huh," I say to myself, looking at the result. I'd expected a 'no address found' or a 'registered to federal services' or something similar. Instead, I get an address. And not just any address, but an address within this city. "So, what are the chances Special Agent Hayes took his wife's car out that day?"

He wasn't wearing a wedding ring, Vega replies, taking my joke somewhat literally. *That's not to say he wasn't using someone else's car. But it's unlikely.*

I grab the address and paste it into a search engine. It takes me to a single, solitary house on the outskirts of town. Loading the street-level pictures, it looks like a cute little house – a single floor and a long dried-up pool by the back. There's a parking lot beside it, which curiously sits empty but for one car. The address is 25 Fenton Rose Street.

"Vega, would that be special agent Hayes' car?" I strain my eyes looking at its slightly pixelated form and try to reconcile that with my poor memory.

It would.

So, we've got our agent's home address. I hit the back button, returning to the original search results and something catches my eye: a headline on a local news site.

APARTMENT BUILDING CONDEMNED IN NUCLEAR ROW

"Nuclear huh?"

The article is two years old and details the city's plan to demolish an apartment building just across the road from the house the FBI agent's car is registered to due to a nuclear cleanup accident at a building within the area. In fact, the entire block was apparently condemned due to dangerous background radioactivity levels.

"Whoa," I say, my fingers pressed to my mouth. "Looks like we've got an answer for our radioactivity question."

I dig in, scouring the internet for as much knowledge about this incident as I can. As I read, memories begin to come back to me. An oft-repeated phrase or a block name etched into my memory from seeing it on the local news so much. I remember parts of this story as it happened, but like so much else I thought it was insignificant – just some unfortunate thing happening to some poor folks across town.

Five years ago a defense contractor went bust. This sort of thing seems to happen all the time. Companies rapidly expand, spend too much, flood themselves with debt, and then crash out in a massive burning wreckage.

But this defense contractor was particularly crooked. Part of their business was creating small nuclear reactors for prototype rockets – the sort of rocket that could fly around the entire planet without having to stop for fuel.

They always had sensitive nuclear materials on-site, and when the company went bust, somebody conveniently forgot about them rather than having to spend the money to clean them up properly.

A year later, some poor guy breaks in, steals a bunch of machinery, and comes down with a bad case of radiation sickness. There's a huge row, some former executives go to jail, others get a slap on the wrist, and the world continues turning.

That is unless you're unlucky enough to live in the neighboring area. The city tests for radiation and quickly realizes they need to re-home everyone on the block and clean the site up properly.

"But," I ask Vega, "why is a man – an FBI agent no less – living on that block still?"

You're still assuming he's a real FBI agent. Perhaps he's a former agent. Or an impersonator.

I'm still scouring the local news pages when I find an image that makes me stop stone cold dead in my tracks. It's our suspect number one – special agent Hayes himself. Only, he's not named Hayes in the caption. Alfred Burden, a 63-year-old male, labeled by the accompanying article as the block's final hold-out against the city's plans for re-homing.

"You know, I think you're onto something Vega."

The article is around a year old. It says he's a retired owner of a printing company, who has lived his entire life in the cute little cottage on 25 Fenton Rose Street.

He was recently widowed, and 'despite generous offers for compensation and accommodation from the city, refuses to give up the house he calls home.' It goes on to state that he's taken a vow to stay there. And while he does so, the city can't demolish the whole block as they'd like to.

I think everything is beginning to make a lot more sense.

"Do you think this man is our bomber? For real, this time?"

I can't stop looking at his image. He even has the same glasses, with both lenses fogged up in the humidity. And a cigarette between his fingers.

He would seem to have motive; unregulated, irresponsible technology use could have ruined his neighborhood and irradiated the home he loves. He seems intelligent, proactive, and he has a lot of time on his hands. Impersonating an FBI agent could grant him a lot of respect and access from the general public that he wouldn't otherwise get. It wouldn't be difficult to create a fake FBI ID, especially for a retired printer.

"But why was he at the aquarium?"

Perhaps he's been following the case of Carver, the copycat, as closely as we have.

"No-one likes a clout-chaser."

I can tell I've stumped Vega; he doesn't reply straight away, searching the pre-programmed knowledge of one trillion nanobots. I bet he understands the sly smile on my face though.

I'm not familiar with that turn of phrase.

"Don't worry about it." I flip back to the picture of the house at 25 Fenton Rose Street. "We're going to check this place out first thing in the morning."

I hear the front door open and slam shut. Dad must be

back. I hear the familiar dragging of feet in the hallway, and in no time the television flips on.

I look back at that image of Alfred Burden – those unintelligible, hidden eyes and that haunting, bereaved look on his face – and I see my Dad. Old and disaffected, living on the fringes of society, left behind by the modern world. Widowed, angry, and handling it in completely different ways.

Before I get my rest for the night, I remember the one last thing I committed to do: text Jessica. I take out my cell phone, navigate to our messages, and then find myself stuck for what to write.

How do I even begin? I know she's suffering, I know she's ill, but equally I realize I'm the last person in the world she wants to hear from. I'm sure there's some magical combination of words out there I could use to make everything make sense; where I'd tell her there's someone out there who understands her.

But I can't find seem to find that combination of words.

For all my cybernetically-enhanced strength; for all my lightning-fast reflexes and heightened sensory ability, I'm still struggling to be *human*.

After sitting and watching a blank message screen for several minutes, vacillating forwards and back over what to say, I send a message apologizing for bothering her on her workday and letting her know I'm here to talk… if she wants to talk. But it isn't enough.

Eventually, I turn out the lights and close my eyes. My mind is racing still, but before long I'm asleep.

CHAPTER 14

I wake up at 5:30 AM from a dreamless sleep. The sun isn't even up yet. In a past life, I'd have been at work at this time packaging sandwiches and dodging egg mayonnaise.

My Dad is evidently still asleep. I quietly traipse around the apartment, showering and getting dressed back into my 'disguise wear' of hoodie, sunglasses, and that tartan scarf. I quickly eat a breakfast bar and work out my travel route while doing so. The buses are unreliable at that part of town, so I upgrade myself to a subway journey. Moving on up in the world, I guess.

Kris, Vega chimes in just before I quietly step out of the front door. *It would be wise to think through your strategy here. This man is evidently intelligent and devious. He knows your face. His home could be a very sophisticated bomb-making site and therefore be very dangerous.*

"And on the other hand," I reply, waiting for the elevator. "We could be completely barking up the wrong tree here. He could just be another one of this city's weirdos."

Yes. There are a lot of missing pieces to this puzzle. If you must investigate his home, I recommend waiting until he leaves.

"Yep, that's the plan."

It's been a while since I rode the subway. Honestly, it has always scared me. Giant, undermaintained boxes of steel, rocketing around underground in the pitch dark. The drip-drip of a water leak; the train of strangers scowling at each other in perpetuity, the hordes of rats and God-knows what else living down there.

Still, that was another me. Another person.

I get to the subway station just after six, and immediately come upon a newsstand proudly advertising my earlier efforts:

POLICE APPREHEND BOMBING SUSPECT

I try to move on quickly – knowing that this small victory is tinged with the bittersweet knowledge that the bigger victory is yet to come – but do allow myself a couple of moments of pride.

As for inside the station, no-one is here but the early birds – the bankers and city workers with coffee cups glued to their hands, and the sad-eyed warehouse and factory workers, trudging home miserably from their night shifts. I know that one well.

Soon the subway train arrives with that classic rush of dusty warm air against my face. I get on board and take a seat. It's relatively empty.

A woman, maybe late twenties with black hair and gleaming white teeth, staring out the window into the black morass between stops. An older man, suit and tie, staring into his cellphone. Streaming TV or figuring out what to text his ex. Around 30 or so other people, differing states of wakefulness, but all of them with unhappy faces.

I wonder if they ever think about the Quiet One. Or the possibility that they could go to work today, go to pick something up from the mailroom, and have their hands blown off by one of his bombs.

After 25 minutes I reach my stop. I hop off, navigate past innumerous ticket gates and escalators, and see sunlight.

I've never been to this side of town before. The defense contractor's building dominates the skyline – a massive warehouse with shiny steel iron ribs jutting out, and dark red panels beneath. No windows, because why would you want to advertise your crimes to the world?

The entire site is fenced off, and I'm sure there's CCTV and guards and dogs and a million other security measures. And besides, that's not where I'm going.

I'm sure this area looked great once; a street of nice, pretty houses, all single floor, with plenty of space for gardens, pools and whatever else passed for middle-class suburbia 50 years ago. Then the city evidently grew outward, like a great polluting tumor, snatching anything beautiful and turning it ugly.

I see where the chimneys shoot up in the distance – a glass factory, a rendering plant, a steel works – and the 20-storey apartment block behind it all, basking everything in shadow.

I walk up to 25 Fenton Rose Street on the opposite side of the road, keeping my distance for now. I see that parking lot to the side, but no car.

"Vega, can you see the car anywhere?"

No.

Finally sure that my eyes aren't deceiving me, I cross the road and take a closer look at the house. It appears just like it did in the article – green grass surrounding it, browning a little towards the edges where it meets the tarmac. An empty pool out the back that somehow hasn't managed to accumulate trash like every other nook and cranny in this city.

The house itself has the curtains open and looks just like any suburban home anywhere in the city, other than the one fact that every other house on this block is boarded up and condemned. It's certainly hard to believe that the entire place must be soaked in deadly radiation.

"So," I say into the scarf covering my mouth. "I suppose I should let myself in."

I walk around the back, taking a peek through the windows as I go. Inside I can see what I can only describe as incredible normality. An old, slightly tattered but comfy looking sofa, a carpet with patterns at least 30 years out of date, and a widescreen television. A kitchen dominated by an old-style refrigerator, a neat and tidy breakfast bar, cooker and sink, and very little else.

Not exactly the dwelling I'd come to expect from this city's mad bombers, judging by the last one I explored.

"Do you think this place is alarmed?" I ask Vega.

So long as we have the right suspect, no. I would suspect he wouldn't wish to inadvertently alert the police to the evidence of his crimes.

With that, I pick up a rock – a nice, smooth igneous rock, evidently formerly used in some garden display – and chuck it through the kitchen window. Then, after knocking the broken shards away from the side of the pane with the cuff of my hoodie, I can climb through.

I'm immediately taken by the smell. It reminds me of my grandparents' home. That old, slightly stale smell of things left untouched. I leave the kitchen, carefully stepping out into a corridor, and look at the portraits on the walls. It's Alfred all right, a little younger, embracing a woman who I presume is his wife. There are pictures of them everywhere. I seem to remember the article stating he was widowed.

I move to the living room and after that the dining room, and see more pictures. In fact, the more I look, the more this place just feels like one big mausoleum but with no body buried there; instead, a once-happy marriage. And there's something very significant that I sense but can't yet see.

"I can't see anything in the way of bomb-making materials here," I say to Vega, walking towards the dining table and pressing both palms onto it. "Can you find anything?"

Analyzing.

Looking around, I can't even see any evidence that this place is actually lived in. It's kept tidy – there's no dust – but there are no items or cutlery left out. No trash. No footprints left in the shaggy carpet.

Along with a lot of radiation, I've found traces of the same chemicals used in the earlier confirmed bombs. The explosives have been here, we've just got to find them.

I look around again, checking inside cupboards and closets but find only the usual boring household items – bleach, scourers, mop and bucket. I walk back to the kitchen, and almost trip over a tuft in the rug.

"Strange place to put a rug, isn't it?" I look down at it – a patterned beige monstrosity. It's no wonder I didn't notice it until now, it's almost the dullest thing I've ever seen. An anti-curiosity field.

I'm not knowledgeable about interior design, Vega says, deadpan.

I flip a corner of the rug, exposing a trapdoor – the same linoleum material as the kitchen floor at the same height, with a small handle set into it.

"Of course you're not," I say, slowly sliding my fingers around the handle. "You missed the trapdoor. An essential feature, you know."

I pull it upwards, revealing a dark, cavernous hole with a ladder affixed to the wall: a secret entrance to the basement. I pull out my cellphone, put the flashlight on, and hesitate for a moment. Then I descend the ladder.

When I hit the ground and step off the rungs, I wave the cellphone around, trying to guide my path. There's a workbench and tools, much like Carver's set up, but that's surely where the similarities end.

This is an organized, tidy, industrious space. A series of magnifying glasses affixed to lamps are the feature I notice first. Then the separate cooking station, no doubt used to brew up the chemicals involved.

I turn around and see other instruments in varying degrees of repair, but all of them very large and specialist. Something that may be a printing press; a huge, industrial scanner; a welding station. There's even an air conditioning box and a vent, through which I can see the tiniest slivers of light. I guess it must surface in the garden somewhere.

"He must have spent months assembling all this stuff down here," I say to Vega. "He's certainly committed."

I feel around for a light switch and find a string cord hanging from the ceiling. I tug on it with some apprehension and the room fills with warm, orange light. The first thing I see is an array of photographs on the wall – all previous targets successfully hit with bombs.

And there's the university, the last on the wall. Looking at it, I'm struck by the number of people the shot. Real living people Alfred Burden snapped in a photograph, who he knew could have been hurt by his bombs. And then he decided to bomb it anyway. I feel something rising in my stomach. It feels like nausea, but the more pronounced it gets I feel I mischaracterized it. It's anger.

"I need to do something about this."

Call law enforcement. Tell them about this basement. And then get out. He'll never use this place again.

Then I notice something – a smell, almost imperceptibly subtle, but present nonetheless. Chemical in nature. I feel as though this basement was used very recently. Maybe overnight. I look over at the pans at the cooking station and feel that whatever liquid was left in the pans here is still slightly warm.

"He must have left just before I arrived," I say, unable to

contain the disappointment in my voice. "I could have caught him here."

And the worst part? There are more bombs out there. He could be setting one right now.

I look around the room again, hoping to snag some more evidence of his whereabouts, but instead just find a bunch of brochures for universities, tech companies, and tourist destinations. And then I look to the ceiling.

Kris, in the corner – look.

I do as Vega tells me, looking up to the corner of the ceiling, and see something – a strange, black hole – beside the cobwebs and the dust. I linger on it for a couple more seconds until I realize it's a CCTV camera.

"A camera?" I ask, surprised. "Who installs a camera to watch over themselves making bombs?"

Then, I hear the first few notes of a tinny ringtone, making me jump out of my skin. It takes me a few seconds until I realize it's my own. I haphazardly pick my cellphone out of my pocket and look at it: an unknown number.

I hover my finger over the icon to accept the call and find myself pausing. Perhaps it's work finally calling to see why I haven't been coming in? I head towards the ladder, begin to climb, and finally answer it with the one hand.

"Hello," I say unassumingly.

"Mr. Chambers," the voice on the other end says, dry and deep. I recognize that voice. "So glad I could reach you."

"Who is this?" I ask as I clamber out of the trapdoor. The line isn't great, but I'm already getting that sinking feeling.

"You know who I am. You're in my home."

Suddenly, I feel myself transported back to school – watching swim class from the stands, feeling that great well of shame and embarrassment rising in my stomach, just a poor, dumb kid. He must have been watching me from one of those intruder alarm apps.

Somehow, I've been stupid. I've been *weak*. Did I fall into his trap?

"Burden," I say, dragging myself back to the moment. "How did you get my number?"

"I thought it very strange that some kid would be saying the B-word into a payphone near where the pretender was at work."

He puts particular venom into the word pretender. And curiously, he doesn't want to say the 'B-word' out loud. Huh. "It was fairly easy to find your employment status and workplace from some social media site or other. They wanted me to ask you if you were coming back to work. In fact, they were kind enough to offer me your number."

Finally, that call from work arrives in the most horrifying way I could imagine.

"I hadn't expected to see you rooting around in my basement though. So, I have to ask, what are you doing in my home?"

His deep voice – like steel dragged along a cast-iron corrugated roof – unnerves me. He has the spoken air of a teacher at middle-school everyone feared.

"It's over, man," I tell him, trying to gain the upper-hand in this showdown. "The police will be here soon. They'll take all your stuff, all your equipment. And then they'll take you."

I pause, deciding whether to say what I want, and finding myself unable to resist: "If I don't find you first."

He laughs; a horrible, deep cackling sound.

"I knew this day would come, but you're not the kind of meddler I anticipated. But no matter, I've already made preparations. Said my goodbyes."

His goodbyes? He seems to imply he knows it's over, but the way he said that word doesn't convey that notion at all. He says it with *hate*.

"So you're handing yourself in?"

"No, not at all," comes the response. "I'm pushing the button that'll start the beginning of the end."

Pushing the button? I'm suddenly struck by a grave, terrible feeling that I'm not nearly in as much control of this as I think I am. The camera; the equipment downstairs; the *trap*.

That horrible pit of dread and fear seizes me again, but this time I act on it. I throw myself through the broken kitchen window, sliding across the sill and feeling the rush of pain and adrenaline as I evidently carve my palm open on an errant shard of glass. I land on the asphalt outside, cushioning my fall with my shoulder. Then I look at the cut on my hand, but not for long.

A deafeningly loud concussive blow hits me; a great rush of warm air, blowing debris and shards of glass from the windows. My ears ring, and I see what looks to be the orange lick of flame above me, as well as a great black billowing smoke that follows. The whole house was rigged to blow.

I clamber away, crawling first, before lifting myself to a run. I get to the edge of the street, shaking glass and splinters of wood off me, before turning to look back at the house, now a giant flaming wreck.

A sick yellow flame pours upwards from every window, and I see the walls and furniture within quickly blacken. Now I know what he meant by *goodbyes*. His beloved home – presumably the reason he started this campaign – is gone.

I remember I'm still gripping my cellphone. I cough a couple of times before lifting it back to my ear.

"What the hell did you do?"

Smoldering panels of wood lie beside me, and as I wipe my face I realize I'm likely leaving blood on it.

"These are the end-times Kris. No time for sentimentality." I'm barely listening to him. My ears are still ringing – the high-pitched drone of the vowel *E*. But he soon says something that convinces me to listen very carefully. "Your number wasn't the only thing I got from your boss. I know where you live."

"What!?" All I can see is my Dad, sitting by the window and smoking a cigarette. Then I find myself running. Sprinting, even. Panic rising within me. I've gotta get home. "Don't do anything stupid, Burden!"

"See you soon, Kris."

And with that enigmatic sign-off, he hangs up.

Kris, Vega says, as I pump my legs and bust my lungs. *You need to think about this. You already ran into one trap today. You're going to run into another.*

"What the hell can I do?" I bark back, catching my breath afterwards. "I can't let him hurt my Dad!"

I sprint past the subway station, reasoning that I can make it quicker if I run. I sprint past dozens of men and women in suits and dresses, all suspiciously looking me up and down as I propel myself along at speed. There's blood on my face; dust all over my hair and sunglasses, but I can't stop to change that.

Soon the cops will find Burden's former house, now a flaming wreckage. For the briefest of moments I wonder if I left anything incriminating behind – fingerprints, blood, CCTV images. But none of that matters right now. I just need to get home.

"Hey, watch ou—" I slam into a large faceless man holding a bag of fast food crossing the road. The force of the impact knocks the wind out of me. We both go flying, but I pick myself up and get right back to my singular mission without a word.

When I reach my block I'm drenched in sweat. I feel my lungs pulsate and burn, and my muscles feel like they're encased in lead. I stop, propping myself up against a lamppost, and catch what I can of my breath. Perhaps it's time to finally strategize.

"Vega," I say, barely able to form the words through my ragged breaths. "Do you think he'll be here?"

It's impossible to tell. I haven't seen his car. But you know he's intelligent enough to plan ahead.

I've got myself in a horrible situation. I thought I was the hunter – that I had superhuman advantages over the elderly, radiation-soaked bomber. As it turns out, I knew nothing. I'm the hunted, running around town like a headless chicken at the whim of the city's foremost terrorist. How did it come to this?

"Well, I'd better go up there," I say, aware I'm walking into the complete, absolute dark. If I walk into a bomb, would I even notice? Would my body be vaporized before my brain even registers the pain?

I climb the stairs, catching my reflection in a glass door panel, and wiping the sweat and blood off my face as I do it. Then, pausing outside our apartment's front door, I screw my eyes shut, clench my fist around the handle, and burst through the door in one fast motion, not knowing whether I'll still be here in three second's time.

"Kris, is that you?"

That's my Dad's voice. His annoyed voice; not scared or under duress, but annoyed. I run to see him sitting at the table, raising his voice with frustration. "Why are you banging the door like that? What's wrong with you?" He looks me up and down, scratching his stubble. Noting the dried sweat and my wild hair, he says, "You look terrible, are you feeling okay?"

"Dad," I say with relief, exhaling deeply and leaning against the wall slightly. Then I look up and see a black briefcase, very conspicuously positioned on top of the dining table, next to where my Dad is sitting. I don't remember him ever having a black briefcase. I point to it: "what's that?"

"What?" My Dad seems confused, straining to follow the line of sight from my outstretched finger. He finally looks over at the briefcase. "You mean this?"

Then I hear a noise from the bathroom – a toilet flush, the sound of the sink. And immediately I know who's going to pop out of that door. It's Alfred Burden.

He bounds out of the bathroom with a smile on his face, looking me up and down, apparently sizing me up once again. He's wearing a large, stuffy black coat, making his true size underneath it impossible to discern.

"Ah, hello again Kris." He strides past me and takes a seat next to my Dad at the table. I look back to the briefcase and can guess exactly what's inside. Burden relaxes on his chair, reminding me who's in charge around here. "Thought I'd never see you again."

I see a couple of cigarette butts neatly placed in the ashtray. My Dad has evidently been smoking with the city's mad bomber. And soon, we'll all be one big smoking hole in the ground, unless I can play this right...

"What are you doing here?" I finally ask, trying to keep my tone controlled and even.

"Mr. Hayes came here to give you some personal news," my Dad says. He's gone back to being Hayes, so I guess he still wants to play games with me. "He says you got the job?"

"I got the job?" I repeat, dumbfounded. An awkward moment passes, and for the first time I see confusion in my Dad's eyes. He doesn't seem to understand that me and the man sitting across the table from him are bitterest enemies, but I think he senses something isn't right.

I look at the briefcase again and wonder just what the detonator is. Timer? Proximity? A button hidden inside Burden's jacket?

"I didn't know you'd applied for a job at the hospital," Dad says, finally. The hospital? Where is this going? "But I'm happy for you. The radiography department, huh?"

The radiography department? What's Burden trying to tell me here?

"Dad," I say, looking at him with serious eyes. "Can you give us both a minute? Just need to, you know, talk about salary."

He gives me a suspicious look before side-eyeing Burden, who still wears that smug smile on his face. Then Dad rises to his feet, taking a cigarette with him, and walks to his bedroom, grunting a word resembling "sure" as he does so. After I hear the door close, I breathe somewhat easier before looking back at the grinning Burden.

"So, what are you planning Burden?"

I speak quietly, but forcefully. He can see that I'm fixated on the briefcase. He leans back in his chair, and for the briefest of moments I think about how much radiation he's spewing into our apartment.

"I wanted to meet you in person once again. I thought you were some undercover cop or a federal agent at first." He pauses, looking around, taking in the shabby apartment my Dad and I live in. "Then I came here and found out you were just some kid."

"Yeah, but unfortunately for you I'm the kid who found you out." I feel myself clenching my fists and gritting my teeth between words. I look between his smug face and his briefcase in quick succession, considering whether I can wrestle it away from him and throw it out of the window before it can destroy us both.

"I'm impressed, don't get me wrong," he says, enthusiastically rubbing his hands together in a strange motion. "You got to me quicker than the police and the federal agencies did. And you found out about Carver quicker than even I did. Someone should congratulate you."

Congratulations aren't what I expected from Burden today. Nor do they make me feel particularly good.

"So I think you've earned an opportunity."

He takes his glasses off and wipes them with the cuff of his coat before putting them back on. Opportunity? Something tells me he isn't actually going to offer me a job here…

"My next bomb is already primed and ready to go. It's on a timer, in a hospital, in this city. I'm giving you an opportunity to find it and do something about it."

He smiles again, baring his yellow, cigarette-stained teeth for the first time. He's evidently enjoying this, making his only known adversary bust a lung all over town. Because he knows that's exactly what I'll do.

"And don't worry, I'll be leaving here shortly. I've got places to be."

I glance back over at my Dad's bedroom and his closed door. Then, with one final look at Burden, I depart, pacing out of the room, and running down the stairs two steps at a time. I push past the door and then I'm back outside.

I have to trust Burden here; in between the bomb in the briefcase and the bomb in a hospital somewhere in town, I know I have to do what he says. Again, I could be running directly into a trap, but if he's giving me an opportunity to save lives – lives at a hospital, no less – I know I have to take it. And, he doesn't know it yet but I have help.

"Vega," I say, beginning to run in the general direction of the city's largest hospital. "What can you tell me? What do we know?"

If we're talking of hospitals in the area, I don't think Burden has explicitly mentioned or shown interest in any of them. But I did notice something when you were in his basement.

"Oh yeah?" I say, expectantly.

A leaflet for a new multi-million-dollar X-ray scanner – the XLA Scopic – built recently and offered for sale to hospitals in this city. Unfortunately, you didn't linger on that leaflet for long so that's all the information I have committed to memory.

A new X-ray scanner? Wanting to blow up a piece of innovative technology would fit the bill, especially one that irradiates the user. I take out my cellphone and look up the XLA Scopic, trying my hardest not to run into pedestrians as I do it.

After sifting through a lot of links to medical journals and sales material, I finally find a press release from a local hospital announcing that a delivery was made a couple of days earlier. *Bingo!*

I think I can make it to that hospital in 20 minutes. I *have to* make it to that hospital in 20 minutes. I begin to sprint, clenching my fists and tensing my muscles, and hope I'm not too late.

CHAPTER 15

I make it in 19. The sweat is again pouring off me; my throat stings with each intake of cold air; my feet and toes are numb with pain and the back of my head is pounding. But I'm here.

The hospital is a small, specialist medical center. I walk briskly past the set of shining double doors and see a tidy reception desk with an older woman sat happily behind it. She looks at me with hopeful eyes, but her expression turns to concern as soon as she sees how I look.

"Hi, sorry, I've got something very important for you," I say, stammering and making close to no sense. I should have planned this out; do I tell her there's a bomb? What if I'm wrong? I pause, take another deep breath, and continue: "I think you need to evacuate the building."

"What?" she says, smiling for a second, perhaps trying to convince herself this is all a joke, and there isn't a sweaty, pallid 20-something telling her to evacuate.

"The hospital, you need to evacuate, I think there's a bomb here."

Her expression turns to stone cold horror, but I still don't think she believes me. She looks at me awkwardly with confused, frightened eyes, before looking down at her desk and reaching for the phone. She dials three numbers and holds the receiver to her ear.

"Hello, I need the police."

"Your new X-ray machine," I say, realizing that standing here and politely waiting for the police to show up isn't a winning strategy. "Where is it?"

I can see her hesitate; the words are on the tip of her tongue, but she doesn't know whether to tell me. Now I can appreciate why Burden would go around pretending to be an FBI agent; the sweat-covered, panting youth just doesn't cut it as an authority figure.

"Down the hall, first right, the oncology department, room 3," she finally says with a hefty degree of nervousness.

"Thanks!" I yell, already turning my back on her and pacing down the hallway. I pass innumerable double doors, dull, sterile-smelling corridors, and pale-faced patients, apparently wondering why I look as bad as I do. A nurse tries to stop me by gripping my arm, but I push straight past her.

Finally, I find the oncology department, and after bypassing the reception desk – and a chorus of shouts from the nurses there – I find room 3, thankfully empty.

It is a blank, expressionless space with white walls and a blue resin floor. I guess they haven't put the machine into use yet, based on the lack of other furniture and materials in here.

The room is dominated by the X-ray machine – a large, shiny chrome piece of future-tech with a massive LCD console – and an adjoining room with a small window and a large lead screen protecting the operator from the rays.

I quickly throw myself to the floor, looking for a package, or a bag, or a steel pipe, or anything that doesn't look like it could be part of an X-ray scanner. Seeing nothing, I crawl to the other side and feel around underneath the scanner.

"Hey, what are you doing?" A man in blue overalls – a janitor, I'm guessing – stands by the door looking at me with feigned anger. I hear other racing footsteps behind him. I ignore him, reaching up into the unseen recesses beneath the machine.

Finally, I feel something distinctly out of place – cold, hard steel, which moves slightly with my touch. I jab it a couple more times and feel around, deducing it's stuck on with some kind of adhesive. Then, I take a deep intake of breath, close my eyes, wrap my fingers around it, and pull…

When I open my eyes again, I'm holding a steel pipe; it's shiny metal, somewhat tarnished by dust and the sticky adhesive that held it in place. It's maybe a foot long, with two distinct sections linked by wires. It certainly looks like a bomb to me.

Suddenly I feel a hand on my shoulder, and then another underneath my arm, yanking me to my feet. I turn my head to see a burly security guard wearing a uniform and sunglasses, strangely absent when I walked into reception. He tries to make a grab at the bomb, but I push it out of his reach and battle out of his grip, gyrating my body clumsily.

"Don't touch me, this is a bomb!" I shout, and the man seems to back off, but he's still blocking my exit. I throw myself past him with all the nanomachine-assisted force I have, knocking him to the ground with a grunt, and head for the blue-overalled janitor next, who courteously stands aside for me.

"Vega, what do I do with this?" I'm gripping the bomb nervously, holding it at arm's length from my body, aware that any moment it could explode and take me with it.

You need to get it out of the building. There is a ward next door with potentially a lot of patients.

"Right," I say, beginning to run down the corridor. I look up to see the exit signposted and follow the signs, frantically pumping my legs while waving the bomb around in the air, obscuring it behind my body each time a confused nurse, doctor, or patient passes me.

Finally, I make it to a set of revolving doors and find myself at a completely different door to the outside than the one I arrived through. I burst through a glass fire exit with enough force that the glass in the door panel shakes, and look around, finding myself in the parking lot, presumably around the back of the building. There's a large empty lot behind it, separated from the hospital building by a wire fence. That's my target.

I grip the bomb tightly, swinging it behind me to wind up to throw the thing, but as I do, I feel something strange; a small, almost indiscernible grinding or vibrating from inside. I feel that panic again; tension accumulating in my fingers, knowing that if I mess this up, I'm dead, or perhaps worse, someone else is dead.

I flex my biceps, swinging my elbow through the air, and throw the thing as far as I can into the empty wasteland ahead. I feel it leave my fingertips and there's a flash of bright light.

And then suddenly, I'm thrown back to the floor, landing on my ass with a thud. The noise is deafening, stabbing my eardrums and bringing that familiar ringing back to my ears.

The impact feels like how I'd imagine a bus hitting me head on would feel, and the skin on my face seems to register a delayed burning sensation, like I'd opened a baking hot pizza oven and stuck my face right in there. My sunglasses are gone too.

My breath is blasted completely out of me; I cough a couple of times, bringing my right hand to my face instinctively to shield my mouth. That's when I feel something quite strange – drops of water on my face, like it suddenly started raining. I'm lying on my back, and slowly turn over to my front, and that's when I see it: my hand, a bloody mess, with no fingers.

"Ohh, God, oh Jesus Christ!"

I find myself yelling, staring gravely at my new bloody

stumps. My fingers are gone! As is roughly a third of my right-hand palm, blasted cleanly away from my body, and only just now beginning to gush blood. It's not raining water – it's blood, my blood.

Kris, keep calm, you need to keep calm.

I barely even hear Vega; I try to move my fingers – my newly nonexistent fingers – and find I still have the sensation of being able to flex them. And then I feel the rush of pain, a pulsating throbbing soreness that seems to increase with each heartbeat.

You'll recover from this, but you need to pay attention.

"Rec-recover?" I stammer, still staring at the space where my fingers used to be.

Get out of the area, find somewhere to hide. The police will be here in no time and you're going to have some difficult questions to answer.

Snapping myself out of my horrified, pained fugue state, I do as Vega says, clutching my stump with my other hand, trying to tighten my grip on it to stop any more blood loss, and I stagger out onto the street beyond the parking lot. Every car here is ruined, but looking around I can't see a single person.

I feel like I'm about to lose consciousness. I'm limping down the block, trailing blood as I go. Teens in big, colorful coats, laughing and joking at curbside, turn around and regard me with horror. Some faceless woman tries to stop me with a firm hand on my shoulder and a question I don't hear, but I power on.

I need to find somewhere quiet and dark. Somewhere I can stop this bleeding.

Finally, I find a set of stairs leading to beneath the street and an underpass reeking of stale beer and urine. I fall against the graffiti-covered wall with my back sliding down it until I'm sitting, and then, with my one good hand, rip the charred and blood-spattered cuff of my hoodie off at the elbow. Then, after pulling off the worst of the scruffy, charred bits with my teeth, tie the rag around my bloody stump of a hand.

"Vega, what do I do?" I cry out desperately, my voice seemingly an octave deeper.

Don't panic, everything is under control. Now that you've quelled the bleeding, you should find somewhere else to hide, somewhere a lot less public.

I pick myself up and notice for the first time that *all* of my clothes are tattered; my hoodie has holes and burn marks in the front and right side; my pants are spattered with drops of blood with a prominent tear in the knee. I've looked worse with each passing hour this afternoon, but at least I'm not a bloody smear on the sidewalk yet.

I pace out of the underpass, climb the stairs, and try to walk casually, but still catch a couple of strange glances. Then I dart into an alleyway, and seeing what I hope is a derelict office, climb onto a dumpster, and then painfully hoist myself through a broken window.

This room is freezing cold – gray, damp walls lit only by the dying sunlight outside, and broken glass smattered across the floor are its main attractions. I clamber over to the corner, where someone has kindly left a decrepit office chair, and sit down. I hear police sirens in the distance – many of them – but hopefully I can catch a bit of respite here.

"What's the damage?" I ask Vega, trying to put that throbbing, aching pain out of my mind.

Your fingers and part of your right-hand palm are gone, and the system of ligaments and bones are destroyed too. You've lost approximately eight percent of your body's blood capacity and you have smaller cuts and bruises on the majority of your skin that wasn't covered by clothing. And you've lost a tooth.

I glide my tongue along my teeth, and find a gaping hole where one of my incisors used to be. My God, he's right!

You have a fractured fibia, which would explain your limp, and a couple of fractured ribs.

Now that he mentions it, I feel a sharp stab of pain upon inhaling. Funny how you don't notice these ailments until you find out about them. Or see the stumps where your fingers used to be gushing puddles of blood onto the ground.

And you have a punctured eardrum. That would be why you can only hear me on your left side.

I hadn't even noticed. And sure enough, that pain is next to arrive; a sharp sting in my right ear.

However, the good news is that all critical functions, for both your body and the nanomachine network, are working perfectly. I'd estimate you need 24 hours or so to heal fully.

"Heal fully?" I say, incredulously. I stare at my hand, bandaged up in a dirty, blood-spattered rag, knowing that the look of what exists below it would make me sick. "What's the point of healing if I'm missing my hand?"

Kris, you didn't listen, Vega says, taking a sterner tone than I'm used to hearing. *Your hand will be returned back to you good as new.*

I get to thinking about that defective heart of mine, made new again by Vega and the robots. I just didn't know it would extend to growing back entire fingers.

"You mean I'll get a new hand?"

It won't be a new hand, it'll be your hand. The network is already interfacing with stem cells specifically cultivated by the nanomachines in your body. These stem cells will be moved into position, and the nanomachine network will gradually craft the tissue that makes up your hand. Skin, bone, ligament, nerve, artery, fingernail, etc.

I sit back on the chair, and gasp with pain and relief. Despite all my suffering, despite all the blood I've spilled around the block, and despite the horrifying vision of my hand spurting crimson and missing all its fingers, I got the bomb out of the hospital. I may have saved lives today. The image of my hand is burned into my memory, but the pride in knowing that I won against Burden today makes it all worthwhile.

"Can you do something about the pain?"

No, Vega replies, surprising me somewhat. *Pain management isn't a capability of the nanomachines. Artificial painkilling stimulants were trialed in earlier versions, but were phased out as they promoted unsafe behaviors in the hosts of the network.*

"Unsafe behaviors? What does that mean?"

Pain is your body's way of alerting you to physical stress and trauma. Removing it enabled the host to surpass their bodily limits, throwing themselves into danger when it would have been wiser to seek aid. It was decided that pain remains an important motivating factor for keeping the host safe.

"Great, so I just have to sit here and watch my fingers grow back in agony?"

Pain is subjective. Consider this: does the fact that you'll be back to 100% in 24 hours dull the pain? Do you feel better knowing that this pain, and indeed all pain, will merely be temporary?

I sit back and think about it. The pounding, throbbing soreness in my palm, and the constraining, stinging sensation in my ribs seem severe by any standards of pain that I've ever known. But yeah, it does feel better knowing that it'll be gone soon. It's just a physical sensation. It won't last forever.

I think to take my cellphone out of my pocket, but predictably it's even more broken than it was before – a larger cobweb of broken glass on the screen, and a visible depression where a small part of the touchscreen now doesn't work, but at least it still dials.

I call my Dad, hoping he'll answer and praying he isn't still sitting in the kitchen, happily smoking with this city's number one terrorist. After a couple of rings, he picks up.

"Hello," I can already hear him exhaling cigarette smoke down the receiver.

"Hi Dad," I say, trying to sound like I didn't just blow my

own hand off. "Listen to me, is that man – that Hayes – still there?"

"What? No, he left." He sounds annoyed with me. That's still far preferable to him being dead. "What's going on Kris?"

His voice is garbled; something tells me my cellphone is on its last legs.

"I can't explain now, but don't let him back into the apartment if he comes back."

"Kris, in the Lord's name, what are you—"

And the line goes dead; the cracked screen is dark and that's my cellphone finally fried. At least I was able to make sure he's okay. I breathe a sigh of relief for that.

I watch the shadows move against the wall as the sun begins to go down. The pain is bothering me less, and soon my ear and ribs begin to feel fine once again.

When it gets dark, I move to the next room, and find a bunch of carpets ripped up, probably in some attempt by scrappers to find copper piping under the floorboards to sell. I bury myself into a carpet, wrapping it around me, and close my eyes, giving my body the opportunity it needs to heal.

CHAPTER 16

I wake up from a sleep I feel I never truly started. It's still dark in here, and cold. So, so cold.

I throw the ratty bit of carpet I've called a duvet off me and walk to the window, noting that the pain and limp in my leg has subsided. In fact, I don't feel bad at all. Illuminated by the faded orange light of a lamppost in the alley outside, I peel the rag covering my wounded hand off.

"Whoa, Jesus!" I cry, looking at my healing hand. Rather than the bloody stumps and exposed bits of bone, it's mostly pink, glistening flesh, with blue blood vessels visible just under the surface. There are five distinct nubs that I hope will grow into fingers.

My tongue darts to my missing tooth and find I have a new one, sitting there as though it was never gone.

The human mind isn't necessarily designed to witness such rapid bodily transformation, Vega chimes in from the shadow realm, *I can see why this would be distressing to you.*

"Yeah, no kidding." I look it up and down, slowly making myself nauseous. "So, is everything going to plan growing these things back?"

Yes, everything is going to plan.

"I guess this is going to take some adjusting to." I pull my eyes away from it, before putting my hand down by my side, out of view. "Will it be the same? Same size, same skin, same grip?"

Yes, of course. It's still your hand.

"My hand was blown off my body," I say, remembering the stump and the gushing blood. "These fingers won't be my fingers. At least, not the same fingers I've had since I was born."

Why not? How much of your body exists as it did when you were born? How many cells do you have today that you had when you were a newborn?

I'm silent as I consider the implications of what Vega is telling me.

Most of your body has replenished itself multiple times since you were born. Your stomach cells are replaced every few weeks. Certain white blood cells live even shorter lives than that. Even bone cells are replaced periodically. The only cells your body doesn't replace are neurons – your brain cells – and there's sadly nothing the nanomachines can do about that.

I close my eyes and think about my right hand as it existed yesterday; the way the bomb felt as I gripped it.

"But, that was *my hand*." I'm not sure Vega's machine brain will ever understand me, even if he was a human mind once upon a time. "I'd had it all my life. And for now at least, I don't…"

You'll get used to having a hand again. And then you'll probably lose it again. If you're intent on chasing down bombers, it will happen Kris.

I pull my elbow up through the arm of my scuffed-up hoodie and carefully maneuver my hand over to my chest, as if I were wearing a sling. I look around, and see my reflection in some broken glass on the floor. Jesus, I look terrible. Dried sweat, blood, and burned, frayed clothing. I look exactly like the person of interest in an averted hospital bombing. Which is what I'm sure I am.

"I need to find some new clothes."

Yes, I agree. You need to be inconspicuous.

I look outside again; it's dark, but I'm sure the sun will begin to rise soon. I should probably get moving while it's still dark, but where I'm going to find decent clothes at this time, I don't know.

I feel like going home would be way too risky. If the cops know who I am yet – and I had surely been spotted at the scene at no less than two high profile explosions yesterday – they're going to want to pull me in and confine me to an interview room for days. All while Burden is out there, rigging up whatever explosives he has left.

No, I can't be talking to law enforcement just yet.

I take one last look at my motel room for the night, and then climb back out of the window, dropping to my heels outside with a splash. It rained during the night, but it seems clear now.

I put my good hand in my pocket, but not before pulling what's left of my tattered hood over my head. Then I start walking, trying to remember all I can about the neighborhood I find myself in.

It's a shadier part of town. Homeless guys are sleeping on cardboard boxes and smoking unidentified substances, all completely oblivious to me. I get to the end of the block and then I realize where I am.

I know this place; this is the area with the pawn shop where I foiled the robbery. I know I shouldn't revisit the scene, but I'm curious and maybe a little too eager to see the results of my vigilantism; did they ever open back up after that harrowing day? Reasoning that a pawn shop is as good a place as any to pick up a new cellphone, I set out on the short walk.

I'm there in no time at all; the dingy street, with trash and newspaper pages sitting unhappily in blocked drains. A couple of neon signs have switched on already – I can hear them buzzing whenever the street is free of cars – and I can see the sun beginning to rise behind the pawn shop in the distance.

As I get closer, I see the shutters – closed until now – begin to open, and an older man walk around from the alleyway beside the shop and duck under them. It's hard to tell in the dawn light, but I think that's the same older man with the head injury. All of sudden I'm filled with a rush of pride. I guess it's business as usual again.

After I see him disappear inside the shop, I shuffle a little closer, taking a look around the neighborhood as I go. Shards of light, peeking from behind the unevenly tall buildings, dance in the puddles of water in the road. There's a smell in the air; the sickly, damp smell of trash, but mostly some food cooking. Chicken, mushrooms? I feel like I haven't eaten in days.

Eventually I make it to the store and peer through a window, seeing the inner layout once again with its myriad of counters and walls and display cabinets.

"Hey, it's you," a deep, slightly accented voice sounds out. I turn around to see the man standing in the doorway. He's wearing a hat that obscures his injury, and a giant smile on his face. "You're the guy who fought off those robbers aren't you?"

The experience of being recognized for something embarrasses me; I feel my cheeks flush, and I struggle to put my words in order.

"Sorry, I know you're probably not open yet, I was just taking a—"

He cuts me off excitedly, stepping to one side of the doorway, and beckoning me in with both hands.

"Come in, come in!"

With some trepidation, I begin to do as he asks, sheepishly walking towards the doorway.

"Sure, I was just—"

"Welcome, welcome!" he shouts at me, far too loud for this time in the morning. I cross his path and make it inside the store. There are a couple of cracked display cases still, and a curious dark smudge on the carpet looking like a cleaning product was applied too liberally, but aside from that, the place looks like new.

Then, catching me in the glow below one of the spotlights, he sees my tattered hoodie.

"What happened to you? You're a mess!"

He shouts something – a foreign language, possibly – to someone upstairs, and ushers me to a seat. Still too embarrassed to talk, I follow his order and sit down.

"Thanks; can I buy a new cellphone?" I take mine out of my pocket with my good hand, revealing the blast damaged screen and shattered glass. "Mine is on its last legs."

"Sure!" he booms, making his way over to a cabinet on the edge of the room, unlocking something or other, and then bounding back over to me holding a tray with both hands. On it is an array of smartphones, some looking new, some slightly scuffed, but all of them undoubtedly an improvement on my current handset.

"What do you think?" he asks, expectantly. I pick the one that's closest to my own in style and reach for my wallet.

"How much is this?"

His eyes light up, before he closes them graciously and waves his hand around madly. "For you, nothing my friend!"

I'm shocked, I can't accept that. I mumble something, and try to wave my hands in some magical formation designed to convey my humility, but it's useless; he's already taken the cellphone and pushed it into the one hand I have that isn't hidden away.

"It's yours!"

I'm still stuck for words, smiling and trying to express my

gratitude, when a woman appears from the backroom doorway holding a large pile of clothes.

"Now, let's get you dressed!"

―――

Around 30 minutes later I'm waving goodbye to my new friends at the pawn shop, wearing a new set of clothes – a secondhand hoodie, one size too big for me with a gaudy sports team motto emblazoned on it, and a pair of jeans – as well as a new pair of sunglasses. I don't know where they got these clothes, but I'm grateful for them nonetheless.

"Thank you!" I call out, before turning and walking away. My cheeks are still flushed with embarrassment. I'm not used to being complimented, let alone recognized and rewarded for any kind of heroism. Praise makes me nervous; shy. The idea that someone will rain down effusive thankfulness upon me makes me shudder, even.

I'm proud of my achievements; I'm delighted to have helped that man out, and he's even more delighted to have paid me back. But this whole experience has proved to me that I'm not in this business for praise and recognition.

"Well, I think that went... well?" I tell Vega, looking both ways and crossing the road.

Indeed.

"I'm just not sure I'm cut out for, you know..." I wonder if Vega will understand my concern this time, "...appreciation like that."

Yes, the blood vessels in your cheeks dilated beyond usual capacity during your meeting with that man. You were embarrassed.

Jesus, I guess I should know better than to discuss such things with the artificially intelligent overlord that has access to all my vital signs. The experiences and emotions of being human – the beautiful highs and the terrible lows – quantified and extrapolated out to a series of blood pressure readings. Human life by the numbers.

"I suppose I never stopped to ask myself, why am I doing this?" I see a police car in the road up ahead and pause, staring into a shop window instead. "I know I'm not doing this for money or fame. There are far easier ways of getting rich or famous than waging a one-man war against the Quiet One. I mean, I slept in a derelict building last night."

Perhaps you're doing it just because you can.

A slightly colder thought hits me. I rub my head, and pause to think about it. All of my life I've been a loser; a nobody. Too fragile to fight; too anxious to relax. Perhaps I'm doing this not for the people I save from the bomber, but instead for me. To prove that I have some worth in this world.

When I see the police car move out of sight, I start walking again. I need to get back on Burden's trail, but before I do that I feel I need to seek Dad out again. I owe him at least some sort of explanation for all of this…

CHAPTER 17

I t's almost evening time; I've idled around the city for most of the day, eating and trying to stay in the shadows. I managed to duck into a coffee store and charge my old, broken cellphone long enough to get my contacts – and that pretty lockscreen with the seagull – transferred from it to my new cell.

The news of the two bombings yesterday has gotten out to the local newspapers, but they're not connected just yet. Neither do they mention a suspect, although I'm sure the cops are already looking for me.

But for now at least, I'm just another dude in casual clothes keeping his head down.

I call my Dad and arrange to meet at the park closest to his church later this evening. I don't know what I'm going to say – I'm certain I won't be telling him he invited the Quiet One inside for a smoke and a chat – but I'll think of something.

Finally, as I see the sun begin to set I duck into a darkened alleyway and take my ruined right hand out from underneath my hoodie, where I've kept it pinned to my body most of the day.

"Well, here goes..."

To my surprise – and wide-eyed amazement – my hand looks totally fine. Same size; same color; same hand!

The nanomachine network store the exact dimensions of all of your body parts, down to the cellular level, Vega tells me. *The network even recreated the small scar on your knuckle.*

I turn my palm over and look at my knuckle. There it is, clearly visible, the small scar I got when I fell over on the sidewalk as a kid. Despite being a different hand to the one I started with yesterday, this feels and looks exactly like *my hand*.

I set out for the park, walking casually; my body entirely rejuvenated but my cover story for the last few days still in pieces.

When I get there, it's dark. This park isn't the prettiest in the city – it's intersected by a big, dirty two-lane road, with the ever-present din of car engines and the occasional truck – but it'll do to meet Dad.

The path is dark and potholed, illuminated only by the occasional circle of light below a lamppost; it reminds me of the park by the hospital where I first discovered these powers.

I sit on a bench near the entrance closest to his church and wait. I study my newly healed right hand, holding it up to the light from a lamppost, and look at the veins and blood vessels inside, my skin translucent and illuminated by the glow.

I felt like a different person a mere week ago, just like I feel now that I have a different hand. Am I even close to being the same man I was? Does it even matter?

Dad's arrival rouses me from my philosophical musings. I see him walking his walk; an unusual limp owing to his old work injury. Eventually, he reaches me and wordlessly sits down.

"Hi Dad," I finally say, breaking the silence.

"So what's going on here Kris? New clothes?"

He asks the questions carefully, with no emotion apparent in his voice. I think he senses I'm *going through some stuff* lately.

"Dad, you need to make sure you don't let that man – Hayes, or whatever he called himself – back in to the apartment ever again."

He looks at me with concerned, stoic eyes.

"Son," he says, after a few moments of quiet. "I can't say I'm not worried about you. Quitting your job, staying out all night. I thought you'd gotten a job at the hospital like that man said."

I wish I had a way of explaining all of this to him. Or at the very least tell a convincing lie.

"But," he says, surprising me slightly, "I can't remember the last time you looked as happy as you do now."

My eyes widen; I thought I was in for a telling off. Instead, it seems he has something else on his mind.

"You've got something; a sparkle in your eye. I don't know. A spring in your step. Like you've been visited by the Lord Himself." I was wondering how long he'd take to bring religion into this. But, he's right in a strange way. I have been visited by something not of this world. "You look like you have purpose for the first time in years."

I smile at him. We've never been huggers, but I almost feel like I could embrace him.

"Dad," I finally say, "what did you and Hayes talk about? Did he say anything… strange?"

"Strange?" He seems perturbed by the question. "No, nothing strange. He was telling me about his departed wife. I guess we share that in common."

He's right; they're both widows. But that's not what I'm looking for.

"He talked about his church a bit; said he hadn't been in a few months though."

Again, not what I'm looking for. I nod, encouraging him to go on.

"And then he said he was looking forward to the parade this weekend."

Parade? The word makes me shiver. I understand enough about Burden to know that he's no ordinary paradegoer.

"Parade? What parade?"

"Some big traveling event coming to the city, a World's Fair kind of thing I think." He shakes his head, as if he's disapproving of it. "They're bringing a load of NASA stuff here and clogging our streets with it."

I think I know what Burden's next target will be.

I exchange a couple more pleasantries with and thank him for meeting me before letting him badger me into attending church sometime. Finally, I shake his hand and stand to leave.

"What about the rent?"

"I'm working on it," I tell him, beginning to step away. "Staying at a friend's tonight!"

I see him nod before taking an inevitable cigarette out of his pocket and moving it to his lips. I can't go back to the apartment; the risk of Burden trying to take me out is too great. As much as I hate being the Homeless Crimefighter, I can't make myself easy to find.

And besides, I've too much work to do.

I walk to a coffee shop around the corner, order myself a soda, and sit quietly in a dark corner by the window. Then, I look up that parade, trying to get to grips with my newly provided cellphone.

INNOVATION ON THE LAUNCHPAD PARADE

The headline jumps out at me; the first thing I see when I search online for this city and parade. I read through the article and it's just what Dad described – a parade of technology with rockets, solar panels, and planned Mars rovers paraded through the streets. It's by far the most obvious target for Burden to hit. A nice, big, public spectacle. And it's tomorrow.

I leave the coffee shop and walk aimlessly down the street, wondering just where I'm supposed to sleep tonight. But putting my powers of deduction to finding a comfortable hotel room can wait.

"Vega, I think we know the next target."

Yes, the parade would make perfect sense. He's a consummate attention-seeker, and disrupting this parade would attract the largest amount of attention he could hope for.

"How is he going to rig the parade exhibits to blow though?"

I pass a drunk guy with a large gut hanging out from the bottom of his jersey. He slurs something in my direction as I stroll by. A month ago I'd have crossed to the other side of the road. Now I don't even flinch.

Knowing his methods, and the planning and research he seems to put into each target, I'd suspect he knows where the exhibits are being stored prior to the parade tomorrow. He's an intelligent guy, he can talk his way past any security, and then it's just as simple as rigging an explosive and setting the timer to blow during the parade.

"So what can I do?"

I find myself in the strange position of turning from the city's biggest introvert to its most obsessive paradegoer in less than a week.

Get ahead of him; find out where the exhibits are being stored and call in a bomb threat.

"But that isn't good enough," I reply, with one single goal on my mind. "I need to find him, I need to stop him hurting people again."

Giving law enforcement the opportunity to find and defuse the bomb could give them the clues they need to apprehend him.

I grunt in acknowledgement, but I'm hardly satisfied. The

cops in this city haven't found him yet, but I have. Why would they catch him after one more bomb?

I duck into another alleyway – my favorite haunt lately – and search the internet for any information I can find, illuminated by the warm green light of an 'exit' sign.

I spend 20 minutes scrolling, but I'm still in the dark though, at least in knowledge terms. Every article I find lists the parade timings, the exhibits, the museums and factories kind enough to donate them, the billionaire donors gracious enough to front the money. No website seems willing to tell me where the exhibits are stored. That is, if they're even in the city yet.

Kris, Vega interrupts me, probably sensing my blood pressure rising with frustration. *Why don't you be a little more direct? The website for the parade lists a phone number. Tell a few white lies and see if they'll be so kind as to tell you where they're storing the exhibits.*

I find myself wincing a little at that idea. I've never been one to tell lies. I've never been one to bullshit my way into, or out of, anything in fact. I don't even know how I'd start with this one.

"White lies?" I finally stump up the courage to ask Vega. "What kind of white lies?"

You could say you're a replacement driver for one of the floats and need to know where the depot storing the exhibits is.

Well, I suppose that's a better idea than calling up and pretending I'm some rocket scientist who wants to make a final tweak or whatever the hell else I would have come up with.

"All right, I suppose I'd better give it a shot."

I copy the number from the parade website and paste it into my cellphone's dial screen. Then, after a few seconds of silent psyching myself up, I hit dial.

It rings and rings and rings. I anxiously pace up and down

the alleyway; perhaps the office is closed already? After all, it's well into the evening.

Finally, to my surprise, someone answers. A female voice, sounding tired and annoyed to have to answer the phone.

"Hello, you've reached Innovation, what do you need?"

"Oh, uhm, hi." I'm already stumbling over myself trying to put the words in order. I close my eyes and try to conjure up the lie. "Yeah, I've just been told to call you, I'm supposed to be driving a float tomorrow, but I haven't received any info yet. Where am I getting the keys?"

Getting the keys? Is that a thing drivers say?

"Hold on," she says, and after some shuffling around, I hear a hold tone. My leg shakes below me expectantly. "Ultra-coach Depot, Jackson Bridge Street. You need to be there for the induction by 8:00 AM tomorrow, so don't be late."

And with that she puts the phone down.

"Thanks," I say to the dead line, before looking up the address on my cellphone. It's an hour away from here at most.

I take a deep breath and pull my hood tight around my face. Then I begin jogging, warming my nanomachine-saturated muscles up, before speeding up a little more.

"Vega, I'm heading there now. I want to watch this place like a hawk. If Burden surfaces, I want to swoop out of the sky and catch him."

Kris, I wouldn't recommend staying awake all night. You may be a cybernetically-enhanced human being, but you still need good, healthy sleep.

It's no use trying to convince me though. I'm determined. I need to haul this man to a police station, dead or alive. That's my job. That's my purpose.

"Your apprehension has been noted," I say to him, panting between steps, trying to mock his calm and robotic tone.

All I want – all I need – is one chance to catch him. I'll stay awake all night if I have to.

I finally slow my running to a standstill when I see the street name. Standing outside a fried chicken shop, supporting myself against the glass window and catching my breath for a minute, I find I can't resist the temptation any longer and head in to grab something to eat.

"So this is the place," I say to Vega five minutes later, leaving the shop and gripping the bag in both hands like it were a newborn baby.

I see a massive warehouse – a fenced-off bus depot, with floodlights illuminating the pathways around it, and a security gate leading to the road outside. It's old – the top of the walls are adorned with windows, but roughly half of them are broken and the other half are fogged up with dark, brown soot.

I pace to the security gate, and check out what I'm dealing with. There's a security guard sitting in the booth, and another posted by the huge, open door to the depot. Inside I can see buses, and behind them flatbed trucks with plastic tarpaulin obscuring the payload.

"I think this is it," I say, speaking into the side of my hood.

You should expect security to be tight, Vega tells me, as I spot one more security guard – a woman, laughing and joking with a guy in dirty red overalls. A mechanic, I guess. *There's a lot of very important and very expensive hardware here.*

I can see the security guards are part of some private firm – the name is emblazoned on the backs of their black coats. Probably a massive upgrade from the security that looks after the buses here. They might even follow the exhibits from state to state.

"Yeah, I'm not going to get in without being seen. So, how would Burden manage to rig a bomb here?"

I'm sure he's been planning this for months. He has most likely forged the correct documents and credentials he needs to slip through.

I walk around the perimeter fencing, but find it's pretty secure. Then I turn my attention to the buildings across the road opposite the security gate. There's a hotel, but it's apparently closed for renovations. Just a couple of CLOSED signs out the front, and the entire building covered in scaffolding.

I amble over there, looking at how stable this scaffolding is, and wondering if I'll actually end up in a hotel room tonight after all.

"Seems cozy enough, doesn't it?"

I pull on the steel bars of the scaffolding; they don't move with my force. I can probably climb this, no problem. I throw my bag of chicken onto the scaffolding surface above me and climb up with both arms, easily hoisting my body onto the second floor.

By last night's standards, I'm sure it'll be a treat.

I climb another floor, and making sure I haven't been seen by the security guards opposite slowly and quietly walk the wooden boards of the scaffolding, looking inside each of the hotel's windows as I pass.

Finally, I find one that's slightly ajar and force it open. The smell of paint is the first to hit my senses. The room is a fairly bog-standard hotel room, with a sink and a mirror, and an adjoining toilet, but missing a bed or any other sort of furniture. The carpet is ratty, specked with paint stains, and I suspect the next thing to go.

I check out the view – my vision of the road below is partially blocked by the scaffold, but I can see the curbside well enough, and I can see the security gates crystal clear. If Burden walks through there, I'll spot him.

I go into the adjoining bathroom and find that some laborer left a couple of items in here – a ladder and a toolbox. I open up the box and don't see anything out of the ordinary. A utility knife, a hammer, some nails. I take the knife – a particularly sturdy type that could cut carpets – and leave the rest.

Then I pull the ladder out of the bathroom and set it up just in front of the window, then I climb onto the fourth step, giving myself a slightly better vantage point. It ain't a bed, but at least it's better than wrapping myself in dusty, tattered carpets while I wait for my hand to grow back.

I tuck into my chicken and start my long night.

CHAPTER 18

I close my eyes for a moment; a wave of fresh, cleansing warmth washes over my eyeballs. Then, knowing I can't afford to close them for long, I open them again.

The sun is coming up – I can see it from behind the towers in the distance, reflected as a dancing orange sea in every glassy window on the horizon. It's around half seven in the morning.

I've witnessed at least one shift change; a new set of security guards came in at some point, swapping out with the old ones. I watched the man in the entrance booth spill coffee on himself. I saw a sketchy pair of guys – one with no shoes – dealing drugs or something beside the fencing. I witnessed a car speed down the street and almost hit a woman crossing. But I didn't see Burden yet.

"I wonder if he's already been here," I say, rubbing my eyes with my knuckle. "Maybe he got here before I did."

It's possible, but rigging the bomb earlier would increase the chance that it would be found. I think it's more likely he wouldn't take that risk. He most likely would plant it just before the parade.

I've been ducking into the bathroom occasionally,

drinking the water from the faucet; a treat I afforded myself from time to time. But now I need to use that bathroom.

I jump off the ladder, stretching my legs, which gladly break out in pins and needles. Then I walk over to the bathroom and use the toilet. When I get back I take a brief look around the street, but see no change. The movies truly don't convey just how *boring* these stake-outs are.

Although my body's fairly acclimatized to sleep deprivation – enduring many hours of gaming into the early hours or packaging sandwiches at ungodly hours – the past few days have been difficult. I've been running long distances, had parts of my body blown off, and enduring mental hardship the likes of which I've never experienced before.

Of course, the next problem I have is that I'm going to have to check out of this hotel room fairly soon. Whenever the decorators are back, I need to disappear.

I climb back onto the ladder and resume my watch. I'm in another world, thinking about when that chicken shop might reopen, when Vega alerts my attention to something outside.

Kris, the man by the security gate. Look.

I focus back on the gate, and sure enough see two figures standing there idly chatting away. One of them is the security guard and the other is an older man with gray hair, glasses, and a long black coat. He's just a figure in the distance, but I instantly feel I know who it is.

"That's him, isn't it?"

I would appear so.

I jump to my feet and waste no time in opening the window and forcing my body through it. Without trying to arouse any attention, I hop out onto the scaffolding and grip the steel vertical bar with both hands, lowering myself down it and landing quietly on the boards below. I repeat that process and land on the uneven tarmac of the sidewalk.

My palms burn with cold, but I barely notice. My attention

is fixed solely on Burden. He's walking down the street by the time I'm on the ground, and I see his car a short walk away. He doesn't see me yet.

I quickly, quietly pace the remaining distance to him, reaching him just as he fishes around in his coat pocket for his car keys. In one rapid motion, I grab his arm, pull it out of his pocket, and maneuver it halfway up his back, holding him painfully in place.

"Surprise," I whisper with barely hidden glee and begin to march him towards his car.

"Kris, is it?" He sounds like he's been expecting me. No matter. I think he knew all of this would come tumbling down around him soon enough. He struggles against me for the briefest of moments, but he quickly finds out it's no use. "So, it seems you got me."

"Not so quiet now, huh?"

I force him against the door of his car, still holding his arm painfully against his back.

"I suppose you'll be interested to know," he says, turning his head to try and look at me. I see the side of his eye and can tell – yellow teeth bared – that he's smiling. "I've already set the bomb."

I look back at the depot, with its army of security guards walking aimlessly around. They'll never find it unless I alert them to it. But, what to do with Burden?

I take a moment to think about it before exhaling deeply, swearing under my breath. Then I kick his legs out from underneath him in one swoop. He falls to the ground with a yelp; he's nothing more than an old, fragile man, but his eyes still stare at me, looking up from behind two foggy glasses lenses. There's hatred in his eyes.

"Stay here," I say to him. Then I take the utility knife out of my pocket, and after enjoying the look of concern on his face for a second, plunge it into the tire of his car, before using every fiber and sinew in my arm to cut downwards, deflating it in a single movement.

It goes flat with a loud, violent rush of air. I leave the knife embedded in the tire and run to the security gate.

"Hey! Hey!" I shout, sprinting the short distance towards the gate. "There's a bomb in the building!"

A pair of security guards look at me like I'm crazy. One tall, the other short, but both of them stocky enough to block my way past.

"Didn't you hear? There's a bomb inside the building!" I get to the gate and bypass them completely, instead electing to vault the barrier standing a meter or so high.

"You can't come in here!" the shorter one shouts, but it's too late, I'm already running towards the depot. Another security guard stands by the huge door and pulls a walkie-talkie off his waistband, shouting something or other about an intruder.

"That man you let in, he's not an FBI agent or whatever he told you, he's a bomber, he's the Quiet One!"

The name buys me a look of understanding from the guard, but he doesn't stop talking into the device. I try to pass him and march into the depot, but he puts a firm hand on my chest, trying to force me back.

"Stay there!" he barks in my face, attempting to sidestep me while wrapping his large bicep around my neck. I push him to the side, knocking him to the floor in a heap. "We're gonna call the police!" he says.

"Yes, the call the police!" I yell, turning my back to the man on the floor, and see the other two on the gate slowly jogging up to meet me. "Call the police and tell them the parade is the next target!"

I see a couple of women in suits inside the depot, nervously adjusting their collars and ties, and whispering to one another before each fishing a cellphone out and dialing. A mechanic runs for the exit and another security guard hesitates, before jogging slowly towards me.

I think my work here is done. A little inelegant, but I think I've created enough of a panic to ensure the bomb is found.

Then I'm bowled over, feeling the full force of a six-and-a-half-foot tall man slamming into me and knocking me to the floor. Another jumps on top of me, wrapping that bicep back around my neck intending to choke me out or something similar. I guess the two guys from the gate caught up.

"Hey, get off me!" I shout into the man's coat, my words muffled. Another guard runs to grab my legs but I kick him off, and then with as much strength as I can muster I peel the thick arm from around my neck, and try to pick myself up on to all-fours.

A kick is aimed at my stomach, knocking the wind out of me and making me gag for air. I block another with my forearm – feeling a pulse of pain that resonates right to the bone – and I manage to get to my knees just in time for another kick to hit my sternum.

I see a fist flying towards me and throw myself backwards to avoid it, doing a clumsy backwards roll and somehow propelling myself to my feet.

"Call the cops!" I shout one final time after a loud and very necessary gasp for breath. Then I sprint as fast as I can for the security gate, hurdle over it, and turn my head.

I see Burden's car, but Burden himself has vanished. I sprint over there and see the tire, still slashed, still with the knife embedded in it, but Burden has evidently split.

"Goddamnit!" I shout, turning myself 360 degrees on my heel, looking for that tell-tale black coat of his. "Vega, talk to me."

He can't have gone far. You left him for just over a minute.

"There's a subway station nearby, I passed it when I got here" I say, beginning to run in its direction. "Plenty busy, lots of room to hide, that's where I'd go."

I sprint to the subway station, jumping down the stairs two at a time, before practically throwing myself down the escalator leading to the bowels of the network. My muscles hurt – my thighs feel like they're pumping acid and my forearm still throbs from that kick – but I absolutely can't stop.

I had him in my grasp; in my mind I can still feel the coarse fabric of his coat. I'm not willing to let him slip through my fingers like this.

I jump over the ticket gate, eliciting a shout from a nosey commuter. Then I race down to the platform. I can see a train has already pulled up.

Kris, I have to warn you, Burden is still a very unpredictable man. Pursuing him into a corner might be a dangerous move.

I barely hear him, sprinting full force towards that train. As I get to it, I see a large, black coat, just like Burden's, boarding further up the platform. He's obscured by numerous people, rushing onto the train like me, but I'm sure it's him.

Hearing that ringing noise signifying the doors about to close, I jump onto the train at the closest door. Then, battling through the crowd of people, I try to reach the train car Burden is in.

I see faces; young people, old people; excited people; bored people. Couples embracing one another; single people staring into their phones. Most of them presumably going to the parade. None of them have any idea who they're sharing this subway train with. And none of them know the mission I'm on as I stride past them, grappling bodies out of the way as I go.

Finally, I make it onto the next carriage, and I still can't see that gray head of hair of his. I walk through the crowd, using my elbows and my palms to move through the sea of bodies ahead of me.

Then I catch a glimpse – a momentary glimpse – of those

hate-filled eyes of his. He's looking directly at me, but someone's head blocks my view. I crowbar my way past another couple of bodies and see the back of his head. He's moving down through the train too, trying to escape me.

I see him make his way past the doors onto the next carriage. I keep moving, knowing that sooner or later he's going to run out of train.

"Hey, watch it man," some guy says out of the side of his mouth. I mumble an apology and keep moving. I step over the legs of a girl sat down by the window, and duck under the arm of a man holding the ceiling strap. At last though I make it to the next carriage.

I fight past another couple of people until I see that black coat directly in front of me. He's an arm's grasp away. I thrust my arm forward and screw my eyes closed trying to grab him.

And then I feel that coarse fabric on my fingertips.

I close my fingers, gripping his collar, and pull him backwards. When I open my eyes again, I can see that I have the right man. That gray hair, those glasses. He turns around, taking a step towards me as he does so.

I see those eyes again. But not so full of hatred this time. They're full of something like glee. Excitement, even. A terrifying rictus grin locked on his face.

I get the feeling that I've made a terrible mistake.

His hands race up to his neck – one of them holding the collar of his coat in place and the other tugging on the zipper fixing it closed. He quickly unzips it, revealing a black jumper underneath and a belt fastened across his chest.

Kris, you're in danger.

And that's when I see the two shiny chrome pipes tied on to that belt with a messy tangle of wires appearing from the bottom of each. I know what it is. It's a bomb! And it's strapped to him!

Someone screams; a high-pitched, feminine yell that seems

to last for an eternity; the whole scene seems to last forever. My fingers wrapped around his collar, and Burden still grinning at me, knowing that with his final act he's won.

Then the scream ends.

CHAPTER 19

I'm still grasping, gripping something in my hand. But it doesn't feel like the coarse fabric of a coat anymore. It feels like gravel. Stony, dusty gravel. I feel nothing but gravel and pain.

My jaw hurts the most; like it has been knocked right out of place. Every other bone in my body aches deeply, like I was picked up by some vengeful god, shook around, and thrown back in the dirt. I see only darkness and hear nothing.

And then I hear screaming again.

I open my eyes and look around, slowly. It's dark; there's the orange, swaying luminance of fire behind me, lighting up the crude brickwork that surrounds me. I look closer to see the subway train; I'm outside of it, and there's a giant hole in the side of the carriage.

I hear people screaming, people groaning in pain.

"Vega," I mumble, still half-in, half-out of this world. But I hear nothing back.

I grasp another handful of gravel and claw my way forward, trying to escape the scene. I'm lying on my stomach, and I can't feel my right arm or my legs right now. I'm just one aching ribcage, pulled along in the gravel by a ghostly hand.

I drag my body across another meter of gravel and grasp another handful of dirt. That handful of gravel is my only reality right now. The only truth in my post-apocalyptic world. I grasp it and pull myself forward again.

The screams behind me are dying down. I can't face them. Agonized cries from the mouth of hell itself. No, I have to escape this place. I have to keep moving. One more handful of gravel, one more yard forward.

I look to my right arm to see it's no longer there. My new hand, gone.

I can't see my legs, but I know they can't be in good working order.

"Vega, Vega," I stammer again, but he doesn't reply.

I keep clawing my way forward. I drag my face along the dirt, tasting bitter mud and soot and God knows what else.

After a while I can't hear the cries anymore. There's no light, aside from the occasional overhead bulb flickering faintly. I keep crawling, clawing my way through the dirt, heading down the subway tunnel into the great darkness.

Until, suddenly, there's light at the end of the tunnel.

And a deafening sound of tracks warping and bending under extreme pressures and a monstrous diesel engine whining and whirring. The sound echoes around the tunnel becoming too loud to ignore.

The lights grow ever brighter. The train is coming towards me! I can feel the vibrations in the dirt!

I engage every muscle in my body; every fiber and sinew I still have left, and roll across to the other side of the tunnel. Over the steel track, vibrating madly, and onto the other track. At last I manage to push my bleeding, almost lifeless body over the next track, and safely onto another set of tracks.

Then I watch as the train goes by, seemingly unaware that

it'll pass the burning wreckage of its cousin just a little further down the tunnel. After a moment, the train is gone, and the noise dies down. I can get my breath back…

That's when I hear something like a garbled radio transmission in my ear. It's brief, but I can just make out a couple of syllables. Then it happens again.

"Vega? Talk to me."

Kris – I've rep – the tympanic membrane, and —

He's getting through, slowly but surely. Clearer and clearer.

"What's happening? Am I dying?"

Not at the moment, but you need to get to a safer place.

I do as he says, grasping another handful of gravel and pull myself along. Then I reach down to feel my thighs. They're both still there, surprisingly. I try to stand, but fall back face first in the dirt again. My feet are both there, but I can't feel them.

"How bad is it?"

The biggest concerns are a bleed on your brain and ruptures to your liver and spleen, Vega says with not much in the way of a bedside manner. *But there are also other hemorrhages of other major organs in your body. The nanomachine network will set about fixing them.*

"Jesus," I say to myself, rising to my knees with great pain. "All those people on the train…"

Vega continues, perhaps trying to avert my train of thought. *However, the nanomachine network itself was damaged; you're running at around two-thirds total capacity of fully functional nanomachines. This is due to the damage they took in reinforcing your body's cells against the blast. They will replenish, but you need to rest.*

I'm barely even listening. I grunt, and suddenly feel that I can hear those cries and screams of the victims again, even though I know that's not possible.

I manage to drag myself along by my knees, trailing my inactive feet behind me until I reach a dimly lit area – a large ostentatious wall of a different brickwork than the tunnel itself. Beside it is a door, large and stained brown from many years of fumes.

I prop myself up against it, finding the handle with my one existing hand, but when I try to turn it I realize it's locked. Devoid of any better ideas, I force the handle, using my remaining strength to pull it down. Eventually, with a clean sounding *clink*, it snaps off in my hand and I drop it to the floor.

Then the door itself slowly falls open. I haul myself up to the ledge it's on and crawl through. Inside is pitch black, but I feel around the walls, dragging myself painfully from knee to knee, until I find a light switch. Then I turn it on.

As the lights slowly flicker on – some bright, some dim, some clearly busted, but all seeming as though they haven't been switched on in years – I look around and see a station platform. There are advertisements from at least 10 years ago and trash and newspapers lying around. I guess this was an older subway station the city closed when I was a kid.

"This is a closed down station. I'm amazed they kept the lights on."

I would presume the city merely bricked it up and called it a job well done.

I find a corner underneath a bright florescent light and get to inspecting my wounds. My legs are in tatters below the knees; my skin and muscles shredded, and my ankle on my left foot seemingly hanging onto my lower leg by a thread. My right arm – where I held Burden by the collar – is blown off above the elbow. And now that I can see the world in full, bright light, I realize I have just one working eye.

I rip a bit of torn denim off my jeans and use it as a tourniquet around my arm, trying to stop the bleeding with Vega's direction. Then I do the same for my leg, fighting through mind-numbing agony to do so. Then I get dizzy – cobwebs forming in my vision – and start to understand I'm done. At least for now.

I close my eyes, and lying down in the dirt and blood, drift into unconsciousness.

CHAPTER 20

I feel myself back on the subway train, gently rocking backwards and forwards on the rails. I open my eyes to see blinding white light streaming in from the windows. I look around and see faces; young, old, men, women...

And then I see Burden, grinning. His glasses are foggy, his eyes hidden behind them, but his smile is unmistakable.

I wake up to the familiar waves of pain washing over me, lapping at my legs and arm.

"Vega," I mumble, looking around, seeing the same closed station platform, "how long was I out?"

Six hours, roughly. You hadn't slept in more than 40 hours. Your body has taken a massive physical toll lately. It seems you managed to sleep right through the pain.

I look down at my right arm; the wound has stopped bleeding and congealed into a pink, fleshy mass. I guess I'll grow a new one. My third hand this week.

"Did I almost die?"

Yes. In the moments just after the blast, your heart suffered atrial fibrillation. The nanomachines that surround your heart began defibrillation, applying electric shocks in an effort to return its beating to a regular state.

"My heart stopped!?"

No, but it was beating abnormally. Your heart is now working perfectly. The bleed on your brain was controlled, and the pressure within your skull returned to normal. Additionally, the hemorrhages elsewhere in your body were fixed too. But you are lucky to be alive.

I think back to those people on the train and the ones unlucky enough to be close to me and Burden when he detonated the bombs.

"I don't feel lucky to be alive. All those people on the train…"

Nothing in Burden's modus operandi as a terrorist indicated he was likely to blow himself up or hit a public transport target. You likely averted a terrible tragedy at the parade, too.

"But then I caused one!" I yell, my words echoing around the abandoned station, painfully reminding me of the reality of what I'm saying. "I'm the reason that bomb went off. If I hadn't pursued him; if I hadn't grabbed him, he might never have…" I can't even finish the sentence. The words are like poison to me.

You did what you thought you had to. You got closer to him than any part of law enforcement. Because of you, he won't ever hurt anyone ever again.

I rub my eyes and realize for the first time that both are working, although one is missing a lot of peripheral vision.

"How many lives were lost on that train? How many lives were saved at the parade? How many people would he have gone on to murder?" I ask the questions frantically, but I know I won't ever know the answers.

We will never know how many lives he'd have gone on to take. He could have continued his bombing campaign for years. Or he could have succumbed to radiation poisoning or been caught by law enforcement. There's no way of knowing.

I look around the deserted station. Dirt and cobwebs adorn every surface and crevice. It's like time stood still in this place; ghosts of past commuters lingering in the shadows. It feels like an appropriate crypt for me to haunt.

"Vega," I say, feeling a tear stream down my cheek. "Don't you get tired of this? Watching the world through my eyes? Having to do whatever I say? Seeing me make these... mistakes. You're the one who told me not to pursue him. I should have listened to you."

I may share the personality of my former host, but my desires and frustrations are artificially limited.

"So you can be a better slave?"

So that I can be a better assistant.

"But you don't have likes and dislikes?"

I hear another train pass the tunnel outside, beyond the bricked-up edge of the station platform. It makes me shudder.

I know the difference between right and wrong, Vega replies. *And, truth be told, I found your effort to catch this man – this terrorist – as quite commendable. You fought through more pain than most humans encounter in their lifetime. And you're still here.*

He pauses, before continuing. *I admire you, Kris.*

I look at the fleshy stump that is my right arm. It's getting to be a familiar sight.

This, unfortunately, is the cost of decision. You made a decision to act, and to try to bring the Quiet One to justice. But decisions like that can bring unforeseen consequences.

I let Vega's words sit with me for a while. Did I trade the lives of the people on the train for the lives of the people at the parade, and the people he'd go on to kill?

It may take 48 to 72 hours to fully regenerate your body. And you're going to need to eat.

"Eat? Look where I am, I'm not exactly going to find a hot dog vendor down here."

I look over the station platform and see a rat, standing still and licking its paws, some two yards away from me. I couldn't possibly, could I?

Maybe you can find something that was left behind when the station was abandoned. After all, they left the lights connected to the grid.

I watch the rat turn and run into the shadows. I pick myself up, rising to my knees, and test my feet out. One of them is a horrible, pink, fleshy mess at the ankle with what I can only presume is the white of inner muscle or bone visible. It still hurts; a throbbing ache with every heartbeat.

I look at my other foot and see that it's a lot more sturdy. My jeans are ripped and tattered beyond any recognition, and the skin below is a mess of pink lacerations and flaking skin, but I think I can use it, if just for a short time.

I try to stand on my one good foot, pushing myself up against the cold, dirty brickwork of the station. It's painful – I feel every ounce of weight on my ankle – but I can do it. Then I slide myself across the wall, holding my shoulder close to it, and use my foot to propel myself along.

I move along the wall, limping to a door beside the entrance to the station. Underneath a buzzing, dim light bulb, I push the door open and feel around for another light switch. When I find it, a large janitor's room is revealed, with blue steel lockers, cabinets full of cleaning products, and a mop and bucket in the corner.

I hobble over to the mop, and try to snap the mophead off by engaging my inner caveman and banging it repeatedly against the wall. Eventually it flies off with a satisfying *pop*. My new walking stick.

I use it to get over to the lockers, and one by one use the strength in my fingers and thumbs to snap the padlocks off. The first few lockers are empty – dust and damp smells. The last locker I explore however is thankfully full.

One folded set of blue overalls; a boilersuit, with bleach and paint stains on it, and a stitched nametag that reads 'Ames.' I push it aside to reveal a set of keys, a 10-year-old soda, and a trio of candy bars whose best-before dates I dare not look at.

You should eat those, Vega says when I grab the boilersuit and leave the candy bars. *The nanomachines in your stomach are able to filter out the inefficient or harmful molecules, leaving you to digest food that will sustain you.*

I pick up one of the bars. It's hard and feels nasty to the touch.

"You have to be kidding."

Vega doesn't reply. I pull it out of its wrapper one-handed, recruiting my teeth with some difficulty, and look at it. It has absolutely no smell, but the surface, rather than an attractive milk chocolate brown, is a lighter shade with green or blue edges. I close my eyes and throw the whole thing in my mouth, chewing despondently.

It's tasteless, which is at least welcome. After a few moments of chewing, I swallow most of it and am left with a million particles of mutated chocolate floating around in my mouth. Gross.

I do the same with the other two candy bars before turning my attention to the boilersuit. I remove my clothes – tattered, singed, and ripped – and throw them into a trash bin in the corner, and then put the boilersuit on. It isn't exactly high fashion, but at least I'll be inconspicuous, sort of.

My new cellphone is already broken; the glass on both sides is cracked and the screen below it damaged. Not that I particularly want to reach out to anyone in the world right now. I throw it in the trash and transfer my wallet to my new boilersuit.

I put my walking stick down and sit in the corner. I'm tired – real tired. I look out back into the corridor outside and see a pack of rats running along the tiled floor. Sitting here – in the rat crap, the damp, the lonely squalor – feels appropriate right now.

"I won't ever forget those people," I say to Vega, but mostly to myself. "I can't ever forget those people."

You tried to do a good thing. That makes you a better man than most.

"What the hell am I going to do now?" I can feel tears at the edges of my eyes. I don't want to sit bawling, but at least the only witnesses are rats and my AI friend. "I can't stay in this city. The cops are never gonna believe my story, and it's not like I'm gonna go back to packaging sandwiches."

I wipe away a tear with the blue cuff of my boilersuit.

You'll have plenty of time to think about that. And besides, I want to show you something. Pick up that mophead.

"What? The mophead?"

I look over – the mophead is sitting there by the wall; sad, lonely, pathetic. I can relate.

Yes. Go and pick it up.

I do as he says and crawl over to the mophead, clasping it between my fingers before sliding back to my grief pit by the lockers.

"Okay, now what?"

Now, nothing. Close your eyes and sleep. Your body is exhausted.

I look over at the mophead in my hand with confusion, but I don't have the strength to argue with Vega right now. I hold it tightly and close my eyes. I'm not awake for long.

CHAPTER 21

I feel it hit me; another blast. The wave of pressure hits my cheekbones, rattling my eyes around in their sockets. The sound is deafening; a loud, fast *clap* of an explosion.

I open my eyes, and find myself back in that janitor's closet, soaked in sweat. I look down at my feet, happily inside my slightly singed shoes. I haven't been gnawed on by rats, so I guess that's a good thing.

"How long was I asleep?"

I remember the mophead in my hand, but it feels different somehow.

Just over 17 hours.

"Did you say 17 hours?! I can't ever remember sleeping that long!" I feel the mophead between my fingers – smaller, harder. I look down at it. "Whoa, what the hell!"

The mophead is gone. Beside my hand is a halo of tiny white fluff, and inside my hand is a shiny gem of some sort. I immediately bring it closer to my eye. It's clear, sparkling, about half an inch in diameter and it seems perfectly round.

"What is this?"

The mophead.

I look closer – the white light from the florescent tube

above seems to bend inside it; a beautiful prism of all the colors appears when I roll it between my fingers.

"Vega, this is not the mophead."

The nanomachines within your hand restructured it on a molecular level. The carbon present in the mophead fabric was restructured to become what you hold in your hand: a diamond.

I'm amazed; I open my mouth but no words come out. Instead, I gasp for breath.

The only difference between carbon molecules that make up the structure of a cotton mophead and the carbon molecules that make up a diamond is structure. The shape the molecules are arranged into. By the same process, diamonds are formed underground at extraordinary pressures.

I remember this lesson from chemistry, but I'm no less surprised to see it in action.

"So I can create diamonds from anything?"

So long as that anything is composed of carbon, and so long as you have the time, yes.

I hold the diamond up to the light. It looks real enough, even if I know it started its life being pushed around the filthy floors of a subway station.

"So, what do I do with this? Start a jeweler's business? Sell diamonds on social media?"

I think we both know that's not to your taste.

I feel like Vega is finally starting to understand me. He's right, it's not to my taste. Still, I know exactly what to do with it.

"Why show me this, then?"

I wanted to show you the extent of your power, and that in this universe there are very fine margins between what is and what isn't. That worthless mophead had all the physical ingredients to become a priceless diamond. They just needed to be put into the right order.

I look at it once more before slipping it into one of the pockets of the boilersuit. Then I take an opportunity to pocket the keys I found. Might be useful to escape this place.

I pick myself up and find that I can use my other foot again. It's not perfect, but it supports my weight well enough to get around this place without hopping and sliding against the wall.

I grab my walking stick and slowly amble out of the janitor's closet. My right arm hasn't grown back yet, but at least I can hide that in the long cuff of my new clothing.

I climb a set of stairs, finding a ticket gate that I can easily push past. I root around in the trash bins and a couple of black liner bags in the corner but find nothing but dusty garbage. Then I climb an inactive escalator and find myself at the street level entrance.

There's a large, cast-iron door that must have been installed when the station was closed. I cycle through the keys, trying each before finally I find one that fits the lock and turns it with a satisfying *click*. The door moves slowly, but after a couple of pushes it's out of my way. I push it back and lock it back up; I don't want anyone to know I've been there.

The smell of the city is intoxicating; I never thought I'd miss it, but after being underground for so long it feels great. The bouts of fresh air between car and bus exhaust fumes; the sweet smell of the trash piling up on the curb. I guess I truly am going crazy.

I hobble up the street, passing a newspaper vendor as I go. With a lot of hesitation – standing lonely on the pavement as it begins to rain – I buy a newspaper.

SUBWAY BOMBING KILLS EIGHT

The headline feels like a spade in my gut, cleaving out my innards and leaving a giant, dark void in their place. I move along, shuffling further down the street, until I find a dark corner I can stand in and open the paper.

The lead story is as expected: a bomb, presumably from the Quiet One, detonated on a subway train and killing eight. The names of the victims are being withheld pending a police investigation, with the exception of two: Alfred Burden, dead in the blast, and Kris Chambers, presumed dead.

It's a strange feeling to read my own name in the newspaper. It's a stranger feeling still to read my own name, followed by the words 'presumed dead.'

I read on: Alfred Burden is named as the lead suspect in this bombing, the Quiet One bombings, as well as the destruction of his own home. Kris Chambers on the other hand is thought of as an associate and an accessory to the crimes.

An accessory?!

I go back to the front page, and that giant, black eight. If I'm counted among the dead, that means six innocent people gave their lives so that I could get my hands on Burden.

I sink to my knees, dropping the newspaper to the ground next to me, where a couple of pages blow away with the passing of a bus.

I killed six people, I'm a wanted criminal, and I'm dead.

After a few moments, I begin to idly collect the newspaper pages at my feet, trying to stop any more from blowing away. Then I see a picture on one of the pages; it grabs my attention instantly.

It's a slightly blurry picture of a child, covered in light-gray dust from head to toe. Her surroundings are dark – a charred, bombed-out building. She sits within it wearing an emotionless expression. It reminds me of that haunting picture of the gull and the dark water. It breaks my heart just to look at it.

I read the article that surrounds it. It's an account of the civil war in Aljarran, a small nation in the Middle East. Government forces, afraid the tide of the war is turning, are shelling towns loyal to the rebels, leading to the destruction of an apartment building, the home of the girl in the picture.

My eyes are drawn back to the picture. She doesn't even look sad. Her eyes are two black holes almost, staring expressionless at the camera, blurred slightly. The look of someone who's way past sadness or loneliness.

I gather the rest of the newspaper pages and read as much about the war as I can. Four years ago, protests began against the unpopular dictator, President Ahab Darida. I remember that much. But as the protests went on, and the protests turned to an armed uprising, the stories dropped from the news.

Four years later, the war continues, still as bitterly fought as ever. Now the president can launch strikes against his own citizens and it hardly gets a peep from the Western-focused media here. Page 15 in the newspaper.

I think about that diamond again. I want to do good things; I want to help people. I want to fight. But doing it here is no longer an option. It's easy to think of myself – with all of my cybernetically-enhanced abilities – as the diamond. But I'm not the diamond – I'm the mophead.

I have everything I need to do good; everything I need to be special. But I haven't worked out how to put it all in the correct order yet.

I turn back to the photograph, and take one last look at it before ripping it out, folding it neatly, and putting it in my pocket next to the diamond. I think I know what I want to do next.

"Vega," I say out loud, beginning to walk along the street again. The rain is coming down heavily now, but I've survived worse recently. "I think I need to get out of the city."

I think it would be wise to avoid being questioned by the authorities, yes.

Vega clearly feels as squeamish as I do about the prospect of landing on some government autopsy table somewhere as a bunch of scientists try to discover what makes me tick. Maybe I'm being paranoid, but I'm always gonna have a hard time explaining the whole nanomachines thing.

"But first, I want to learn all I can about this Aljarran civil war."

Vega seems to pause for a couple of moments. Processing my request perhaps? Or just computing how to comprehend my latest insane desire to put myself in harm's way...

You're thinking of traveling to Aljarran, a Middle-Eastern warzone?

"Yes," I say, without any trace of hesitation. I pick up my pace, limping a little still as I hop over the puddles forming from the rain.

I suppose I don't need to inform you of the extreme danger that would involve?

"Nope."

Okay. We should learn as much as possible about this nation. The rebels, the government, the war, the weapons, the climate, and the terrain.

At last, we're on the same page.

I look around, and realize I'm 20 or so minutes from the city's public library. Seeing as I can't seem to hold onto a cellphone for longer than a couple of days without it being blasted into a thousand pieces, I should probably do this the old-fashioned way.

With that haunting picture still on my mind, I limp to the library.

CHAPTER 22

It's getting dark when I make it out of the library. I guess I was in there for hours. Luckily, no-one seemed to bat an eyelid at the presumed-dead-man browsing the internet with one arm from the comfort of his dusty boilersuit.

And I did manage to learn a lot.

Aljarran used to be a shining beacon of democracy in the region, with flourishing industry and a vibrant set of universities. And then a military coup installed the nation's current 'president,' a dictator by the name of Ahab Ebu Darida, around 10 years ago.

He began brutally crushing all forms of dissent; unfriendly journalists were hounded out of the country or put in jail on phony charges, and anyone involved with any of the previous political parties quickly found themselves scared into silence or dead. Fairly standard stuff for a dictatorship, of course.

Where it all became complicated is when a fruit-seller decided to protest against the president after his license to sell in the market was rescinded. One man's protest turned into a marketplace on strike, which turned into a town holding new elections, which turned into several cities voting to secede and start their own nation.

President Darida wasn't going to take that lying down, and the two sides – Darida's government and the seceded rebel nation, led by a charismatic woman named Cantara, have been fighting ever since in a brutal civil war.

Darida has been getting ever more desperate using horrifying incendiary bombing against civilian cities, and rumors abound of him procuring chemical weapons: nerve gases or similar.

I've already learned I can fly to a neighboring nation, and then attempt to cross the border into rebel territory. Leaving the United States may be difficult, but I'm sure I can think of something.

Now, I'll be the first to admit I'm no soldier. I've held a gun precisely once – a BBQ at my uncle's before my Dad and him stopped talking for whatever zany reason. I didn't get a chance to fire it because it was neither the time nor the place, and because I was six.

But I surely have a lot to offer. I'm willing to learn, I've got a good pain threshold, and I'm the strongest, fastest human being alive. And that's not even mentioning my ability to grow back the right hand that keeps getting blown off.

"I need a way to get out of the country Vega, but first," I look around, taking in the sights, sounds, and smells of the city, "there's a couple of things I need to do before I leave."

It's 10 o'clock or so by the time I make it back to mine and Dad's apartment building. I stand across the street, watching to make sure the coast is clear. The last thing I need is one of my former neighbors calling every newspaper in town and saying they've seen a dead man.

When I'm satisfied I can run to the mailroom without

arousing any suspicion, I cross the road and let myself in. The lobby of the building is the same as ever – bland, cold, and strange-smelling. Can't say I'll miss it.

I get to the mailroom and pick an empty envelope out of the trash can. Then, taking a biro pen I pilfered from the library, I scrawl one word on it: 'RENT.' Then I carefully deposit the diamond inside it before posting it through our apartment's mailbox. It'll even be enough to cover that hospital bill I've been dreading.

I think about dropping in and saying a few words to him, but I quickly change my mind. I know he thinks I'm dead by now, but the diamond should hopefully dispel that notion.

Besides, he'll rationalize it all to himself somehow; he'll reason that I'm some resurrected prophet or that our family is on some divine course to change the world. I just don't wish to be part of that conversation.

Sorry, Dad.

I jump out of the mailroom, out of the building, and bound away down the street without once looking back. It was a crummy apartment anyway. Dad will be happier there alone; just him and his cigarettes.

"So," I speak into the collar on my boilersuit, trying to arouse as little suspicion as possible. "How do I get out of the country?"

It will be very difficult using conventional means. I can't help but notice you don't have a passport with you either.

"Yeah, I haven't left the country since I went on vacation to Mexico as a kid."

That means the easiest route would be to procure a fake passport or steal one.

"I don't know anyone who could fake a passport." I think of Burden once again, and that fake FBI ID. I didn't realize I'd be descending to his level quite yet. "And I'd have to steal a passport from someone who looks just like me."

Not necessarily.

I pause, coming to a standstill in the middle of the street. Some guy in an obnoxiously loud coat walks towards me on the sideway; I wait until he passes to speak.

"What do you mean?"

Do you remember when you had to call the police and the nanomachine network was able to re-sculpt your vocal cords for a short time?

Again, I think of Burden. I met him for the first time right after that. Two imposters going about our days.

"Sure, I remember."

The same process can be applied to your facial structure. If you happen to find yourself with someone else's passport, the nanomachine network can restructure your brow, nose, lips, etc., to roughly match their picture. It wouldn't fool a sophisticated facial scanner, but it could fool a human.

Huh; how did I never think of this before? I mean, I can grow a new arm. Why not assume a new face?

I set out for a bar near here. I've never actually been in there, but I know from just the look of the place it's full of asshole frat-boys my kind of age. Hopefully it won't take long for me to find someone stupid enough to use a passport to prove they're legal to drink.

"So, I just grab someone's passport and we'll re-sculpt my face?"

Yes. The process should take six hours.

My arm still isn't repaired yet; I can't quite rub my fingers together within the arm of my boilersuit. Perhaps tomorrow, with a new face, a new arm, and a new sense of adventure, I will be ready to travel.

I soon get to the bar. It's a real classy joint; a pink neon side out the front advertises a terrible home-brewed beer that illuminates every puddle on the street surrounding it, looking like some drunk halo. There's a large man outside with cold eyes and a warm fleece jacket.

There's a puddle of something beige, wet, and bitty just

outside the door. I don't look down; I already feel like I know what it is. The sound of nu-metal from 20 years ago is practically vibrating the door off its hinges.

Jesus, I really wish I didn't have to go in there.

I stand by the entrance to a pizza parlor, ignoring the fantastic smells of cheese and tomato, and trying to work out how I'll handle this exactly. Even if I manage to get past the burly guy on the door – and he doesn't recognize that I'm a suspected of being a dead terrorist – how am I going to steal someone's passport without them realizing?

I look around the area, desperately ignoring the thoughts of pizza clouding my mind. A group of men in smart shirts pass by me, walking past the bar and laughing and joking as they go. By the time they're out of earshot, I see that the bouncer on the door has disappeared. Perhaps this is my time to sneak in.

I tentatively approach the door, trying my best to stroll up casually as if I hadn't been nervously eyeing it up for the past five minutes. I'm about five steps away when the bouncer suddenly emerges, dragging another man out by the shirt collar.

In one ungracious movement, he throws the man to the ground. The man – drunk and slurring his words – tries to protest, but it's clear to everyone but him that his night is over. He wallows in a puddle for a moment before clambering to his knees, and then awkwardly to his feet.

"Whoa, hey bud," I say, as he stumbles in my direction. He reeks of beer, and I'm not sure he knows where he is exactly. "Are you all right?"

"Take your friend and get out of here," the bouncer snarls at me. I guess he thinks we know each other. "And he ain't coming back til he learns not to be creepy around women."

He has shorter hair than I do, and he's shorter than me – around 5'6" – but his hair is the same color as mine.

"Hey, I'm sorry, I'm sorry," the drunk guy slurs, holding

his arm around me like he actually knows me. Another man emerges from the door of the bar – this one looking decidedly unimpressed with his evening, wearing a black T-shirt bearing the name of the bar. He hands the bouncer something and heads back inside.

"And take this with you."

The bouncer hands the man a small blue book. Could that be a passport? I think I may have found my mark.

"Hey, thanks, I'll ensure he gets home all right."

I swoop in like a vulture, leading him away from the bar and into the street proper. His white dress shirt is stained yellow, and a brown coat clings to him unflatteringly. If I hadn't heard he'd been creepy to women, I'd feel almost sorry for him in this condition.

"Where are we going?" he asks, looking me in the eye for the first time while draping his arm further around my neck.

"I'm getting you home buddy."

I can tell he doesn't like that answer. He squirms around on my shoulder, his eyes lazily swimming from side to side in their sockets.

"What? No way man."

This really doesn't have to be painful. I just need to grab the passport and get out. We stumble to the curb and stand there like a couple of scarecrows, wavering in the wind.

"Okay, another bar, fine."

He starts talking; slurring his words and repeating himself, telling me how good a night he's had and that his friends abandoned him. I don't think he'll even remember this in the morning.

Watching him grip his passport, waving it around in the air violently as he talks, I decide to make my move. I grab it out of his hand, which elicits a look of confusion from him, but he doesn't stop talking. After a few moments, he seems to have forgotten he ever held it in his hand. I slip it quietly into my pocket.

"And that's – that's where my friends went, I think."

"Uh-huh," I grunt in acknowledgement.

I finally see a taxi and wave an arm around to flag it down. When it arrives by the curb, I tell the driver to take this man home and chuck him a few dollars for the journey. The drunk guy looks at me dejectedly from the backseat, like he'd expected me to join him. At least he'll get home safe.

I close the taxi door and take one last look at the man. His face – small eyes and a small mouth – isn't offensively ugly, but the thought that I'll look exactly like that tomorrow is enough to turn my stomach.

The taxi speeds off and I walk away from the scene. When I'm comfortably far from the bar, I take the passport out of my pocket and open it to the photo ID page.

"Dyson, Colton," I read from the page, looking at the photograph of the man. His hair is different to mine, but surely that won't be a problem. "He's 22 years old. Is this a decent enough match?"

Yes, Vega says confidently.

I lose myself in his image; a dull, unremarkable passport photo of a dull, unremarkable-looking man.

"I just hope this guy isn't on some sort of watchlist."

You should find somewhere quiet where you're not going to be seen or disturbed. The process of restructuring will take approximately six hours, but you shouldn't let anybody see you as it's happening.

"Yeah," I say, averting my eyes and closing the passport at last. "Roger that."

I can't afford to spend any of the last few hundred dollars I have on a hotel room, and my other natural habitat – the closed-down subway station – is probably still crawling with emergency services. I guess I'll treat myself to another derelict building.

I walk in the general direction of the airport until I reach a real seedy area on the outskirts of town. There's a perpetual smell of smoke in the air hanging thick on every street corner. Sirens are almost ever-present; a wailing going on long into the night, and yet never a single police car in sight. Seems a perfect place to become a new man.

I glance around the neighborhood, seeing a dingy hotel on a street corner that I quite like the look of. I hop inside, bypassing a sleeping man on the reception desk, and take the stairs down to the parking garage, but not before swiping a few towels from an errant cleaning cart in the lobby.

Then, from the parking garage, I go next door; a derelict office by the looks of it. Using my one good arm, with the towels bunched under my other, I pull myself up to the fire escape and climb the staircase a couple of floors. Then, after carefully climbing through a broken window, I'm in.

It seems I've become quite the expert at sleeping rough.

I find a dark room, free of the glow of streetlights, and pick a cozy corner before wrapping myself in the towels. It's cold and it's uncomfortable, but it's far better than the dusty subway station and its clientele of rats.

"So is this gonna hurt?" I ask Vega. I feel like pain has been almost constant for the last few days. But like Vega suggested, pain just doesn't have the same sting when you know you're going to wake up healthy.

A little. A dull ache in your face as the bones and cartilage are re-arranged.

"Great."

I take the passport out, and take one last look at it, straining to see it by the thin strands of car headlights that occasionally light up the room.

I do feel bad about taking the guy's passport. And, you know, his identity. My excuse is that I need it more than he does, at least for a short while. I don't plan on being Colton Dyson for long, and when I'm out of the country I can return to my own name and my own face.

Kris, I have to ask, Vega says, evidently analyzing the exact amount of time my pupils are lingering on the passport. *Going to fight a war is a very courageous thing to do. Fighting a war in which you have no personal stake or obligation is even more so. But, if you're looking at this at a cost-benefit point of view, what's in it for you?*

"What?" I ask, putting the passport away. "I mean, I don't feel like I can stay in this country, and I want to prove myself."

I think of those people on the subway train. Six killed, probably many more injured. Maimed. Their lives changed. I can feel anger rising within me; Burden's grin locked in my memory forevermore.

"This is a war with an absolute, obvious evil. President Darida is a tyrant. He shells his own cities – his own people – with no thought or compassion. This war has killed hundreds of thousands of civilians and it's because of *him*."

I realize I'm picturing Burden as I say that. I rub my eyes, feeling that dull ache in my brow for the first time.

There are ways you could use your abilities to benefit the people of Aljarran without putting yourself – a man with no combat experience and no familiarity with the psychological rigors of battle – in harm's way.

"What am I going to do? Brew up a diamond daily and open a jeweler's store? Donate all the profits?" I can feel myself getting frustrated.

"I need to do this for me. I need to prove that I'm not just some moronic kid, making everything worse."

Vega is silent. I know he feels my blood pressure and my heart rate rising.

"I've had a whole lifetime of inaction. Of being wrapped in cotton wool. Of being mocked, picked on, and told I was fragile. I just want to prove that I can fight. That I can make a difference."

But you did make a difference. You uncovered Alfred Burden. Because of you he'll never plant another bomb ever again.

"And six innocent people died." I sink back against the wall, pulling the towels up around me, really feeling the cold for the first time. "But this war will be different. I'll join the rebels; sell myself as a mercenary. I'll learn. I'll be a soldier."

And I'll help you every step of the way. I just want you to know that war is hell.

I grunt in acknowledgement.

I've slept in derelict buildings and cold, hard subway station floors. I've had parts of my body blown off repeatedly. I've seen more of my blood spilt than most humans can surely tolerate. And all of this has been easier to stomach than the first 24 years of my life.

I think I'm ready for war.

CHAPTER 23

I feel the steady rocking of a ship; forwards and backwards, moving myself with the waters. It's night; pitch black, and I find myself on a cruise ship of some sort. An older style with a wooden deck.

I look out into the sky and see complete darkness. No moon, no stars, no lights on the horizon. Just me and this large, gray ship.

I walk a little further along the deck and see that I'm no longer on a ship at all, but some sort of carnival. There's a merry-go-round and a helter-skelter. And people dressed in bright colors, smiles on their faces.

And I just know there's a bomb here, waiting for me.

I wake up with the sound of a bus's exhaust chugging along outside. I put my hands to my face, wiping away the tears that have begun to form in my eyes, and immediately panic when my fingers touch my cheek.

My entire face feels different; my teeth sit differently in my mouth, my nose is smaller and pointier. I puff air in and out of my nose and find it sounds different. Even my ears feel weird, seated in an almost incalculably different position, but noticeable nonetheless

"Whoa, I forgot about the new face here." My voice still sounds the same, thankfully.

I'm sure it will take some getting used to. As I mentioned last time, the human brain isn't particularly good at processing rapid change to the body.

I stand up, folding the towels and putting them to one side before searching the rooms in these abandoned offices for something I can use. Eventually, finding a bathroom partially destroyed by scrap hunters, I find it: several broken shards of a mirror.

I look like him alright. Colton Dyson; the last time I saw him he was fidgeting in the back of a taxi. Now he's staring right back at me; my own ghostly reflection.

I pull my right hand out of the cuff of the boilersuit and see that it's good as new. I rub my face with it, savoring that tactile feeling I've missed. Then I go back to my sleeping spot, gather my towels, and leave this building via the same fire escape I came in from. I head back into the hotel and nonchalantly leave the towels by the door.

Then I'm ready to make the walk to the airport.

The city's airport is a dump. I really shouldn't be surprised; every other building in this dark and gloomy city is derelict or a pawn shop or a liquor store. But the airport is really something else.

It looms on the horizon like some giant, sickly animal. Its huge concrete façade is gray and crumbling. The floors are sticky, the windows cloudy, and there's an ever-present smell of diesel fuel and desperation in the air.

Worse are the passengers; despondent and beaten down by their time in this city and desperate to escape it. Or even worse, those having just landed, their enthusiasm turning to despair in no time at all.

I hop into a store to buy some exceedingly cheap clothing: a T-shirt, shorts, and a new pair of inoffensive-looking sneakers. Anything to get me through the flight with as little suspicion as possible.

Then I spend the last chunk of money in my account on a ticket to Mehdirran, a small, oil-rich country on the border of Aljarran. My research tells me I can travel there visa-free. After that, it's just a matter of crossing the border.

I sit in the departures lobby, watching a group of women laughing, joking, and downing glasses of white wine. There's one last itch that I haven't managed to scratch: Jessica. She probably thinks I'm dead right now, and there's nothing that I – with an entirely different face – can do about that.

I tell myself I'll see her when I return, whenever that may be. I tell myself that I was the jerk; I was too wrapped up in my own dramas to see that she was hurting too. I tell myself everything will be better someday, for me and for her.

And I tell myself that flying out of the country to fight in a war I barely knew about a week ago is a good idea.

Am I crazy?

Am I self-absorbed?

Am I in way over my head?

Probably. But for the first time in my life, I'm fighting.

CHAPTER 24

I'm standing in a small queue clutching Colton Dyson's passport nervously. For all the worrying about my chances of dying a brutal death on a Middle-Eastern battlefield, I didn't expend much energy thinking about a more mundane threat. Namely, that I'd be turned away at passport control.

The flights were practically supreme luxury compared to the discomfort I've endured recently. First to Europe with a short layover, and then a relatively quiet journey to Mehdirran. The only real difficulty I had was trying to avoid prodding and poking my own face.

But, standing here behind the giant crystal-clear windows and the relentless sun beating down from outside, I feel a little more exposed. The airport itself is gorgeous: marble-like tiles and Hellenic-style columns adorn the arrivals lobby. When I look down, I can see the strange and unsettling silhouette of my face reflected in the tiles.

Finally, I'm called forward to a small booth, behind which sits a dour-looking man wearing a blue military-style uniform. He has a nametag on, upon which an entirely illegible name is scrawled.

I hand my passport over, trying to maintain an utterly expressionless look on my new face. I look at him directly and feel my eyebrow twitching already. When his eyes meet mine, I instinctively look away – an unhappy remnant of my shyer school days.

He looks down at the passport, looks at me one more time, and then grabs a stamp nearby and puts one big, wet imprint in Colton Dyson's passport. He smiles and waves me along. I feel a wave of relief pass over me, which is reflected in the wide grin I give him as I grab the passport back and move on.

I was worried that the travel ID would have been cancelled already or placed on some international blocking system. But I guess Colton is a chaotic enough character not to have noticed he's missing it yet, or more likely not to even care.

I pass through the spotlessly clean corridors and lobbies, free of the burden of waiting to collect a bag. Then I get to a huge, golden set of doors.

As soon as I'm through them, I feel the heat hit me; a dry, intense warmth that already feels burning on my pallid skin.

"It's hot."

Yes Kris, Vega says, *it's going to be a challenge to regulate your temperature in this climate.*

"I should have brought sunscreen."

The nanomachine network can shield you from the most problematic of the sun's rays to a certain extent. DNA damage due to ultra-violet radiation can be limited. Your greater challenge is staying hydrated. Your organs, despite being ably assisted, are still human.

For a moment I wonder if Vega is trying to insult me, but quickly move onto my next goal: getting to the border. Mehdirran is a small nation, but it's 25 or so miles to the border with Aljarran.

"How hot is it?" I ask Vega, hoping to God that he tries to dissuade me from walking it.

It's 82 degrees Fahrenheit.

"I think I'll thumb a ride."

Saying those words seems foreign to me. I've never hitchhiked or 'thumbed a ride' before. I walk out to the largest road leaving the airport and sit by the side of the road in the sand and dirt, holding my thumb out and looking entirely out of place.

Mehdirran is a strange place; every car that passes me is one of only three things: an expensive-as-all-hell sports car, most probably with some sheikh behind the wheel; a tiny, Eastern-European brand of car, sputtering along belching foul blue-black smoke behind it, or a truck of some sort, invariably white or grey, packed with food or boxes or the like.

The heat is beginning to sap my energy; I wipe the sweat off my brow – battling a moment of slight alarm when I feel the topography of my face again – and wish I'd picked more appropriate clothing than my gaudy T-shirt and shorts. I look up and down the road but see no shade.

I begin to count the number of vehicles that pass. I lose count after 230. This already feels like a mistake. I begin to wonder if I should ask Vega to magic up another diamond; something I can flash in a truck driver's face in exchange for a ride, but just when I expect it least I get lucky.

A small truck – a flatbed, empty in the back – pulls up. I look over and see the man inside smiling politely in my direction. I smile at him and walk over. I find the door slightly obstinate, but it opens when I apply a bit of force.

The man – tired-looking with a wispy beard and warm eyes – says something in the native language. I try to say the name of the city I'm trying to get to – Aminabal – but can see I'm utterly hopeless. After I say it a fourth time he nods and gets to driving, humming along with a song on the radio as he goes.

I'm idly watching the sights pass by when I turn to my driver and see he has large scars on his neck. Two circular scars, appearing pink on his tanned skin. They look suspiciously like in-and-out bullet wounds. I don't ask – I don't know how to – but I do wonder how far that civil war next door will reach.

―――――

The drive takes half an hour or so; I'm unceremoniously dumped right next to a sign that says 'AMINABAL,' one of the few examples of signposted English I've seen. I wave the driver away with not a single word spoken between us, but plenty of gratitude conveyed on my face, or so I hope.

With the sun beating down on me once again, I walk into town.

"So, what's my best chance of crossing the border?"

I read a hell of a lot at the library, but I'm no human encyclopedia; half of it I feel I've already forgotten. Luckily, I've got one trillion sets of eyes on everything I do.

The border with Aljarran is heavily guarded, being the entrance to a rebellious, diplomatically unrecognized territory, as well as being a warzone. You might find a section of unguarded border within the desert, but the journey across will be treacherous.

"Right."

I'm walking casually, but I can already see I'm getting a lot of funny looks from the city folk here. I'm a pale, tastelessly dressed tourist and undoubtedly look completely clueless.

You'd be better off stowing away inside someone's vehicle when they cross the border. That's what a lot of the accounts we read from veterans suggested.

I got lost reading a bunch of accounts of the war from Americans who'd travelled to fight. Former soldiers who missed the battlefield, professional thrill-seekers who wanted camera footage to boost their YouTube channels or true-believers who wanted to will the new breakaway nation into existence.

They all seemed to go with bright-eyed enthusiasm and returned home with PTSD, tinnitus and broken limbs. The overwhelming sentiment: war is hell, and this war is hell on steroids.

Eventually I make it to the center of town; a large marketplace within an ornate, glass-domed building. The walls outside are adorned with multi-colored, shiny mosaics, and stained glass windows. It looks like a former palace or mosque but seems now to be dedicated to the almighty free market.

There is a mixture of other buildings around – large sandstone brick apartment blocks and Western-style hotels and offices decked out in shimmering crystalline glass. But the marketplace is the first to really catch my eye, and by far appears to be the busiest.

I go inside and spend half an hour or so walking around aimlessly, taking in the sights and the sounds and the smells. There are spices, breads, curries, meats, wines, and everything in between. But there seems to be no opportunities to jump into a truck and go over the border. I don't know what I was expecting.

I think you'll have to look elsewhere.

Evidently Vega has seen enough; he's tired of me looking wistfully upon a market stall selling cured meats and wants me to get to the task at hand.

"Yeah."

I'm starving by now; I nab a couple of free samples, but it isn't enough. The sellers look at me like a tasty piece of meat; one even licked his lips upon seeing me. Half of them know English it seems, but no-one deigns to offer me a ride across the border. Eventually I have to turn my back on the marketplace and leave to preserve my own sanity.

I walk around the building, finding a few hastily assembled market stalls outside but nothing of real interest. Another half-hour is spent doing this, before I lean against a building and watch an immaculately dressed man direct his five servants to unpack the shopping from the back of a sports car.

"It's like I never left the States."

Vega makes a noise in acknowledgement.

After I'm done watching the exploits of the rich, I find myself walking down a series of winding alleyways, just wide enough for a car, mostly to seek the shade.

As I leave the town center, I get to the warrens of houses and apartments where the populace lives; the gorgeous smell of food hangs in the air, and I hear voices – singing, talking, shouting – emerging from the open windows.

There's a strange noise coming from this alley, though. A sputtering, idling engine. And then frenzied shouting.

I can't make out the words, it's undoubtedly in a language I don't understand, but something I've been learning more and more about is the language of violence. And this sure sounds like violence.

Turning a corner, I find myself inside a small square of sorts and see a dirt-covered truck with a bed full of sacks and boxes. The driver's side door is open, but the driver is nowhere to be seen. The windows and shutters all around are closed and grey, and a shopfront is sealed with a huge metal shutter obscuring it.

I follow the sounds of shouting and see a man squatting on the floor behind the truck, holding his hands out defensively. Above him is another man wearing an improbable leather jacket considering the searing heat.

I walk around slowly, and only when the leather-jacketed man sees me do I realize he's holding a knife; it catches the sun and shines brightly. I guess I ran into something here; my habit of finding dicey situations in dodgy alleyways continues.

The man on the floor holds something out: a set of car keys. The robber is distracted though; he's more bothered about the pale American witness who just strolled into the scene of his crime. He's young, maybe late teens, with deep brown eyes and large lips, and his hair is gelled back.

He yells something at me. I play dumb, looking around, and approach him with a hand out, all conciliatory. The robber steps over the poor guy on the dusty ground, holding the knife in my direction before swiping it in a threatening manner.

"Hey!" I say, trying to appear even more like a dumb tourist, if that were possible. "I just want to find my hotel!"

I take another step towards him, and he seems to be in two minds; he doesn't know whether to actually try and stab me or just turn and run. I see fear in his eyes. Maybe this is his first time dabbling in knife crime.

"Calm, calm, calm," I repeat, taking another slow step towards him. His eyelid twitches and he lifts the knife above his head. I dive forward, grabbing his wrist and pushing his body to the ground. He wilts like a decaying flower, dropping the knife and collapses. Then he jumps to his feet, and after looking one more time at the stricken driver he turns and runs.

I look down at the man on the floor; he's middle-aged, wearing a set of thick-rimmed glasses, and with receding hair. When he smiles at me gratefully, the first thing I see is a gold tooth among some very shiny white teeth.

"Thanks man!" he yells. I hold out my hand to him and pick him up from the ground. Then I put two and two together and grasp that he spoke to me in perfect English. "These kids, ya know, little terrors!"

"You speak English," I say to him, slightly dazed. He dusts himself down and rubs his head thoughtfully.

"American TV," he says, with a sly smile.

I watch as he walks around me, looking his truck up and down before turning to the cargo. He has a strange walk; he bobs from side to side as though he's nursing some sort of old hip injury. When he's satisfied nothing from the bed of the truck has been stolen, he turns back to me.

"How can I repay you my friend?"

Repay me? I hadn't even thought of that, but now that he mentions it...

"Well, there is some place I need to go."

He smiles receptively, showing me that gleaming gold tooth again. I rub my forehead, trying to think of a way to say the next part without wiping that smile off his face.

"I need to cross the border to Aljarran."

Well, technically he doesn't stop smiling. Instead he laughs, disbelievingly at first, before really leaning into it when he sees that I'm not joking.

"You do know there's a war going on there, don't you?"

I nod. He shakes his head before wiping his eyes with his hand, nudging his glasses down his sweaty nose.

"You're not the first American to tell me that," he says. He walks around to the driver's side of his car before re-adjusting his glasses again. "The last American to tell me that didn't make it out of there in one piece."

"I think I appreciate the risks," I tell him, only half-heartedly.

"You're not dressed like a soldier. And you're not equipped like a soldier." He looks me up and down and sees a mid-twenties kid. A mid-twenties kid who just disarmed a mugger, but a kid nonetheless. "But, sure thing. It's a funeral right?"

I wonder if he means to say 'it's *your* funeral,' but nod along anyway.

"My name is Kris," I say belatedly, holding out my hand to shake his. He takes it eagerly; his palm is clammy with sweat, but his grip is firm.

"Saad," he says in reply. "So I have deliveries. A couple here, a couple there, and then I can cross the border."

"So you cross the border often?"

"Fairly often," Saad replies, the warmth in his eyes suddenly draining. "I have family there. Most of us in this town do."

I get in the passenger's side and feel the heat from the idling engine immediately. My shirt is sticking to me; I couldn't look more like some stupid American kid who wandered off the beaten track and into a situation he neither understands nor can survive. Feels familiar.

Saad gets in the car and drives around the rabbit-warren of alleys and side streets with commendable skill, darting and weaving around corners and dodging oncoming cars like he's done this a thousand times before.

He tells me more about himself in-between hopping out to deliver a box or two and take a fistful of bank notes. He says his father was from Aljarran and his brother taught there prior to the conflict. After the civil war kicked off he was unhappily conscripted into the government forces. And then he stopped so he could reply to texts.

Saad says he never heard from his brother again. He has no idea if he's alive, dead or imprisoned.

After he makes one final stop and unloads a burlap sack of something red – vegetables, by the looks of it – he tells me it's almost time.

"The border security... it's not great," he tells me, before his expression hardens. "But I don't want to give those guys any excuse to take my beautiful truck."

I look around at the tattered upholstery and the paint peeling off the hood, before smiling and nodding with some degree of irony.

"So, we're going to hide you in the back. Shouldn't be for too long; no more than half an hour."

I climb out of the truck at his direction and walk around the back. There, Saad reveals the luxury carriage that'll get me into Aljarran: a dull burlap sack, formerly full of some sort of peppers and spices. As he ruffles it and opens it up, there's a dust arising that makes my eyes itch.

"I'm getting in there?" I ask, even though I know the answer. He nods with that gold-toothed grin again and opens the neck of the sack even wider.

I dutifully hop over the side of the truck then put both feet in the sack; there are seeds, dust and other remnants of the previous occupant in the bottom, but I try to put it out of my mind. Then I sit down and pull the sack up around me. Saad assists me by drawing the cord tighter, and before I know it I'm fully within.

There's nothing but dull brown light making it through the material, and the air is thick with the intense smell of spice. I can taste it. But not just through my mouth and nose; it almost feels as though my eyes are tasting it, stinging with every blink. After a minute I learn to just keep them closed.

I feel the truck begin idling below me, and before long it shudders into motion.

"I guess I found a worse way to travel than the bus," I say to Vega, satisfied that my voice is masked by the engine.

It isn't the most comfortable way to travel, but I believe it will work.

I inhale another nostril-full of spice fumes and begin to mentally count down the time I'll be stuck in this burlap sack. Half an hour or so and I'll be over the border. And then the real fun can begin.

CHAPTER 25

It feels like an hour has passed when the engine stops. I want nothing more than to poke my hand through the closed neck of the sack, open it fully, and inhale a full breath of clean air. But I wait until I'm told the coast is clear. I feel like I'm burning up.

The journey itself seemed to go without incident; a small pause – the whine of the engine never ceasing – and the sound of muffled voices outside my small world of the spice sack. Words in a language I don't understand, followed by laughter, and the wheels coming to turn again.

I wait a little longer, and suddenly I'm bathed in light. I open my eyes again and gratefully see the clear blue sky above me, and Saad's face, grinning that grin with the golden tooth glinting in the sunlight.

I try to speak, but with my lungs coated in spicy peppery dust I just end up coughing.

The nanomachine network is working to scrub the alveoli in your lungs of foreign contaminants.

I put my hand to my mouth and hack my lungs out for a minute. I feel and sound like Dad.

"The best spices in Mehdirran. My berbere will turn any dish into a Michelle star!" I'd tell him he means Michelin, but I can't even speak. "I should be charging you for the privilege of sharing a bag!"

"Thanks," I finally manage to say in between coughing and spluttering. My eyes are burning still; I wipe away a tear or two, and try to adjust to the intense, bright light.

"No problem." He shakes my hand again before walking back to the driver's side of his car. I look around, and see that we're at a crossroads, in the middle of a huge, flat void of rocks and sand. Just a great beige desert underneath a majestic blue sky.

"Where do I go?" I call out, as he climbs into the truck. I begin to walk to meet him in the driver's side window, catching the sun directly in my eyes as I do so. "Like, which way to the nearest rebel town?"

He points down the road to our right, grinning that same hospitable grin.

"Right that way." The engine starts, and I feel like our time together is coming to a close. "Good luck, whatever you're planning on doing here."

He puts on his seatbelt and puts the radio on. It seems like he's about to accelerate away, but hesitates before turning back to me. His expression is serious again; his eyes draining of any warmth.

"Don't get too involved. There's nothing to love here."

He slowly drives away, kicking up another cloud of dust. I watch him leave before turning and walking in the direction he told me to. I see buildings on the horizon; large, dark monoliths shimmering and dancing in the heat.

The sun is beginning to go down at last; it's nowhere near as hot as it was earlier in the day. As I walk I begin to take in the reality that I'm in a foreign land for the first time in years. Lost in a foreign country, with no language skills, money, or cellphone. Under normal circumstances it'd be a living nightmare.

But right here and right now, it feels like an adventure.

When I finally reach those shimmering buildings, I see that they're not grand monoliths at all, but dilapidated apartment buildings, overlooking a dusty road. Part of one of them is collapsed, leaving a heap of bricks and other asserted trash in its wake. I see three people – elderly, and similarly run down.

This place feels both far away from the war, and at the same time very close to it. I hear no gunfire, and see no soldiers, but the war has starved this place; its battered buildings and hopeless people are evidence of that.

I walk over to an older man sitting by the side of the road, reading something on a cracked smartphone. He's selling newspapers and magazines, all of them in the native language.

"Hey, hi, speak English?"

He looks at me curiously, taking in the full, strange sight of me. Then he says a few words in his language, and I know that this is fruitless effort.

After trying and failing to speak to a couple of other folks in this fashion, I begin to worry. I knew there'd be no recruitment center; no big, signposted buildings for volunteers and mercenaries to join the war effort. But as it is, my only options seem to involve asking around the tired, very suspicious populace. And I wouldn't want to speak to me either.

"Vega," I finally say, hoping to allay my uneasiness in the final way I can think of. "Can I get my face back?"

Yes. The process will be quicker than before; the topography of your face is stored within my memory. Two hours.

"Do it."

I walk around some more, finally finding an area in the shade. There's a tall building; what perhaps used to be a mosque or other temple, but having caught a few shells it lies partially in ruins. There's a set of trash cans beside it, with another helping of black bin bags rounding out the picture.

I'm hungry. Starving, even. I check to see the coast is clear – the town is pretty deserted, it seems – and jump into the trash, splitting the bin bags open with my fingers, looking for any leftovers or food that I can grab.

But there's nothing. No scraps of green leaf, no moldy bread or pasta. No spices, although I can't say I'm sad about that.

I should have known better than to expect surplus food in the middle of a war-torn, developing and desperate nation. I sit by the trash and feel the dull ache in my brow and palate. At least I'll soon be able to feel my own face again without freaking out.

Then I wait, watching the very occasional car go by, and observing the sun fall from the sky.

―――

The process is complete.

I feel like I nodded off. I hadn't realized how tired I was. I've been traveling for a couple of days, and that's before we talk about whatever amount of calories I expend in sculpting my facial bone structure back to how it was.

The sun is lower in the sky, but it's still bright. I pick myself up, dust myself down a bit, and get walking again.

Most residences here seem lifeless; either shelled and partially collapsed or boarded up to protect against bullets and sandstorms. If anyone is living within these walls, they're surely hiding from what this country has become.

I walk beside what could have been a department store once, noting the presence of myriad bullet holes against a wall at roughly torso height. Then I notice a motorcycle engine behind me. I turn to see it; a green dirt bike, with a slim figure stood beside it. Squinting against the sun, my hand to my eyes, I can see that the driver is a woman.

"You American?" she asks in English, before taking off her helmet, revealing long strands of slightly greasy black hair.

"Yeah, I am." I reply. I consider joking what it was about my appearance that gave me away, but think better of it.

She waves the hair away from her face with one hand, while holding her helmet in the other. She looks to be my age; she has a small nose, thick dark black eyebrows, as well as deep brown eyes that I can see even from across the road. She's attractive; I notice that immediately.

"Why are you here?"

Her tone is terse and impatient; like I've strayed somewhere I shouldn't have, or mistakenly taken a trip to a war zone while trying to get to the beach. Her accent is thick, but I can understand each word perfectly.

"Well, I was hoping to help."

Her expression is entirely unchanged; she looks at me with a sort of incredulous contempt. She knows I'm way out of my depth.

"Help? In what way?"

"Yeah, with the war effort."

Another moment passes, and her stony expression is still locked on her face. This is beginning to remind me of high school again. Then she seems to chuckle to herself, and smiles at me.

"You want to help with the war." She shakes her head, still smiling. "Are you a soldier?"

"Not really," I say in reply. Then in the resultant awkward silence, I feel compelled to explain myself more. "Well, I mean I can handle myself. I've been in fights, I'm smart. And I know who the good guys are and who the bad guys are."

She smiles again, and I could swear that something approximating gratitude flashes across her face.

"I can take you somewhere you'll be appreciated."

She turns the motorbike engine off, before stooping over

the backseat to pick something out of storage. She's wearing a black leather jacket – what is it with folks in this climate wearing leather – and beige pants, as well as motorcycle boots. Her clothes are dusty, like she'd been riding a long way to get here.

After she grabs a green rucksack from the motorcycle, she leaves the bike behind and walks past me, beckoning me to follow her. We walk behind the building with the bullet holes, her boots leaving footprints in the dirt and sand. Then we pass something that looks to have been a building once, now collapsed into concrete chunks with rusty rebar sticking out.

"Are you with the rebels?" I ask, watching her hop across the concrete skeleton of a building, before doing the same myself.

"We're all rebels," she finally answers, coming to a set of stairs set uneasily within the ruins. I look down, seeing the passage has been cleared of debris. It's a door to a collapsed building's basement, quite naturally ingeniously hidden within the corpse of the structure. "Every citizen in this country is rebelling."

I remember this is a breakaway region of Aljarran. Two nations both calling themselves Aljarran, fighting between each other for legitimacy. One of them fighting for hope and democracy, the other to crush dissent. Brothers fighting brothers, sisters fighting mothers.

"Well," she says, pointing to a cast iron door at the bottom of the stairs. "After you."

I begin to feel uneasy; I have no idea what's beyond that door. This could be a trap; there could be a dentist's chair and a government-enlisted torturer waiting to painfully extract every single one of my molars. Or maybe I still just can't get Saad's gold tooth out of my mind.

I slowly walk down the stairs, pausing when I reach the door. The girl follows behind me, until she's beside me. Then she knocks on the door, and says a word in the native language.

After a few seconds – uneasily spent exchanging glances with her – the door opens.

"Come on," she says, walking into the dark recesses of the basement. I follow her, seeing the last shafts of light disappear, until I hear the door close behind me with a deafening metallic *clang*. There's a man beside us; he's tall, and powerfully built but his smile seems warm and genuine.

"I'm Kris, by the way."

"I'm Dina, this is Mo." She points at the big man. He smiles, and I see for the first time that he's missing fingers on his left hand; a series of scars snaking their way up his arm are also apparent. Dina continues on: "He doesn't speak English."

"But you do," I say, looking around the room. There's a couple of bulbs illuminating a dusty, dingy basement. There's a large table, with a pack of cards splayed out and slightly unnervingly, a large machine gun. I look back at Dina. "How did you learn?"

"My mother was Professor of English Literature at one of the universities here" she says, somewhat dismissively. I get the feeling she doesn't wish to elaborate.

"What is this place?"

"Safety," she answers tersely.

I watch her walk over to the table and take a seat. Mo disappears behind me into what appears to be a small improvised kitchen with a camping stove and a microwave held together with duct tape. She beckons me to sit at the table, and I do.

"So, you're not a soldier." She leans back in her chair, staring me directly in the eyes. Her gaze carries an authority that seems way beyond her age. She may not be pulling my teeth out, but I feel like I'm in an interrogation nonetheless.

"Do you do IT systems? Communications? Connectivity? Are you an engineer?"

I shake my head nervously at each question, and with each question her expression seems to coarsen, like I'm wasting her time.

"Have you used firearms before? Can you repair cars or bikes? Do you have medical knowledge? First aid?"

I keep shaking my head.

"Any experience with explosives?"

"Ah, yes I do."

She looks surprised. Shocked, even. I open my mouth to speak, and then realize that this is going to be a difficult one to explain. How do I recount my dead ass is caught up in a domestic terror investigation back home, or that my greatest experience with bombs is being blown to pieces by them?

"I helped investigate a, uhh, bombing suspect back home."

"Oh, right." Finally she looks at me with interest. "So, you're police?"

I pause; another awkward silence passes between us.

"No, I'm more of a..." I can't even think of the words. Concerned citizen? Civilian investigator? Suspected dead accomplice? "A private detective."

"Right." That look of exasperation is back on her face. She bats away a few errant strands of hair and looks over to Mo, who's standing watch in the kitchen. She doesn't take me seriously. I wouldn't take me seriously either.

"Look, I want to fight. I'm strong. Strong of mind, strong of body, strong of will."

Another moment of awkward silence before my stomach grumbles loudly and embarrassingly. Loud enough for everyone to hear, and loud enough to mercifully get me out of this jam.

"You're hungry," Dina says, before looking over to Mo. She says something to him in the native tongue and turns back to me. "We'll feed you, we'll make sure you're rested, and then we'll find you some work."

I relax back in the chair and smile at her. Then my attention wanders back to the gun. I know from endless films and videogames that it's an AK47, but that's where my experience ends. I wonder how many people it has killed. And then, for what feels like the first time, I consider the very real prospect that I'll soon have to shoot people.

I'm certainly no stranger to death, and I've come close to meeting it once, I guess. But up to now, I've felt like everything I've done has been in service of trying to save people. Being in combat – shooting people dead – feels entirely different.

The ceramic *plonk* of a bowl on the table in front of me shakes me out of my reverie. It looks like a watery soup of some kind; hard for me to discern in the poor light of this room, but there could be vegetables floating around in it. Either way, it's a hell of a lot better than eating out of the trash. A small loaf of bread soon follows, and I'm sold. I tuck in greedily.

I'm busy digging into my soup when Dina rises from the table, and exchanges a few words with Mo. Then she takes a couple of things from the backpack, and goes to leave.

"You're going?" I say through a mouthful of bread and carrot.

"I have work to do, but you'll be fine here. I'll be back in the morning to pick you up."

I look over at the big man. He smiles at me awkwardly. I'm sure he doesn't want a scrawny American staying over in his mancave, but this will be the most comfortable shelter I've had in days.

"Get some rest. You'll need it."

She puts on her motorbike helmet and departs, opening the cast iron door before slamming it shut with an almighty loud *clonk*.

I finish my soup and thank Mo with a smile and an awkward bow, clasping my palms together as I do it. He leads me to another door and I open it. Inside is a small room – uninviting brick walls and a sole lightbulb hanging lonely from the ceiling. But, significantly, a bed.

"Here, here," he says in heavily accented English. I make the thanking gesture again, and he waves goodbye with a fingerless hand, closing the door behind him.

I sit on the bed at first and take a look around. There's a wooden bedstand with three legs, home to a bunch of foreign language books. Then there's a basket full of cleaning products at the foot of the bed. The bed itself is a slim steel frame, which creaks musically with every movement I make.

I lie back, quietly content in my achievements of the day. It hasn't been easy, and it definitely hasn't been comfortable, but I feel I've accomplished everything I needed to, at least for today.

Sure, to an untrained observer, I've touched down in a country I know almost nothing about, with no money and no clue. I've wandered around aimlessly, hid in a bag of spice residue, and then took a nap next to a trash can, only to get lured to a strange place by a pretty girl. I can see how an untrained observer would think that.

But, looking at it from another point of view, I've successfully navigated my way around a foreign land, ingeniously crossed an armed and fortified border without incident, and then, having successfully changed my disguise, located a rebel safehouse and ingratiated myself with the freedom fighters.

The uncharitable view, and the generous reading. The mophead and the diamond.

I pull the sheets – coarse white fabric – over me, and feel the exhaustion wash over my body like waves on some beautiful white sandy beach. I sink into the mattress like sand. It ain't perfect, but to me it feels like heaven. It must be no later than 9.00 PM local time, but I should sleep.

I close my eyes, and the first thing I see is Burden; those glasses, that grin, that coat, and the screaming…

I open my eyes again; I don't feel like I'm on a beach anymore. I'm in the same cruel world. The world with bombs and machine guns and missing limbs and death.

But I will work to make it better.

CHAPTER 26

'm walking by the river in the city. It's a place I haven't been to recently. A place that you wouldn't want to walk alone these days. But a place I remember my Dad and Mother taking me to when I was younger.

I'm walking there, looking at the sun reflected in the water. And then I hear a bang; one that vibrates my teeth in their sockets and makes my bones writhe around in my muscles. I look up to see a large black cloud. A mushroom cloud; a black, grinning skull in the sky.

I wake up in a panic again. I rub my eyes and see that I'm still in the same basement room. I didn't even turn the light out. My heart is beating; I feel the adrenaline coursing through my veins again. I never used to have dreams like this. Psychological wounds that Vega can't heal.

I try to get back to sleep – reasoning that I shouldn't leave this room until they come and get me – but find it impossible to after that moment of panic. I sit up in bed and wait.

Eventually I hear a certain shuffling around in the room next door and words exchanged in the native tongue. There are three voices this time; two men and Dina's. I'm relieved she came back for me at least.

A knock on the door follows, and Dina's face is the first I see. I smile at her, clamber out of bed, and go to join them in the next room. The cards are arranged differently, but everything else seems the same. There is, however, one more face. Another man, with short black hair and a raspy beard.

"We're leaving," Dina says to me abruptly. Thankfully I travel light. I motion goodbye to the big man Mo, and follow Dina and the new, nameless guy out of the basement into the brutal dry sun once again. Then I hop along the rubble and walk with them back to the road.

"My friend Adnan here is integral to the war effort," she tells me, motioning towards the man who looks me up and down with a stony expression, like he's judging my usefulness. "You'll be stationed with him. Our commander in the field requested it.'

"Commander in the field, right," I say, immersed in language of the battlefield for the first time. "Hi Adnan."

He doesn't say anything, but instead holds a hand out for me to shake. I do so.

We walk to a car parked by the side of the road; a small two door automobile, with five seats inside. It's messy; food wrappers and empty bottles fill the back seats. I clear one side and sit there. Dina and Adnan get in, and after a conversation I don't understand, Adnan begins to drive.

Now I begin to get a strange feeling. I don't feel exactly like a soldier in this army of rebels. I don't even feel like a recruit, being shepherded to whatever passes as training around here. I feel like cattle trafficked to the slaughterhouse, with barely a word or a glance acknowledging my existence.

I look out of the window, watching the great, flat expanses of land at every side. This landscape is a huge, dusty blanket, speckled with jagged rocks and spans of treacherous looking sand. There's almost no vegetation, except for the occasional tree that seems to exist impossibly, standing alone in the wasteland.

No animals, no people. No buildings, save for the occasional farmhouse or ranch, long since abandoned. Occasionally we pass another car or truck coming the opposite direction. Or a burned-out vehicle a couple of times.

Finally, breaking up the silence inside the car, we pass a military convoy. Humvees and 4x4s, along with the occasional covered truck. Finally, the artillery shows up; trucks with massive machine guns and other artillery pieces strapped to the back. Dina and Adnan begin speaking again.

"What's that?" I ask, watching the last artillery piece pass us.

"They're going to the frontline. It's always moving," Dina says, before exchanging a couple more words with Adnan.

I notice we're moving away from the frontline in that case.

When we reach an even smaller village than the last one – appearing merely to consist of a couple of townhouses, a farm, and what appears to be a factory or warehouse – Dina parks up by a well and tells me we've arrived.

We all get out of the car, and I see a couple of soldiers here – AK47s slung around their shoulders, regarding me with interest and suspicion.

"This is it," she says.

I look around, and wonder, is *this* really it?

We walk into the largest building here; there's a precariously placed air-con unit jutting unsettlingly out of the wall. It hums like a rusted chainsaw. Inside, I adjust my eyes to the darkness. The building is falling apart; paint flakes off the walls in huge chunks, and garbage bags litter the hallways.

"Adnan will need your labor here."

"My labor?" I ask, getting horrible flashbacks to the fun old days of packaging sandwiches. We walk past another armed man smoking a cigar, and I see the factory floor – rows of sewing machines, although only a handful are attended. I look behind me and see kitchens. "What is this place?"

"This is the war effort," Dina says, refusing to look me in

the eye. "This is where the ceramic protective vests are sewn up. This is where the meals for the soldiers are cooked and filled. This is where uniforms are sized up and where new tires are fitted to vital vehicles."

I look back upon the sewing machines with a feeling close to horror. I came half-way across the world, risking my life, to be condemned to another factory.

"Hey, I can't stay here, I'm a fighter, not a—"

She cuts me off; her eyes full of fire.

"Not a what? A worker? You wanted war, here's war. This." She gestures madly around her, pointing to each figure manning each sewing machine. "*This* is war. It's not glamorous, it's not heroic, it's not some Hollywood movie."

She steps closer to me; I find myself backing off instinctively.

"This isn't a game to us. This is our lives. Our freedom."

Finally she relents, turning around and moving out of my space. She starts to leave, abandoning me on the factory floor, but says one final thing:

"If you're not useful to us here, you won't be useful to us anywhere."

And she's gone without even giving me one final glance.

Adnan walks towards me, and for the first time speaks English.

"So, you want work?"

"You speak English?" I ask him, amazed. He's been keeping that fact quiet.

"Sure. You want work, yes?"

I pause, rubbing my temple. Then I nod despondently. This hasn't work out how I wanted it to. But now that I think about it, it makes perfect sense.

He leads me back out into the corridor, and into the kitchens that adjoin the factory floor. There, he takes me to a set of industrial ovens. It's hellishly hot here; the heat is a veil of stuffy, choking air that hits you full on in the face. The wall tiles are stained with dirt, and what were probably once windows are boarded up.

I watch him lead me through bunch of motions, teaching me how to knead bread. It's stuff I already know, but I'm too humiliated by this whole situation to protest.

I swanned in here acting like some superhero; like I was a legendary soldier who had deigned to donate his precious time and ability to the cause. That's what I feel like, with my machine-augmented strength and energy.

But to everyone else, I'm a liability. A weak link that will break under the faintest of pressures. An untrained, unseasoned war tourist.

I have to prove myself.

CHAPTER 27

Eventually, Adnan leaves me to my own devices and I spend the next few hours kneading dough, putting it in the oven, and taking it out when it's done. A nameless, dour old woman works beside me, who I'm sure doesn't speak English. Either that, or she doesn't wish to talk to me.

When I'm reaching my limit – drowsy from the heat and covered head to toe in sweat – I duck out of the kitchen, walking past a soldier with a rifle slung over his shoulder, and go outside.

The sun is high in the sky; it can't be any later than midday already. I walk 20 yards or so away from the factory and into the wastes. I hop over a couple of rocks until I find one I can sit on semi-comfortably. There's still no respite from the heat, though.

"Vega," I say, after making sure I'm out of earshot of any onlookers. "I need to get out of here. I need to prove I'm worth a damn in this war."

I understand you'd like to be involved in the fighting, but Dina's point was a saliant one. You are helping the war effort here. Meals are important to soldiers after all.

"I don't feel like I'm helping. I could have baked bread from home." I feel myself shifting around on my warm rock like a hyperactive tortoise. "I mean, what's the point of me being here if I can't use my abilities to their fullest?"

You would need someone to take you to the frontline or to embed you within their combat team. Neither looks likely at present. But there is some value in being eased in gradually. You have no combat experience. There are weapons here that will blow you apart.

I grunt. I've been there before.

I decide to take a walk around the village. Call it a lunch break, I guess.

There's a farmhouse with a few slightly emaciated cattle beside it. Nobody is working the farm, nor are there any viable crops. The wind picks up, blowing dust into my eyes, forcing me to seek shelter beside one of the old townhouses here.

I'm blinding feeling along a wall, trying to find a surface to lean against while I get this crap out of my eyes, when I accidentally break through a rotten wooden shutter on a window. The reaction is immediate; a frenzied, surprised shouting coming from inside.

I quickly rub my eyes and yell my apologies, but two inhabitants come running out; two figures, shouting at me in the native language. One of them has a rifle.

"Hey, sorry, my fault, accident!" I yell, trying to defuse the situation.

"American?" One of them asks. I open my eyes again to see the two men – one of them pale and blond; not exactly what I expected. His accent isn't familiar to me though.

"Yeah, I'm American."

The blond guy relaxes his posture. His friend then does the same. They're both wearing beige camouflage like soldiers, but there's something distinctively casual about their appearance still. The blond wears a bandolier filled with bullets, like he's starring in a western.

"You're about 5000 miles from home, stranger."

He smiles; he's wearing large sunglasses, and his blond hair blows in the wind. It's difficult to tell his age behind those sunglasses, but he seems to be in his thirties. His friend beside him looks around, slightly nervously.

"Yeah, I know," I reply. "You don't seem to be from around here either."

"Poland, actually." We shake hands. His buddy remains still, watching the horizon. "This beats a Polish winter. My name is Tomas. This is Darius."

I nod at his friend, who nods back before going back to surveilling the environment.

"So, what are you doing here?" Tomas asks.

"Well, I just got here yesterday. I wanted to help the war effort so was working at the factory, but I, uhh…" I feel a bead of sweat drop off my nose. I need to get to the point here. "I'd like to be a bit more involved, you know? I want to show how useful I can be."

"Is that so," Tomas says, his intent masked behind those wraparound sunglasses. He looks around, as if he's looking to see if I've been followed, then speaks once more: "why don't you come inside with us? We might have something for you."

I look back to the townhouse and the broken shutter before turning back to them both and nodding. I follow them both inside the townhouse; it's a largely empty series of rooms, with a very basic kitchen and a rundown living area.

There's a battered sofa that dominates the living space, situated directly in the middle. None of us sit on it, curiously. Instead, we stand around it.

"We're on guard here until sundown," Tomas says. I notice he's talking quietly; I can't hear anyone else in this townhouse besides us, but there seems to be an element of discretion about all of this. "And then we're transporting some equipment to the front line. Come with us if you want to be useful."

"Sure," I say, with barely any hesitation. Something about this seems slightly off. The pair of them are evasive and jumpy, like they're hiding something. However, I can't turn down a chance to get out of the kitchen. "Absolutely I will. Where shall we meet?"

I have the strangest juxtaposition of feelings. I'm getting into something distinctly dangerous and treacherous, and I'm excited about it. It's not that I don't feel afraid; I'm in a foreign war zone, putting my trust in a bunch of people I don't know, so of course I'm afraid. But, for the first time since pursuing Burden, I feel ready for the fight.

"Meet here at 7.00 PM," Tomas tells me. "Don't be late."

I give my assurances and walk back to the factory, intending to immerse myself in the kitchen until then. The heat is intolerable, and Adnan walks up and down checking on us periodically, reminding me of Pedro at the sandwich packaging plant.

I see Tomas' buddy Darius walking up and down the corridors too. I guess their duty here is to guard. Reserve duty. Make sure no saboteurs disrupt the breadline or whatever.

I lose myself in the work. Before I know it, the sun begins to hang low in the sky; a couple of stray rays intrude through a cracked ventilation duct and momentarily blind me again. I leave my post to go look for the time and see that it's 6:50 PM already.

Adnan's busy with the sewing room; I sneak out without him seeing and walk over to the townhouse again. When I'm inside, I stand by the sofa again, still feeling like I'd rather be on my feet than take a chance with its rugged, bug-infested upholstery.

I wait a few minutes, looking at the floorboards in here and how they've warped in strange directions, before Tomas, Darius, and one more man – a short guy with darker skin and similar sunglasses to Tomas – walk in. Tomas says a few words in another language – Polish? Aljarrian? Who the hell knows – before addressing me.

"All right then, you're here."

"I'm here," I repeat, putting my most confident of voices on. "So, what are we doing? You guys are soldiers with the rebels, right?"

Tomas looks at his two buddies before looking back at me. I can't discern his expression behind those sunglasses though.

"Yeah, we're with the rebels all right." He moves over to the window; the one with the shutter that I broke earlier. "We're waiting for a car with a shipment then we're taking it to a town near the front."

He looks back at me; first my feet, then my shoulders, then back at my face. Sizing me up, I would guess.

"Always good to have back up," he continues in that Polish accent, "but you need some appropriate equipment."

My ears prick up immediately, and I feel an involuntary grin creeping across my face. *Finally*, someone taking me remotely seriously.

Darius disappears off into a backroom of the townhouse and re-emerges with a water-damaged cardboard box. He drops it on the floor at my feet and I kneel down to take a look.

There's two pairs of boots, seemingly of different sizes. They're black – similar to hiking boots – and pretty worn, but obviously far better than my sneakers. One of them has a badge fastened to it. When I look closer, I see that it's the peace symbol.

I dig both sets of boots out and look below them. There's a pair of sand-colored pants, a belt, and a green T-shirt. Below that, a jacket with a pixelated camouflage spanning three colors: sand to beige to brown. Looks like army gear to me...

"All you'll need to do is stand there and back us up," Tomas says. "Guns are hard to come by here, though."

I shrug at him. I didn't expect to be given a gun without being trained to use one anyway.

"All good," I say, picking up the pair of boots with the badge, and taking the box into another room. There I get changed out of my hideous tourist-ware, and into my new camouflaged apparel.

I walk back to a mock round of applause from the three; it feels like I'm in high school again.

"Beautiful, beautiful," Tomas says, grinning inanely. "We're gonna travel to a nearby location to deliver the stuff."

The three of them get back to conversing in that other language, and I'm left feeling like the gatecrasher again. I watch Tomas walk back to the window, look through the shutters for a minute, before turning to the rest of us and ushering us out.

When we get outside, the light has turned decidedly golden; the sun clings to the horizon, with a shimmering haze below it. There's a truck outside; a 4x4, absolutely filthy with dirt and dust. Tomas and the other two walk towards it, beckoning me to follow them. I guess this is our ride.

I climb into the backseat and see that there's a driver – a shaven headed man with darker skin and a slight mustache. He's glugging from a sports bottle, and when he's done he passes it to Tomas who's gotten into the front passenger seat. When we're all in, the driver starts the engine and we're back on the road.

"Here, you want?"

Tomas thrusts the bottle into my face. I take it from him, thinking I haven't quenched my thirst in a while. It's half full of liquid.

"What is it?"

"Vodka of course!"

I look at him in surprise; my eyes widening. Then I look back at the bottle and shake it again for some reason. I'm mostly just too dumbfounded to think straight.

"Vodka!?"

Tomas laughs, turning back to the road. I grip the bottle for a little longer before the short guy with the sunglasses snatches it from me and takes a full-throated gulp. Tomas, on the other hand, puts the radio on.

I guess I shouldn't be surprised. It's a battlefield; I'm sure these guys have seen horrifying things, and if we are about to head to the front maybe it's just liquid courage. Then again, I don't know anything about these guys. I don't even know if we're really going to the front, or just going on a drink-fueled joyride.

"So," I finally say to Tomas, rising above the sound of glugging vodka and shrill dance music. "You said we're delivering equipment?"

"In the trunk," Tomas says, focusing on drumming out a rhythm with his palm on his knee. "All we need to do is deliver it."

"What is it?"

He doesn't answer right away. Did I ask something I shouldn't?

"Let's just say it'll be of great use to our men."

The guy next to me – Darius, I think – begins to laugh. I feel like I'm very slowly descending into boiling water. I'm not submerged in it yet, but I'm beginning to feel the heat. Something definitely isn't right about this.

Kris, there's something I should make you aware of.

Vega's statement seems quite timely. I remain quiet and let him continue.

The nanomachine network is always studying your environment. It's a basic safety measure to ensure there are no toxic substances or gases. When you entered that car, trace readings of a certain substance were detected: diamorphine.

I raise one eyebrow quizzically, hoping that Vega gets the hint that I don't know what that is.

On your streets, I believe the substance is named heroin.

I raise both eyebrows this time; my quizzical sentiment turns to horror. I feel my face begin to heat up; my cheeks flushing red, no doubt.

Heroin!?

How did I get into this!?

I try to act calm; try to remain a casual onlooker in this whole thing. Maybe this car was used for nefarious purposes a week ago, but it's squeaky clean now. Maybe we're delivering bullets or whatever else is small enough to fit in the trunk of the 4x4. Or maybe we really are drug-running in the midst of a civil war.

Trying to distract my mind from the multiple extravagant ways I could get blown to pieces in the middle of this, I look out of the window. The sun has disappeared behind the flat desert horizon now. The sky is a blue mask, and the only sources of light I can see are the 4x4's two white headlights in front.

"We're almost there," Tomas says, finally turning the obnoxious dance music off. I look around at the others. Casual drinking and jokes between song lyrics has turned into steely, focused stares. "Like I said, we just need you to stand there. You're on guard duty."

"Right," I reply, before audibly gulping.

We come up to a strange feature in this otherwise barren waste. A large rock, with jagged edges and a curiously flat top, like a plateau. The 4x4 is parked and everyone gets out, including and hesitantly, me.

"There's no-one here" I say to Tomas, who's circling the car, looking across the landscape. I didn't notice when it happened, but his sunglasses have disappeared. There are slight wrinkles around his face; maybe he's older than I thought or maybe this war's just been cruel to him.

"Yet," Tomas replies. His buddies walk to different places around the car, taking up defensive positions by the looks of it.

My curiosity finally gets the better of me. There's only me and the driver who aren't armed here, but even so, I'd like to know if I'm liable to die in a giant cloud of bullets and heroin or not. I approach the trunk slowly.

"So what's in here?"

Tomas walks to meet me at the trunk; his eyes look deeply into mine, like he's searching for my intentions, trying to decipher if I'm really some dumb American he picked up or something much more sinister.

"Well," he says, confidently and swaggeringly. "What do you think?"

"Something…" I hesitate, trying to figure out the best way of playing this. "…illegal?"

Tomas laughs again; a deep, warm chuckle. his friends are silent though.

"This is a civil war, there are no laws, there are no rules."

He pushes the logo on the trunk, springing it open slightly. Then he nods in my direction, as if prompting me to open it. After eyeing him and the trunk suspiciously, I put my fingers underneath the bottom lid of the trunk and pull it up.

Inside are a bunch of blue plastic sheets, illuminated in the dim white light of the trunk. Below them, however, I can see something that looks like parcels or bricks. Immediately I can't stop thinking of all the cop shows where they'd haul a bunch of bad guys in and parade a table loaded with drugs, all packaged and compressed into bricks.

"Is it drugs?" I ask Tomas, finally. As soon as I say it, I regret it; I somehow manage to sound both naïvely dumb, and at the same time like I know way too much.

"Of course not," Tomas replies with that cheeky grin on his face. He rips away the plastic sheeting, revealing something else entirely. "It's cash!"

They're not bricks of drugs, but giant wads of dollars, all taped and bound up into blocks, perhaps two inches tall apiece. I look down and see rows upon rows; more money than I ever thought I'd see in my lifetime.

"Oh my God," I say absentmindedly, my mind transfixed by the money. "There must be tens of thousands of dollars here."

Tomas looks up at me and nods excitedly. Finally, after staring at the dimly lit wads of cash for another few moments longer than I should, I open my mouth again:

"What are we doing with all of this?"

Tomas doesn't answer. Instead, he looks over my shoulder and nods at something in the distance. Then he whistles to the others and I feel the whole scene become a lot more tense.

I turn my head, and see two headlights in the darkness, off-road, driving slowly towards us. I back away from the trunk, leaving Tomas there alone, and instead take up a position behind the car.

My leg trembles; I shift my weight onto it, hoping to hide that fact.

The car moves in closer, finally coming to a stop around 10 yards from our own. Three men get out, including the driver, and one of them walks towards our position. They're military men, in similar camouflage to ourselves, but they all have intricate badges and equipment; guns and bullet-proof vests. They look much more like a professional army than we do.

For the first time I notice a chill breeze; I feel my arms turn to goosebumps under my jacket. Is it the desert night or am I that nervous?

Tomas approaches the driver, and then speaks with him in hushed tones. Then they both erupt with laughter; Tomas slapping him on the back and guiding him to the trunk. They both greedily take a look at the money – the other man rubbing his hands together – before both going to the other car.

The wind picks up again, blowing sand into my eyes. I rub them, and when they're clear again Tomas is directing Darius and one of the other men to lift a bunch of boxes out of the other car.

I watch as they exchange items; all the wads of cash we have in the 4x4 for the boxes. When the trade is complete, Tomas shakes the three men's hands and walks back to our position. The other men, talking between themselves slightly above a whisper, get back into their car and start the engine.

"So," I ask Tomas, unsure exactly of what I just witnessed but having a pretty good guess. "What was that?"

"That was free enterprise," Tomas says with a smile on his face and glint in his eye. "And when we offload this stuff, we'll be laughing."

I feel like these guys are already laughing. It doesn't take a genius to work out what they are. I watch the other car drive away before I turn back to Tomas and speak.

"You're drug traffickers?"

Tomas rakes his fingers through his long, blond hair. Then he looks over to Darius – who's looking at me with a stony, emotionless expression – before walking over to me, slowly.

"We're men who gave everything for this war." I see a spark of anger in his face for the first time; a vein begins to pop out of his forehead. He points to the driver: "Adil lost both of his brothers, one of them was only 11 years old."

He looks over at Darius, still looking stoic.

"Darius lost his sister and his mother. An artillery shell hit his home, putting his mother in hospital. His sister visited, and then they both got killed by a cruise missile aimed straight at the ward."

I say nothing, just listen and grit my teeth.

"I've been here for two years. Do you know how many friends I've seen die in the sand? This desert is baying for blood, and however much we give it, it will never be enough."

He pauses, regaining his composure.

"We all came to this war with good intentions. And then

the war took everything from us. And now we just want to take a little in return." He turns back to the car and walks to the passenger door, before turning back to me with that smile back on his face: "And you'll soon feel the same way."

I watch as everyone gets back into the 4x4. The driver flicks away a cigarette; I still see its red embers in the darkness.

"Come on," Tomas shouts to me, "you wanna walk back through the desert?"

It's a tempting prospect. I don't know where I am; I can't see any form of civilization or life from here, just black shadows on a dark blue horizon. Yet it still seems a better idea than getting back inside that 4x4.

After kicking up a cloud of dust below me, I finally saunter over to the car. I can ditch these guys as soon as I get back to civilization, forget I ever took part in this. Chalk it up to my youthful exuberance, whatever...

I get in the 4x4 and shut the door behind me, aiming a look at Tomas intending to be grateful, but probably appearing nothing like that.

I'm crestfallen. I came here to fight with good versus evil. To help the people of Aljarran overthrow their dictator. The man who kills, tortures, and maims them. Instead, I'm riding around with thousands of dollars of drugs in the trunk.

My 'tremendous, potentially world-altering power' as Vega put it, utilized instead to move the most dangerous drugs across the most dangerous borders.

What a mess.

Suddenly, the driver slams on the brakes, snapping me out of my stupor of self-resentment. The five of us are flung forward and I catch a moment of panic in Darius' eyes.

"What's wrong?" Tomas' question is answered by the driver pointing ahead of him. I lean over Tomas' seat and squint my eyes to see. A couple of white headlights sit in the distance, maybe a 100 meters or so away. Another car?

"Huh," Tomas says, his voice wavering a little, "how about tha—"

Something hits the 4x4; a loud, short, metallic *thunk* like an extremely heavy drop of rain, pranging against the frame of the car. Four or five more follow so quick I can't count them, and the rear passenger side window farthest from me breaks, shattering into 5000 tiny chunks of glass.

"Ambush, get down!"

Tomas' voice fills the interior of the car, followed by more deadly raindrops from outside. I glance to my right and see the two bodies beside me slump down, followed by specks of crimson on the upholstery of the back of the driver's seat.

I catch a glimpse of the world beyond the broken window; a row of short, bright yellow lights, like fireworks, far away in the distance.

Panicking – feeling every muscle in my body begin to tense up, and my heart drop to the middle of my belly – I reach for the door handle to my left. As I pull it, I feel I get hit with something like a punch. It knocks the breath clean out of me.

I summon every last bit of breathless strength I can to push myself out of the door and land face first in the sand beside the car. I look up and see Tomas running and disappearing behind a rock. One of the guys in the car is still groaning, but soon he's quiet too.

I gasp for air, breathing in the dirt, blowing clouds of dust with each breath. I cough a couple of times, seeing a couple of drops of blood leave my mouth as I do. Then I look down and to my left side, and see blood beginning to pool in the sand. My eyes widen and my heart skips a beat.

Kris, don't panic. You've been hit twice, but it appears the bullets passed cleanly through you.

I close my eyes and do as Vega says. I try to control my breathing – resisting the urge to cough – and feel for the first time that old familiar pain like my previously broken ribs, but sharper. A sharp stiletto dagger between my ribcage, pulsating with every heartbeat.

The nanomachine network is working on clotting the entry and exit wounds, as well as repairing the damage to your lungs, large intestine, and liver.

My liver? Large intestine? I try to relax my body; slow my breathing to a pace more manageable and make myself feel at home in the dirt. But then I have another dreadful thought.

I open my eyes and look around; I can't see the ambushers yet, but they're bound to turn up and take what they came for.

Close your eyes. Lay perfectly still. You're not armed, and the ambushing party will hopefully think you're dead or unconscious.

Again, I do as Vega says. All I can hear is the engine idling and the occasional breeze blowing over us. It almost sounds peaceful.

Then I hear footsteps, distant at first but growing ever closer. When the footsteps – tentative, slow crunches in the dirt and sand – are getting to be loud, they suddenly stop. Then I hear the trunk pop open.

I tell myself to stay calm; I take a small, shallow breath, hopefully too faint to be seen.

There's the sound of rustling plastic and cardboard, and then the footsteps sound out again. Loud, but growing ever quieter. I allow myself to gasp – a sigh of relief.

A few minutes pass; the pain is ever increasing, but equally I find myself less and less concerned by it. I open my eyes, and seeing no-one around I try to pick myself up from the dirt. I push my body up with one palm, and succeed in turning on my side. There I lie, like a stricken jellyfish, breathing more heavily now, but growing in strength.

I finally manage to pull my entire torso up and lean with my back against the side of the 4x4, sitting in the dirt. My new jacket is ruined – blood streams down the inside of my shirt and I can see two dark bullet holes and the deep red wounds within.

Your injuries are still clotting, but they've stabilized. Your internal bleeding is under control and the network is beginning to patch up the damage within your internal organs – your right lung, your liver, and your large intestine.

I don't even want to know what the inside of the 4x4 looks like. I can't hear a thing from the occupants, just the gentle humming of the engine.

I can fairly confidently say you'll survive your first bullets, Kris.

I make a noise in acknowledgement; it still hurts to breathe. I cough out a bunch of thick liquid and the pain increases still.

Then I feel my blood turn to ice in my veins; there's a faint light in the distance getting closer. I rub my eyes to take another look – hoping it's some pain-inspired mirage – but it's definitely there.

A frenzied shouting follows; I feel my heart begin to race again. I consider dropping to the floor and biting the dirt again, but surely it's too late by now. They've already seen me; I can see two cars approaching, and a motorbike – two horrible, dark monsters bearing down on me. All I can do is hope for mercy.

I close my eyes and wait.

"Hey, buddy!"

Among all the shouting in languages I can't understand, I hear two words; a male, deep voice, saying those two words in a distinctly American accent.

I open my eyes; there's a group of men wearing military camouflage fatigues and military-style helmets. They're holding rifles, pointing them towards the car and the surrounding wastes.

The motorbike rides up beside me, making my eardrums ache with its noise and kicking up a storm of sand as it screeches to a halt. On it is a female figure that I think I recognize.

"What the hell are you doing here?"

I recognize her voice instantly. She takes off her helmet and drops it to the floor, sending her black hair tumbling to either side of her face. She looks at me like she's looking at a ghost. Maybe she believes she is.

"I got—" I gasp, catching my breath in my damaged lung. "I got caught up in something."

She doesn't seem satisfied by my understatement of the year. She jumps off her bike, grabbing something from the side as she does so. Then she moves to my side, and I see for the first time that it's a first aid kit with a huge, red cross on it.

"Mikey, help me turn him over."

One of the military men paces over to me, grabbing me under the arm. Dina takes the other arm, and they lay me down in the sand. I groan with pain as they do so, not quite able to gather enough breath to speak yet.

"You're hit," she parts my jacket, looking at the two bloody bullet holes in my T-shirt underneath. "Two entry wounds."

She opens the box and takes out a pair of scissors. Before I can protest, she begins cutting my shirt open.

"You don't need to do that," I finally manage to say.

"If I can help you, I will."

Dina is still cutting, but I block her path with my forearm. She looks at me with disdain, horrified that I'd try to stop her saving my life.

"No, I mean…" I hold my breath, picking my shoulders up from the ground, before bending upwards at the waist as far as I can so that I'm seated in the bloody sand again. "I mean you *really* don't need to do that."

She's silent; she seems dumbfounded. I look around and everybody – six people I now count – is staring at me, some amazed, some horrified.

"Jesus dude," the American says; he has medium-length, light brown hair and stubble; he's wearing a bullet proof vest on top of a shirt with no sleeves, with two tattooed, muscular arms exposed to the elements.

"Lie down," Dina says, her tone urgent, "you've been shot, you need treatment."

"I don't think I'll lie down" I say in reply. I don't know if it's the adrenaline or a desire to perform for my audience, but I'm starting to feel better now. "I think I'll sit up."

I slowly maneuver myself around on the spot, and finally manage to rise to my knees. Then, after a few more deep breaths, I climb to my feet.

Don't go too far Kris. You're still healing.

I take Vega's words seriously.

"But you've been shot twice. You have a bullet hole entering your chest; your lungs." Dina is still battling against me with her knowledge of human physiology. "Aren't you in pain?"

I look back at the 4x4; it's smattered with bullet holes and specks of blood. Inside are three bodies – the three men who accompanied Tomas and I on our little adventure tonight. Tomas is nowhere to be seen.

I take a step towards the 4x4 and stoop a bit. I look at Darius, or rather, he looks at me. His eyes are open wide and staring directly into mine. But there's no life in them. His desert camo is stained with dark red blood and his body slumps slightly and unnaturally to the left within the backseat. It's a terrible sight.

"Yeah, I'm in pain."

CHAPTER 28

I'm sitting on a towel in the back of a Humvee with its door wide open and my legs hanging out. I'm still fixated on the 4x4 some 20 yards away. My clothes are sticking to me with congealed, half-clotted blood, but I'm feeling good.

I managed to convince Dina that I'm not going to die. I demonstrated to her how my wounds had clotted already. I even managed to convince her to let me walk unaided. Now they're looking over the 4x4 with flashlights, trying to figure out how what the hell happened.

After a few minutes of this, Dina and the American guy with the tattooed arms finally begin to walk back over to me.

"So," Dina says, looking at me with inquisitive eyes. "What can you tell us about all this?"

I lean back into the seat a little; my breathing is easier now, and I can talk without gasping for air. Not bad for a guy that was almost Swiss-cheesed I guess.

"Well, I won't accept rides from strangers in the future."

"Funny," Dina says, allowing a small, sly smile on the side of her mouth. "We were on a reconnaissance mission around three miles away. The mission was cut short, and while we were returning to base we heard gunshots. We came to investigate, and who do we find…"

"Three dead men," the American says in a Bostonian accent, "and a dead man walking."

He's smiling; he's evidently happy to see someone shot twice and survive. I'm just happy to meet another American.

I recount the day's events to them both; Tomas, the 4x4, the money, the drugs, and the ambush. Dina looks on with ever-increasing disbelief. The American just grins, enthralled by my story.

"The name's Kris right?" Dina asks. I look up at her and nod. "You've got yourself in some big trouble here Kris. The men you were buying drugs from are most likely government forces. They also probably ambushed you to take the drugs back. You're lucky to be alive."

Government forces!? I'd expected to meet the government forces on the battlefield, not the black market.

"Speaking of being lucky to be alive," Dina continues, "how are those wounds holding up?"

"I'll be fine," I grimace

'Lucky to be alive' is practically my superpower. Looking at their expressions, though, I can tell they're not going to be satisfied by that answer.

"You have two entry wounds and two exit wounds, corresponding with paths through vital organs," Dina says, laying out the case for me being dead. "And judging by the color of your clothes, you've lost a hell of a lot of blood. I've never seen a man walk around after wounds like that. You should have died half an hour ago. In fact, I'm expecting you to die imminently."

I think about those dead bodies in the 4x4 again – Darius' eyes looking back at me, empty – and swallow hard. Then I look at Dina, who by now has her arms crossed like a teacher reprimanding me at high school. I shrug at her.

"We're gonna stick to you like glue," she says tersely. "I

don't believe you really intended to join a drug trafficking operation here tonight. You're much too stupid to know what you're doing."

I open my mouth to protest, but after realizing that she's mostly correct I close it again.

"But there's something very strange about you. I feel like you're a lot more dangerous than you look. You'll be coming back to our forward operating base with us and we'll decide what to do with you there."

In classic style, I guess I'm getting to my intended destination. All I wanted when I got here was to join the rebels. Now, in a strange sort of way I guess I am.

It's another 10 minutes before the soldiers are done with the 4x4; in the end Dina calls someone about retrieving the bodies and arranges for Mikey, the American, to drive me back to the base.

"How you holdin' up?" he asks courteously.

I tell him the truth; I'm fine, and will be fine. He sniggers and climbs into the driver's seat.

After an hour's drive, we get to the base camp I've been hearing about – a city of tents, maybe 20 or 30 of them surrounded by a hastily constructed barbwire fence. I see men and women with body armor and rifles walking the outside perimeter.

We pull up to the entrance; a checkpoint with a moveable steel fence. Mikey says a couple of words to the soldier standing guard, who then shine a flashlight in my face and then at my chest with its numerous blood stains. After that, we're waved through.

"Don't get too comfortable here," Mikey says, parking up beside another Humvee and turning off the engine. "The camp moves all the time."

We get out, and I follow my host. There isn't much in the way of lighting; maybe a camping light every few meters to illuminate the path. We pass men and women in combat fatigues, smoking or vaping or otherwise walking around like zombies.

Everyone looks tired, but they become a lot more animated when they see me walking around, covered in my own blood. Maybe I'm the zombie after all.

We walk into a large tent in the middle of the camp; there's a table with wooden chairs and a camping light swinging overhead. I look to the right and see an adjoining room filled with beds side-to-side. The floor is a plastic tarpaulin that crinkles beneath my feet.

Mikey sits on one of the chairs, and signals for me to do the same. He grabs a rucksack that sits upon the table and takes out a large bag of chips – some sort of Middle-Eastern Cheetos knock-off. I'm fixated on it; my stomach is hurting from hunger. Mercifully, he tosses the bag to me.

"I guess if you survived two bullets, you'll survive a bag of these."

I open them immediately, sticking my hand inside. The smell of cheese is overpowering and majestic. I take out a handful and shove them into my mouth; they're slightly stale and absolutely delicious.

"So," Mikey says, crossing his arms and leaning back on his chair. "What's your story?"

In between chewing mouthfuls of cheesy chips, I give him a carefully abridged version of it all. I tell him I quit my job, foiled a robbery, and discovered a lot about myself; that I want to fight, and that I want to fight for good. I tell him I spent my last money on a plane ticket and got smuggled across the border.

Then I explain again what happened with Tomas and the ambush. He laughs, rubbing his eyes with the back of his hand.

"I'd heard whispers there were troops on our side doing drug deals with troops on their side for a while. Aljarran is one of the biggest highways for opium in this region." He laughs again. "One hell of a way to get inducted into this war."

"So, what's your story? How come you volunteered here?" I ask.

"I did eight years in the marine corps. Joined right out of high school. Then I went home and found that I couldn't do civilian life. I couldn't own a car. I couldn't pay a mortgage. I couldn't settle down and have kids. It just didn't excite me."

I nod along, thinking I couldn't do those things either, but only because of my own uselessness.

"Then I read about the rebels, the dictator, and the breakaway region here" Mikey says, continuing. "And I got on a plane, got across the border, and picked up a gun. That was a year ago."

I hear an explosion outside, far away. It echoes through the tent; a low, deathly rumble. I get off the chair, rising quickly to my feet, but to my surprise Mikey stays sitting, laid-back as ever.

"You'll get used to those. Artillery fire."

"They know where we are?" I slowly drop back to the chair.

"Sure." he says, "Their artillery isn't accurate enough to precisely threaten us. But occasionally they hit some poor fella. Think of it like buying a lottery ticket every day."

I'm beginning to understand Mikey's dark sense of humor.

"And what do I win?"

"A free trip out of here!" Mikey laughs and slaps the table with his hand. I chuckle and shake my head. This mad man.

"Nine years I've been in the military. I've fought in three different countries. Had countless buddies. Lost a few of them." His expression becomes a lot more somber. "But I've never seen a guy take two bullets, refuse treatment, and walk around afterwards."

He leans closer to me, looking me in the eyes. The white

light above us, swinging gently in the night's breeze, seems brighter now. Suddenly, this feels like an interrogation.

"What really happened back there? They looked a hell of a lot like bullet wounds to me, but the way you recovered makes me think otherwise."

"I know this looks weird," I say, in another massive understatement. "But, take me out with you. Let me fight alongside you. I'm made for this. You'll see."

He's silent; he looks at me warily before looking back at all the dried and congealed blood on my clothing, and the holes in my jacket. Then he slowly rises to his feet.

"Stay here."

He disappears out of the tent. A breeze rushes through the fabric door as he leaves. It's enough to make me shiver. There's a smell I keep encountering. It's metallic, coppery, like a gone-off pork sausage. I realize for the first time that it's the smell of blood.

A couple of minutes pass and then Mikey re-enters the tent. He's carrying a large bottle of water with one hand, and a pile of clothes with the other; sand-colored military fatigues, just like my last ones, only thankfully free of blood and bullet holes.

"Here, get changed into these. Our team leader will decide what to do with you tomorrow, but seeing as you're here, you might as well be comfortable."

I do as he says, taking off my top and checking out my bullet wounds. They're beginning to heal; tissue forming within the holes already. There's no more bleeding and barely any pain.

"Jesus," Mikey says, looking at the wounds. "You don't even need stitches."

I take the bottle of water outside and wash the dried blood off me, arousing some funny looks from onlookers, but thankfully no remarks. Then I go back inside and put on the clothes Mikey gave me.

"I don't know what the hell you are, dude," Mikey says, as I sit down again. "But I guess we'll soon find out, right?"

We spend the rest of the night comparing stories of our childhoods in the States. He was born and raised in Boston. A troublesome kid at school, with a deadbeat dad and a single, overworked mom. It feels like I don't have a lot in common with him, but I do enjoy his company.

Eventually, he shows me to my quarters: a small, unappealing-looking mattress on a steel bedframe. I lie down on it and feel I could fall asleep instantly. I wonder what kind of physical toll getting shot twice has on my body, but I don't wonder for long. Before I know it, I'm fast asleep.

CHAPTER 29

When I open my eyes, the first thing I see is Dina looking over me. Her expression is quizzical; she's staring at me like I'm a cadaver on an autopsy table.

"So," she finally says, "he's still alive."

I sit up in bed and rub my eyes. When I open them again, I see Dina, Mikey, and another man: he's older, perhaps in his forties, with a dark complexion and a scar on his lip. He's wearing a beige camouflaged jacket with a set of three stripes on the arm.

"And he was shot?" the man asks. He's got a Aljarrian accent, but I understand every word.

"Twice," Dina says in reply.

They allow me the honor of getting away from under their analytical gazes and out of the bed. We all go to the next room and sit at the table. The fabric flap that serves is a door is open, and the warm, dry air is billowing through the tent.

"I'm captain Mahmoud; I'm the man in charge of the recon teams here. And what's your name?"

I tell him, as well as retell the story of how I got here. He listens, never once changing the expressionless look on his face. I get to explaining the ambush and lift my shirt to show them the wounds.

"What on Earth?" Dina says, her jaw dropping. Then she evidently gets the self-conscious feeling that she's gawping and picks it up again. "They're perfectly healed."

I look down. Sure enough, the wounds are gone. There's just a small, pinkish discoloration of my skin in place of each one. And tomorrow I know that'll be gone too.

Captain Mahmoud tells me to leave the tent for a moment. I comply, walking outside, and smell the morning air for the first time. The sky is cloudless, and the heat already feels close to intolerable. There's the odd soldier around, but the place is a lot quieter than it was last night.

After a couple of minutes, they call me back in.

"So you want to fight?" Captain Mahmoud says. "We'll let you fight."

Dina's sat with her arms crossed. She rolls her eyes. Maybe she thought I wouldn't notice. Or maybe she doesn't care.

"There's a village close to the frontline; I need to know if there are government forces there, and if there are, how many. Mikey will be leading you."

Finally I get an actual assignment. I smile, nodding my head with enthusiasm.

"If there are no forces there, then I want you to remain in place and, uhm, what's the saying?" He strokes his chin for a second. "Hold the fort."

I look at Mikey who's enjoying my enthusiasm. Dina is still sitting there with her arms crossed. Obviously, there's one last heart and one final mind to win over.

"But don't get into a firefight. If there are troops there, surveil them from a distance and then leave. You're a recon team; you're not equipped to go all – what's his name – Rambo."

Mikey nods sagely.

"Sorry we can't provide you any training. Training exercises are a luxury we just don't have anymore." He pauses, looking at my body once more. "But my father always said that nothing prepares you for war better than taking fire. I suppose you already know that."

I nod again and thank him. He rises from the table and exchanges a few words with Dina in their native tongue. Then he says his goodbyes and leaves.

"So, when do we go?" I ask; I can't wait to finally be useful.

"Within the hour" Mikey says in reply. "That is, if you're definitely feeling up to it."

"I feel great," I tell him truthfully. "This is what I've been waiting for."

Mikey gets up from the table and leaves, pushing me playfully as he passes me. I'm left with Dina, still crossing her arms, still regarding me with suspicion.

"You'd better pull your weight Kris. This war isn't a joke."

I wipe the smile off my face and nod. She rises to her feet and walks outside, but not before pausing by the door and saying one last thing:

"And maybe you'll make a good human shield."

Ouch. But, you know, maybe she has a point.

I wait until I know the coast is clear, and then get my damage report.

"Vega, how am I holding up?"

Your liver and large intestine are fully healed. Your lungs are a very delicate organ and so that damage will take a little longer to repair.

I'm just about to respond when Dina walks back in. She tosses me a rucksack, which I just manage to block from hitting me in the chest.

"Here," she says with urgency. "You'll need this."

I go to unzip the rucksack, expecting guns, knives, body armor, or something equally spicy. Instead, I find it filled with green plastic packages adorned with strange lettering and barcodes.

"What are these?"

"Meals ready to eat, or as we say, MREs," Dina replies.

We go to a short briefing about the mission and the location. It's a small village called Shahassi located just behind the frontline, with a smattering of farms, houses, and a school. It's apparently empty – evacuated of its occupants long ago – but remains a strategically important location if the rebels are ever going to win the war.

Then, Mikey leads me to another tent – an armory of sorts – and gives me a couple more items: some sort of protective vest with ceramic plates inserted, as well as a light brown desert hat. Given the scorching temperatures here, maybe the hat is more the lifesaver than the vest, but I accept both nevertheless.

We pack a car – a small hatchback that's seen far better days – and I meet the remaining member of our team: an Aljarrian man named Salman. He's strong; rippling with muscles, and a black, bushy mustache. He bumps fists nonchalantly and gets into the back of the car with me.

I wind down the window beside me, and as we set off enjoy the sensation of the warm breeze against my face.

The village is around 40 miles away. It doesn't take long before we're close by. There's a couple of plumes of black smoke in the distance rising high into the sky. Then I hear a low, distant rumbling, like a hellish, infernal engine. I quickly grasp that it's the low rumbling of artillery and gunfire.

"The front line moves every day," Mikey says, turning to face me from the seat ahead. "Sometimes by a little, sometimes by a lot. We've gotta make sure we don't lag behind. We're a small squad. A recon squad. We're not going to be getting into firefights, you hear?"

I nod and he turns back around. Dina is driving and

uncharacteristically quiet. After a minute, she pulls over by the side of the dirt road we're on and turns off the engine.

"Close enough?" she asks, before taking her hand off the wheel to part the black locks of hair from her face.

"Sure," Mikey replies enthusiastically.

I look out of the windows; I can't see a village. I can't even see any buildings. Just the thick columns of the smoke, the blue sky, and the relentless sun.

"We're here?" I ask.

"We're a mile and a half out" Mikey replies. "We're going to walk the remainder and surveil the village from distance."

Seems pretty obvious now that I think about it. We unpack the car – taking several bags from the trunk, as well as a trio of rifles – and prepare to set out. I sling a rucksack across my back and begin hiking.

The ground here is treacherous as always; sandy recesses that want to gobble you up whole, or jagged rocks that stick out of the ground at improbable angles. No vegetation, no reliable track, just a constant calculation over where to put your foot next.

Before long, Mikey signals us to stop with a wave of his hand. We crouch behind the rocks and look to the bags. Mikey and Salman pick out a set of binoculars each. I look out into the distance, and sure enough see a couple of buildings blending in with the horizon.

"So that's the village?" I say, before looking over the rest of the horizon. "And all of that could be the front line?"

"Correct," Mikey replies. "I'm seeing no activity from this distance. No vehicles. No evidence of occupation."

"So we walk in?" I ask, perhaps letting my enthusiasm to do something other than traffic drugs get the better of me.

"You want to eat another couple of bullets?" Dina asks curtly. I look over at her; her large, brown eyes are reflecting the sun.

"She's right, we wait." Mikey pulls the binoculars away from his face and turns to face me. "Besides, it's dinnertime."

At his direction, I pull four MREs out of my rucksack and distribute them to everybody. I tear mine open, finding a bit of stale bread – at least I know where that came from – as well as a candy bar, and finally a dried noodle dish, evidently intended for boiling water, which we do not have. I tuck in, eating the noodles dry.

Then we wait. Salman watches through the binoculars. Mikey hands me his pair, and I take a look. Indeed, two sandstone and concrete buildings sit on the horizon, with a larger one partially hidden behind them. They look empty. No vehicles, no smoke, no soldiers, no signs of life.

"So what do you think of the frontline, Kris?"

I put the binoculars down, and see Mikey waiting expectantly for my answer.

"Well, I think I..." I stutter a little, trying to find the words. "...I think I expected a little more action?"

Mikey laughs before looking to Dina, who shakes her head at me, but not before allowing the tiniest slither of a smile on her face.

"Dude, you got shot *twice*, like, *yesterday*. And you want more action!?" Mikey is incredulous. I guess he makes a good point. "You're incredible man."

"We just sit and fire shells at each other," Salman says, still peering through his binoculars. "Maybe take a bit of land here, maybe lose a bit there."

"It's a stalemate," Dina adds. "We don't have the manpower or the resources to make any kind of breakthrough. But we're also sure that Darida's goons don't either."

"But we can take this village, right?" My question has Mikey smiling again, through admiration of my courage or mockery of my stupidity, I'm not sure. "One small battle, on the road to winning the war."

"Yeah man," Mikey says, "something like that."

After an hour or so, we walk a little closer before taking up a position a 100 yards or so away from the buildings. Salmon and Dina watch through the binoculars as Mikey and I crouch behind a small rockface, hopefully out of view.

Mikey sits with his rifle in one hand – supported against his shoulder, with the barrel aiming upwards – while throwing pebbles with the other. I'm drawn to the tattoos on his arm. There looks to be a list of names in a cursive font, along with dates.

We wait for another half hour or so before Mikey gives the order to advance. We slowly approach the first building; Salman, Mikey, and Dina with their rifles drawn, and me behind them carrying a couple of bags.

Mikey signals me to wait behind, as the three of them assume positions outside farmhouse number one. They work as a team; Mikey first, with Salman and Dina backing him up, opening each door slowly and exploring each room with their rifles drawn.

"Clear!" Mikey yells, and they move onto the next building. I hang behind, watching their movements, and then watching the rest of the village when they disappear into another building. A cloud of dust is blown softly across the road that intersects the farmhouses, but other than that it's a ghost town.

Finally, after checking on every other building in the village – just over a dozen – they move on to the larger building: the schoolhouse. Mikey whispers into my ear to wait outside and keep watch. With a small pang of disappointment, I stand beside the door, trying my best to be useful under the circumstances.

After a couple of minutes – and a few shouts from inside – Mikey emerges and beckons me into the building.

"Looks like the intelligence was correct," Mikey says as I

follow him inside. "For whatever reason, they gave this village up."

Inside is ruined; there are still kids' drawings on the walls and colorful paintings scattered around the floor, but all of the furniture has been broken and repurposed as barricades, beds, or just sadistically destroyed by the former occupants.

We walk down a corridor, heading to a large room that I gather was once a gymnasium. As we go, I peek past each door. One former classroom is a bombsite, quite literally; a giant crater sits inside, and the ceiling and adjoining wall is entirely absent. Shards of wood and plaster sit strewn around and the walls are black with ash.

I look at the corridor wall; there's a finger-painting mural of a group of children along with a taller figure who I assume is their teacher. There are animals: dogs, cats, horses, camels. And each figure has a bullet hole in its head. The adults, the kids, the animals, used as point-blank target practice to stave off boredom.

I don't think any child will ever be safe here again.

When we get to the gymnasium, it looks to have been used as a barracks by Darida's men. Filthy sleeping bags surround a pressure cooker and camp fire in the center of the room. The windows are blasted out – probably by the shell that hit the school – and broken glass litters the wooden floor.

We find Dina and Salman sitting in the center of the room; Dina is already radioing our findings back to basecamp. Salman is perusing a Aljarrian language magazine he found. It seems like a job well done, even if I didn't actually do anything.

"So what now?" I ask Mikey.

"We wait for a platoon." He looks restless, like he expected more of a fight. The muscles in his arms are twitching. "I imagine 50 or so soldiers will come here and fortify the place. Then we can move on."

I nod in acknowledgement, but I can see he isn't done

around here yet.

"C'mon man," he says after a couple of minutes of being unable to sit down. "Let's take a better look around here. Sometimes these goons can leave ammunition behind."

I begin to follow him out, arousing Dina's attention:

"Where are you going?" she asks, putting the mic-side of the radio close to her chest. "We need to take up defensive positions."

"We're gonna take a look around," Mikey replies with a sly wink. "Won't be long."

We walk out of the gymnasium and down the corridor.

"I don't think she trusts me yet," I remark to Mikey, when we're out of earshot of the gymnasium.

"She's a tough nut to crack," Mikey says, leading the way. Eventually he finds the kitchen. "But she's a good soldier. And she's been through a lot."

I contemplate what he's said and watch him open several cupboards, but find nothing of note. Eventually he waltzes over to the corner, containing a large refrigerator, and begins to size it up.

Watch out, Vega says, making me jump on the spot. *There's a trap.*

I look over at Mikey, and see his hand darting to the refrigerator door. Beside the door, for one split second, I see something like a shiny wire, sparkling in the light.

"Hey, hey, wait!" I cry. I watch his hand clasp the refrigerator door handle; his fingers close around it.

"Don't open that!"

He pauses, before looking back at me quizzically.

"Look," I say, approaching tentatively, with my arms out defensively. "There, attached to the handle, there's a wire."

He turns back to the handle, and sure enough we both see it; a tiny, plastic wire tied around the handle of the refrigerator. We both simultaneously follow it upwards, trying to find what it's attached to. And then we see it.

A hand grenade, taped to the top of the refrigerator, almost out of view. The other end of the wire is tied around its pin, intending for the unlucky fridge-raider to be blown to Kingdom come as soon as it was opened.

"Jesus H. Christ," Mikey exclaims. He lets go of the handle, instead staring morbidly at his hand. Then he looks at me with an expression I've never seen before. "I think you just saved my life man."

He tosses himself at me in an embrace, throwing his arms around me and squeezing me. We hear footsteps down the hall and he lets go.

"What's going on?" Dina shows up in the doorway, looking ready to admonish two misbehaving school kids. "We heard shouting."

"Here, look, this refrigerator is rigged to blow," Mike says as Dina approaches slowly. Mikey carefully unties the wire from around the grenade's pin, and then prizes up the tape that attaches it to the refrigerator. "We should be careful, there may be more traps."

I watch him carefully take the grenade and examine it. Then he fiddles with something on the top, unscrewing it until it comes off in his hands.

"See, the fuse. It won't explode without this."

He places both – the grenade and the fuse that sat atop it – down onto a kitchen counter.

"Nice find," Dina tells Mikey. He shakes his head, grinning from ear-to-ear, and waves his hand in my direction.

"It was all our bulletproof friend here. If it hadn't been for him, I'd be painted all over this kitchen right now."

"Huh," Dina turns to me, her expression a strange mix of surprise, relief, and begrudging appreciation. "Is that so?"

"Always good to have another set of eyes watching," I tell her.

Oh, if only they knew.

CHAPTER 30

After much backslapping and many high-fives from Mikey – and a little guarded admiration from Dina – we head back to the gymnasium.

There, we decide our next moves. Mikey sends me and Salman out to look for more traps within the village, and he and Dina look to barricade the building, blocking the broken windows of the gymnasium with the intact remnants of desks and cupboards.

After a couple of hours, neither me, Salman, nor Vega can detect any more traps. We return to the gymnasium and gather around a gym bench someone has dragged into the middle of the room. It's hot as all hell in here – the air con is long gone, if this building ever had it – but as the afternoon goes on, it's getting mercifully cooler.

I wipe away a palm-full of sweat from my forehead and from my hair underneath my hat. This is a ruined mess of a place – like exploring a shipwreck in a drained sea – but I can still recognize the gymnasium. The latches on the ceiling for the ropes, the benches, the shiny wooden flooring.

I close my eyes and can almost hear my old classmates shouting, running, crying, and jumping. And then me, sat to one side, always having to watch, never made to participate. Humiliating.

"I hate gym class," I finally find myself saying, speaking my thoughts out loud. "I mean, you know, I used to hate gym class."

"Wasn't your thing, huh?" Mikey asks. He has his rifle – I can't identify it from any videogames I've ever played – laid out in front of him. He's meticulously unscrewing each part. "It was the only part of school I ever enjoyed."

"I had a heart condition" I add, still lost in my own thoughts and unhappy memories. "Everyone had me wrapped in cotton wool. They thought I was too fragile to take part in any sport. Too much of a liability to join in."

"And look at you now," he says, laughing. I watch him finish dissembling his rifle and pick up a cloth. "Soaking up bullets like a west-coast rapper."

I snort in appreciation. Then I realize Dina's eyes are burning a hole in me. I turn my head to look at her.

"Is that why you're doing this?" she asks; those brown eyes are interrogating me. Searching deeply into my soul. She still doesn't trust me; doesn't understand me. "You're doing this to prove you're no longer that kid?"

I dither, avoiding her gaze and trying to find the words. Of course she's right. I tell myself I'm out to use my abilities for good, to depose the dictator and become the hero. But I'm still that fragile, stupid kid at heart.

Finally, I shrug.

"I don't know," I say, looking her in the eyes at last. "I can't tell you what I've gone through in the last week or so. I've discovered things about myself I never knew I had. Discovered strengths and tolerances I could never have dreamed of. Maybe I just want to push myself to the limit."

"And what's the limit?" Mikey asks, "finding that one bullet too many?"

He chuckles to himself and goes back to cleaning his rifle. Dina still isn't finished staring me out, though.

"We've had all sorts of Americans join us," Dina says. "Some of them are real, full-blooded soldiers like Mikey here. They're at least useful. Some of them are crazed, psychotic losers who are convinced Darida is the antichrist. And then some of them are the war-tourists; the guys who want to stream video of a real-life battle scene for likes and followers."

She shakes her head, seemingly disgusted with her memories of them.

"They're the ones who charge into gunfire, and we're the ones who are sent to fish their corpses out of a ditch."

I gulp, thankful she didn't have to drag my corpse out of that 4x4 last night.

"But you, you're different. I've never met anyone like you in this war before. You look like you've never been in a fight, let alone fired a gun. You've no experience of war, but you've got this dumb confidence that you're going to survive anything."

I hesitate again, feeling embarrassed to be the center of attention.

"Hey," Mikey interjects, "maybe he's a superhero."

Dina crosses her arms and exhales in annoyance. Salman looks over with a smile on his face before going back to his magazine.

"No, no, hear me out." He excitedly drops his rifle and readjusts his seating on the bench. "Infused with plutonium in some CIA laboratory, with a chip implanted in his brain so his every movement can be tracked. They've sent him here, to some dumb war no-one cares about, to gauge his abilities."

I laugh, somewhat nervously. He's so preposterously far from the truth, while still being too close for comfort.

"What can I say, you got me."

Mikey sniggers and turns back to his rifle and picks the

cloth back up. He doesn't even seem to care who I am, even if I turn out to be some CIA super soldier. He seems to live for the thrill of all of this.

"This war has been everything to me," Dina finally says before looking at Salman. "For every Aljarrian citizen, it's been life and it's been death. This war takes everything from you. I don't know why you Americans would want to come here and fight but I should say I appreciate it."

I'm shocked; it's the first I've ever heard Dina sound grateful for my presence here.

"I was a medical student at university here when this all began," she continues, "I'd never held a gun. I never wanted to hold a gun. I thought my purpose here was to heal the sick, not kill the living. And then the war began and we all got dragged down to this."

Her voice is monotonal, and yet conveys four years of torment. She pulls out a necklace from underneath her shirt, worn tightly around her neck. On it is a small, circular silver locket. She opens it and closes it again in rapid succession.

"My mother was one of the first to die. Probably put against the wall by Darida's men. An intellectual who couldn't be trusted. We never even recovered her body."

I think of my own mother, and the way in which she died. The catastrophic shockwaves it wrought upon us; upon my dad, warping the way he saw the world. Then I think about that on a national scale: hundreds of thousands of families devastated.

"My mother died a while back," I say, looking Dina in the eyes again. "She was murdered. Killed by a stray bullet, shot from God-knows where, by God-knows who. We'll never know who shot it. The cops said it could have been from miles away. But who knows? Just another bolt from beyond."

I feel myself beginning to well up at the side of my eyes. I quickly turn my head away from Dina's. Then I hear a low rumble from far away – an artillery shell landing, ripping another hole in the earth.

"What I do know is, it leaves a wound. A wound that never heals."

We sit in silence for a few minutes before Mikey finishes cleaning and re-assembling his gun, and has us patrol the perimeter of town, ensuring no-one can get the drop on us. After that, we sit in a spot by the boarded-up windows and play cards, enjoying the gentle evening breeze as darkness falls.

We take out a battery powered lamp from one of the bags and set up around it. I never went camping as a kid. I barely ever left the city. But this feels comfortable.

After a few games, I can see Dina is tired; she has deep, dark circles around her eyes that seem to grow with every hour. I don't know how much sleep the others get; I was out like a light last night. They could have slept beside me and I'd have no idea.

"How long have we gotta, uhh, hold the fort here?" I ask, practically jolting Dina back to life. "How long until we can reinforce this village?"

"Probably the morning" Mikey says, looking over to Dina. She nods.

"But" I add after a moment, "we can't sleep, right?"

"We've got to keep watch," Mikey replies. "This is still the frontline. Still no man's land, still liable to be attacked."

"Right."

After an indeterminate amount of time, Salman informs us it's past midnight already. My legs are beginning to ache from sitting on this cold, hard wooden floor. Eventually, I stand up and excuse myself.

"I'm gonna take a walk outside, get some fresh air."

"All right, don't go far," is Mikey's response as he throws another set of cards in the others' directions.

I walk down the corridor, straining my eyes trying to

avoid debris and shards of wood and concrete on the floor. When I get to the door, I hop outside and take a look around. It's a full moon, and it seems especially large in the sky tonight.

The desert looks sublime in this light. Silver sands and strange, sharp rocks, lit by the faintest white light. Perfect silver silhouettes against the black horizon.

"Vega," I say, confident the others can't hear me. "I thought I should check in."

All vital signs are returned to optimal levels. The damage to all of your internal organs is fully repaired and all are functioning perfectly.

"Cool," I say, still unsure how I should react to the 'damage report.'

Kris, I didn't know your mother died in that way, Vega then says, shocking me. He's never enquired too far into my past before, but I suppose we're almost one and the same now.

"Yeah," I say after a few moments. "That's why everything is so messed up. Well, part of the reason anyway."

Losing a parent so young will always be a traumatic experience, especially in a manner such as the one you describe. You spoke of it as a wound that never heals. I think that description is apt.

"Yeah…"

I stand out in the moonlight for a little longer. I look up at the moon, almost directly over me. Some 11 years ago, my mom walked to her car and fell down dead in an instant. Two weeks ago I was working the sandwich conveyer beat, terrified of any smallest twinge in my chest.

It's an unpredictable world, all right.

I walk over to one of the farmhouses, trying to stretch my legs a bit. It's easy enough to see the path out here; the tiny bits of moss on the brickwork glisten in the moonlight, illuminating my path.

I lean against the farmhouse door and hear something strange from inside; a scrape of one surface against another.

Like that of an animal quickly trying to escape a corner or a boot scraping across a concrete floor.

Kris, be aware – I don't think you're alone.

I turn around before pushing against the door, trying to take a look inside. That's when I hear it for sure: a scrape of a boot, and right after that a kick to the back of my knee. I drop immediately and feel a hand around my throat, and a cold, steel blade against the side of my head.

A couple of men burst out of the farmhouse door. One of them is frantically speaking at me in a language I don't understand and the other begins tying my wrists together behind me. I mumble something, which is answered with another flurry of words.

It all happens so quickly, I don't have time to gather my thoughts and react. I turn my head slightly and see that cold, steel blade is actually the barrel of a rifle. My heart skips a beat, but I don't panic. I take a deep breath, close my eyes, and talk:

"Hey, look, I don't know who you guys are, but—"

I get struck with something; a cold, hard blow to the side of my temple. It knocks me funny for a second or two. My eyes dart to my right, and see one of the men holding his rifle butt close to my face. I guess I got smacked with that…

I hear something like tape being unwrapped and feel a sticky sensation over my lips. I try to cry out, but find they've taped my mouth shut. Then I taste blood; that old, familiar flavor.

"American?" one of them whispers forcefully. I focus my eyes on the guy to my left; he's wearing black gear and a balaclava with intense hateful eyes staring at me from within.

I nod. They exchange more words that I don't understand before I see a couple more men ahead, slowly walking into the schoolhouse with their rifles drawn. I think I count four in total. Two of them are still beside me.

Regaining my wits after that blow from the rifle butt, I try to discern what my wrist ties are made from. They're thin, sharp plastic. I think back to the cable ties I put Carver in, all the way back in the aquarium. I can't let the others get ambushed by these goons. I *must* get out of these ties.

Keeping my hands innocuously behind my back, I twist my wrists together, hoping to use whatever nanobot-augmented strength I can muster to break them without raising any attention. It hurts – the plastic ties are like razors cutting against my wrists – but after a couple of sustained motions, I feel them break suddenly.

My body judders upwards as I break my way out of the ties, but my captors are momentarily distracted watching their buddies disappear into the schoolhouse. With my arms finally free, I can plot my next move: the steel barrel of the rifle pressed painfully against the side of my head. And they don't expect me to be able to move…

With one final look to ensure they're not watching me, I move my right arm upwards, grabbing the barrel of the rifle. I tear it away from his grasp, pulling his finger from the trigger as I do so.

Rising to my feet and grabbing the gun with my left hand too, I swing the rifle butt into the face of the other balaclava-clad goon – the one on my left - as hard as I can and then some.

"Oomph," he groans, holding the side of his face as his body hits the ground. He drops his own weapon as he goes down, and I desperately kick it away; the only thing I can think to do in the situation. Then I wrap my finger around the trigger and aim it at the guy to my right again.

I see his eyes – they're no longer filled with hate. Instead, they're fearful; like he knows he's in deep water. I find myself pulling the trigger – a panicked, involuntary muscle movement – but the gun just produces an audible *click*. I jam the trigger another couple of times, but again nothing happens.

He turns to run, but I manage to trip him as he does so; he

staggers and falls. I jump forward onto him, and like some enraged caveman, and begin clubbing him with the rifle butt – four or five times – until he stops struggling beneath me.

I drop the gun and rip off the tape from my mouth.

"Mikey, Dina!" I yell, as loud as I possibly can. "Watch out, two guys entering the building!"

There's silence, other than the occasion groan and gurgle from the guy I first hit with the rifle. Then I hear gunshots; multiple loud bangs coming from the schoolhouse, echoing through the corridor and throughout the moonlit village. I wipe a trickle of blood from my temple and run to pick up the rifle I kicked away. My hands are shaking – through adrenaline or sheer nerves, I can't quite tell just yet – as I pick up the gun.

I run over to the door of the schoolhouse and crouch beside it, frantically trying to adjust my grip on the rifle. The gunshots are still ringing out, echoing into the night's sky; a series of sharp stabs directly into my eardrums.

And then silence.

CHAPTER 31

As quickly as they began, the gunshots end. Quiet reigns once more.

I peer around the door and see a whole lot of dust kicked up. Then I see the two men lying still by the bottom of the corridor, close to the door to the gym.

Slowly, I walk down the corridor, aiming the rifle towards them as I go. As I get closer I can see they're not moving. They'll never move again in fact. Multiple dark red stains cover their clothing.

"Hey, it's just me now," I yell down the corridor, belatedly realizing that I don't want to get shot by my own side. "Don't shoot!"

After a few moments of stillness, I hear some shuffling from beyond the corridor inside the gymnasium.

"Kris!" Mikey shouts excitedly. "Are you hit?"

"No!" I shout back, the single word echoing across the bare walls of the corridor.

Mikey strides out, stooping over his rifle as he walks. He sees me in the corridor and eases his posture a little. Then he makes a signal with his hand and Dina and Salman follow.

"How many?" Mikey asks, approaching me slowly.

"Two here, two outside," I say, turning back to the door. He puts his hand on my shoulder as if to drag me back. I let him take the lead, and we slowly walk outside looking down the length of our rifles.

When we get outside, the man I'd hit with the rifle butt repeatedly is still lying there in the shallow moonlight. The other, who I'd kicked the gun away from, is nowhere to be seen.

"He's gone," I say to Mikey, pointing to the cobbled road he lay on – groaning and moaning – when I left the scene.

I run back to the farmhouse and take a look over the landscape. Mikey and Salman talk between themselves and set out searching for him, while Dina goes back to check on the man I left lying.

My hands are shaking still; I try to rub the sweat off my brow, but find my fingers don't work as they should. I rake them across my forehead and take a moment to breathe deeply.

I see Dina pick herself up and walk back into the corridor. I can't help but look over at the man laying there in the gutter. He's still not moving.

You seemed to handle that well, Vega says.

He's perhaps sensing my heartrate hasn't quite slowed yet. I feel the wound on my temple for the first time. It throbs painfully, but I've survived far worse. I'm kind of glad I have it; something to make me remember I just fought for my life.

A couple of minutes later, Dina appears at the door to the schoolhouse holding the first-aid bag. She beckons me inside, and I slowly walk in.

"You're hurt," she says, forcefully turning my head round in her hands. Then she sets the bag down, opens it, and takes out a large bandage, which she rubs hesitantly between her fingers. "Here, let me help you."

She begins to wrap the bandage around my head, but I block her with my hand. She surely must have seen that coming.

"I don't need that," I say to her, still looking at that lifeless body splayed out on the floor. She gives me a look halfway between annoyance and understanding, and I take the bandage from her, dabbing my head a couple of times. I point at the man. "What about him?"

She's evidently surprised to hear me ask.

"He's dead Kris."

I feel the hairs on my forearms begin to stand on end. I can't believe it. *Dead?* I just hit him a few times. I didn't mean to kill him.

"What happened?" she asks, surprised at my reaction. "Didn't you shoot him?"

"Shoot him?" I find myself shouting the words, frantically. "No, no I didn't shoot him."

"Well, whatever you did worked," she replies sardonically. I guess she has no time for my crisis of conscience. "He has no pulse and a massive head wound."

"I hit him with the rifle butt," I say, trying to explain my actions. She begins to pack her first aid kit away. "Only, like, a couple of times. Why didn't they kill me?"

"I don't know. You're white and look pretty stupid," Dina says without looking up from her kit. "They probably guessed you were American. Big ransom fee."

I slowly approach the body, fearing what I'll see. Wherever I've gone, whatever I've done, I've left a trail of bodies but this is the first time I've actually killed someone.

He's lying motionless on his back with his arms limply by his sides. One of his hands is curled into a fist, like he tried for the briefest of moments to defend himself. His head is a black mass of balaclava fabric, blood, and mashed up flesh glistening in the moonlight. I can't look for long.

"Of course, it's obvious that he has one single, notable defect that made him especially susceptible to that mortal wound."

"What?" I ask, somewhat hopefully.

"He isn't made of whatever the hell you're made of."

She turns and heads back down the schoolhouse corridor without a second glance. So much for psychological support.

Mikey and Salman arrive back, walking with their rifles held passively across their stomachs. They find me meandering around outside the schoolhouse still.

"He's long gone," Mikey says, resigned to losing him. "Slipped into the night. I'm guessing it was just the four of them, but we've got to be vigilant until reinforcements arrive. He could come back with a platoon."

Mikey walks to inspect the body weighing heavily on my mind. He ducks to a squatting position and examines the head wound.

"What the hell happened here?" He turns to me with a devilish grin. "You did this?"

I swallow nervously, then look at him and nod my head.

"How?" He looks around, before seeing the jammed rifle on the ground. "You shot him?"

I can see that my unusual super abilities has some drawbacks. Chiefly, I don't know my own strength. And second, neither does anyone else.

"No, I hit him with the – uhh." I motion to the butt of the rifle.

"The stock," he says, finding a descriptor I'd barely heard of. He looks at the rifle butt, shining a flashlight on it. "Jesus Christ, you must have crushed his skull, man."

He laughs and begins to clap. I rub my head with both of my hands. I can see that I'm going to get nothing but lurid praise for the killing I just committed.

He and Salman come over and chest-bump me, which I

half-heartedly try to reciprocate. They tell me they were alerted to the attack by my call. That they would have been ambushed and killed in the gymnasium if it wasn't for my warning. That I almost single-handedly saved their lives tonight. They tell me I'm a hero.

A *hero*.

It's strange. I don't feel that way. I feel like I crossed a dreadful line, and there's no returning back over it. Whatever I was a couple of weeks ago, I'm something different now.

I follow Mikey and Salman back into the gymnasium, stepping over the dead bodies of the two men they shot. Mikey and Salman are jubilant; they look like men who love every minute of this. Dina is her usual self: steely, steadfast, reserved. No-one even knows who shot the bullets that killed the two men.

Mikey pours us all a coffee from a flask he picks out of one of the rucksacks; he quaffs it like a frat boy drinking beer. I put the cup to my mouth and drink it slowly. It's tasteless.

Again they toast me, and tell me I'm the reason they're all here. That I've been an indispensable member of the team. Even Dina kicks in: "I guess we found a use for you after all," she says begrudgingly, with the tiniest hint of a smile.

Everyone keeps their rifles close by, but they mostly seem to be enjoying themselves. I just look down and rub my forehead. My temple throbs with pain again as I do so. I'd forgotten about it again until now.

"It doesn't feel good, does it?"

I look up to see Salman addressing me directly. He's staring me deep in the eyes, his chin twitching slightly beneath his thick, black beard.

"What?" I ask, playing dumb. I think I know what he means, though.

"Killing someone," he clarifies. Mikey stands and walks over to the barricaded window of the gymnasium. "I hate these men, these thugs Darida sends after us. I hate what they've done to my country, I hate what they did to my family. But killing them still doesn't feel good."

"Hell, I remember my first time," Mikey says from across the room. He sits by the window with his rifle on his lap. "When I was a marine. Clearing a building in some town I don't remember the name of. We thought we'd smoked everyone out, but he came at me with a knife. Shot him through the chest at close range."

"I shot a guy hiding behind a door," Dina says somberly. "I heard him move behind it, just the smallest of sounds. I fired a few rounds; he fell to the floor, as did his revolver. But he had no bullets; he was unarmed. It never goes the way it does in the movies."

I take another sip of tasteless black sludge.

"Human life seems so valuable," Dina continues, "until it doesn't. Something will cheapen it and then you won't think twice."

I want to mention the Quiet One. The bomber I caught. The lives at the parade I likely saved. And the people on the train who died because of me. I feel I already know how valuable human life is. I've been trading in it for weeks now: a merchant of death.

After finishing the once in a lifetime treat that are our coffees, we go to different positions in the schoolhouse and keep guard. I stay in the gymnasium and Dina and Salman patrol the corridor and classrooms.

Maybe it's the night weighing heavily on me – maybe the sheer weight of it all compresses time itself – but morning rolls around in no time. As soon as the sun breaches the flat, rocky horizon, we hear Dina call out.

"They're here!"

Mikey and I walk to her position, and sure enough a convoy of Humvees and other vehicles are heading towards the village. Our reinforcements, at last.

Dina marches off to greet them. Mikey, on the other hand,

thumps me on my shoulder. I turn and see him smiling gratefully.

"I'll never forget what you did for us man."

He swings a rucksack onto his back and paces out to join Dina.

I'll never forget this either.

CHAPTER 32

Our remaining time in the village is short. We meet Captain Mahmoud again, who points out the lieutenant of the platoon whose name I instantly forget. We're thanked for our efforts and told we'll be returned to base camp.

Then the four of us climb into a Humvee, and we're driven back.

The journey is quiet, save for the humming of the engine and the occasional jolting of the vehicle handling rough terrain. Mikey seems to fall asleep immediately, whereas Dina looks out of the window, fumbling that locket around her neck between her fingers. Occasionally she opens it and closes it quickly, without looking inside.

My mind is busily going forwards and backwards through all the images it's amassed lately. Dina's interrogative gaze, looking through me; Mikey's effortless smile; that horrible, black mass of blood and gore of a face I created; Burden's horrible, diabolic grin, knowing that he's about to play his final card…

"Home sweet home," the driver says suddenly, jolting me

upright. I guess I fell asleep. We all climb out of the Humvee and stagger back to the tent I spent my first night in.

As we get there, Dina turns to face me. Those big, brown, searching eyes are on me again. She studies my face, and my temple, and the wound that I suffered there.

"Your wound is gone," she points out, sounding neither shocked or impressed.

"Yeah, it tends to happen," I say sheepishly, stepping past her and into the tent.

This is getting to be a problem; one that I hadn't anticipated when I came here. Sure, I can impress Mikey with feats of miraculous strength and recovery. I can sway the guys who believe in battlefield gods, with their pagan tattoos and appetites for chaos.

But I can't fool Dina. She's an ex-medical student. You don't need to finish medical school to know a gash – which should have required stitches – can't heal overnight. And there are two bullets embedded somewhere in the desert which should have been the nails in my coffin.

She isn't stupid. She's going to want to know how I keep doing this.

I sit at the table at Mikey's direction. He tells me he'll be a minute and disappears out of the tent. When he reappears, he's holding something in his hand.

"Here, we've got these."

He hands me a cellphone. The screen is cracked, but I'm of course used to that.

"We've just got some kinda satellite signal dish installed. You should be able to get on the wi-fi with that. It won't be quick, but maybe you can send a message home, if you have anyone."

I try to put on my most grateful face and thank him. The cellphone is old; maybe a model from five years ago. It's scratched to hell and looks like it's been through the wars. But it turns on. That's a start.

Of course, there's no one I wish to call. Everyone at home surely thinks I'm dead. And I'm not keen to correct them of that falsehood quite yet.

I take the cellphone into the room with the beds stacked side-to-side, and fall onto one of the mattresses. I'm immediately stabbed by a 100 sharp, malevolent springs, but as I shuffle around I begin to get comfortable.

I turn to the cellphone, and I've got one thing on my mind: I open the browser and look up news from home. It doesn't take long to find the name Alfred Burden in thick, block lettering.

Those bungling cops have managed to pinpoint Alfred Burden, former owner of a printing business, as the Quiet One. They explored his destroyed home forensically and found evidence of bomb-making materials. They even have a motive: industrial pollution from a defense contractor nearby.

Good job guys, only one week after I solved the case.

Then, scouring down the lines of text, I see my name: Kris Chambers, thought at the moment to be an accomplice who suffered a crisis of conscience. An accomplice: great, just *great*.

I keep reading, hopping from article to article. Going back a few days, I find the one I'm looking for:

BOMB DISCOVERED AND DEFUSED, PARADE CANCELED

I throw my head back into the pillow and breathe a sigh of relief. I feel like a certain weight has been lifted. They found that bomb after all. I really did save lives at that parade.

My eyes drift over another headline: one about the subway train bombing. I try to put the phone away. I pull my fingers from the screen and squeeze them tightly to my palm, but it's no use. I click the link.

Nine confirmed dead now, including Alfred Burden, the suspected mastermind of the bombings, and Kris Chambers, his alleged apprentice, whose arm was found close by. And one more person was taken off life support a couple of days ago. *Jesus*.

I messed up on the train. Those people didn't have to die. One day I'll be able to bear to read their names. One day I'll memorize them, so that I can never forget them.

But it's okay, I tell myself. I'm halfway across the world now, fighting a merciless war against a brutal dictator. I've already achieved things I can be proud of. How many lives can I save here – 100?, 1000? *More*?

Maybe this mode of thinking is illogical. Maybe I shouldn't think about it in terms of trading one life for 10. But that's what I seem to be doing here: justifying my actions by telling myself I'll do more good in the world than I'll do bad.

I put the cellphone away and close my eyes.

CHAPTER 33

I wake up confused again.

For a moment I feel like I'm back at home, in that miserable apartment I shared with my dad. That I'd woken up in that same bed, with the relentless sound of the city outside hammering against the window.

I feel the drudging disappointment of waking up as the person I was before all of this.

And yet, my hands feel clean.

Then I open my eyes and see I'm surrounded by the green fabric of the tent. I turn over to see another sleeping body in here, but other than that the scene is remarkably tranquil. I can't even hear the distant gunfire today.

I pick myself up and walk over to the main room in the tent; it's empty, with just a packet of crackers and a plastic bottle of water laid out on the table. I eagerly tuck into both. I'm so consumed by the food in front of me that I don't notice Dina walk in.

"Don't let me disturb you," she says. I look up from my meal and try to say something with a mouthful of crackers. She waves her hand dismissively. "I can wait."

She's wearing a yellow T-shirt with black pants. Not

exactly combat-ready; I guess we're not going to war today. I haven't seen her in casual-ware before. She looks good, but I can't say it suits her.

"Sorry," I finally say. "What's going on?"

"Lieutenant Al-Shabbasi wanted me to convey his gratitude for…" she pauses, curiously. "…for everything you did for us yesterday."

"Oh, yeah," I scoff with another mouthful of crackers. "All in a day's work, eh?"

She hesitates again. I feel like she's struggling to tell me the whole story.

"And he wants me to teach you how to shoot."

Ah, there it is. I turn in my chair to face her properly and finish chewing.

"That'd be great."

"All right," she says, before awkwardly crossing her arms by the fabric tent door flapping in the breeze. "Well?"

"You mean now?" I ask.

"You want to be a soldier, don't you?"

"Sure, but I—" I don't finish my sentence before she turns and paces away. I stand up, knocking the chair over behind me, and rub the crumbs away from my mouth before marching out to follow her.

We walk to the boundary of the camp, passing an entrance checkpoint, and find a slapdash, improvised firing range just beyond the perimeter fencing. In the distance I see a bunch of cans lined up atop a large, flat rock. There's a couple of guys here already – both lying prone, firing shots from rifles – and a wooden box with a couple more firearms in it.

We wait a minute until the two guys are done. I feel my heart beating again. I've never fired a gun before. Sure, I tried – last night – but for whatever reason it jammed.

When they finish up, walking past us and nodding to Dina as they do, she picks out a handgun from the box and hands it to me, being careful to point it away from us. She tells me the name of it – some Middle-Eastern model I can't possibly hope to remember right now – and shows me how to unload and reload it.

I try to commit it all to memory. Then she has me look out onto the range and the cans on the rock. I stare at them; they seem to dance in the late afternoon heat. She hands me the handgun and I aim, adopting the position she demonstrates.

"Breathe easily and squeeze the trigger," she says.

I aim down the iron sights on the handgun and then I squeeze the trigger. The sound of the first gunshot makes me jump slightly. I fire a few rounds, missing all but one of the cans, which I'm pretty sure I didn't even aim for.

"One out of six," she says emotionlessly. "You'll get better."

You know the sights are misaligned, Vega says. *The iron sights are slightly out a half millimeter to the right.*

I think about it, and then take a look down the sights again.

"These sights are misaligned," I tell Dina. "They're off ever so slightly. Enough to compromise the shot."

She chuckles to herself before turning to face me. "Do you know how often I've heard that?"

"No, I'm being serious." I reload the handgun, remembering what she showed me. Then I take another look down the sights.

Aim slightly to the right of the cans.

I follow Vega's advice, aiming slightly to the right.

Slightly more.

I do as he says and aim a little further to the right of the target. Then I steady myself as best I can.

Okay, fire.

I squeeze the trigger and hit the very can I was aiming for. Then I repeat the process for the remaining cans, aiming the same distance to the right of them. To my burgeoning sense of smug pride, I hit every single one.

When I put the handgun down and unload it, Dina says nothing. She's just staring at me in that incredulous, interrogatory manner she does so well.

"What?" I ask.

She takes the handgun from me, takes a look down the sights, and then inspects the sights again from the top.

"How did you know that?" she finally asks, doubtingly.

"I dunno," I tell her, lying through my teeth. "I got lucky, I guess."

"Lucky, right." She stands up, and I follow, climbing to my knees and then my feet before dusting myself down. "You're a lucky guy Kris."

She begins walking back to basecamp. I follow close behind.

"Or there's something you're not telling us," she finally adds, without looking back at me or even breaking her stride.

I don't know how to respond. So I don't.

We go back to the tent; Mikey is awake and dressed in some real garish gear; a black wifebeater vest with an obnoxious logo of a topless woman on it, along with cargo shorts. He looks like every paralytically drunk guy hanging out at a tailgater.

I'd have avoided him at all costs in my previous life. I'd have crossed the street just to avoid smelling the beer and cigarette smoke on his breath. I'd have prayed he didn't sit beside me on the bus and cursed my luck if he had. Now, I feel like his like equal; his brother, even.

"Hey, look who it is," he says with that welcoming grin on his face. "We were just talking about you."

I didn't even notice the other guys. Salman sits behind Mikey, and behind him another man, with bronze skin and a shaved head. They all look at me and grin and clap in my direction. I can't remember the last time I entered a room and elicited a reaction other than indifference.

"Here's the guy who took back Shahassi!"

They all clap again; even Dina gets in on the action, slapping her palms together with a wry smile, although her eyes are still suspicious.

"Thank you," I say, trying to hide the fact that this much attention instinctively embarrasses me. "First time lucky I guess!"

God, I sound like a bore; first time lucky? Maybe I can trot out a couple more cliches while I'm at it. Perhaps I could add that 'they'll have to kill me to stop me,' or that I 'don't want to live forever' or something equally corny.

Still, no-one seems to care apart from Dina. She stops clapping and crosses her arms. I suppose she noticed me using the L-word again.

Dina and I join them sitting at the table. Mikey pours us all a drink of something; it's brown and smells like vinegar. He later informs us it's beer. I put the plastic cup to my lips and regrettably let some of the liquid into my mouth. Stale, warm beer of a brand I couldn't identify if I tried. I swallow and let Vega worry about digesting it.

"So, captain Mahmoud was telling us," Mikey says, between gulps of beer so large I can only imagine he has no tastebuds. "The entire frontline moved forward yesterday. Shahassi is just the start; we're hoping to take a bunch more towns next week."

"Oh, cool," I say, before burying my head in the cup and taking another wretched gulp. "Do we know why they'd abandon that village yet? Or why they'd send four guys back for it?"

"They abandon villages when it suits them," Dina replies. "Sometimes they lack the manpower to hold onto it. Sometimes the frontline moves and they don't want to be surrounded."

"And sometimes," Mikey interjects, "it's a trap."

"They'd have sent more men if it were a trap. Heavier equipment. Armor maybe." Dina shakes her head. She hasn't touched her beer; I guess she doesn't drink. "Those guys were probably just recon or they came back for something they'd left behind."

Salman, Dina, and the other guy begin talking in Aljarrian or another language I can't identify. Mikey leans back in his chair, drinking the last of his beer. I take another sip and try to maintain my composure in the face of absolute disgust.

"So, right," Mikey says, slamming his empty cup on the table. "They're gonna host a barbecue tonight to celebrate our gains, and then we move the camp forward next week."

"We're moving the camp already?" I ask the question, but I'm not sure why. It just spills out of my mouth. It's not like I'm particularly wedded to this tent, although I much prefer it to my old hangout of derelict buildings.

"Gotta be movin' forward, always. We take each town, drive Darida's thugs out, and eventually we march on the capital."

My stomach grumbles. Only now do I recall the other thing he just told me.

"Wait, a barbecue?"

Mikey laughs and picks up his cup, before placing it down again, seemingly forgetting he just finished it.

"You've never been in the army, huh."

He says it as though it's obvious that going to war would involve copious amounts of barbecue. I finish my beer and ask Mikey if he'll find us another, despite the taste.

I'm enjoying myself. I feel like I'm part of something. And I feel like, for the first time in my life, I really mean something to the world.

CHAPTER 34

It's dark, and evidently it's party time.

Someone, somewhere managed to dig out a bunch of torches – a kind of Middle-Eastern tiki torch – which are arranged haphazardly around the center of camp. Beer, wine, and soda flows freely, and we haven't even got the barbecue started yet.

Mikey's already shirtless, wearing just an apron. He's swigging beer, dancing around an ice box. Someone is playing a strange-looking pear-shaped guitar, and the mood is jovial. All the higher-ups – the captain, the lieutenant – are nowhere to be seen yet, but seeing as we're all volunteers I guess we get to do what we want.

There's a group of around 30 people – a lot of men and some women. A few are dancing, some are stood in circles chatting and laughing. I count a lot of smiles on a lot of faces. These people seem to think we're winning the war.

I sit a few meters removed from it all on a wooden bench. I'm not exactly a graceful dancer, but I'm enjoying the evening breeze combined with the ambient heat from the torches. The swaying, pirouetting flames remind me of sitting by my grandfather's fireplace when I was a kid before mom lost her life and dad lost his mind.

I stare longingly into the fire. I lose myself, and I'm transported suddenly back to that dank, dreadful subway tunnel. The subway train broken and bent into dangerous angles by the force of the bomb, and the windows consumed by flames, licking outwards and upwards. The cries, the screaming…

I shake myself out of it, tearing my gaze away from the fire. This is the consequence of spending any time by myself: stoking the embers of the past.

Standing up from the bench, I think to go over and give Mikey some words of encouragement but seeing him and a bunch of others standing over a barbecue, pouring gasoline over the coals, I decide to let him get on with it.

Instead, I look behind him, beyond the circle of torches, and see Dina. She's sitting alone, staring into the flames. Or perhaps staring into another world, just beyond them. I quickly realize I just did the same.

I walk over to her – past the torches and a group of dancing soldiers – and sit on the bench beside her. She doesn't notice me at first; she's staring into the flames and rolling her locket between her fingers absent-mindedly.

"Hey Dina," I say, hoping to get her attention. She looks away from the flame at last. "Not dancing then?"

"No," she says with a wry smile. "Not my scene."

"What was your scene?" I ask after a couple of moments, "I mean, before the war?"

She looks at me improbably; like she didn't expect me to ask the question. When she does, I see the fires dancing in her large brown eyes.

"I really didn't have time to do anything besides my education," she says with a sigh. "I was in my third year of medical school. My mother was at the same university in the languages department. We hung out a lot."

She plays with the locket around her neck again, opening it and then closing it as if by muscle memory.

"I mean, I was just a teen, ya know? I was lucky enough to understand English, so I could enjoy all of the movies." She laughs, as if remembering something embarrassing. "I even played in a band. Didn't exactly go down well in the traditionalist suburbs, but my mother was always supportive."

She pauses again; I can tell this is difficult for her.

"This country wasn't exactly a great place before the war," she goes on to say. "Darida ruled brutally. No one was really free. But you could be happy. We were happy."

"I can't imagine what it's like," I say, trying to sympathize with her. "But, feeling the mood here tonight, it feels like we're winning."

"Maybe," she says, brushing her hair away from her face. "And then what? We spend the rest of our lives rebuilding, hoping that whoever we install in Darida's place, whether it be Cantara or some other politician, is charitable enough to let us live our lives in peace?"

I'd never thought of what happens after Darida is ousted. I just wanted to come here to help depose a tyrant, but I'd never considered that for the people living here, the story doesn't end there.

"You don't trust the rebels to put someone decent in Darida's place?"

She looks into the fire again.

"I don't trust anybody to do the right thing anymore."

"So why do you fight?" I ask, trying to decode her. "If you have no hope in this country's future, why fight at all?"

"Because I'm angry," she says, succinct and emotionless. I can't think of a response; she sums it up perfectly. Maybe if I wasn't such a gutless coward when my mother died, I'd have been angry too.

"I've got a question," I finally say, breaking the silence after a few awkward moments. "What's inside your locket?"

"Oh," she says, seemingly only just now aware that other people can see it. "This?"

She twists and turns it between her fingers again.

"Yeah, I see you holding it, and I—"

"Nothing," she says, interrupting me. "Look, it's empty."

She opens it, and sure enough, it's entirely empty. A circular locket with nothing inside.

"My mother always wore a sapphire ring, kind of a family heirloom," she says with palpable reluctance in her tone, "the same morning she went to work for the last time, the gem broke off the ring. Loosened over time or something like that."

I listen patiently.

"When she didn't come home, I found the sapphire and put it in this locket. Back then, I hoped to give it back to her."

"So," I say after a few moments, "where is it?"

She pauses; if I didn't know better, I'd think she was about to shed a tear.

"I lost it. I was on a supply run a couple of months ago 100 miles from here. Fell out of the locket and lost in the desert. Probably buried under a foot of sand by now."

She exhales and slaps both of her palms onto her knees, as if to draw a line under this whole conversation.

"So now I just have the locket. A reminder of a reminder."

She stands, gives me a small, playful salute, and walks away back into the camp and into darkness.

I think about everything she said. I don't have anything of my mother's; I can't even think of many pictures that still exist from back then. When she died, I spent my childhood sliding into gloom and apathy; Dina picked up a gun.

I'm distracted from my thoughts by a great pillar of fire, and the hooting and hollering of Mikey and the rest of the barbecue boys. I guess they managed to ignite the coals, gasoline and all.

I stand up and queue behind a bunch of guys for a bread

roll. Mikey's enjoying himself; laughing and dancing in front of the barbecue, sticking a bunch of sausages and burgers on the grill.

The rest of the night is spent speaking to Mikey, trying to communicate with the guys who don't speak much English, drinking this terrible beer, and eating hot dogs. Dina spends the night alone; I'd worry about her, but I know she'd hate that.

I feel that warmth again; the feeling of being close to these people. Sure, I had friends at school; we'd gather in the corners at breaktime, talking videogames and TV and the like, but I never felt I truly belonged. My life always felt so brittle, like I could drop dead at any moment. What's the point of making friends?

Now I'm here, I feel like I belong to something. The weather is hellish; occasional sandstorms; cold, dark nights, and heat during the day that'll melt the soles of your boots. The food is terrible; the beer is stale; most of these guys don't speak my language, and someone tried to kill me yesterday.

So how come I feel more alive than ever before?

CHAPTER 35

The next morning I'm awoken from a mercifully dreamless slumber by Mikey's infectious laughter in the room next door.

I take a few minutes to wake up before slowly sliding out of bed and sauntering over there.

Mikey is defying the laws of physics and displaying no indication that he's hungover. He's shirtless, banging a bottle of water on the table, making a strange noise like one I'd imagine a pterodactyl or other long extinct dinosaur made. Maybe he's still drunk

"Game day, bro!" he shouts in my direction.

I'm too tired to work out what 'game day' is right now. Luckily, he goes on to explain.

The camp is moving soon. But we needn't worry about that, because we're being sent on a new recon mission. As the frontline moves forward, Darida's men begin to abandon more towns, either because they consider them strategically unimportant or they lack the manpower to keep hold of them.

"Or they've managed to suck every last bit of worth out of it and left the town a smoking hole in the ground," he adds.

So we're being sent in to investigate. We've got to find out if there are any of Darida's goons left, find out if there are any civilians still living there, and report back.

But what Mikey is really so happy about – why he's making ungodly noises and slamming the table with glee – is that our success the other night has gotten him a promotion of sorts.

As part of the informal 'foreign legion' of English-speaking volunteers here, we don't have ranks per se. But, Mikey tells me, we'll be assigned a bigger squad with Mikey in charge and Dina his deputy.

"This is it, brother. Leading from the frontline, socking Darida in the mouth, one town at a time!"

He's delighted. I'm delighted for him. He grabs me, wrapping his arms around me, and squeezing. Is this what it feels like to be a 'bro'?

"Ahem," someone says sheepishly. I turn around and wrench myself from Mikey's grip to see Dina stood at the door – her arms crossed in that pose we all know and love – interrupting our traditionally American show of fraternal love.

"And here she is," Mikey says, his eyes lighting up again. "my deputy!"

Dina doesn't uncross her arms, but she does feign a smile.

I go to get a shower – enjoying the cold water on a blistering hot autumn day – before getting another set of clothing. Then we attend a briefing for the recon mission ahead of us, and we're given the opportunity to tuck into a tasteless ration as we do so.

There, Captain Mahmoud explains the mission: Kolajje is a small town that before the war was populated by more than 400 people. It's a former mining settlement, where coal would be mined from the veins deep underneath the town. However, the coalmining operation was ceased in the 80s and the town dwindled in size.

We're told the town would make a great place to situate

the basecamp, and that if it really has been abandoned as reports indicated, we must strike and take it back immediately. Seems simple enough.

I'm given an assault rifle for the first time. Mikey spends 20 minutes going through the basics; loading, unloading, and safe use. The rifle itself is old – there's small bits of rust along the barrel of the gun – but I'm told it works just fine.

"Besides," Mikey says with a cheeky glint in his eye, "you have most of your fun with the stock, right?"

I guess he has a point. I make a point to keep it unloaded until we get there. The last thing I want is to accidentally blow my balls off in the car, and then have to explain to everyone how I can miraculously grow them back.

Mikey then gives me a canteen full of water and an old walkie-talkie with Cyrillic lettering on it. It looks like something out of a crappy 80s Cold War action film.

We walk to the entrance of the camp and meet our squad for the first time. A few faces I recognize – Salman and a couple of guys from the barbecue – but most of them are new. There are 15 men and three women stood in slapdash military gear, swaying on the spot as if they're crops blowing in the wind.

Mikey addresses them in English – we're told everyone assigned to us speaks it – and gives them the plan: that we'll approach in four different cars from four different directions and co-ordinate our efforts to surveil the town for enemy activity, and then clear each building for enemy combatants and traps.

"Good luck folks!" he yells as we all begin packing the four cars. They're pretty beat up; I can see bullet holes in the door of one of them. Still, it's not as though we're a well-funded operation; we're a rebel insurgency. I didn't expect to be riding a limousine into battle when I got here.

Mikey sends Dina to lead one of the teams, Salman the

other, and a Spanish man I haven't met before named Estevez to lead the third.

"Kris, this is Abbas," he points to the shaven-headed man I saw in the tent yesterday, before pointing to another man, with a large beard and fierce eyes, "and Fadi. We're all riding together today."

We get into our car – a beat-up two door, four-seater of presumably Russian import – and set off.

"Abbas here was a famous actor, you know," Mikey says, wrestling with the gearbox of the car. "Before all this went down."

The car shudders into motion, kicking up a cloud of dust behind us. The engine sounds like a transformer being drowned in a bathtub.

"Ehh, I don't know about famous," Abbas says in broken English, leaning back in his seat. "I was on a show, Love and War. A daily show."

"Like a soap?" I ask, wondering if I'm traveling with Aljarrian television royalty here.

"A soap, yes."

"He got a medal from Darida," Mikey adds.

"Oh yeah?" I ask. "What's he like?"

"How you say, boring."

He tells me the cast was invited to the presidential palace and Darida held a banquet for them, speaking about nothing but Hollywood movies, before giving them all a cheap-looking medal of presidential freedom. Then he disappeared with the female cast, and the male cast was kicked out of the palace. I guess politicians are the same the whole world over.

"And you met Cantara too, right Abbas?"

He nods.

"What's she like?" Mikey asks.

"Busy."

I'd read a little about Cantara before I flew out here. A daughter of the last democratically elected president, she was living in exile until the civil war kicked off. Now she's back, trying to rally support for the rebellion.

I've seen posters depicting a woman with long, black curly hair, in inspirational speaking poses back at basecamp. I hadn't paid much attention until now, but it occurs to me she's one of the images of inspiration around here. The possibility of a modern, benevolent leader.

"You trust her?" Mikey asks Abbas, who's drumming some song out on the dashboard.

"Who else is there?" Abbas replies.

We're in that car – sputtering along, praying the engine doesn't give up the ghost – for another hour. I begin to feel the adrenaline again; my fingers trace the metal of the body of my rifle, up and down. We pass a bottle of energy drink around the car reminding me of Tomas and his boozy drug deal. And then, as I drink the last drops, we get as close to Kolajje as Mikey allows.

"All right, we're approaching from the west," Mikey says after sticking the handbrake on and turning the engine off. "The others will approach from the north, south, and east."

We climb out of the car, grab our rifles and bags from the trunk, and begin walking.

The sky is overcast right now; it's one of the first days I've been here that I haven't been able to see the sun.

A battle was fought here. Among the remorseless, rocky desert that I've come to know and love lie burned out Humvees turning to rust; craters now half-filled with dirt and sand, and trenches dug into the earth.

Looking out, there are tens, maybe hundreds of these burned-out vehicles. Tanks – old Soviet ones you see in films with the turrets blasted off – and the pulverized remains of trucks and buggies. It looks like the remnants of a toy battle between two clumsy, juvenile gods.

"It looks like someone fought to keep hold of this town," I

point out to Mikey as we come to a stop by one of the trenches. "Why would they give it up so easily?"

"Hard times for Darida, huh?" Mikey says, retrieving a set of binoculars out of his rucksack. "We got them running scared."

He hands me the binoculars, and I look upon the horizon. It's difficult to see – there's a haze of smog or dust in the distance – but after some time I can pick a few buildings with blasted-out windows and blackened, charred roofs.

"Looks like a graveyard," I say, turning back to Mikey and lowering the binoculars. "No sign of anything alive."

The other man with us – Fadi – looks at me with intensity in his eyes. He doesn't say anything at first, but I can't help but wonder if I've offended him.

"Don't call it graveyard," he says, finally, in slightly broken English. I look at him, understanding his meaning, and then nod in his direction appreciatively. I forget that a lot of these people had family here once.

We wait for a period of time, then take a walk closer, ducking behind the long-since abandoned skeleton of a supply truck. After we all confirm that the town looks empty, we communicate with the others and tentatively begin our approach.

We agree to take the west of the town, clearing every building, checking for signs of life or life-endangering traps. The four of us move methodically through the streets, our rifles raised, checking every building for activity. The more we search, though, the more we see that the hope of finding anyone still alive and living here would be way too optimistic.

Every other building is blackened and burned out by fire or incendiary shelling or some other hellish assault. Every schoolyard and parking lot ripped asunder, crammed with craters. Every shopfront blasted of its glass and looted.

Mannequins sit in the windows, riddled with bullet holes, seemingly used for target practice.

We find a dentist's surgery with the roof shelled and caved in; we find a once proud home, now lying in pieces with a burned out APC driven through it. We find a hospital with every building, department, and ward desecrated, looted of any valuable-looking equipment and left as rubble.

"Jesus," Mikey finally says, looking upon a stack of hospital beds piled 12 feet high and set alight in a giant bonfire. "They really did leave us nothing."

Deeper within the hospital, we find our first corpse. One of Darida's men, according to Mikey, dead of a shrapnel wound. He's curled into the fetal position, lifeless and harmless. Still, it's a shocking sight.

"Looks like they forgot someone," Mikey says, examining the nametag before losing interest and forging ahead.

We soon clear every room in the hospital and make it outside, and agree to meet the other teams in the center of town. There, we sit by the former city hall, which seems to have escaped the worst of the battle other than the typical broken windows and smashed furniture inside.

Dina's team is the first to rock up with tired, ashen faces, looking like they'd all seen ghosts.

"Did you find anyone?" Mikey asks, expectantly.

Dina hesitates before replying. "Not exactly," she finally says.

When the other two teams arrive, Dina leads us all past the railway station – a formerly bustling transport hub, exporting the coal mined here across the country – and to the outskirts of a town to the east. There, she leads us to what appears to be freshly dug soil, and the next thing I see turns my stomach.

A hand – its fingers bloodied and stretched in morbid directions – reaching out of the earth. It looks almost like a small, deathly tree poking out of the ground. And the disturbances in the soil around it feel like it's the first of many.

"A mass grave," Dina says, her voice emotionless and unwavering. "I think there was a ravine here. They probably just filled it with bodies and pushed the earth over."

We all look on in silence before Salman begins to walk the edges of the hastily moved dirt. I look up and see two crows nesting in a rooftop, making grim-sounding calls. Then I look over to see Abbas, wiping tears away from his eyes, before disappearing into a nearby house.

"This is graveyard."

I turn to see Fadi, pointing and shaking his head. My adrenaline from earlier is gone. Now I just feel a sober sense of shame and anger. I don't say anything; just meet his eyes with my own and shake my head too.

CHAPTER 36

"Well, I suppose it's mission accomplished," Mikey says, his rifle hanging from his shoulder and his arms crossed defeatedly. "For now, at least."

"The camp is already on the move," Dina says. "I've heard that an entire battalion is headed this way. Could be 1000 people headed down here. The leaders want to solidify this new territory and add it to our own."

I look around – at the devastation, the dust-filled craters, the bombed-out houses – and wonder what there is to add. Dina sees my quizzical expression and feels compelled to explain.

"This could be a defensible position for us. And if we get the rail network here running again, we can resupply the front line with ease. It was important to Darida once. Until this whole withdrawal."

Yeah, *the withdrawal*. I'm starting to get more and more suspicious about Darida's intentions. The mass graves, the bloodthirsty armies here one moment, gone the next, sometimes so quickly as to be unable to take home their dead.

"It won't be long now," Abbas says, his eyes reddened from his own tears. "Darida will be the one in the grave."

All of us suspect Abbas knew someone here, but so far none of us have dared ask him. Everyone's in a strange mood. Some of us are quiet and sullen – Mikey isn't even his usual brash self – whereas others seem barely able to contain their anger.

I can't get the hand – twisted, poking out of the dirt – out of my mind. I wonder how many other bodies are in that mass grave, and what Darida and his government are trying to cover up.

Everywhere I look, I see something that reminds me of the horrors of the last few days. There's a strange, dark brown spatter against one of the walls nearby. It could be paint, or then again it could be the telltale dark crimson of old, dried blood. I flash back to the man I killed and the dark, bloody mess of his balaclava…

I excuse myself from the group, telling Mikey I need to go for a walk. He gives me the usual platitudes about being careful, and I walk away from everyone, heading around the outskirts of town. I feel I need a different perspective on all of this.

"Vega," I say, watching the late afternoon breeze raise a cloud of dust across the horizon. "What do you make of all of this? Mass graves?"

Despotic regimes can be brutal. Especially so in times of war. Without an in-depth investigation there is little more to say.

I step across a set of rail tracks. They've been blasted at a couple of sections – warped and twisted by the damage – but Mikey seems to think we'll get trains running again with some repair work.

There's an old building composed of corrugated metal and empty panes, long since relieved of their glass. It looks like it was once used to house trains. I walk up to it and take a seat on the concrete indoors, escaping the harsh sun on the back of my neck.

There is something of note, though.

I sit up, anticipating what Vega has to say. Clues of secret weapons of mass destruction? Strains of a zombification virus hiding out here?

There's a lot of gunpowder residue – smokeless powder, to be exact – here. It's apparent in the sand, on the walls, and seems especially high in this hangar you're currently sitting in.

"Gunpowder residue?" I think about it and recall the hundreds of destroyed, burned-out vehicles nearby. "There was a battle nearby. It doesn't seem unusual."

Perhaps. But I'm detecting evidence of large amount of unburned, unused explosive primer. Ordinarily the gunshot residue would be burned in firing, but very recently this town hosted a massive stockpile of relatively fragile, unsafely secured ammunition. It might even still be here.

I stand back up and take a look around, my interest finally piqued. I follow the rail tracks out of the building and deeper into the desert. After 10 minutes of walking I see them descend a dune and meet a small cliff-face, plus a couple more buildings. In the cliff-face is an entrance to the underground, boarded up with scrappily constructed wooden planks.

"I guess this must be the entrance to the mine, right?"

Yes, it appears so.

I make the walk over there and take a look at the boarded-up entrance. The nails are new – they shine silver in the sun – and the wood hasn't long been exposed to the elements judging by the condition.

I place my palm against one of the planks and wait for Vega's response.

There's a lot of unspent primer residue here. I think there will be more beyond these planks.

I take a step back and look at the entire structure again. Then I take the crappy radio out, push a couple of buttons, and hope I get through to someone. To my shock and amazement, Mikey answers.

"I've got something you'll want to check out."

———

"Huh, so what am I looking at?" Mikey is scratching his head underneath his helmet before adjusting his sunglasses. It took him, Dina, and Fadi about 20 minutes to make it down here, and they're all looking confused as to why they bothered with the walk.

"This is the entrance to the mine," I explain, hoping to talk them round without mentioning that my fingertips can detect gunpowder residue. "Look, these nails, these planks, they're all new. Can't be older than a couple of days, right?"

Mikey looks at Dina. She shrugs but doesn't look completely opposed to my reasoning.

"Why would they board up this mine without leaving?" I ask, trying to tie this all together. "What are they hiding inside the mine that they don't want us to find?"

I can see I've asked Mikey a question he can't leave unanswered.

"Yeah, we should open it."

"Shouldn't we wait 'til the battalion gets here?" Dina asks. She has her arms crossed again, ever the killjoy. "I mean, there could be evidence of war crimes."

Mikey turns to her with a sly smile.

"Ahh c'mon, aren't you curious?" He begins trying to prize the planks off, but after a couple of attempts he gives up.

"We need a crowbar or—"

I interrupt him, quickly stepping up and beginning trying

to prize a plank off. I dig my fingers into the wood, sending a couple of splinters into my fingertips, but after a few moments of effort, I manage to prize it away and throw it to the ground behind me.

"Oh 'kay," he says, shocked at my strength. "I did not expect that."

I look at Dina, but she isn't impressed. Again, she's entirely suspicious of me.

"C'mon," I say, stepping up to prize out another plank. "Maybe I loosened it for you."

Mikey and Fadi begin pulling the planks off with me, sending nails flying as each is prized off. After a few more we see the dark at the end of the tunnel. After a couple more we can finally climb through.

"You can't honestly be going in there," Dina says with palpable disbelief.

"Why not?" Mikey asks, already sticking a foot through the exposed entrance. "Where's your sense of adventure?"

Dina looks on disapprovingly. I shrug at her and follow him into the mine. Inside, he switches his flashlight on and we begin to walk slowly into the depths following a series of cables that probably once carried power into the mining complex. It isn't long before we find something else, though.

"Huh," Mikey says, stumbling on something on the rocky ground. "Take a look at that."

He shines his flashlight downwards and I see something gold and shiny in the dirt.

"These are 7.62mm ammunition rounds, Soviet," Mikey says, and I see that they're barely shiny and gold after all. Instead, they look like the bullets I've been loading and unloading into my rifle. He picks one up and examines it closely. "They seem to be intact."

We press on, coming to a series of turns in the mine and a ladder. We climb down it with only Mikey's flashlight to guide our path. I should probably suggest we turn back –

maybe Dina was right to suggest waiting for reinforcements – but my curiosity gets the better of me.

The air is warm and acrid; there's a damp, pungent smell in the air, but also something I can't quite identify. It brings back memories of the fourth of July, somehow, and the cloudy haze of fireworks.

"The briefing said these mineshafts go all the way under town, right?"

"Yeah," Mikey replies, as we slowly saunter onwards. Then he pauses, shining his flashlight onto something in the distance. "What's that?"

I see something like a wooden pallet or crate, and beside it another one. When we draw closer, we see the entire mineshaft is full of them. Box after box, crate after crate, pallet after pallet.

Then I put my foot down into something that feels different from the uneven, rocky ground I've been used to. It feels almost like metallic gravel, shifting and clinking underneath my feet. Mikey evidently feels the same and shines the flashlight down to see dozens of unspent bullets. All different sizes, shapes, and colors.

"Wow," Mikey says, shining his flashlight into a nearby crate. "They must have used this place as an ammunition dump. Underground, easily defended from the town above, close to the rail network, it's perfect."

"So why'd they leave it behind?" I ask. I'm not exactly a master strategist – I couldn't even get a hang of how to play *Risk* – but even I know there are plenty of unanswered questions here.

"Beats me man," Mikey says as he continues walking forward with me following behind. "Maybe it was too much to carry. There could be millions of bullets, shells, and other explosives here. But one thing's for sure…"

He turns to me, placing his flashlight below his face, lighting it from below.

"It's a great find."

I look back at him uneasily. We come to a pause as Mikey pulls out his radio and begins to report our findings to the others. Only now, in the overwhelming darkness, do I remember I have a flashlight of my own: the cellphone Mikey gave me. I pull it out and use the flashlight function.

Taking a few more unsteady steps on jagged rock and loose bullets, I shine the light in my path and take a look at the crates on my own. There's Middle-Eastern lettering on the crates and each one seems to be at least three-quarters full of bullets or magazines full of bullets.

I walk a little deeper into the mineshaft and come upon something else: a larger crate, loosely sealed with a wooden lid. I force the lid off with ease and shine my light inside.

"Hey Mikey," I call out, "take a look at this."

"Oh, crap," he says when he gets here; I see his eyes widen. "Artillery rounds. I think those are 122mm shells."

They're large – five inches, perhaps – in an array of colors from green to red to metallic brass.

"This stuff could really come in handy for us," Mikey adds.

Kris, Vega says, with such vigor that I almost reply out loud. *What are those cables underneath the box?*

I shine my flashlight down, and sure enough Vega saw a couple of cables that I didn't: two white wires, bound together, snaking out of the bottom of the crate. I follow them along, and see a couple more join the bundle from another large box. I keep following the cables eventually coming to a large, metallic box almost like a fuse box.

"Mikey," I shout, my voice echoing across the rocky walls. "Here!"

He slowly makes his way over. I point out the cables and the box, and he scratches his chin. Then, he opens the fuse box, shines his flashlight inside for a moment, and suddenly ceases all motion.

"What's the matter?" I ask.

"Well," he hesitates, before slowly pulling his hands away from the box. "I think this is a remote detonator."

"A detonator?! That means…"

"I think this place is rigged to blow."

CHAPTER 37

I watch as the last few black buildings of Kolajje disappear behind the great cloud of dust our vehicle kicks up as we speed away from there.

Dina is speaking Aljarrian over the radio, frenetically pronouncing syllables of words I don't understand, repeating herself occasionally, and shouting occasionally. They almost sound like swear words.

The last hour has been a blur; Mikey and I took some very quick photos of everything we found before finding our way back to daylight and gathering the rest of the group as quickly as we could. Then, we all ran back to our vehicles and decided to race out of there and back to base camp as quickly as possible.

Dina suddenly ends her call and looks to me, Mikey, and Abbas in the car, exhaustedly.

"They're going to postpone the move to Kolajje, at least for now."

I feel a surge of relief. Everything I've seen today – the burned-out husks of tanks and vehicles; the blackened, destroyed buildings; the mass grave – has been a prelude to one, big, explosive final act. The detonation of the ammunition stores under Kolajje and the destruction of the entire town.

"I can't even believe he'd plan something like this," Dina says, rubbing her fingers against her temple. I look over at Abbas who sits next to me in the backseat, staring out of the window intensely, his eyes burning a hole in the glass. He looks way beyond tears now.

"I guess Darida knew he was laying a trap all along," I reply.

It makes sense in a twisted way. Everyone knows Kolajje is an important strategic location. Darida gets to hide evidence of his war crimes and the mass graves; he gets to kill thousands of rebels as we rush to take back the city, and he gets to blame us for blowing up the town as soon as we retake it.

"Those tunnels could go on for miles," Mikey adds, gripping the wheel as he speeds away into the dusk. "If all those tunnels are full of old ammo, there's no telling what the explosive power of it all will be. The entire town will be reduced to one smoldering crater."

When we reach base camp, I can see everything has been turned upside-down. Tents are half-dissembled, with tired-eyed soldiers slowly putting them back up. Men hang out of the back of trucks, throwing boxes back out of them, and we're greeted by an array of incredulous, frustrated expressions, like we just pulled the plug on everyone's new dream home purchase at the last minute.

We park up and head straight for Captain Mahmoud – sweaty and irritable – who yells at Dina in Aljarrian, who promptly yells back. Then she paces over to me, grabs the cellphone from my pocket, and shows him the pictures I quickly snapped of all the ammunition, the shells, and the fuse box.

His expression soon changes. He crosses his arms and softens his tone, before looking Mikey and I in the eyes ruefully. I feel like the prospect of your new camp going boom in the night will change your mind like that.

Everyone seems to be running around, bobbing up and down like emperor penguins, trying to make head or tail of this entire situation, but at this point I'm just tired. I tell everyone I'll be elsewhere in the camp if they need me, and walk to the showers hoping they haven't yet been disconnected from the well here.

They haven't, and I spend a good 15 minutes standing under the freezing cold water, washing off all of the dust and the dirt and the gunpowder residue and the decaying asbestos, and whatever else Kolajje imprinted on my skin today.

What Kolajje imprinted on my mind, though, will take a lot longer to wash clean.

When I get out and put some clothes back on, Dina is waiting for me outside.

"Kris," she says, her arms crossed as ever and her dark brown eyes inquisitive, "I feel like we've got some talking to do."

It's dark at this point; she's lit only by a couple of camping lights still left out, but I can see her stern expression perfectly well. I feel like I'm running out of time with her.

"Oh yeah?" I ask, hoping to disarm her before she explodes in my face. "It was a job well done today huh?"

She doesn't reply; she just harshens her gaze. I gather my towel and walk past her.

"You wanna talk?" I finally say without turning to face her. "Let's go to the firing range."

I hear her following me, and immediately feel that old, familiar feeling of dread in my stomach; a cold, tight knot of nerves that embeds itself below my sternum. I take a deep breath and try to put together what I'm going to say here.

She's been suspicious of me for a while. I don't think she

suspects me of being a 'superhero' as she's not stupid enough for that. Instead, she sees me for what I am; a strange, supposedly inexperienced American 20-something who turns up and miraculously finds himself at every right place at every right time.

Or, of course, the times I get shot, or wounded, and heal as if by magic. Not even a dent on the fender.

The 'firing range' is lit by one single camping lamp, knocked over by the wind. I pick it up, stand it the right way up, and sit beside it. Dina sits beside me with the lamp between us. The light illuminates her features, making her eyes and eyelashes stand out quite beautifully despite the demanding look on her face.

"Kris, you and I both know you're not a normal volunteer. You're not a regular, out of his mind American veteran with a death wish. You're not even some young volunteer who thinks he can change the world."

I swallow dryly. I'm dehydrated, but I haven't noticed until now. Being under Dina's intense, blazing-hot spotlight would dehydrate anyone.

"Look, I—" I try to interrupt her and regain my chance to shape the narrative, but she interrupts me.

"A young, physically strong American with a mysterious backstory, and an unusual introduction to us, designed to make us sympathetic to you. We find a man suffering gunshot wounds and left to die in the desert. How can resist taking you in?"

"Hey," I bark, trying to make my point. "That wasn't the first time you met me, you remember?"

"And then," she goes on, ignoring my protests, "he recovers almost overnight. Almost as if those gunshots were staged, right? We take that man out in the field, and he proves his worth by repelling a night-time assault, killing two of the bad guys with his bare hands and alerting us to the other two."

I open my mouth to argue, but quickly realize it's useless. She won't be deterred.

"This strange and marvelous man then uncovers a plot to destroy a town and obliterate our entire battalion, potentially saving 1000 lives. Why, he's amazing, how does he do it?"

"You know, everyone else thanked me."

"At first," she says, ignoring my smart little comment, "I thought you were CIA, either sent in to gather info on our side, to discretely help us, or just playing both sides for the hell of it. Who knows how decisions are made in the deepest, darkest corners of the CIA's imagination?"

"CIA?" I ask skeptically. I'm about as far from an international spy as I could imagine.

"But then," she says in a tone of voice that tells me she's close to revealing her big discovery. "I found this."

She holds a cellphone out to me; on the large, conspicuously undamaged screen sits a screenshot, and on that screenshot, a headline: one that I'm sadly too familiar with.

NINE DEAD IN SUBWAY BOMBING

"You died last week in the USA, Kris. It's right here."

She scrolls to the next screenshot and holds it close enough for me to see. Sure enough, that's my picture, next to my name, next to a paragraph reading that I died. That knot of dread in my chest is back and growing bigger with each passing moment.

"How did you find this?" I ask in disbelief, my vocal cords completely on autopilot. My mind quickly searches for an easy way out of this, but I know it doesn't exist.

"It's the first search engine result for your name, Kris."

She puts added poison into her pronunciation of my name. Like it's a cursed word: the name of a dead man.

Why didn't I keep Dyson's face? Or change my own, even just slightly? Why didn't I use a fake name? Why didn't I try to conceal the gunshot wounds, or let Dina treat them and take time to recover like a normal human being?

I mean, I know why: because I'm not CIA and I'm not smart. I'm a stupid kid who's doing all of this for the first time.

Somehow, I doubt Dina will accept that excuse.

"I didn't tell anyone about this," she then says. It almost sounds like she's throwing me a lifeline. "I wanted to get your story first."

"Well," I say after a few moments. "I can tell you first, I'm not in the CIA."

She raises her eyebrows briefly as if that's some great revelation. I briefly meet her eyes with my own and find them still as intense as ever, looking into me deeply. Searching me. Interrogating me. There's only one way out of this...

"I'm not CIA, I'm not a spy, I'm not a soldier, or any sort of agent of the United States. And I'm not dead, but that's obvious, right?"

She says nothing.

"Instead, I—" I pause, and try to think of a way to phrase it. "I, uhh, found something."

"Found something?" she repeats incredulously.

"Technology. Something that shouldn't have been here, that I shouldn't have found, but somehow made its way to me regardless."

I finally got her to change her expression. Now she looks at me like I'm crazy; she can't believe *this* is the cover story I've come up with.

"Look," I say, racking my brain for a better way of explaining this. "Like, tiny robots. Billions of them. A trillion, even. Living in my body. On my body. Able to make me into a superhuman."

"Nanomachines," she says, skeptically. "We've all seen sci fi movies, Kris."

I think of something. I look around, behind us and beside us both. Everyone's still re-assembling the camp, paying little attention to us.

"You've got a knife on you, right?"

She immediately looks at me suspiciously, and backs off a little while still remaining sitting.

"Dina, you can trust me. If I wanted to kill you, I could do it with my bare hands. I think I've proved that haven't I?"

She still has her eyes locked on me – part suspicion, part horror – but her hands move to a pocket on the thigh of her pants, unbuttoning it slowly, and withdrawing a switchblade. With a bit of reluctance – I'm sure I see her hand waver – she hands it to me.

I place my right hand on a rock beside us, lit by the camp light.

Kris, Vega says; I did expect some input from him. *Are you sure you want to do this?*

I ignore him and flip the blade out. It's three inches or so long, and hopefully sharp enough to do the job in one motion.

"Those gunshots weren't staged. I recovered from that subway bombing. I recovered from those gunshots, and I'll recover from this."

I place the blade down across my index finger horizontally. The blade is cold; I brace myself for the pain that will follow.

"Kris, Kris, what are you—"

I push down on the blade, making it about half way down at first, meeting something hard on the way down. I guess that's bone.

"Kris! Stop!"

I push harder and make it all the way down to the rock. Then I slide the knife upwards, separating my finger from the rest of my hand. Blood shoots out in spurts. The whole spectacle is enough to turn my stomach, and I can't even feel the pain yet. I can't imagine how Dina feels.

She grabs the finger and stands up, looking around her. I quickly grab the finger with my intact hand and hide it within my palm.

"Just calm down, just wait," I tell her, carefully planting it back onto the rock beside me. "The nanomachines will do, ya know, their thing. They just need a bit of time."

Someone within the camp yells something to Dina in their native tongue. I guess they heard the shouting. She looks at me apprehensively, then at my finger, and then yells back; it sounds almost like she's telling him there's nothing to worry about.

Slowly, hesitantly, she sits back down beside me.

"How long?" she finally asks. "How long until I force you back to camp and sew your finger back on?"

The network can sew the external tissues back together within 15 minutes. It'll be fully operational within an hour.

"About 15 minutes."

I move the bloody stump of my finger to meet the disembodied finger, and only then do I feel the pain. By now I'm used to it – the pulsating, throbbing sting; the leaden ache that underlies it all; the sensation of being able to move every ligament in my finger, despite the fact it's no longer connected.

"This is sick," Dina says, finally breaking the tension.

"You never really left medical school, did you?"

We wait together in an awkward silence. I hear her breathing heavily. I don't know if it's the image of my finger being cleaved away from my hand or her uneasiness of letting me do it in the first place, but she's more distressed than I've ever seen her.

"Wait," she says after a couple of minutes, standing up again. "At least let me get some disinfectant."

I grab the cuff of her jacket with my good hand.

"Not necessary."

And she sits back down again, slowly, uneasily.

"I've had fingers blown off repeatedly. This isn't my first right hand. It isn't even my second."

I look at her; her eyes are fixated on my finger and the

slowly drying blood around it lit in warm, golden light. A perverted, sickening candlelit date.

A few more minutes pass, but between the tension, the pain, and Dina's silent horror, it feels like an eternity. Eventually, I hear from Vega who tells me I should be able to pick my hand up by now.

"Okay, here's your moment of truth."

I pick my hand up from the rock – my disembodied finger, thankfully attached – and rotate it around in the lamp light. Dina watches: amazed or horrified, I can't tell anymore. She seizes my hand between both of hers, and examines the wound. Sure enough it's reattached, the formerly red, bloody clotting having now taken on a pinkish tone.

"This is impossible," she says, clearly not yet buying into the nanomachine excuse. "This requires stitches. Surgery."

"Time to leave medical school," I reply. "We're way past that now."

CHAPTER 38

I spend the night telling her everything: the dead body, Vega, the nanomachine network, my short abortive career as a crime-fighter. I tell her about the Quiet One, the parade bombing I managed to avert, and the subway bomb I couldn't. I tell her about the passport I stole and how I changed my face overnight.

"And now you're here," Dina says, quizzically. "Why?"

"Because I'm a nobody; I'm a loser. A kid who packages sandwiches for a living. And yet..." I look up; the stars are plentiful in the sky. "...and yet I find myself with all this power. All this potential. This *gift*. I'm the strongest, most effective fighter in the world. I've got to do something with it. I've got to try and help people, don't I?"

She doesn't soften her expression. If anything, she's more confused than before.

"And you found it from a dead naked man in an alleyway?" she says. I nod. "Who you suspect of being a time traveler, or at least not of this world or time?"

I nod again. She seems more fearful of me now; like I'm a ticking bomb waiting to go off. Like I'm a genie, and now I'm out of the bottle no one never get me back in. Her eyes are wary.

"Did you not think about how you acquired this technology?"

I pause; it's not the question I expected her to ask. I ask her what she means, exactly.

"I mean, aren't you worried?"

Worried? I've been worried for my entire life. I worried about my heart, I worried about school, I worried about my job, I worried about my dad, I worried about how long my life would be.

I didn't worry about the time-traveling nanobot technology that came to inhabit my body. Should I have?

I shake my head at her.

"You call it a gift, but it isn't. It's a debt" she says, her tone of voice grave and foreboding. "When you acquired that technology, you incurred a debt. You took something that wasn't yours, and someday, perhaps someone or some *thing* is going to want repayment on that debt. You understand that, right?"

I look at her and then down at the dirt. My index finger – my newly connected digit – has been tracing shapes in the sand the entire time.

"Did you not wonder why that technology came here? What the purpose of that man lying in that alley was? We don't know why, but there has to be a reason."

She makes a good point. I'd accepted Vega's word that he didn't know why the man – the original Vega – had ended up here. And then I'd assumed that it was a mistake; an accident.

"I always thought it was an accident. I mean, he was dead. What else am I supposed to think?"

Dina laughs. A low, regretful laugh, but a laugh nonetheless. She doesn't seem to do that often.

"You gave me an excuse for all of this that's way more chilling than you being part of the CIA, you know that?" She begins to rub the locket around her neck between her fingers again, opening it and closing it in quick succession. She looks like she doesn't even know she's doing it.

"But" I say after a few awkward moments, "at least I've been honest?"

She laughs again.

"Kris, thank you for your honesty." She stands up; this time I don't try to stop her. "I won't tell anyone else about this. You're a real live super soldier, and obviously we need you for the war effort."

She turns to leave before turning her head to face me one final time.

"And, for some stupid reason, I feel I can trust you."

She walks away.

Dina *trusts* me? She seems almost afraid of me. But at least she believes me; medical miracles are a compelling way of getting your point across. After all, as my dad is so fond of thinking, it worked for Jesus.

But there are no miracles. Not anymore. Just technology beyond anyone's wildest dreams.

"Hey, Vega," I say, looking down at the rock beside me with its spatter of blood and slight, horizontal cleaving indent. "What's a sapphire composed of?"

Aluminum and oxygen, mainly, along with some smaller trace elements.

"Beer cans are made from aluminum, right?"

I begin to wonder where those beers Mikey and the others were drinking the other night ended up.

Correct.

I stand up and move my index finger for the first time. It's slow and slightly painful, but it works already. Other than a diminishing pink horizontal scar, you'd never know I brutally chopped it off 45 minutes ago.

I take a walk back to the camp and begin rooting around in the dustbins that surround the canteen tents. It doesn't take me long to find a bunch of crushed-up cans. I grab a plastic bag, empty it of some foul-smelling food waste, and bag up six cans, crushed into circles. Then I go back to that tent I was calling home for the last few days.

Inside, Mikey is setting up the tables and chairs once again. I suppose they were taken down when everyone thought the camp was moving to Kolajje.

"Hey man," he says, greeting me warmly. "We did some great work tonight. We could have saved hundreds of lives."

"Yeah," I say, sheepishly. Dina's interrogation of my supernatural abilities still lingers in my mind. I can't afford to celebrate my own achievements too loudly.

"And it's all down to you, my friend!"

I feel my cheeks burning up; I've never been one to enjoy the limelight, and especially if the limelight could expose me as nanomachine-assisted superhero.

"It's a team effort Mikey, I couldn't have done it without you." I give him a good-humored salute before turning my back and walking to the bedroom beside us.

"What's that?" he asks, noting the metallic noises of the cans jostling together in my bag. "Couple of brewskis for a job well done?"

"Not exactly," I reply.

I get in the bed furthest from the fabric door and take the cans out one by one, stashing them under the bedsheet. I climb in, and then grab the cans, compressing them together as much as possible between my fingers.

"Okay Vega," I whisper, hoping not to alert Mikey. "Can you make a sapphire?"

I can.

Hopefully I can repay Dina for keeping my secret.

I turn over, trying to get comfortable, and close my eyes.

CHAPTER 39

I'm on a subway train again, only this time I know I'm dreaming.

I'm looking down the train, trying to see past the throngs of people – men, women, and children – standing around, nonchalantly trying to get on with their day. I crane my neck from side to side, trying to find some light at the end of the tunnel or whatever else will liberate me from this dream.

Then I hear a great, overwhelming bang. It isn't the loud, quick whip-crack of a bullet or a shell landing that I've grown used to. It feels larger than that. A great, thunderous roar of a million fireworks exploding all at the same time.

The walls on the subway train begin to shake; the people fall down beside me. I hold onto a pole for dear life, as everything rattles and breaks around me...

And then I open my eyes.

I'm back in the tent, and the fabric walls are blowing inwards, as if we're caught in some great storm. I jump out of bed and run to the door. It's the very crack of dawn; the sky is a watercolor mix of blues, reds, oranges, and yellows.

But that's not what grabs my attention first.

The huge mushroom cloud on the horizon is what I see rising high into the sky. A black, angry blot on the otherwise beautiful sky. I can't see where it began, but I certainly have a very good guess.

I see folks running outside to look for the source of the noise. People half-dressed stare in dreamlike disbelief and soldiers on guard stand dumbfounded. Everyone seems to know that what we're seeing is a town going up in smoke.

Mikey emerges from the tent, looks up with sleepy eyes, and crosses his arms.

"Well," he says, his voice tired and an octave lower. "I guess it happened, then."

He goes back into the tent and I follow.

Then I remember what I was doing prior to putting my head down.

I quickly make my way back to my bed and find a pile of metallic dust and shavings, like someone had put those six cans through an industrial shredder. I dig through the pile, and inside find a small blue sapphire.

I hold it up to the small amount of light filtering through from outside; it's slightly dirty, but I can see the light shimmer and dance within it like an endless ocean. I clear the pile of dusty metal pieces from my bed and pocket the sapphire.

Inside the main room of the tent, Mikey is already pouring himself a coffee. He's wearing a dirty white vest; I can see those names and dates tattooed across his arms again.

"Rise and shine," he says with an element of sarcasm in his voice.

I smile at him and rub my eyes. Then I head back outside. The mushroom cloud is still there, higher in the sky and a lighter shade of grey than before. I look around and see the faces of the men and women gathered to see it.

It's a strange mood. Some are clearly experiencing feelings of relief; they're not the ones sat directly above the source of that explosion. Hopefully, no-one is. They smile and joke between themselves. Others are more subdued; a man I can't name wipes tears from his face.

Another is frenziedly shouting words I can't understand, other than one: Darida.

When I walk back to the tent, Mikey greets me with a cup of that putrid coffee. I take it, knowing that whatever it's made of will at least be rendered nutritious by my stomach. I take a seat and Mikey sits across from me.

"Well, I gotta say," Mikey breaks the silence, "as a marine, it feels weird to be saving people from a huge explosion rather than causing it."

I smile at his gallows humor and slurp my coffee.

The rest of the morning is spent downing coffee, eating bags of Middle-Eastern potato chips, and speaking about what comes next. Dina ducks in and out, telling us the captain and lieutenant are rolling around the camp, trying to get word on what happens now.

Eventually, sometime around 10:00 AM, Dina returns to the tent and tells Mikey and I that we're wanted elsewhere.

"And you'll need to pack a bag."

"A bag?" I ask, relieved to be getting the chance to get out of here. "Are we moving the camp now?"

"No," she replies. "We're taking a trip to Rachiya."

I think I remember reading the name of that city in my research. Mikey certainly recognizes it; he claps his hands and laughs joyously.

"Finally," he exclaims, "someone is taking notice."

"What? Who?" I ask, completely in the dark as usual.

"The rebel leadership," Dana says, with noticeably little joy in her voice. "Cantara."

She explains that the four team leaders of the four recon squads that explored Kolajje – Mikey, Dina, Salman, and the Spanish guy – are being invited to Rachiya for recognition of their great insight into uncovering the trap. And furthermore, the team member who first discovered the suspiciously boarded-up mine is invited too.

"You," Dina says to me, with one eyebrow raised.

I feel a rush of excitement, but it doesn't last long. The threat of the limelight looms again.

"We're going at twelve," Dina adds, before taking her leave.

Mikey seems excited enough; he begins rooting around for a rucksack, telling me eagerly that he's never met a famous leader before.

"Famous leader?" I ask, slightly worried about the potential for all of this to reach the world's press. One week I'm a terrorist's accomplice – and dead – and the next I'm a war hero?

I try to put it out of my mind for now and leave Mikey to his own devices while I go on the hunt for a rucksack I can borrow and some clothes I can pack it with. After all, it's not like I have any clothes or possessions here. I travel light.

———

At lunchtime we all meet at the edge of the camp with our bags on our backs; me, a tired-looking but dutiful Dina; an enthusiastic Mikey; a nonchalant Salman, and Estevez, the Spanish volunteer I've barely met.

I see that we get an upgrade on the vehicular front. No more scratched up, sputtering hatchback. We get an armored, tan Humvee with a large grill in the front, adorned with various badges and bows tied around it. The windows are small and dimmed, and the wheels huge with sand embedded in the tire tracks.

"So, what's the big deal here?" I ask to a clearly unenthused Dina as we pack the Humvee. "Like, why bring us all the way to the big city and commend us in person?"

Dina looks at me with a caustic expression; she evidently

feels the same way. It almost feels as though she thinks a medal won't be the end of it.

"I don't know," she says, getting in the back of the Humvee. "Maybe we're very lucky. Or maybe it's the opposite."

The opposite of very lucky? I follow her inside and sit beside her and Salman. Mikey drives and Estevez sits beside him in the front; I brace myself in my seat as the engine roars to life.

"Just don't expect things to be the same after this," Dina says ominously. "We're so-called heroes now, with all the crap that entails."

"If you don't want to be a hero," Mikey says, tapping his fingers against the steering wheel as if he's drumming out a beat, "why fight at all?"

"I fight for revenge," she says in a cold monotone. "Not to be a hero. Not to be famous. Not for some hokey leader."

"What's the matter Dina?" Salman says in his thick accent. "You don't like Cantara?"

"I don't like any politician," she replies, tersely, "especially one who was never elected, who never fought, and whose only claim to power is nepotism."

Geez, Dina is a tough crowd.

"You don't think the people need a figure to gather around?" Estevez asks, "to inspire them? To show them what's possible if Darida is defeated?

Dina snorts, and looks out of the window at the dirty, dusty sand dunes passing us by. I take a look behind us and see the camp disappearing in the distance. Then I check my pocket in a panic and confirm that the sapphire I had the nanomachines craft is still in my possession.

I see the camp disappear completely and replaced by a cloud of dust kicked up behind us, a sight I'm beginning to get used to. Then I figure this may be the last time I see it. It'll have surely moved on by the time we get back, as was the plan.

I can't help but feel like I'll miss that camp if I never return. The sandstorms that whip abrasive particles into your eyes until you're blinded. The putrid coffee and horrific, cardboard-flavored MREs. The wiry beds that feel like lying on nails. All of those things felt homely to me. I was somewhere that accepted me.

Mikey begins humming to himself. He's still in a good mood. Of course he wants to be a hero. But even that wouldn't satisfy him. He lives for the adrenaline, for the rush of battle, for the camaraderie. He wants to feel like he's fighting for the good guys, forever.

Similarly, I don't know when Dina will stop fighting either. What will it take? Her hands wrapped around Darida's neck? Nothing will bring her mother back and she knows it. So, I believe she lives in limbo, waiting for that moment of revenge that will most likely never satisfy her. She'll fight, and she'll fight, and she'll fight, and seemingly never tire.

I sit here with my nanomachine infused blood and super-optimized muscle fibers, and yet both of them are way more heroic than me.

CHAPTER 40

When we reach Rachiya after some six hours on the road, it's nothing like I'd expected. Before the war, it was the third largest city in Aljarran and it was the first city to rebel against the government.

The first thing I notice is the hustle and bustle. There are cars on the roads and people in the streets. Buildings are four or five stories high in varying states of repair but none of them lying in ruins. Streamers and banners span the space high above the roads, with various messages and one picture: that of Cantara.

Occasionally we drive around a crater in the road or a building recently burned out, no doubt from one of Darida's errant bombs or missiles. But I also see the steely resolve in people's faces; the desire to get from A to B and to live their lives without fear.

It's the first time I've seen such a place in Aljarran, and it's inspiring.

It's almost dusk by the time we get here; streetlamps turn on slowly or flicker, and I can see traders walking home with trolleys full of goods and crates. I even see children playing in the street, kicking a soccer ball around, despite mopeds trying to weave between them. The air is rich with exhaust fumes, something I haven't smelled since the city.

Rachiya's architecture is like a beautiful, broken gemstone. Huge glassy domes and windows adorn most buildings – some smashed, some sparkling clean, and plenty in between – as well as picturesque arches and mosaics. Every so often I see one destroyed or burned almost beyond recognition, bringing me back to the cold reality.

We're far out of artillery range, but I do remember reading about airstrikes earlier in the war. Darida's planes have been decimated since then – shot out of the air by dogged rebel defense – but the reminders of the destruction they once wrought is everywhere.

"So what's the plan?" I finally ask as Mikey carefully steers between cars. "Where do we go from here?"

"Honestly, I don't know," he answers, pulling up at a red light. "We were told to go to a hotel here. There's a presidential residence– one of Darida's old ones – but it's just for show. Cantara is too smart to actually go there."

"How come?" I ask, rather naïvely.

"Because Darida would hit it as soon as she steps in the door," Dina replies.

Finally we pull up to a sparsely populated parking lot boasting a couple of nicely sized craters in the tarmac. This area is dimly lit; the dusk sun doesn't reach this far, and every building around is taller than six stories, seeming to arch inwards like grasping trees in some haunted forest. Seems perfect to hide away.

I get out of the vehicle and look around; there's the remnants of what could have been a luxury hotel here, but the signage is beaten up and missing a few letters. Instead of a doorman, we're greeted by sandbags and a man in military fatigues standing guard.

We unpack the Humvee and walk slowly towards the

guard. Dina says a few words in their language and shows a couple of papers, and we're let in by the dour-faced man.

"This is a hotel?" I ask, looking around. What was obviously once an opulent reception – with gold upholstery and chandeliers – is now covered in military regalia. Slogans spray-painted on the walls, banners hung from light fixtures, and wooden crates piled high.

"Surely you noticed we're at war?" Dina replies sarcastically. "War changes everything. Nothing remains untouched."

I guess it wouldn't be an authentic Aljarrian experience if I didn't get roasted to within an inch of my life by Dina.

We're led through the reception, up a flight of stairs past a non-functional elevator, and led to a former meeting room – once used for business discussions and functions, but now full of maps and whiteboards with inscrutable arrows and diagrams scrawled on them. Curiously, they didn't remove the opulent satin curtains.

There, we sit on some chairs and wait 10 minutes or so before an Aljarrian military man – wearing tan fatigues and a black beret – marches in with panache, salutes us, and speaks for way too long in Aljarrian. I can't understand a word, so I watch Dana's emotionless face and as a result gain no more insight.

Eventually, he leaves, and the non-Aljarrians amongst us crowd around Dana to find out what was said.

"He says welcome to alpha base; there's a banquet tonight," she says, way more succinctly than the military man put it, "followed by a meeting with Cantara."

"Banquet?" Mikey is already interested; he's rubbing his hands together and licking his lips in a cartoonish display of hunger. "I've eaten nothing but rations, bread, and potato chips for months."

Even Dana manages to crack a smile. Salman immediately whips his cellphone out and begins texting, and my own stomach produces a rumble in anticipation. Mikey sits back on his chair and begins leaning back on the rear two legs in quiet satisfaction.

I've lived in squalor for the past week. I've been dirty, dusty, and bloodied, and can't remember the last meal I ate that didn't taste like peppered cardboard. And now we're being treated to a 'banquet'?

We pass the time until another military man – smaller than the last – wearing the same outfit comes to get us. Then we follow him to a larger room: a banquet hall, obviously used within the former hotel for that purpose, but now emptied of all of its furniture and character other than one long table in the center.

Yet again the room is decorated with large banners depicting Cantara and various slogans. The same luxuriant satin curtains are still there, and the wallpaper is impressively patterned, although dirtied in places.

"So, do we dine with Cantara, or—"

Our guide beckons us to sit; the five of us do so, and then he disappears from the room.

"I don't know," Dina says, "it all feels very weird, doesn't it?"

I feel like we're VIP visitors to an abattoir, treated to eat the wonderful meats it produces, but forbidden to go into the factory and see the real horrors.

"Whatever man," Mikey says, leaning back on his seat again. "I just want to eat a real meal for a change."

After a few minutes, a man in chef whites brings out a number of dishes for us – no menu, but we didn't need one of course. We tuck in; starters of fish and salad; mains of chicken, beef, and potato, and desserts of some sort of Middle-Eastern sweet biscuit. Dina tells me the name and I immediately forget it.

The food is, of course, mind-bendingly awesome. I'm barely even conscious while eating it; I enter a trance and shovel as much into my mouth as I can manage. Back home, restaurant fine-dining was never to my taste, but right now I feel like I'm as big a foodie as you'll ever hope to meet

As I'm finishing the dessert, I look over and see Dina idly pushing her dessert around on the plate with a fork. I get the feeling she isn't quite as enthusiastic about this as I am.

"Dina," I say, looking over to her, as the chef comes back to clear our plates and put them on a trolly. "What's the matter? Not to your taste?"

"No, I suppose you could say that," she says at first. After thinking about it for a bit, and waiting for the chef to depart, she continues: "Doesn't it bother you that we're being served a three-course meal here? Some towns are struggling to feed their citizens."

"Dina, it's one meal, dude," Mikey quickly intercedes. "We could have saved a 1000 lives. Soldiers, fighting men and women. Aren't we allowed to celebrate?"

She doesn't respond, she just continues pushing the biscuit around.

Salman and Estevez talk about something or other, and Mikey closes his eyes, enjoying the feeling of being gluttonously full, I guess.

In 10 minutes or so, we're summoned by yet another military man – one with a large, gnarly facial scar over one eye – and asked to get to our feet and follow him.

We walk through a number of corridors and climb a couple of flights of stairs. We pass by the former hotel's gym, full of grunting, sweating soldiers, and past a bunch of former hotel rooms, now doubling up as small barracks and offices.

I now see that beyond the dining room the hotel is a hive of activity, with soldiers and bespectacled plain-clothes administrators pacing the corridors, carrying reams of documents and laptops and other devices.

I feel as if the entire war could be planned from this building, and yet nothing is bolted down here. Everyone looks like they could drop everything and move to another safehouse at a moment's notice.

We're ferried like cattle deeper into the building, finally being deposited inside a waiting room of sorts filled with chairs and a drinking fountain. There, we're patted down by two, large Aljarrian men who remind me of the bouncers back home. Dina loses her knife, and I'm lucky not to lose the sapphire, which they don't seem to notice.

After another 10 minutes, sitting in uncomfortable silence together – all of us probably trying to think of an appropriate way to greet Cantara – we're finally summoned through a set of large, ornate wooden doors. We walk through another corridor – decorated with red walls and paintings I'm walking too quick to look at – and finally reach one more door.

Another large bouncer-like man opens it for us, and I'm wondering just how many corridors exist in this building. What I instead find behind the door is a small room with that same red wallpaper and a large wooden desk, and behind that a small-statured woman with black curly hair. I immediately know who it is.

She stands up with a smile on her face and greets us in the native language. She looks a little different to how she appears on the banners and posters; she has bags under her eyes and her skin is paler than it appears on the propaganda. She looks tired – entirely fitting for a wartime leader – but her eyes are full of intensity.

Salman salutes her. Dina follows suit, somewhat reluctantly. Mikey and Estevez do the same, and I'm the last; I'm unsure exactly how a salute is meant to work, but I try to mimic what I see in the movies.

The woman wears a green jacket, embellished with several badges which I presume are military insignia. She's older than I expected – maybe late thirties to early forties – but even without her propaganda reinforcement field, she carries an indescribable aura about her, like seeing a movie star or a notorious mafia boss.

She's small, Vega chimes in to say, *but don't let that fool you. She must have acted decisively and ruthlessly to rise to a position of leadership within the rebels.*

"And to our western friends," she says, addressing Mikey, Estevez, and I, "I am Cantara Hafeez, and I am in your debt."

She speaks English very well with a slight American accent. She walks around the desk and approaches us to shake our hands. I'm conscious of the burly soldier standing behind us still – I can almost feel his eyes burning a hole in the back of my neck – so I wait patiently for her to shake Mikey's hand before approaching her myself.

After we've all shaken hands and exchanged pleasantries, she goes back behind the desk and sits down as a couple more military people dive in with steel foldable chairs for us, before disappearing just as quickly. The five of us sit down in front of the huge, imposing desk, and the small but equally imposing woman behind it.

In front of her is a mess of papers, books, and a scratched-up laptop. There's a green lamp and a set of photographs behind her, where she appears to be younger, accompanied by an older man: her father, I presume. Curiously, a snow globe sits on her desk, depicting a city. It's engraved 'Haramat,' which I remember is the name of the capital. I wonder how often it snows in Aljarran?

"I heard all about you," she says, stroking her chin and looking at us each in turn. "The tiny, fearless recon squad who saved a battalion. A lot of men and women owe their lives to you."

"All in a day's work, ma'am," Mikey says, as cocky as ever. I can tell he's enjoying this. "We just want to sock Darida in the jaw."

She nods in his direction.

"I've also heard the troubling reports of mass graves," she

continues, her tone shifting. "The loss of Kolajje is a terrible scar on the face of our country. It must be avenged. It will be avenged."

Even Dina seems to like the sound of that. She licks her lips, like she's anticipating a meal. Then she side-eyes me, wondering if I saw it.

"However," Cantara then says, "I have to be honest, I didn't bring you here with the sole intention of feeding and thanking you."

Mikey's eyes grow wide with expectation. He looks almost the same he did as that massive meal was brought out to us.

"I want to offer each of you an opportunity," she says, maintaining that steely, intense eye contact, and moving it between us like a laser. "I want to offer you a chance to alter the course of this war. I want to give you the chance to be heroes once again."

I feel a rush of excitement; my heart beats out of my chest. This is like a scene in a movie: recruited directly by the rebel leader for a special mission? Maybe I'm getting ahead of myself, but this seems perfect for me. Mikey obviously thinks so too; he leans forward, his chin resting on his fist.

"If you accept, you'll be taken away from Lieutenant Al-Shabassi. You'll be taking orders from me and my generals directly. You've proven yourselves in combat, you've proven yourselves in reconnaissance, now it's time to really put those skills to the test."

Mikey is already rocking around in his chair with enthusiasm. Everyone else looks a little bit more guarded.

"Can we know anything more about the sort of missions we'll be sent on?" Salman asks.

"No," Cantara replies. "I'm sure you'll understand. That information is secret until the point you're given the mission."

Silence follows. Everyone seems unsure to commit right now. I watch as she taps her fingers on the desk.

"If you accept, you'll remain here and be briefed on the mission tomorrow. If you don't wish to accept, I'll have one of my men drive you back to your forward operating base."

"I don't want to stay here forever," Estevez says, defeatedly. "I never asked to be called a hero. I never even asked to be a squad leader. I'm sorry, it's no from me."

Salman is the next to speak, exhaling deeply before he does so.

"I have a kid. I'm happy to fight for my country, but I can't put myself in harm's way unnecessarily. I'll have to say no as well."

I'm beginning to wonder if we're embarrassing Cantara here. I shift around in my seat and open my mouth to accept, but Dina beats me to it: "I'll do it," she says, terse and to the point as always. I'm surprised at first, but thinking about it I shouldn't be. Anything that gets her hands closer to being around Darida's neck, right?

"Hell yeah," Mikey says next, apparently waiting to see if one of us volunteered first. I suppose he doesn't want to do it alone. "I'm in too."

"I'd like to do it," I finally say, sounding a little less assertive than I'd like. To be fair it's my first time being handpicked by a national leader. Surely I'm allowed to be a little overawed by the situation?

"Good," Cantara says, standing up behind her desk again. She walks back around, shaking Estevez and Salman's hands, exchanging a few warm-sounding words with Salman in Aljarrian. And then she has them both escorted out.

"Okay then," she says. She looks at the wall as if there were once a window there, but instead she looks at a painting stuck haphazardly onto a metal sheet bolted to the wall. "Dina, Michael, and…"

She doesn't know my name. That's quite a relief. The last thing I need right now is a background check.

"Kris."

"Kris, right," she sits down again. "We're very thankful to the foreigners fighting for our nation's freedom. And Dina, I promise you that someday we will unite Aljarran again."

Dina smiles, but I know she thinks they're hollow words uttered by a consummate politician. Maybe she's right, but I don't much care right now. This is all I've wanted: to prove myself.

"You'll be accommodated here overnight, and after you're well rested you'll be briefed on the mission ahead of you."

We stand up to make our way out, saluting her as we do.

"Before you go," she says, her tired expression turning to gratitude. "I'd like to say thank you for all you've done. If Darida's plan had succeeded, we might already be on the path to losing this war by now."

I smile, trying to hide how utterly delighted I am inside. Finally, I'm making a difference.

CHAPTER 41

We're taken up another floor and shown to a room that seemed to have been one of the hotel's luxury suites at some point, but has been looted and repurposed into a self-contained quarters. The room number is still embossed on the door: 422.

"I guess this is where they're keeping us," Dina says, taking a look around.

There's fluffy carpeting and beautiful mosaic wallpapering, but that's where the luxury ends. Anything like a four-poster bed and TV and bathtub are gone, replaced by three sleeping bags on a gym mat and a plastic table and chairs. There's a small kitchen area – and a refrigerator stocked with bread and vegetables – and a small electric cooker.

Unusually, however, the windows here haven't been boarded up. Instead, we get a door to a balcony outside.

Our guide – another faceless military man wearing a beret and tan fatigues – says some words to Dina, then salutes us and leaves.

"What'd he say?" Mikey asks, before sizing up the balcony outside.

"To stay off the lower floors."

"Right, cool," he says, before heading out of the balcony door and closing it behind him.

There's a moment of awkward silence between Dina and I. I pretend to take another look around the room until it dissipates.

"You don't think there's something weird about this?" Dina asks. When I look at her, her arms are crossed. Classic. "A day ago we were an expendable recon squad; not even a part of the real rebel army. Now we're handpicked by the leader for a special mission."

"I guess we impressed her," I tell her. "You heard her – we averted disaster. It isn't every day you save the world."

"True," she says, sarcastically. "Unless you're a technological superhero, right?"

I smile at her nervously. I'd almost let myself forget she knows everything.

Mikey bounds back indoors, telling us in lyrical terms about the fantastic view. Then he offers us both a cigarette and when neither of us take him up on the offer he disappears outside again.

"Dina," I say, remembering my gift. "I wanted to give you something. As a thank you for, you know, keeping my secret here."

She looks at me quizzically, like I really surprised her.

"I remembered what you said about the sapphire you lost in the desert, and, well," I reach into my pocket, and pull out the sapphire I made. "Here, have this."

I walk over to her and drop the sapphire into her palm. She looks at it with wide, suspicious eyes.

"What is this?" she asks.

"It's a sapphire. Aluminum, oxygen, and a few other trace elements."

She turns it over before pressing her fingers down on it, expecting it to shatter into pieces. When it doesn't, she looks up at me again, shocked.

"How did you—"

We're interrupted by one of Cantara's men entering the room without knocking and confidently announcing something to Dina. She seems flustered, and quickly pockets the sapphire.

"He says he needs us for some photographs, one at a time."

"Photographs?" I feel that nervousness again. The last photograph taken of me was probably on some subway CCTV prior to my 'death.'

"I'll go first," she says, "Tell Mikey that you'll both be next." And then she follows the man out of the room, into the deeper bowels of the hotel.

It isn't long before she returns, finding Mikey and I sitting at the table. Mikey has already found a box of electrical items under a kitchen counter and is rooting around inside it, digging out anything that interests him.

"Kris, you're up next," Dina says, dismissively.

"What is it?" I ask, maybe giving away a little too much of the fact that I'm uneasy about this.

"Passport photos," she says unenthusiastically, before fishing around in her pocket for something.

Passport photos? I think about what that could mean as I'm led down the labyrinth of corridors. My only guess is that we're being given fake passports for something. But why?

During a very awkward experience with a couple of guys with black berets, one camera, and no knowledge of English, they take a picture of my face with a white sheet behind hanging behind me. Then, they give me a thumbs-up and direct me back upstairs.

When I get back to our quarters Mikey is listening to an old CD player, having apparently found some CDs elsewhere. He's next to head to the photographer's studio, and Dina and I are left alone again.

"Passport photos?" I ask her.

"A sapphire?" she asks back.

Ah yes, the sapphire.

"So, I should probably explain." She nods at me, expectantly. "The nanomachines can alter the molecular structure of anything I'm touching. I don't know exactly how it works, but within reason I can create diamond from coal, wine from water."

I didn't mean to make the similarity between Jesus and me. It was just the first thing I could think of.

"So, wait a minute" she says at first. "You can create guns? Sniper rifles? Bombs?"

No, Vega says. *Nothing complex; no moving parts or complicated chemical interactions like what exist in guns and explosives. Just simple objects with repeating molecular architecture.*

I repeat what Vega said.

"Kris," she says, looking at the sapphire between her fingers again. She peers into it, seeming to lose herself briefly. "This isn't my sapphire. I can't accept this."

"I know it isn't, but surely it just the same? It's the exact same elements that have gone into making it."

She stops looking at it, but curiously she doesn't give it back to me.

"If I give you an old, rusty rifle," Dina says, rubbing her forehead, "and over the course of a year, you fire it so often that you have to replace the barrel. Then the stock breaks, so you replace that. Then the magazine jams. And eventually you replace every single, smallest component. Is that still the gun I gave you?"

"Well," I say at first, thinking about it. "It never left my side, did it?"

Then I look at my right hand and think of the same conversation I had with Vega. Is this my hand, or isn't it? Is my heart the same heart I was born with?

Dina smiles at me, and puts her hand on my shoulder. Her

touch surprises me – it's uncharacteristic of her – and I flinch slightly.

"But, it doesn't matter," Dina says, looking deep into my eyes. "I appreciate the gesture, Kris."

She rolls the sapphire between her fingers one final time before opening her locket and putting it inside. She closes it, and exhales, closing her eye, and saying a silent prayer, I presume. When she's finished, we endure another slightly painful silence.

"Beer cans," I say, thinking of something to dispel the quiet. "Aluminum beer cans. That's what I made it from."

She smiles at me incredulously, then laughs, shielding her mouth with her palm.

"You know just what to say, don't you?"

Another moment passes between us, but this time it's far easier. I stare into her deep, brown eyes, and feel almost like we could *be something*…

"Well, that was a waste of time," Mikey bounds through the door to say. I lean back, getting out of Dina's space. "Neither of those guys could speak English. I spent 10 minutes trying to figure out they wanted my sunglasses off. One of them threw me a comb; I thought I was going to lose an eye."

I snort in acknowledgement but curse his timing. Or maybe I should be thanking him, interrupting something that probably shouldn't happen…

"What the hell do they want our photos for anyway?"

Dina looks between us. She's giving me the impression that we're missing something here.

"Isn't it obvious?" she asks. It is not obvious. "We're going behind enemy lines: into the territory Darida holds. I presume they're mocking up fake IDs for us as we speak."

Mikey grins infectiously, punching the air. His enthusiasm makes it to me, filling me with adrenaline before I think again and get to wondering just how we're going to make it behind enemy lines.

"Wait a minute," I say, thinking this through. "How the hell are we supposed to get behind enemy lines? Mikey and I are American. You're the only one who speaks the language here, Dina. We're just about the worst secret agents you can find in this city."

She crosses her arms.

"I'm sure the fact you're American is part of the plan," she says monotonously. "I did think it strange that she invited three Westerners up here. No offence guys, but you're hardly the posterchildren of Aljarrian liberation."

"Well, I don't care," Mikey interjects. "I'm James Bond now. I'm Jason Bourne, I'm, uhm, I'm that other guy."

I laugh, trying to figure out what other movie superspy he's talking about.

"You're out of your goddamn mind, man," I tell him. He shrugs and grins that grin of his.

Mikey and Dina begin speaking about some other mission they were on a month ago before my time. I take a trip outside and check this balcony out. It's almost dusk now; the sky is a mixture of gorgeous reds and pinks.

The view of the city from here is a series of rooftops and minarets, jutting high into the sky like grasping hands. Some were unlucky enough to catch a missile. Always something to look forward to here, I guess. There's a slight chill in the air; the season is turning. Soon there will be a new spring in Aljarran.

Well, Vega says, waiting for the right moment as ever. *You're really living the dream now.*

I can tell he's being sarcastic, but I appreciate the sentiment nonetheless.

"Cool, right?" I say, quietly.

It is ironic that the nanomachine network would facilitate you being the perfect secret agent, if you were to use it. You can change your face and voice at will. Instead, it seems you're having to make do with a fake ID.

Huh, I hadn't even thought of that.

"I guess it's too late now. Also, I don't know if you'll ever understand this, but I've grown quite attached to this face. Despite its disadvantages, it's very, well, me."

Then we will see how far that face gets you.

CHAPTER 42

"Good morning soldiers."

Standing before us is a very tall man – 6'5" perhaps – wearing the customary tan/sand colored military fatigues and black beret that seems to be the uniform within this building. He has glasses on with a yellowish tint and thankfully he speaks English.

"I'm general Major General Rahal, and I'll be the one delivering your briefing."

Last night was spent nervously anticipating the day's events with Mikey and Dina. Despite our enthusiasm, we're all aware we're entering the unknown here. Hell, if Major General Rahal knew that a month ago I was packaging sandwiches and playing videogames, he'd call this mission off right here, right now.

The four of us are piled into a small former hotel room. Room 413, as a matter of fact – they didn't pull the numbers off the door. It's completely empty, except for a projector sat behind us, three steel folding chairs, a white bedsheet hung in front of us, and a large, almost out-of-control houseplant, conspicuous by its presence here.

The three of us sit awkwardly on the chairs. It's early –

maybe 6:30 AM or so. Dina and Mikey seem wide-awake. I'm still getting used to this military schedule.

"A few days ago, we arrested an American national here in Rachiya. After further investigation, he revealed his identity: Paul Elphick-White, a black-market weapons dealer. We heard reports that he was trying to set up arms deals here, and that he was also trying to cross the border into Darida's territory."

I look at Dina; she has one eyebrow raised. I think she's beginning to see where this is going.

"After a..." he pauses, before finding the right words, "...frank discussion with Mr. Elphick-White, he divulged certain information that we found useful. Namely, that he has a meeting set up with the Butcher of Ben-Assi tomorrow."

Dina's eyes widen. The Butcher of Ben-Assi? He sounds like a fella from a horror film.

"For those of you who might not have heard of him, General Bedoussi is one of Darida's most trusted generals and confidantes. He's also responsible for the slaughter of 300 men, women, and children in Ben-Assi, one of the first villages to pledge allegiance to the rebellion."

"Jesus Christ," I say, disgusted. An unsettling atmosphere descends on the room. I look around and see Mikey staring on with fire in his eyes. I presume he's heard of him.

"You may be wondering why we had your photographs taken yesterday," the Major General says, although it's becoming very clear. "We want one of you two Americans to impersonate Mr. Elphick-White. A fake passport will be issued to one of you and you'll attend the meeting with the Butcher."

All of a sudden this all feels very real. It's so far from our silly ambitions about becoming James Bond or whatever. One of us will soon have the pleasure of sitting down with a real-life genocidal maniac.

"And there, during this meeting, you must kill the Butcher of Ben-Assi."

Mikey exhales deeply; I can almost hear him saying 'whoa, man' in his head. Dina, on the other hand, doesn't make a sound. If not Darida's neck yet, I think she'll happily get her hands around this 'Butcher' character's throat.

"How do we kill him?" Dina asks.

"We've manufactured a poison," the Major General replies, straightening his posture. "One of you will need to smuggle it into Darida's territory, and one of you will somehow need to administer the poison."

Poisoning? Here I am again on the precipice of killing a man. That man is a murderer of hundreds – if there's anyone I should kill, it's him – but the thought still makes me queasy.

"Hell, I'll do it," Mikey says, throwing his hands up in the air dismissively. "I'll be this weapons dealer and get that poison into his body, no problem. I'll feed it to him if I have to."

"Our suggestion is that both of you Americans attend the meeting. One as Mr. Elphick-White, the other as his assistant. That would leave you, Dina, to act as their support staff."

She nods once.

"How old is this guy?" I ask, my mind teeming with questions. "I mean, if there's a 20-year age gap, this will look suspicious right?"

"He's in his mid-thirties," the Major General replies. "I would suggest Michael here be Mr. Elphick-White on the day, and you, Kris, be his assistant."

Too baby-faced to play an arms dealer. My acting career over before it's even begun.

"You'll be given appropriate attire – suits, an expensive watch, etc. We're assured that the Butcher doesn't know what Mr. Elphick-White looks like, so with the appropriate knowledge and documentation, you should hopefully be able to walk straight into the meeting."

The Major General pauses before looking at Mikey. "And yes, feeding the poison to him would be a preferable mode of delivery. It is designed to be colorless, odorless, and can be added to food or drink without the victim being aware. It's delayed-acting. You should have between 30 minutes and three hours to escape before he begins suffering the effects."

He then turns on the projector, giving us a series of notes about the town we're due to meet the Butcher in. It's close to the frontline, but very well-fortified by Darida's men still, so the chances of a bomb going off beneath us this time seem slim.

Apparently, the three of us are to cross no man's land and the frontline on foot tonight, just after nightfall. This will be the first challenge: ensuring we're not seen. Then, we should find a vehicle stashed away earlier by another team of rebels and can drive into town.

We have a safehouse set up there where we can finalize our plans and rest before the meeting, which is set up tomorrow at 12:00 PM. The venue is a former rec center – once full of rich Aljarrian businesspeople playing racquetball, but now another dilapidated husk.

After we're done with the meeting – if we manage to escape with our lives – we're to meet Dina, who will drive us back over the frontline and no man's land. Our forces will allegedly be told to expect our crossing and won't shoot at us.

If all goes to plan, we'll have a leisurely walk over the frontline, find the car for a nice evening drive, get well-rested in a comfortable safehouse, and then meet our friend the Butcher for dinner and discuss an arms deal. Then we'll take our leave, meet up with Dina, and make our way out of town, all while the poor Butcher chokes on his lamb chops.

If it doesn't go to plan, we'll all be dead.

Mikey and Dina ask a couple of follow-up questions, but I'm still grappling with the logistics of it all. It's clear now that Cantara needed us because Mikey and I are real, authentic

Americans, with real American accents and real understanding of the culture back home. We're the only people who could convincingly impersonate the weapons dealer.

But there are so many ways this could all go wrong…

I look over at Mikey and Dina; Mikey asking questions and joking with enthusiasm. Dina listening intently, determined to finally begin striking back at the generals who put her mother up against the wall. They're my friends; the closest friends I've had in years, perhaps. I don't want to lose them.

I must do what I can to protect them.

"Kris," Dina says, snapping me back to reality. "Do you have any questions?"

"Uhm, no, I don't think so" I answer. It's not true. I have many questions, but I doubt they can be answered until we begin the mission.

"Thank you for listening," the Major General says. "Thank you for volunteering for the mission, and above all, good luck."

We leave the room and go back upstairs to our quarters. When we get there, we sit down at the table in contemplative silence. There are muffled voices down the hall, no doubt officers and generals planning out more elaborate schemes. Players plotting the pawns' next moves.

"We're living the dream now," I finally say, repeating what Vega sarcastically told me last night. "I suppose we'd better get ready."

I take a shower and change into the clothes provided: desert camouflaged pants, T-shirt, and jacket, along with a similar colored baseball cap. Mikey and Dina are dressed the same; the gear that will hopefully get us across the frontline. In addition, we get some kind of co-ordinate tracker to help us find the vehicle.

After an hour or so, the Major General comes up to our

quarters and hands Dina a small box: plastic, but heavy and robust. Inside is a tiny glass vial – maybe an inch and a half tall – which we're told contains the poison.

"Taped to one of your bodies, the vial won't trip any sort of metal detector and shouldn't be discovered in a pat-down," he says, articulately. "Whatever you do, don't ingest the poison. It'll wash harmlessly off your fingers, but if you somehow swallow it, it will kill you."

Don't swallow the poison, got it.

"Also, this goes without saying, but you won't be taking weapons with you," he goes on to say. "The risk of one of you being caught with firearms, and thus derailing the mission, is too high."

He bids us good luck again and tells us they'll come to take us to no man's land at 3:00 PM, before leaving with a grateful smile and a salute.

"All right," Mikey yells, far too loud for this time in the morning. "I'd better get acquainted with Mr. Elphick-White, huh."

He grabs a handful of documents from the arms dealer's interrogation – provided to him in the briefing – and takes them onto the balcony, closing the door behind him with a thud.

Dina looks at me with her eyebrows raised high. Her expression is one of excitement. Funnily enough, since the briefing I'm not feeling it.

"How are you feeling?" she asks me, seemingly reading my mind or at least my face.

"I don't know," I reply, somewhat truthfully. "There's a plan, but it's long and complex. There's many places and ways in which it can go wrong."

She nods in agreement, although her enthusiasm doesn't seem to be quelled.

"And, you know," I go on, with plenty on my mind,

"we're amateurs at this. We're not spies, are we? We were selected because two of us are American."

"It's war," she simply replies. "You have to do what you can. Fight until they corner you, and then fight some more."

"Aren't you afraid?" I ask. "Even slightly?"

"No. Not anymore."

There's a silence between us. I take a deep breath and try to regain my composure.

"Are you?" Dina eventually asks.

I think about it for a moment. "I've spent my entire life being afraid. Up until recently, I woke up every morning thinking death could be just around the corner."

She snorts with laughter. I look her in those deep, brown eyes.

"You're not exactly easy to kill, Kris. I think we both know you'll survive this mission."

I turn away from her, breaking eye contact at last.

"Maybe it's not me I'm afraid for."

I sit up in my chair and rub my head. This is the kind of scenario that would disable me with a migraine for an hour. Now I know I don't have to worry about that. Nanomachines in my cerebrospinal fluid, yadda-yadda-yadda. But I still have that instinctive reflex to rub my head.

"I can look after myself," Dina says with the same implacable courage as ever. "So can Mikey. And besides, if we get into trouble, you'll be there to throw your body in the way of their bullets."

She smiles at me with that same fiery doggedness in her eyes. I can't help but admire her. Dina and Mikey – Dina the fearless freedom fighter, Mikey the thrill-seeking American hero – are everything I ever wanted to be. Adventurous, courageous, heroic.

She's right. I would take bullets for them.

CHAPTER 43

I'm looking out onto the vast dunes of Aljarran again. An expanse of rolling sandbanks and catastrophically jagged rocks that seemingly never end. Barren wastes, the occasional bit of thorny scrub, and sparse patches of brown grass. I didn't miss it.

At least the sun is going down. Its golden glow illuminating the sharp rocks, casting horrifying shadows on the horizon. It's an appropriate setting for no man's land. A harsh and unforgiving place, but also one of peace and solitude, right until the next artillery shell lands.

We're traveling in a 4x4 driven by one of Cantara's men. We've just left the road, and now we're bumping over sand, dirt, and rock. The motion is enough to make me feel slightly sick. I guess the nanomachines can't compensate for travel sickness.

By the time the sun goes down and the unforgiving dunes are bathed in darkness again, the 4x4 comes to an abrupt stop. The driver says some words to Dina, and she beckons for us to get out and unpack the trunk. Then, with a couple more words, the 4x4 speeds away, leaving us in a cloud of dust.

"This is it then," I say to them both. "No turning back."

"No turning back," Mikey repeats with a smile.

He takes the GPS tracker out of his rucksack along with a small flashlight. And then, over treacherous rocks and sands, we begin to follow him.

Kris, be careful, Vega tells me. *This is a battlefield. It's no man's land. There could be any number of hazards here.*

"Better keep our eyes open," I say to the others, trying to inspire the same level of care and attention as Vega tries to inspire in me. "There could be anything here waiting to kill us."

"Yeah man," Mikey says, trudging forward at a brisk pace. "This terrain is no joke. All we can use to light our way is this stupid little flashlight, so try to stay behind me."

We walk for what seems like an hour, talking, laughing and joking occasionally, trying to keep the mood jovial but mostly just concentrating on not falling and cracking our heads on a rock.

It's difficult work – always second guessing yourself, wondering whether the darker patch of terrain you put your foot into is a bit of dirt or a foot-shaped rut in the rock hungry to break your ankle. I'm so busy concentrating – cold sweat emerging from my pores like bullets – that I forget Vega is doing the same.

Kris, there was a landmine to your right. You just passed it. You'd better alert the others.

"Guys, I—"

They don't even have time to turn and face me before I see it: something dark, raised, and most worryingly perfectly circular. A shape that couldn't exist out here among the dangerous shapes and angles. And Mikey's just about to put his foot onto it…

"Mikey, Mikey! Don't put your foot dow—"

He steps on it.

And we wait.

It feels like an eternity. I know it's only one single

moment, but I feel as though my heart beats a 1000 times. We're all paused on the spot – frozen in time – until finally Mikey speaks.

"Well, how about that?"

He carefully adjusts his position as Dina and I watch, unable to move, talk, or ask him what the hell we do. Then he slowly steps off it, eliciting a moment of panic that grips my body coldly.

"Looks like it doesn't work." He kneels down beside it, analyzing it closely with his flashlight. "The fuse has been knocked out of position. It's disabled."

Dina begins to laugh. She carefully steps forward and slaps him on the back. I take a deep breath; I'm not quite able to cope with this just yet. I think back to the first time this happened – the grenade taped to the refrigerator door – and know that this time I couldn't have saved him in time.

"I'm guessing these landmines were dropped by plane," Mikey says, picking it up and throwing it off into the distance like a frisbee. "It's a quick and easy way to lay a minefield, but occasionally the impact on the ground can jolt the fuse loose."

"Jesus Christ," I say at last, putting my hand over my heart. "You could have been killed."

"Oh no," he says, wagging his finger at me like I got a quiz question wrong. "These things aren't designed to kill you."

"They're not?" I ask, showing my battlefield naïvety again.

"No, they're designed to maim. Blow your foot off. Sometimes even your leg. You're a bigger hindrance to your own side if you're bleeding out on the battlefield. And, you know, you'll never fight again."

I think about it, and it makes sense in that logically pure, yet absurdly cruel way I've come to expect from this war or any war for that matter.

"Shall we head on?" Mikey asks, before walking – both feet intact – slowly ahead.

"Wait," I call out. Mikey pauses and turns to look at me expectantly.

"I should go first. I'm good at spotting traps, I'm observant. If there are any more ahead, I'll see them."

Mikey's expression turns to doubt, and we both look at Dina. She nods in agreement with my suggestion, understanding the greater sense in having me blow my feet off rather than Mikey.

He relinquishes his flashlight to me and we trudge on again.

Vega is useful in pointing out one more landmine. I in turn point it out to the others, and we pace around it. It isn't long before Mikey's reading of the GPS tracker has us in the vehicle's planned location. Sure enough, hidden inside a small ravine with a brown fabric draped over it we see the vehicle.

It's a rather shabby saloon car, stained light-brown from the dirt and the sand. But, so long as it has four wheels and a working engine, it'll suit us just fine.

"So we're through no man's land, past the frontline, and inside Darida's territory," Dina says, tired and relieved. "Now we've just got to find that safehouse."

Mikey and I sit in the back, trying to make ourselves comfortable while Dina fumbles around with a map to the safehouse the resistance left us. Then she finds the key in the glove compartment and the engine soon purrs to life.

We endure a nervous hour of driving – first through the rocky wastes, and then on dirt roads and across arid farmlands. Mikey and I look at our passports for the first time, knowing that they'll be needed should we run into a military checkpoint.

"Paul Elphick-White, just as promised," Mikey says, reading from his new passport. "How about yours?"

"Mark Cochrane," I reply, reading from my passport in the glow of a passing streetlight. "I'm your assistant, right?"

"Say you're my cousin," Mikey responds. "Family connections are more easily trusted."

I look at my picture in the passport; my face, looking entirely listless, staring down the camera. Mark Cochrane, cousin and assistant to an arms dealer. I've never so much as appeared in a school nativity play, now I'm impersonating arms dealers and performing in front of bloodthirsty, genocidal generals.

We finally make it onto an asphalt road, and it isn't long before we come up to our first military checkpoint: a couple of armored cars blocking all but one lane of the road and two rifle-toting soldiers beside it.

We pull up beside them and Dina exchanges some words with the soldiers, before pulling out her fake passport. Then she beckons for us to do the same.

The soldier takes my ID, shines a flashlight on it, then shines the flashlight directly in my face. My eyes strain under the bright light, but it doesn't last long. He quickly moves to give Mikey the same treatment. After a couple more words with Dina, we're free to continue on.

"That was easy," Mikey says as we speed away from the checkpoint.

"Plenty of Americans on Darida's side of the frontline too," Dina says bitterly. "The war profiteers looking to make a quick buck. Arms dealers; oil and gas companies; lithium miners all wanting their piece of Aljarran if Darida should win the war."

Darida's Aljarran is very similar to the rebel territory, it seems. Passing military convoys, hearing the occasional low boom of artillery, and seeing ashen-faced citizens walking by the side of the road, just trying to get on with their lives. We speed past a couple of villages, festooned with banners 12 feet high bearing Darida's face on them. His smug grin, watching our every move.

We pass a bombed-out village; blackened farmhouses with their roofs caved in, walls reduced to scattered bricks and splintered wood. The ground is pockmarked with craters; scarred with the tormented memories of the horror that once occurred here.

I think again of that photograph I found of the little girl amongst the wreckage of the destroyed apartment building and find myself ready to shed a tear. Is the Butcher of Ben-Assi responsible for this too? Or one of a 100 military officers loyal to Darida?

They've all got to pay.

It's another hour or so before we reach the town we're due to meet the Butcher in and our safehouse. Our shelter for the night is a small farmhouse just on the outskirts of town. It's no more than a couple of buildings with an outhouse for a toilet. Cattle was probably farmed here once, but any signs of livestock are long gone aside from a large steel trough outside.

We park the car, and taking a key from a pre-agreed hiding place we let ourselves in.

The smell of choking, stale air hits us immediately. This place hasn't been cleaned for years, let alone lived in. There's one small bed in the corner – good thing we brought sleeping bags – and a couple of cupboards stained grey with dirt.

Seems homely.

Vega gives me his thoughts out of nowhere, sarcastic as always. Life is good for him; he gets to live in the temple that is my body. I have to endure the real world.

I go to check the other room out and find it completely empty, except for some straw in the corner. The floors are hard, cold stone tiles, and the ceiling above us is flimsy wood.

"Not the kind of accommodation I had in mind," I say to the others. Mikey has already found a small, rickety wooden stool perched beside one of the cupboards. "Hard to imagine James Bond living like this."

"What, you expected the VIP suite at the casino? Did you forget your tuxedo?" Dina asks. "Sorry to break it to you, but you're not James Bond."

She smiles sardonically at me. Harsh, but probably fair.

We unpack the car, and I watch as Dina very carefully brings in that plastic box with the vial of poison inside.

"We've got to think of a way of getting this inside the General's body," Mikey says, looking at the box with a sort of fascinated respect. "One of us has to take the vial in there."

"I should probably do it," I say, surprising Mikey somewhat. "You're doing most of the talking right? If I'm the silent assistant, I can concentrate on delivering the poison somehow."

Mikey nods and Dina hesitantly murmurs her agreement too.

Alleged bomber's accomplice to silent assassin, all within a month. What a career path.

Dina heads outside to unpack the last of the things from the car, and Mikey whips his jacket and shirt off, complaining that the clothes fit poorly. I know I should go out to help Dina, but then I see those names and dates tattooed on his arm once again, and my curiosity is too much to resist.

"Can I ask, what's your tattoo there?"

He looks at his arm, reading them silently for a moment, before turning to me.

"These are my friends. They're no longer with us."

Brett West, Marvin Thoms, Stef Schindler... the list goes on. It's at least a dozen long.

"I'm sorry to hear that."

"Don't be, they were heroes," he says, rooting around in his rucksack. He takes out a suit jacket, slightly crumpled. "They died with smiles on their faces."

"From your time in the marines?"

"Yes," he replies. "I never really had much of a family. I never knew my dad, and my mom was busy with work."

He takes out a set of pants to match the shirt and a slightly creased white shirt.

"I found my real family on the battlefield. These people would have thrown themselves in front of a bullet to save me. They'd have stepped on that landmine so that I didn't. I owe them all a lot more than a tattoo."

He seems to speak for the first time with a weariness, like he knows he has a debt to his fallen friends that he'll never pay off.

"We all fought together, because that's what you do in a family. You're a team, linked together with an unbreakable bond. That, to me, is what being a warrior is. It's what gives my life purpose."

Purpose. I sure know how it feels to search for your purpose.

Dina comes back in, and the three of us unpack our clothing for tomorrow. Mikey's crumpled and slightly shabby suit, my casual shirt and jeans combination, and Dina's hoodie. All very drab, but inconspicuous enough to hide a trio of amateur assassins.

"There's still one big, glaring question," Dina says, taking a flask of coffee out of her bag and holding it close to her. "How do we give him the poison?"

"We're meeting him at a former rec center," Mikey says. "You know, racquetball, tennis courts, yoga studios, whatever. It's not a crazy prospect that they'll have a kitchen there. And we are meeting at lunchtime."

Mikey is maybe thinking with his stomach again, but he does have a point.

"And if worst comes to worst? If we can't sneak it into his swan and veal pie, or whatever these guys eat?"

My question is met with silence.

"Well, in that case," Mikey begins by saying, "I'll hold his jaws wide open and you just shove the vial in there."

I laugh; the smile on my face hiding my swelling feelings of worry.

We're amateur assassins all right.

CHAPTER 44

I'm sitting in a room; it's dark, but I can make out a coffee table visible in the few, gray rays of light that make it through the closed blinds beside me. There's a number of items on the coffee table: a gun, an empty plate, a cellphone, and finally a pipe bomb – just like Burden used to make – shining slightly in the pale light.

I'm sitting on a sofa of some sort; a figure is beside me. After a moment, I have the imperceptible feeling that it's Mikey. We're both looking at the table, trying to decide which items belong to who.

Kris, it's time to wake up. It's a big day ahead.

Vega's disembodied voice forces me back to wakefulness. Sure enough I see Dina getting out of the bed. Mikey's bedroll is empty; he must already be up. After a minute of trying to shake that dream out of my head he bounds in, enthusiastic as ever.

"Mornin' folks, it's game day!"

We eat a bland breakfast of bread and some dried noodle mixture we find in our rations, heated up and made somewhat edible by boiled water, and then we talk over our plan again.

Mikey and I are to be dropped off a short walk from the venue by Dina – our cover story is that we travelled via civilian bus from the capital. Dina will then wait inside the car at the venue, and as soon as we emerge from the entrance of the rec center, we're out of there.

We're going to try to avoid checkpoints, but if we hit one we pass through it as though nothing is wrong. The poison should take a while to work anyway, and the full alarm won't be raised until a period of time after that. We then have an agreed point within no man's land we can cross without being fired on by our own troops.

Very important, that last part.

The only real wildcard is what happens when Mikey and I are in there with him. We know absolutely nothing about how the meeting will go down. Will there be food? Drink? How many bodyguards will he have?

Hell, we don't even know what kind of arms deal he wants from Elphick-White. The file Mikey received mentions a shipment of grenades and hollow-point ammunition smuggled in from Greece, but what if he wants something else? What if he doesn't want to buy from us at all, but to jail us and ransom us back to the United States?

Mikey tells us he'll improvise; string him along as much as he can.

"I know how these sorts of guys talk," he says, crossing his arms. "I've hung around with dodgy-ass characters slinging dodgy-ass firearms. I can BS with the best of them."

Mikey is confident enough. Dina seems determined as ever, if not especially confident, but I want to get a second opinion.

"I'm just going to get some fresh air guys," I tell them. "Need to gather my thoughts."

I head outside and walk a minute away from the farmhouse. There's a large sandstone rock out here, and I take a seat on it with the relentless sun beating down on me.

"Vega, is there any easy way to deliver this poison?"

The Major General said it has to be ingested. There would conceivably be a way to deliver the poison via the nanomachine network.

"Oh yeah?" I can barely hide my eagerness; I almost shout it. "How would that work?"

The nanomachine network could create a series of 1000s of tiny nanomachine spikes – think nanobot on top of nanobot, repeated millions of times – over your fingers and palm. If you were to soak your hand in the poison, these spikes would be able to deliver the poison into his skin and into the blood vessels, eventually.

"All right, great, how long would it take?"

Two minutes, perhaps more.

"Two minutes?!" I rub my head, anticipating another headache that'll never come. "So, you're saying I've got to hold this bloodthirsty General's hand?"

I'm sorry Kris. Even technology has restraints. Your body is strong, fast, and durable but you can't kill someone out of thin air.

I see a large plume of black smoke erupt on the horizon. Then the low, terrifying rumbling sound of the explosion.

"So, we'll have to do this the old-fashioned way then."

I'm afraid so.

I stand up and begin the walk back to the farmhouse, watching the smoke rise in the distance.

It's a strange mood back in the building. The atmosphere is tense. Everyone understands this is the most dangerous day of our lives.

"Okay folks," Mikey says when the hour is upon us. "Someone's gotta die. Let's make sure it's him and not us."

We get changed; me into that gaudy shirt and jeans combination, Mikey into his suit. His hair is unkempt and wild, but with the suit and sunglasses it does at least make him look like a Hollywood arms dealer. I look like I did before: a dopey American kid.

"Do we look good? Good enough to make this work?" Mikey asks Dina. She looks at us with unimpressed eyes.

"If I say no," she says, "does that mean we're all going to die in one of Darida's jails?"

"Sure," Mikey replies. He's grinning, but I'm sure he must feel at least some amount of nerves.

"Then yes, you both look great."

We say goodbye to the farmhouse and pack the car. Mikey goes over Paul Elphick-White's backstory again – taking his notes with him – and I tape the vial of poison in my armpit.

"Careful you don't break it accidentally," Dina tells me, watching me button my shirt back up. It's uncomfortable, but that's good. I need to remember it's there.

Then we get in the car and finally set off.

The route to the town isn't far. The town itself is like a mirrored-universe of Rachiya; the same small craters and fissures pockmarking the roads; the same damaged buildings with once beautiful domes now in ruins. The same civilians – men, women, and children – purposefully walking the streets, living their lives in the shadow of war.

The only real difference is Darida's face, looming large over us. A banner hung from every arch or bridge or advertising hoarding. Grinning at us; promising a prosperous future, trying to pretend he isn't trying to murder half the population or that he hasn't already filled mass graves with his own countrymen.

I look at that smile and imagine the expression on his face when he finds out his top general and confidante is dead. And then I recoil backwards in my seat a little, shocked by how bloodthirsty I already sound. This war is changing me.

After 20 minutes of driving on almost empty roads, it's nearly showtime. I rub my head, feeling the pounding of my heart in my ears and throughout my body. I feel sick with anticipation.

I haven't felt like this in a long time – maybe back when I

found Alfred Burden and my dad sitting and talking over breakfast. That time Burden held all the cards; this time I have the ace tucked under my armpit.

"All right, I think this is as close as I should get," Dina says, parking the car. "The rec center is two blocks away. I'll let you guys out, and then I'll circle around and park a short walk from the entrance."

The engine shudders to a stop and then goes quiet.

"All right, let's do this." With that, Mikey opens the door and leaps out. I do the same. We take our fake passports and begin the walk. After a couple of steps, we hear the engine start again and Dina speeds ahead without acknowledging us again.

"You nervous?" I ask Mikey.

"I don't know," he replies, assertively. "Maybe earlier I was. But now? I feel something else. Like this is a dream, you know?"

Living the dream, I think back to myself. Vega's words in my head.

When we get to the block with the rec center on it, my heart sinks into my stomach. There are already soldiers here. I count four of them, stationed at various points across the street, but there have to be more inside.

I look at the buildings on the other side of the road; they seem to be apartments, slightly dilapidated, all needing a lick of paint, but every single one of them has a large, spacious roof terrace. There's a man watching the scene from above. I wonder briefly if he's a civilian or not.

The rec center itself is just a large, concrete building with mosaic tiling clinging to the walls for dear life. Its brutal architecture stands out like a sore thumb here; a most conspicuous building. It doesn't strike me as the sort of place a general would hang out, which is presumably exactly why we're here.

We walk past a couple of Darida banners to the entrance

of the rec center. A couple of soldiers walk up to us and say a few words in the native tongue. They're tired looking – one of them has crazed eyes, darting from side to side, as though he's high on something – but their rifles seem vigilant enough.

We make a show of being dumb, ignorant Americans – yelling loudly and slowly, before showing them our fake passports. They take a look and direct us inside the building, where another man – wearing a shirt, tie, and glasses – waits for us.

"Mr. Elphick-White?" he asks us both. Mikey speaks up in the affirmative. He then looks at me keenly. "And who might you be?"

"Mark," I reply, trying to sound as professional as possible, "Cochrane."

"Mark is my cousin," Mikey says, as one of the soldiers begins patting him down as expected. "It's a family business, you see."

"Ah, right," the bespectacled man says. The soldier finishes patting Mikey down and begins on me. "Good to meet you both."

I feel palms aggressively pressing every surface on every limb, along with my back and chest. I wonder if he can feel my heart beating out of my chest. The palms soon brush over my armpits, but don't find the vial.

"Follow me please," the man says, as he turns his back and begins walking.

We follow him through the building, past a set of tennis courts and down a couple of corridors – glass crunching underneath our feet – until we reach the former swimming pool. It's a huge room with dusty, Victorian-style tiled walls. On each wall is a large mural – a dolphin, a whale, an octopus – looking down on us.

The vast empty expanse of the pool dominates the room, 50 or so meters long and half as wide. It's long since been drained, and now all that remains is a large, dusty bed of turquoise tiles, reaching out before us like a field of ice.

I look up, and immediately I'm blinded by the sun. There were glass roof panels here once, but they were blasted out long ago. There's a steel ladder leading down into the pool, and inside the middle of the pool – directly in the center of the room – a red couch, a table, and a set of two chairs.

We're directed by the English-speaking man to climb down the ladder and sit on the sofa together. As soon as I approach the ladder, I get that foreboding feeling; there's no canteen as we'd hoped. No restaurant setting. Just a gigantic, turquoise arena with the potential for many eyes to watch over us from above.

"After you," Mikey says to me, pointing to the ladder. I climb down it and jump into the empty pool. The feeling of claustrophobia is sudden; all around me there are walls, stained and chipped tiles that seem to be closing in from every angle. A vast ocean without a sea.

Mikey climbs down and we both slowly walk to the couch in the center, its red upholstery sticking out like a bleeding thumb. I look up and see the presence of a couple of soldiers standing on the edges of the poolside, holding their rifles close to their chests. The Butcher couldn't have picked a more intimidating venue, that's for sure.

"Some place, huh," I say to Mikey. He looks around, no doubt scouting the soldiers looking on from above.

The thought occurs to me that this is maybe the first time I've ever been in a pool. My parents would never let me as a child owing to my heart condition. I can't help but smile to myself at that.

We sit on the couch – first Mikey, then me. It seems comfortable enough, but that doesn't stop me feeling my heart beating all the way into my fingertips.

Sensing an uncomfortable itch in my armpit, I realize now is the time: I go to scratch it, putting my arm through the space between buttons in my shirt, and while I'm there quickly grab the vial, tearing it from my skin. I conceal it inside my palm, and after a moment put my hand into my pocket, leaving the vial there.

Eventually, after several minutes of tension – Mikey and I awkwardly sitting on the couch, as we watch armed guards patrol the sides of the pool above us – we finally hear a door slam and loud footsteps echoing across the tiled surfaces.

Our appointment with death is here.

CHAPTER 45

"I guess that's him," Mikey says, motioning towards a slightly overweight man in a green military jacket and tan pants climbing rung by rung down the ladder. When he hits the ground, he turns and re-adjusts his jacket – revealing for the first time a row of colorful medals – and begins walking towards us, smiling graciously. The English-speaking man in the suit and tie follows behind him.

The man saunters over to the couch; we both stand to meet him. Surprisingly – to me at least – he shakes our hands, saying something warm-sounding and enthusiastic in Aljarrian. The English-speaking man translates.

"General Ali Abdal Bedoussi welcomes you," he says. The sun shines onto his glasses, hiding his eyes in its glare. Suddenly I have an unsettling memory of Burden. "Please sit."

We sit down again. The Butcher and his translator sit opposite us on the slightly more professional and dignified couple of chairs. The General himself is covered by a sheen of sweat – seemingly exhausted by the climb down the ladder – and a thick, gray mustache sits below his red nose.

I look up and see the two soldiers still patrolling the pool side, like a couple of military-grade lifeguards.

Mikey begins talking, but I'm in my own world. Counting the guards outside, and the guards inside, there are at least six rifle-toting bodyguards here. Six men with six guns we'll have to dance the tango with if things go wrong. And that doesn't include the General or his translator.

"By the way, can I get a drink?" Mikey asks, snapping me back to reality. The General waits for it to be translated, and is then effusive in his reaction, gyrating his arms.

"Yes," the translator says, "of course, refreshments are already on their way."

That gets our attention all right; I feel Mikey relax his posture beside me. Nothing would refresh me more than a cold glass of water and a dead Butcher of Ben-Assi right now.

"So, yes in terms of artillery shells," Mikey says, his voice shifting out of its usual surfer guy cadence and into a professional tone I've never heard before, "our organization can supply as many as 500,000 per month, all shipped from Greece."

After he hears the translated version, the General looks surprised. He whispers something in the translator's ear and I get that sinking feeling. The great, turquoise sea opens up and begins to swallow our couch whole. Did Mikey say something outlandish? Are we rumbled?

We're interrupted by one of the military lifeguards saying something. The translator stands up, adjusts his tie, and walks over there slowly, all as the General sits watching us, smiling. The translator is passed down something – a shiny, silver tray.

I briefly wonder what's on it – a bomb? A loaded gun? A copy of a newspaper with my mugshot on it?

When he walks over, I see for the first time that it's a teapot with four small cups on it, as well as a jug of water with accompanying glasses. I have to restrain myself from breathing an audible sigh of relief.

"British tea," the translator says, "very refreshing, I think you'll find."

Ask to smell the tea, Vega says, thankfully monitoring my every opportunity. *Pick up the teapot and smell the tea. As you do so, bring it to your face, hold the teapot towards the top of the pot, and break the vial inside as you do it. You can hide it all behind the teapot.*

I try to swallow the lump in my throat. All I've ever done with my hands is play videogames and package sandwiches. I'm no Houdini. And I hate tea.

I nervously grasp the vial in my pocket. Then I close my eyes, take a breath, and speak: "I love British tea," I say, trying to sound as courteous as possible. "Can I smell it?"

The translator passes the message along to the General, who grins and nods.

I hold the vial between my thumb and the inside of my palm and go to pick up the teapot with slightly trembling fingers. I lift it to my face, but not before checking the two lifeguards can't see what I'm about to do first.

Then, I lift the teapot and put it directly in my face, arching it slightly, and lift the lid. I close my eyes, take an audible sniff, and break the vial between my thumb and inner palm. I feel the cold, viscous liquid run down my palm and hopefully into the teapot. Then I breathe out deeply – with relief or dread, I'm not yet sure.

When I lower it from my face – still concealing the broken vial between my thumb and palm – both the general and the translator are looking at me with expressionless, hard to read faces. I feel Mikey's posture tense beside me. Then the general's lips start to contort at the sides and he smiles again.

"Good?" he says, in heavily accented English. I nod. "Good!"

You can drink it, Vega informs me. *The nanomachines in your stomach will ensure the poison is rendered inert.*

I take the teapot and begin to pour it into our tea cups – one for me and one for the general. He says something to the translator as I do so, but he sounds happy enough not to be pouring his own tea. Mikey takes the initiative and pours himself a glass from the jug of water.

"To good health," I say, before picking up the teacup, putting it to my lips, and drinking from it. I enjoy the moment, supping my cup of poisoned tea, amazed that I've actually gotten away with this.

When I turn around to meet Mikey's gaze, he's looking at me with desperate eyes – his face is blank, but I can see his eyes are frantic. I put my cup down and wink at him, hoping it'll pacify him, at least for now.

When I look back up to our host, he's happily sipping his tea.

"Uhhm, well, what I was saying," Mikey begins talking, but is clearly thrown off. He evidently thinks I'm trying to give my life to assassinate this man. "The shipments, we hide them inside tankers."

He seems to get back on track and keeps talking, but aside from the rank taste of British tea in my mouth, I've got one more worry: we need to get the hell out of here before the poison kicks in.

I think Mikey senses that too. He begins talking about shipment numbers and commitments, but the Butcher begins thinking to himself – pulling out a cellphone to add sums together even – and talking to his translator in a language neither of us understand. Before I'm even aware what's going on, 10 minutes have passed.

"So, we agree," Mikey says, clapping his hands together. I didn't hear what came beforehand. "Can we finish this via phone call?"

"No phone, please, we do everything face-to-face," the

translator says. We're badly burning time here. Mikey feels it too; his legs begin getting restless, juddering up and down.

I take another ominous look at the teapot, the great pandora's box that'll open when that poison begins to take its toll on our host. Then I feel a bead of sweat forming at the top of my forehead. The lifeguards are circling above still and we need to wrap this up.

"I need to speak with someone about the supply route," Mikey says, fumbling for something to say to get us out of there. "How about we arrange to meet again later this week?"

Upon hearing the translation, the Butcher throws his hands up, exasperated. He evidently hasn't gotten what he came for yet. However, after checking his watch – and taking another sip of deadly tea – he says something else to the translator.

"The General is willing to meet you later this week."

"Great, that's perfect," Mikey says, standing up. I follow him around the couch and we exchange some more pleasantries, shaking the General's hand again.

We all slowly saunter over to the ladder and climb out of the empty turquoise pool. Mikey and I try to make a fast exit, only for the translator to ask us to wait while the General climbs out first.

He does so – huffing and puffing and covered in sweat – and I'm gripped by panic already. He says a few words to his translator before trailing off, repeating the same word over and over. The translator looks at him with concern, and then with alarm, asking him a question in Aljarrian and then repeating it

I tap Mikey's arm with my elbow, as if to tell him we don't have much time. And then I look around the room; there are six of us in here – Mikey and I, the Butcher and his translator, and two rifle-toting bodyguards.

I sense Mikey take two steps backward, and I follow, but we're quickly joined by the two bodyguards, ambling over to see what's wrong with their General. The bodyguard to my right is within touching distance. His gun isn't pointed at me yet, but it's surely only a matter of time.

"Are you okay sir?" Mikey asks half-heartedly, feigning concern for the General. He doesn't seem to hear; instead, he clasps his hands around his throat and begins coughing, which turns to choking and I see that his lips are a shade of purple.

I feel my heart racing. We've got to act now.

"Kris," Mikey says, "the guy to your right."

I don't need to be told twice. I turn to the soldier to my right – whose gaze is still locked on his General – and quickly clasp my fingers around the barrel of his rifle. I pull, using every hyper-optimized sinew in my bicep to wrench it away from him. He tries to hold on, but he's powerless; I pull the rifle away from him, sending his body stumbling before me.

He looks at me with horror, realizing only too late that I just disarmed him. He goes to grab something on his belt, but I act faster, forcing the stock of the rifle I now hold into his jaw. I miss, hitting the underside of his nose, but it doesn't matter – he falls to the floor unconscious.

Then a couple of gunshots blast out, echoing rapidly. My heart beats a frenzied rhythm; I spin around on my heels, expecting to find myself face to face with a gun barrel. Instead, I see Mikey holding a rifle and the second bodyguard crumpled on the ground face first; his limbs splayed out unnaturally.

We both then turn our attention to the Butcher – now on his knees, both his hands clasped around his neck – and his hapless translator, frozen in terror of witnessing everything unfolding before him.

Mikey wastes no time in checking his rifle – unloading the magazine, looking at it, before reinserting it with an audible *click*. Then we both turn our attention to the General, who gasps and chokes a couple more times before slumping forward onto his face, falling like an enormous dead tree.

"I guess it worked," Mikey wryly remarks. Then he looks at me. "What about you? Didn't you drink it too?

"I've got a strong stomach," I tell him with a grin. He looks back blankly, not appreciating my attempt at humor. I nudge him in the shoulder, attempting to move us on. "I'll explain later, let's get out of here."

I let Mikey take the lead; the two gunshots must have alerted the other four soldiers by now. Mikey adopts a combat stance, stooping slightly as he walks and pointing his rifle as he goes. I follow him, leaving the translator bent over the Butcher's corpse.

We leave the swimming pool via the old changing rooms rather than the way we came in, slowly walking across the dirtied and cracked tiles. The room is a labyrinth of open lockers, punctuated by mirrors – some broken, some reflecting our hostile stances back at us. My finger tightens on the trigger, but I manage to avoid blasting my own image.

We quietly and methodically move through the room, waiting to cross each corner before springing out, anticipating danger in every shadow.

"I hear shouting," Mikey whispers to me. "We need to find our way to the car."

"I counted no less than four, not including the two guys we took out," I whisper back at him.

We exit the changing rooms and find ourselves in a large, open atrium, complete with a large dome composed of shattered glass panes. The sun is unbearable as ever, blinding me in its glare as I look around.

The sound of another gunshot – a loud, painful bang – makes me jump out of my skin, or rather fall straight onto my side with a sharp, throbbing sting in my thigh accompanying it.

I yelp out in pain as I hit the ground, making a noise like a wounded animal, a sound I've never made before. I look over to see two men in beige military fatigues pointing a rifle and a pistol our way. Then I screw my eyes shut, resisting the pain, and pull my rifle up in their direction.

A handful more deafening gunshots ring out. I open my eyes again and prepare to squeeze the trigger...

But both guys are already down, and a wave of heat from Mikey's rifle barrel hits me. The smell of gunpowder fills the air, and then I see the spatters of blood on the tiled walls behind each body; each one looks like a Rorschach test, and I only see relief.

"They're down," Mikey says, "we have to keep going."

He grabs the back of my shirt collar and pulls me across the floor through the dirt and the sand and flecks of broken glass. I try to pick myself up, but immediately get put down again by a lightning bolt of pain through the thigh. That bullet hit a nerve, literally.

There's a bullet embedded within your thigh, Vega says, as Mikey continues pulling me across the atrium floor. *It missed the femoral artery, but the bullet will cause you some pain.*

I don't even have chance to think about Vega's glib observation; Mikey drags me to a wall, and stoops down to my level before wrapping his arm around my back and under my arm and pulling me up to my feet. I wince with pain as he does so but manage to stabilize on my good leg.

"I'm good, I'm good," I say to him, trying to put the pain out of my mind. "Let's keep moving."

Mikey still has his arm around me, and we stumble slowly towards another set of double doors. When we reach them, I push one open with the barrel of my rifle and see the beautiful sight of sunlight on the street outside; we're finally out of the rec center. But there's one more problem...

"This isn't the way we came in," I say, looking left and right, trying to square our whereabouts with my memory of entering this place. "Dina isn't here."

We continue to stumble up the street – me hopping along on one foot and Mikey bearing most of my weight – until I see the car on the horizon and Dina stood beside it, far further up the street than I'd hoped.

And then we both fall to the floor in a hopeless heap of painful, tangled limbs.

Half a second later, my brain registers the sound of a gunshot, sudden and violent like a thunderclap. I look around and see a man aiming down the sights of a rifle far away in one of those apartments overlooking the rec center.

"Kris," Mikey says, coughing a little. I look down to see him lying on his back, with a small crescent of deep red by the side of his lip. Then my eyes are drawn to the large, red stain on his shirt and my heart skips another beat. A gunshot wound in the middle of his chest…

"Mikey!" I yell.

He's motionless, but his eyes follow me intently. And then, with another cough that sends a fine mist of blood through the air, his lips contort into a smile.

"It's okay," he says, his voice thinning out into a whisper. "It's all right, it's all right."

I hear footsteps behind me and yelling in another language. Then I feel us being cast into shadow – some deathly eclipse of the sun; one of the general's bodyguards towering directly over us, his gun pointed in our direction.

"You're a warrior now," Mikey whispers to me, blood seeping out of his mouth and the red stain on his shirt growing ever larger. "You're a warrior."

"You're gonna be okay man!" I yell, cradling his head. He smiles at me, and with one final cough all the life drains from his eyes. He begins to look through me – no longer focusing on my face, but instead on something beyond – and I see him take a final breath, his chest falling and failing to rise again.

"Mikey!" I cry, but it's no good. The wound is directly over his lung and heart. There's no saving him. That smile is etched onto his face still; a warm, contented smile. I want to cry, but I can't find the tears.

A rifle barrel is pointed in my face, resting itself perilously against my forehead, but I'm too distraught to care. Then I feel hands on me – two biceps underneath my armpits, pulling me up to my knees with great pain. I make a bunch of horrible, undignified sounds.

And then I see Dina in the distance; she's stood beside the car some 100 yards away with a hand over her mouth. I see her begin to pace toward us, but I shake my head at her, stopping her in her tracks. I won't let her get killed too.

She clenches her fists and turns her head, seemingly unable to look upon the scene anymore.

I look down at Mikey one more time – at that smile and his apparent glee of dying on the battlefield – and feel a sharp, sudden blow to my temple. It knocks me off balance, taking me completely out of the moment.

Finally, I feel tears in the corners of my eyes.

I regain the presence of mind to see the stock of a rifle on a terminal path towards me, and then it's lights out.

CHAPTER 46

I feel like I'm still lying in the shadow of that horrifying eclipse. The soldier standing over me, monolithic and indomitable. I look down beside me and see that Mikey isn't there. Instead, there's just dirty brickwork, lit by a sickly orange glow. It reminds me of that subway station; I've been here before all right.

I sit up and look around. I'm inside a small room – no bigger than six feet by four feet – with just a stainless-steel toilet for company. Above me hangs a solitary lightbulb; it sways from side to side, guided by some air current from places unknown.

Three walls within this room consist of brutal, insurmountable bricks with flecks of paint and jagged chips providing extra decoration. The last wall is a series of steel bars. Indeed, it doesn't take me long to figure out I'm in a jail cell.

The floor is greasy and dirty – my hands are stained just from touching it – and the air is warm and unbearably humid.

I can see there's a corridor beyond the steel bars and an empty jail cell opposite my own. Down the corridor, I can hear something. Sobbing, or similar indeterminable noises made by another human being.

"Vega," I finally say, before looking down the length of my own body. "Are you there?"

My leg still hurts, but not nearly with the force and intensity of before. My pants are stained with dark blood all around the wound, though – it appears black in this light – and my shirt is covered with small bloody droplets. Mikey's last breaths…

I'm here, Vega says. *You took a bump to the head, but all your body's processes are now stable.*

I sit up, drawing my legs closer to me. I'm not sure that I can put any weight on them yet, but it's not like I'm going anywhere anytime soon.

The bullet in your leg will be slowly destroyed by the nanomachine network. The process of healing the damage caused with its entry has already begun.

I close my eyes again and see only one image, burned into my retinas: Mikey's ghostly smile. A display of glee from a man beyond the grave.

"Mikey," I mumble.

He died with a smile on his face, having successfully completed his mission. I think if you'd asked him, that's how he'd wanted to have died.

"If I hadn't taken that bullet," I say, recounting the memories that are way more painful than the bullet in my leg. "If I'd have been more attentive. If I'd opened my goddamn eyes…"

You put yourself into a dangerous situation. You were vastly outnumbered and outgunned. You were lucky to survive. Despite all of this, you did everything that was asked of you. The Butcher of Ben-Assi is dead.

I couldn't care less about that right now. If I could trade it all in – if I could turn back the clock and throw that stupid vial away before we ever made it to the meeting place – I would. Mikey would still be alive. We would both live to fight another day.

I think again of Dina and that distraught, discouraged look when I shook my head at her, telling her not to bother coming to our aid. I have to believe she'll manage to cross the frontline safely. I absolutely must believe that one of us managed to escape: the one light at the end of this very dark, dank tunnel.

"So what's the deal with this?" I ask Vega after a couple more minutes. "Why did they throw me in here? Why not kill me?"

I'm sure they have a lot of questions they'd appreciate you answering about the death of the General. If you'll recall, it's been said they prefer taking American captives for ransom or as political bargaining chips.

"Yeah, I remember Dina telling me that."

They most likely saw the wound in your leg and decided you no longer pose a combat threat. That too explains why they didn't treat it. They want you to never fight again.

I snort in derision. A strange sobbing noise re-emerges from down the corridor again, and beyond that snoring. I wonder how large this prison is; I can't see any further than the empty cell opposite, but there could be dozens of people here. There are very faint voices far away. I can't tell if they're captive or captor.

I reach over to the bars on my cell. They're steel – slightly rusted in places, but very sturdy. I apply some force to them, pushing, before pulling. They don't move. Even my robot-augmented strength doesn't shift then.

"Can we do anything about this?"

Yes. The nanomachines on your fingers and palms can work to degrade and destroy the steel they touch in much the same way they will destroy the bullet inside you. You'll just need to hold onto the bars for a few hours.

I think of Dina again and find myself tightly gripping the bars, making my knuckles turn white. I've got to get out of here, if only to ensure she's okay. My last memory of Mikey will be that gleeful smile etched on his face. My last memory of Dina hopefully won't be in the same bloody, sun-scorched street.

I don't know how many hours have passed. I've been sitting here uncomfortably on the squalid brick floor with my palms wrapped around the bars the entire time. Every time I blink I see Mikey staring back at me with that smile on his bloody lips. It's unbearable.

Eventually I allow my palms to ease up on the bars. I move them away and rub my fingers along the sides of the bars where I've been holding them. They still feel rigid, but parts of them are already flaking away, dissipating in a fine dust.

I move my palms back to their former positions before taking the opportunity to change my stance, with my legs growing numb underneath me. But I don't have to wait long until something exciting happens...

I hear the sound of keys being jangled and a door being unlocked and opened. Footsteps begin to echo along the corridor, quietly at first. And then they get louder – booming strides from somebody walking with purpose. I soon hear that it isn't one set of footsteps, but two.

I remove my hands from the bars; a small cloud of dusty steel particles follows my fingers as I move them away, but otherwise the bars still look untampered with. I turn my head up and look my captors in the face.

Two men – one of whom I recognize – stand in the corridor adjacent to my cell. One is doubtless one of Darida's goons, with a thick beard and eyebrows, and no spark or warmth in his eyes. He carries a rifle slung over his shoulder, and he chews something slowly.

The other man, however, I know well enough by now. The Butcher's translator – I don't think he was ever important enough to give us his name – stands beside the goon, looking down on me like I'm some sort of animal.

"Hi buddy," I say to him, trying my hardest to smile. "Fancy seeing you here."

"Mark Cochrane," he says with a cold, stony face. If looks could kill, he might actually be able to murder me here. "But that's probably not your real name, is it?"

"You wanna know something else?" I ask him, greedily taking the opportunity to twist the knife. "I don't even like British tea."

His hateful stare seems to intensify.

"It's bad for you, you know," I add. "I mean, just look at your old boss…"

"What are you?" the translator asks. "CIA?"

I shake my head. Why does everyone think I'm in the CIA?

"Well, I can tell you this," he says, kneeling down to look me closer in the eyes. "Whoever you are, we'll find out. We'll make you talk. That bullet in your leg? A papercut compared to what we have planned for you."

I feel he's really playing to the wrong crowd here. This kind of talk would be much more threatening if I hadn't watched so many pints of my own blood spilled already. Hell, I'm even quite curious to learn what those plans are.

"And after we're done with you, we'll throw you in the same grave as your friend. I promise you that, 'buddy'."

I don't say anything; the thought of Mikey alone in some shallow grave is enough to stop me trying to play around with this guy. With one final smirk, they both leave – I hear footsteps echoing out again, growing quieter and quieter until they're both gone.

And I still don't know that translator's name.

I place my hands back around the bars, roughly in the same area they were in before. As much as I'd like to find out what that geek calls torture, I shouldn't waste any time in getting out of here.

An hour later, I'm stuck within my own torrid thoughts – that mental image of Mikey's dying smile haunting me whenever my mind wanders – when I suddenly feel one of the bars give way. Not a lot of movement, but enough to give me the faintest slither of optimism that I'll be out of here soon.

I move my hand away and rub my thumb along the bar. The steel is crumbling away in small, dusty chunks. I use my thumb to push against it, and to my surprise I push through the entire bar, sending chunks of it flying across the corridor on the other side. I watch as they land and explode into fine dust.

"That was quick."

That was a billion nanomachines working towards a single goal. From my point of view, it's anything but quick.

I don't respond to Vega's passive aggression, and instead break the bar my other hand was holding. It requires a tiny bit more force, but it too soon gives way. Now I have large, glaring gaps in two of the vertical bars, side by side.

"So, what now?"

The structural integrity of the two bars is compromised. You should be able to bend them both out of position and clamber through.

I grip both bars again above the break, and pull them towards me. Lightly at first, before really wrapping my knuckles around each bar and engaging my muscles, pushing my feet against the bottom of the bars as I do so.

It takes a lot of force, but sure enough I manage to pull each bar towards me at a 90-degree angle.

"I never expected I'd end up in jail," I say to Vega as I prepare to grip each bar below the break and pull those bars out in the same fashion. "I definitely never expected that I'd break out of jail."

It's an occupational hazard if you'll insist on fighting other people's wars.

I succeed in bending the lower half of the bars toward me, and for the low price of a couple of burning palms, I'm staring at a gap in the bars, maybe two feet tall and a foot wide.

I take one last look at my cell – my home for the briefest of stays – and squeeze through the gap.

As I suspected, the corridor outside is long, stretching maybe 50 yards in both directions. There's not a ray of natural light; we're deep underground by the looks of it. One of Darida's subterranean torture dens.

I begin to follow in the direction the translator and his friend walked from earlier. I go slowly, trying not to let my footsteps echo out across the corridor. There's a dimly glowing lightbulb every few yards, each swinging with the current of air or blinking erratically.

The next couple of cells are empty, but the ones after that are both occupied: in one, a sleeping man, laying on the floor with a coat over him, and in the other, a man looking at me with wide, watery eyes. He grips the bars of his cell, and I can tell he's silently trying to communicate to me. I understand him perfectly – he wants me to help him.

I put my finger to my lips, hopefully making the international signal for quiet, before moving on. I see another couple of men in the next two cells, and they both make the same pleading, hopeful expression. I carry on, limping along the corridor, with a mass of dried blood still making my pant leg stick to my thigh.

I keep on moving and keep seeing prison cells full of quiet, silent people, watching me with haunted but expectant eyes. None of them seem to want to cry out and alert the guards upon seeing me; they all understand that I can release them if I play this right...

Eventually, the corridor ends with two doors: one, a jailhouse style consisting of vertical and horizontal steel bars with a staircase going upstairs behind it. And the second, a large, characterless iron door aside from the numerous bolts and rivets decorating it.

I put my ear to the steel door and hear something like the low droning of a TV with accompanying static. I try to adjust my position, but accidentally drag the sole of my foot along the floor as I do so. The sound is slight, but it fills the corridor.

When I hear movement from within the room, my heart jumps to 200 beats per minute. I step aside, flattening my body against the wall beside the door, hoping that whoever steps outside won't see me here.

Sure enough, a bolt behind the door is slid out with a screeching metallic wail, and I hear the door opening out into the corridor, swinging on its hinges. My position is thankfully obscured by the door, and I hear a couple of footsteps echo out behind it.

This is your chance, Vega says. *You can push the door closed and attack the guard from behind.*

I do as Vega tells me, pushing back on the door with my palm, and seeing the clueless figure of the prison guard from earlier emerge. He's facing away from me, and hasn't yet realized I'm here or that the door is closing.

As soon as the door slams shut, I charge forward, clenching both fists and aiming a punch at the back of his head. I connect with a sickening crunch – a noise that seems to reverberate throughout my body – and earn a throbbing pain in my knuckles.

The man falls forward onto his face and chest, tumbling lifelessly into the hard brickwork of the corridor floor. I ready another punch, but he's not moving. I think he's out for the count.

You fractured your fourth metacarpal in your hand throwing that punch, Vega tells me. *It isn't a problem, but you should really work on your punches.*

I ignore him, while of course appreciating that he's 100% right. I guess that was the sickening crunch. I shake my right hand out, straightening my fingers with some pain. I crouch down beside the guard's lifeless, unconscious body, and slowly take his rifle from the ground beside him.

Then I rest my palm on the handle of the steel door, take a deep breath, and open it.

I find a small, somewhat grimy room, similar to the cells in decoration. Inside there's an old television displaying misty, blue pictures, and a steel desk and accompanying lockers. There's a green lamp on the desk, and on the wall a notice board with various Polaroid photographs of prisoners, not including me.

But none of that grabs my attention quite like the room's main exhibit: the translator, sitting alone on an office chair at the desk, watching the television and writing something on a piece of paper. He's facing away from me and begins speaking to me in Aljarrian; he must think I'm the prison guard.

I take a couple of silent, slightly painful steps towards him, and by the time he turns around to see me it's too late. I grab the back of his neck with my right hand and push his head down onto the desk so that his cheek is touching the cold steel.

"Whoa, how did you—"

He cries out, but I interrupt him.

"Be quiet," I tell him, taking a more extensive look around. "How many prison guards are there here?"

After a few seconds, he still doesn't answer so I tighten my grip on the back of his neck and exert a bit more pressure downwards, forcing his face into the metal surface of the desk.

"You're going to need to tell me."

"Just the one down here," he splutters, clearly panicked. "There's another two guards upstairs."

"Keys?" I ask. He begins trying to wriggle free of my grip, but I dig my fingertips into his neck, putting a stop to that.

"They're here," he cries, half-whispering. He slowly moves his hand to a drawer within the desk and pulls it open, revealing a set of four keys on a large keyring. I let go of the rifle for the briefest moment and pocket the keys.

"What is this place? A torture den?" I ask him after a couple more moments and he whimpers and hesitates to answer. "Come on, we're almost done."

"I just worked for General Bedoussi, I don't know!"

He's growing more and more restless beneath my grip; he's clearly agitated. I think back to what he told me an hour earlier: that he'd throw me in the same grave as Mikey. And then I see Mikey's dying smile once again.

And then I get mad.

"My friend gave his life so that your boss couldn't kill again," I tell him, grinding my teeth on every consonant and spitting every vowel with venom. "What should I do with you, huh?"

He doesn't answer, but I can hear him breathing heavily with panic. Then I notice for the first time that he has a wedding ring on. My anger subsides and I'm filled with pity for this character: an apparent family man who just so happens to work for a bloodthirsty tyrant.

Then I'm beset by a certain disgust; not at the translator, nor at the Butcher, particularly, but at myself. What the hell was I going to do? Kill this unarmed, whimpering man?

I loosen my grip on him; he looks up at me, as hopeful and optimistically as the prisoners in the jail cells did, but I'm not quite done with him yet. I let him go, clench my first, and punch him across the jaw, spinning him around 360-degrees in the office chair. Wow, that was cinematic.

And then I remember my fracture, and the adrenaline-summoning rush of pain soon follows. Oh well, he deserved that one.

I clamber over to the cabinets in the corner and fumble around with the keys. After a couple of unsuccessful attempts, the third key unlocks it and I stand in wonder at what I find: four firearms – two assault rifles, and two handguns, as well as a few clips of ammunition – waiting for me.

These weapons could be your easy ticket out of here. Free those prisoners, arm them with this weaponry, and escape with the crowd.

Vega makes a compelling argument. I pocket the ammo clips and grab the four firearms, slinging the three rifles I have over my shoulder, and make for the door. I pass the translator, lying with his head on the desk, mumbling something in semi-consciousness and bleeding from the mouth.

Hardly payback for Mikey, but then what would be?

CHAPTER 47

I push the door open and see that all eyes are upon me within the corridor now. I see hands wrapped around bars, hear a quiet but excited murmuring among the inmates here. I step over the unconscious body of the prison guard and place the weapons on the ground. Then I take the key that looks most like a skeleton key and begin to open the first cell.

When it turns in the lock with a satisfying *clink*, I see the cell's inmate's eyes light up. A tall, rotund man, wearing a stained white vest takes a step back, and allows the jail door to slowly swing open. It's a prison break, all right...

I hold out my hand to fist bump him. He obliges. Weird, I don't remember ever fist bumping anyone ever before, but then I've never broken anyone out of prison either.

I move onto the cell opposite, and the murmuring soon turns to chattering, and the chattering soon turns to cheers. I free another five inmates, who promptly talk between themselves and pick up the firearms I left on the floor. Some of them offer a handshake or a single word of thanks in broken English.

The seventh cell I come to, however, holds a real surprise.

When I walked past this one earlier I'm sure the resident was sleeping. Now though, he's awake and looking me straight in the eye.

"Well," I say, recognizing the man sitting opposite me immediately. "Howdy, stranger."

He looks back at me with both hands wrapped around the bars. His expression is hopeful, but possesses an element of mistrust. At least he recognizes me.

It's Tomas, the Polish mercenary and drug trafficker. The man who got me mired in a drug deal gone wrong during my very second day here, and left me in the desert to bleed out along with his other friends.

He's wearing a slightly blood-stained plaid shirt, with black pants and no shoes. His blond hair is greasy and matted, and his nose looks slightly out of joint. I suppose he crossed paths with our erstwhile friend the Butcher at some point.

"Hey, Kevin? Is that you?"

He doesn't remember my name. I suppose that's okay; up until a moment ago he thought I was a dead body collecting sand in the desert.

"It's Kris."

I think better of freeing him right now, and instead walk past his jail cell and go to open the next along. I've got another plan for Tomas.

"Hey, hey!" he shouts, "aren't you going to let me out?"

"I'll be back for you," I promise him. His eyes turn from expectation to dread.

I finish up freeing the prisoners; 10 men and one woman stand by the end of the corridor, waiting for me it seems. I motion to them to pick up a firearm – while I take the prison guard's rifle I got acquainted with earlier – and clutch the first key on the keyring.

With the 11 former inmates behind me – some laughing,

some murmuring, but most attentive and determined – I unlock the jailhouse door leading to the upward staircase.

After trying to communicate to them that there are two guards upstairs – motioning guns and holding up two fingers – I let them pass me to fight their way past the security upstairs and on to freedom.

They file past me one by one; smiling, willing each other on in hushed tones. I get one final fist bump, and then they're gone. I walk back to Tomas' cell.

I hear gunfire above – the muffled thunderclaps makes me jump a little – but I know my guys will do all right. They have the element of surprise, after all.

"So, Tomas, it's been a while hasn't it?"

He's still waiting patiently inside his cell, his hands wrapped around two vertical bars. He smiles at me, but behind his eyes is uncertainty. He's wondering if I'm going to leave him for dead.

"Heh, sure, I'm so glad you're alive." He looks down at my thigh, with the thick, sticky blood stain over my pants. "Are you hurt?"

"It's just a bullet," I reply. He tries to feign concern, but I go on: "And it's not like it's my first."

"Look, Kris, I feel terrible about what happened, and I—"

"Shut up," I say, cutting him off. He closes his mouth and listens, "I'll release you, but I need you to do something for me."

He waits; he loosens his grip on the bars and leans back a little.

"I need you to get me back across no man's land and into rebel territory. That is without getting us shot up this time."

His eyes light up again. He thinks he's got his ticket to freedom.

"Sure, I can do that. I know exactly how to get across the frontline."

I lean forward, putting the key into the lock, but before I

turn it I look at him one final time and wait for him to address the latter part of my request.

"And we won't get shot this time," he says.

I turn the key and open the jail door. It swings open with a rusty whining screech. Tomas stands up and steps out with some trepidation. He evidently doesn't fully trust me yet, and of course he'd be absolutely right not to.

I allow him to walk ahead of me, and I limp on behind him with that rifle slung over my shoulder. He pauses to check on the guard I punched out before stooping beside him to pull off his boots.

"First rule of combat," he says, looking up at me. "Look after your feet."

When he's done stealing the man's shoes, we climb the stairs to the floor above; a dark, tiled area with plenty of broken glass and smashed furniture. What appear to have one been desks have been cleaved apart with a crowbar and used to set up makeshift defenses long ago.

Planks are affixed to windows and the lights are seemingly out. I can't find any evidence of the inmates I released, but we do pass a couple of corpses: men in mismatched military outfits with very recent bullet wounds lying lifeless on the ground. I guess they'd be the prison guards I was told about.

"This is an old police station," Tomas tells me. The jail downstairs, the office furniture, the pervasive sense of dread; it all checks out. "We need a car. I think there's a parking lot beside this building."

We continue on, navigating our way around dimly lit corridors and open plan offices. We pass a radiator with numerous sets of handcuffs affixed to it and blood stains beside it, as well as a large office chair with a selection of knives, pliers, and other tools beside it; these too are soaked with dried blood. I'm thinking this is the torture that the translator promised…

When we come to the reception area of the former police station, we finally see through a set of large wooden double doors that it's nighttime. Tomas vaults over the reception desk and finds a notice board in an office out back with several keys hanging from it. Car keys, in fact. He's nothing if not resourceful.

"All right, be careful – there are soldiers all over this town."

I take heed, and we both check the coast is clear before pushing our way past the double doors and leaving this place behind.

I wonder how long it'll take this town to return to normality, whoever wins the civil war. Rec centers become military headquarters; police stations become torture chambers, and the populace becomes accustomed to the possibility of death at any moment. It's no way to live.

Tomas paces to a parking lot opposite, and I follow. It doesn't take him long to find that one of the car keys opens up: an old, beaten-up police car. It's white – or at least it was white once, now it's a dusty beige with a red stripe going down the middle and a blue siren on top of the roof.

"This is perfect," Tomas turns back to me to say. He clambers into the driver's side, and I go around the other way into the passenger's side. The car smells terrible – stale, greasy fries and rubber – but the seat is the comfiest thing I've experienced since *that* sofa.

The engine rattling to an unhappy start puts that thought out of my mind. Tomas looks back, reverses out of the parking lot, and we're soon chugging along the road in this hunk of junk.

"So," Tomas says, looking over to me keenly. I look back at him with tired annoyance. I'm not exactly well-rested, and some time spent unconscious following a blow to the head is not an acceptable substitute for sleep.

"So?" I finally ask.

"So, how did you end up here?"

He drives carefully, and we pass in and out of the orange halos of streetlights as we motor on.

"You mean, how did I end up here after we got ambushed in a drug deal gone wrong?"

He's silent; he looks ahead at the road.

"Let's just say I managed to find my way into the real rebel army."

"You're not exactly dressed for battle," he looks over at me again and at my blood-stained shirt and pants combination. "How did you find yourself in Darida's territory?"

I'm not going to go over the whole poisoning thing. It's still too painful. I don't even know if I'll see Dina ever again, and yet I know I'll be seeing Mikey's dying smile until the end of my days.

"Me and a few friends were posted here on a mission. I don't want to talk about it," I reply dejectedly. After a few moments of awkward silence, I ask him the same thing: "What were you doing in an underground jail cell?"

"After that deal went bad, I fled to Rachiya. I wanted to stay out of the way of the buyers. You know, the people who supplied the cash."

I see a military checkpoint up ahead, but Tomas is already wise to it; he turns left into a parking lot, drives through it, and crosses an embankment to emerge on the adjacent street.

"Of course, they found me, stuck a black bag over my head, and smuggled me into this town so they could hand me over to General Bedoussi and collect the ransom on my head."

"How did they find you?"

He hesitates to tell me; I get the sudden feeling he's ashamed to say.

"I met a couple of other contacts I had. I wanted to get some more cash together for another deal. I guess they turned me over to them."

I begin to laugh. *Unbelievable.* This guy barely escapes a deadly ambush with his life, and rather than getting the hell out of here he goes straight back to inept drug deals.

"You're an idiot, you know that?" He looks at me with barely concealed scorn.

I can't help but think about how quickly things have changed for me in Aljarran. A week ago, I was the rookie looking up to this guy, trusting him to get me into the rebel army. Now I'm springing him out of jail and laughing at his naïvety.

"You know," he says, back to concentrating on the road, leaning over the steering wheel in barely concealed frustration. "I could say the same things to you. You just took a bullet for Cantara…"

I look down at my leg again, and the rank, dried blood sticking my thigh to the leg of my pants.

"And yet here you are, asking me to ferry you right back to rebel territory. Back into the jaws of hell."

"You surely can't think we're similar," I laugh again, rubbing my fractured knuckle. "I'm nothing like you. I'm trying to help these people take back their country. You're out here running drugs, putting money in the pockets of drug lords and corrupt generals and God only knows who else."

"And you really believe that, do you? That you're taking back their country?" His fingers seem to tighten around the steering wheel. "You're just another stupid Westerner in a place you don't belong making everything worse."

I seem to remember him saying something similar the night of the drug deal. I shake my head and look out of the passenger side window, but he isn't finished yet.

"I came here with big ideas too. I thought I could change things. Help people. But this war chews you up and spits you out. I bet you've already seen a friend die, haven't you?"

I don't answer. I'm still running my fingers along my

broken knuckle; it stopped hurting a while ago, but something makes me want to keep rubbing it…

"We're not these people's saviors. I'm just some dumb European and you're a scrawny American. This is a brutal civil war, and the longer we're here playing army men, the more likely someone's going to get hurt, I'm sorry to tell you."

"You don't know anything Tomas," I say emotionlessly, trying to give the impression that he didn't hit a nerve.

"I know, I'm sure you're one gnarly dude. You got us out of that jail, and I haven't seen many men walk around with a wound like that." He nods at my leg. A huge, crimson badge of honor, I guess. "But this war wasn't made for us."

I don't reply. I just carry on looking out of the window at the dimly lit sidewalk and dilapidated, battle-scarred buildings passing by.

He's right about one thing: I did lose a friend. It hurts, and I can see how it'd drive an optimistic man to deathly cynicism.

But I'm not willing to give in yet. General Bedoussi isn't here anymore. That's because of me. No more genocides, no more mass graves, no more massacres by his hand. That's what I'm most proud of. If Mikey were here, he'd be proud of that too.

Tomas carries on with some small talk before he finally switches the radio on, and soon the town disappears behind us into the night.

Goodbye Mikey.

CHAPTER 48

Tomas is at least good for his word this time.

We pass through no man's land with no problems, taking a detour beside a river and finding part of the frontline free of active conflict or landmines. The whole journey lasts a few hours; I even let myself fall asleep for part of it.

When I wake up – jolted into life by the car bumping over a large curb and onto a road – it's almost dawn. The sun is beginning to peak out from across the horizon, and the sky is littered with blue and red clouds.

"Where are we?" I ask, looking at Tomas. He doesn't even look tired.

"Probably half an hour from Rachiya if that's where you want to be dropped off."

I could tell him I'm returning from a mission across enemy lines, having been handpicked to do it by the leader of the rebels herself, but he'd only launch into another bitter screed. I'd rather keep my morning free.

We finally make it to Rachiya, with its beautiful and tarnished glass and its gleaming arches and domes. I dearly hope Dina made it back across no man's land to see it too.

"What are you going to do?" I ask Tomas. If he tells me he's going in for another drug deal, I think I might just strangle him myself.

"I don't know. I'll hang around town for a bit and see if there's any decent way of getting paid around here. Mercenary work, ya know?"

"Lay off the drugs," I tell him with a wry smile. "They're not good for you."

He smiles back, raking his hand through his mane of blond hair.

He drops me off a couple of blocks away from Cantara's converted hotel. I climb out, stagger a little, and hold my hand to my eyes to shield myself from the sun.

"Thanks for the ride, Tomas. Keep the rifle."

He nods, and I slam the door closed; the entire rickety car seems to shake, but the engine picks up and he drives on.

Alpha base looks as quaint as ever; a large building nestled in a larger square. It's quiet at this time of morning, besides the chattering of a couple of gun-toting military men outside.

I walk up to them like a zombie; my leg is healed now, but I'm covered in dried blood – both mine and Mikey's – and I don't feel all that reinvigorated after my stay at the Butcher of Ben-Assi's underground spa.

When the soldiers see me shambling towards them, they hold their rifles up and aim them in my direction, barking orders in their native tongue. Some welcome, but I didn't expect anything less.

I drop to my knees and clasp both of my palms on my head. And then I try to communicate that I'm one of them, but it doesn't work. Only when one of them rummages through my crimson-stained pockets – while the other points his gun at me – do they find something that'll hopefully get me in.

The passport – Mark Cochrane's, that is – is deep red with

blood stains, and slightly grazed and charred, presumably by the flight of the bullet that dug itself into my thigh. They both look at it, talk to one another, and one of them begins to yell down their radio.

After 10 minutes of this charade, they allow me up and warily follow me into the building.

Inside, I'm greeted by loud applause; the four of five soldiers in the former reception area are clapping jubilantly. I smile, somewhat confused by it all. Then I'm greeted by the tall Major General; the same guy who gave us the briefing for the previous mission.

He sees my leg, and the mess of blood caked on me, and his applause turns to frantic concern.

"We need to get you to a doctor."

"I'm fine, it's just a scratch," I say, somewhat underselling the sheer amount of blood on my pants.

"I'd heard you were captured, we're delighted to see you here," he replies. He'd heard I was captured? Does that mean Dina lived to tell the tale? "Go to the doctor's office. When you come back, we'll debrief you."

A young-looking soldier with slightly nervous eyes and a twitching eyebrow leads me up a flight of stairs. He tries to help me – offering a shoulder to lean on to ease me up the steps – but I wave him away.

This reminds me, I really need to find a way of explaining how I can rebound from these serious injuries so quickly. Dina figured out there's something very strange about me, and anyone else with a couple of brain cells and an inquisitive nature would surely think the same way.

To alleviate that fear, I decide to feign a bit of injury, limping up the steps. The soldier beside me watches with concern but doesn't offer to help me again. Instead, he looks at me with respect and admiration, and I have the strange and somewhat unsettling thought that he's awed by me. By *me*.

On the fourth floor, we stop climbing the stairs and I'm

led to a featureless room with a desk, a couple of chairs, and a large, locked cabinet – another converted hotel room I assume – and told to wait. There's no doctor here yet. I take a deep breath and close my eyes, but soon see Mikey staring back at me, forcing them open once again.

Something about this reminds me of my first hospital stay after finding the body.

I rub my forehead and try to keep my eyes open. But I'm tired. I'm so tired I don't register the footsteps in the corridor.

"Kris?"

I turn my head and see her: Dina, clad in unassuming olive military fatigues, with a very big smile on her face. Her eyes are huge, and she's grinning so widely I can see dimples on her cheeks. She paces towards me and embraces me, hugging my body tightly and warmly. I didn't expect that...

"Dina," I say, with my head buried in her shoulder, "you got out okay."

"I got out okay," she says, letting go of me and stepping back a little. Then her expression sours; the light in her eyes goes out and I can tell what's coming. "What about Mikey?"

I avert my eyes from her own, look down, and shake my head.

"He didn't make it."

There's a painful silence between us. When I finally look back up at her, she's got that emotionless expression again; like she's so experienced in receiving bad news by now that she's got an impenetrable, protective wall she can put up at any moment.

"I saw you both on the street outside the rec center. I saw you both covered in blood, surrounded by the Butcher's men. And then I saw you shake your head at me. You told me not to intervene."

"There's nothing you could have done," I tell her.

"What about you?" she asks, looking at the various dried blood stains all over me. "What happened to your leg?"

"I got shot," I say, referring to a bullet embedding itself in my thigh muscle as casually as eating a hot dog. "But it's fine. It's fixed, if you know what I mean."

She knows exactly what I mean. She leaves to go find another set of clothes for me, and I'm left with the memory of her arms wrapped around me in a tight embrace. I liked the feeling.

When she returns with an armload of folded, tan camouflage clothing, I manage to peel off my blood-stained pants for the first time in two days and take a look at my bullet wound, or rather the complete lack of one. It's already fully-healed; I don't even have a patch of scarred flesh to show for the fact I was shot behind enemy lines.

I throw the rest of the clothing on and follow Dina downstairs. We pass a few military men and women as we walk, all of whom smile and speak warm, enthusiastic-sounding words to us both in Aljarrian.

We end up in the large banquet hall where Dina, Mikey, and I ate that three-course meal. Thankfully, the banners hanging from the walls are the only thing that might still remind me of that night. Everything else has been re-arranged and redecorated.

The dining table has made way for a number of folding chairs, and a wooden table lies at the back of the room, filled with various cold meats and other buffet foods on small paper plates. I soon as I see it, I'm willed over there by a higher, irresistible power. I greedily tuck in, shoveling ham and cheeses into my mouth with my fingers in an undignified fashion.

Dina follows me and watches me disgrace myself with a smile. Under normal circumstances I feel like she'd make some smart remark – compare me to a pig or the like – but I guess she thinks I've earned some slack.

When the room suddenly fills – several older military men, as well as the Major General from earlier – I barely notice. I see that Cantara is the last to arrive, flanked by two bodyguards, but my mouth is full of pastries. I turn to salute her, and slowly try to chew the remaining food away. Quite uncouth, but quintessentially American I suppose.

She smiles awkwardly before saluting me back. She's wearing a purple suit jacket with a couple of badges on it, and a surprising amount of make-up: lipstick, mascara, foundation. I look at her and can't get the image of a TV news presenter out of my head.

"Kris," she says, pointing to the center of the room and the array of chairs laid out. "I'd like to commend you for a successful mission."

"Sure thing," I manage to say, having swallowed most of what I'd stuffed into my mouth.

We all take a seat – Dina and I on the front row beside Cantara, and the faceless, nameless crowd of military men behind us – as Major General Rahal recaps the preparation for the mission. He mentions Mikey's name – a painful couple of syllables that stab at me as as any bullet – before asking me to come up to the front to give my own account.

Nervously, I stand up and they give me another round of applause.

"Well," I begin, "I'm not exactly used to public speaking, so I'll go through this quickly."

I tell them about our journey to the rec center, about the military presence, and about the Butcher. I tell them how I managed to poison his tea and how readily he drank it. Of course, I don't tell them I too had a sip. And then I tell them how the poison worked too quickly, and we didn't have time to escape before it started taking an effect.

"Or," I say, unhappily reliving that day's events once again. "Maybe I applied the poison too soon. Maybe I could have waited. This guy, the Butcher, he wouldn't stop talking. And Mikey tried to end the conversation, but, but…"

My eyes meet Dina's; she can see me trailing off,

drowning in the muddy memories of that day. She narrows her eyes at me sympathetically. I think she knows exactly how I feel.

"You shouldn't be ashamed, Kris," Cantara says, throwing me a lifeline. "You did your part in the mission perfectly."

I smile, and go on to recount my escape from the jail with plenty of white lies thrown in. My story doesn't perfectly add up, but everyone's so caught up in the killing of the Butcher that they don't seem to notice.

"You can sit down," the Major General tells me after I waffle on for a bit longer. I do as he says, nodding my head awkwardly and smiling to another round of applause.

Then, Cantara stands and begins speaking.

"The justified killing of The Butcher of Ben-Assi is just the first step in bringing Ahab Ebu Darida's inner circle to justice," she says with vigor. She talks with a smile on her face, clearly relishing this fight. "The wheels of destiny are turning and they won't stop until they crush Darida beneath them."

She continues, and I find myself getting into the speech; I feel goosebumps rising on my forearms. She can talk a good game, that's for sure. I hear mumbling behind me, take a look back, and see that this whole speech is being recorded on camera. When I look beside me, Dina has her arms crossed skeptically.

Cantara closes her speech and we all give her a round of applause. Everyone stands up and begins milling around the room, speaking in groups of two or three and eating the food. Cantara, on the other hand, makes a beeline for Dina and me.

"It's great to have you both back," she says, her eyelashes catching the sublime white light in here. "I'm truly sorry we lost Mikey, but he gave his life for a just cause. He gave his life for the people of Aljarran."

She salutes us again and we salute back. And then she leaves to join the company of a circle of generals.

"I guess we're dismissed," Dina says.

I take one last look at the gaggle of generals and other military men, chatting and enjoying our success. And then we quietly leave.

I follow her back up to the fourth floor and into room 422 – the same room we shared with Mikey before the mission. It looks the same; the box of electronic items Mikey was rummaging through is still here.

"I managed to get across no man's land last night and spent the night here," Dina tells me. I sit on a chair and sink down to rest my cheek on the table. Then I exhale the content of my lungs, making a noise akin to a wounded beluga whale. I'm exhausted.

"Well, we did it," I finally say. "We killed the Butcher."

"Yeah, we did," Dina replies, mournfully.

"So what do we do now?"

She looks at me blankly, like I suffered a knock on the head in my captivity and lost a few IQ points.

"What do we do? We fight the next battle," Dina says. She sits down opposite me, and stares into me with those intense, laser-focused eyes of hers. "What else can we do?"

"You don't think there could be another role for you in all of this?" I ask her. This has been playing on my mind ever since my conversation with Tomas. "You've got medical knowledge, you're smart, why do you have to risk your life?"

She leans back in her seat, rubbing that locket between her fingers again, and smiles at me bashfully; something about her posture reminds me of Mikey and his laidback attitude to life.

"Didn't we have this conversation? You don't have to be worried about me Kris, I can handle myself. I know my way around a gun. And you said it, I'm smart."

"Yeah," I say after a few moments of hesitation.

"Get some rest," she says, picking up a book and flipping

through it. "You're our super soldier, we need you ready for battle."

I snort in acknowledgement, but I wish I could change her mind.

"To glory," she says, with a coy smile, "or the grave."

I make a slightly bemused face. She sees and seeks to clarify: "Someone I used to fight alongside. He'd say 'to glory, or the grave'."

Someone she *used to* fight with. I'm not going to ask what happened to him, but I can guess he never found the glory he was seeking.

It's useless to argue with her, though. She's made for this war. Or, more worryingly, this war was made for her.

To glory, or the grave.

CHAPTER 49

I'm sitting on the balcony of room 422 watching an enormous flock of birds in the blue sky. They're flying in strange shapes and patterns. I think I see something I recognize from time to time – a face; a flower; a gun – but the flock shapeshifts again before I can see for sure.

I can't ever remember seeing flocks of birds like this back home. There's a chance they all died out from the noxious exhaust fumes, maniacal populace, and radioactivity disasters, but it's probably more likely I was never in the mood to look to the skies like this.

It's 11:00 AM or so. I don't even remember what day it is. It could already be November for all I know. I spent yesterday catching up on sleep, playing cards with Dina, and exchanging stories from our childhoods. Or at least whatever passes for a story when you had as wildly fun a childhood as I did.

It was an unusual feeling to a day relaxing, rather than growing back a blown-off fingers or languishing on the stained floor of some torture jail cell. But I liked it.

Dina is good company. I feel I don't have to try my hardest with her. Everything seems natural.

"Vega," I say, thinking now of the very unnatural presence within my body. "Are we all healed up?"

The bullet in your leg has been destroyed. All of your biological processes are working optimally and the nanomachine network performing at peak efficiency.

"Ready for battle then."

Dina's own words tumbling out of my mouth.

Ready for battle.

I stop watching the flock and walk back into the hotel suite. Dina is sitting at the table again reading a Aljarrian-language newspaper. When I take a seat opposite her, she closes the paper and dumps it on the table in front of me with its first page facing upwards. It's a picture of General Bedoussi, the butcher of Ben-Assi. I don't know what to make of it; I can't read the headline.

"He didn't spring back to life, did he?"

"No," Dina says with a grin. "In fact, he's still very dead."

"I suppose that's a relief," I say, thinking of the reports of my own death back home.

She tells me the newspaper is native to Rachiya and loyal to the rebel regime ever since the civil war kicked off. She stands up, walks besides me, and translates the article.

"General Allam Bedoussi, otherwise known as the Butcher of Ben-Assi, the fearsome general and confidante of dictator Ahab Darida, is thought to have been assassinated by rebel forces Friday."

I laugh to myself. That was Friday, so it must be Sunday today.

"The killing marks the latest victory for Cantara's forces, who are anticipated to make greater gains in the coming days."

"They make it sound like we're really winning," I say, still amazed at my own presence in the newspaper headlines for the third time or so.

I flip a couple of pages and see stills from the video

Cantara recorded at this very hotel and the back of my large, dopey head.

We eat some dinner together – the noodles from the terrible rations along with some leftover potatoes we managed to snag from the kitchens downstairs last night. And then we begin thinking about checking out of this place, as nice as the food is.

"Where would we go?"

"Back to Captain Mahmoud's unit," Dina replies without skipping a beat. "Good, honest work for a good, honest leader."

"I don't know why you don't like Cantara," I say, noting her implied diss. "She's inspiring. She's turning this war around, isn't she?"

"We're turning the war around," she replies with scorn in her voice. "Not some politician sat by the minibar in a luxury hotel."

I can see how Dina would be distrustful of politicians. The same way I was distrustful of the outside world, I guess. Her mother died by a politician's order. My own mother died by a stray bullet. It shaped us both.

"Well, I'm ready to go any time."

"All right," she says, a lot more upbeat this time. "We'll say our goodbyes and find out wherever Mahmoud's base camp moved to."

We finish up dinner, and Dina packs her worldly possessions away while I sit and rue the fact that I myself have nothing.

She's halfway through when we hear the thunderous noise of heavy footsteps in the corridor outside, running or pacing away somewhere. Not an unusual occurrence in itself, but when we hear a three or four more runners it's a monstrous racket that shakes the walls of our room. We both look at each other with the same curious expression.

Dina goes to the door, opens it, and looks out. Another

couple of heavy footsteps, making an urgent run for somewhere sounds out in the corridor, and Dina is quick to ask a question in the native tongue.

"They're saying part of Darida's forces on the frontline have collapsed," she tells me, walking back with an excited spark in her eye. "They're in retreat. We want all the people we can muster to push forward and take as much land back as we can."

"So, what happens now?"

"We should join them," she says, eagerly and predictably. "This could be it; we could chase them all the way back to the capital. This could be the end of the war."

Part of me is filled with apprehension; an unfocused, unplanned push into Darida's territory without any support or intelligence? We could be walking into a buzzsaw. But whatever apprehension I'm feeling doesn't make it to my mouth.

"Sounds good enough to me, let's go."

I quickly pack a bag with water and a few other essentials, and put my boots on – still slightly stained with my own blood. Dina grabs her medical bag and a few other items, and we're on the move.

We join a couple more guys in military gear running downstairs, and soon find ourselves back in the banquet hall. The whole place is a buzzing hive of activity now; soldiers run past us in both directions, other people queue for rations and whoop and holler as if the war is already won.

We move on, and Dina says a few words to the tired-looking guys behind the desk in the front lobby, and one of them disappears underneath it to produce a couple of rifles that he hands to us, along with three magazines of ammunition for each.

Meanwhile, I hear a delirious commotion from every corridor. The building is shaking in its foundations. I begin to feel those goosebumps rising on my forearms again; my heart is beating out of my chest, but not with panic this time. This feels big.

We march outside and see a queue of soldiers lining up to jump in the back of a personnel transport truck: a roaring beast of a cab, with a flatbed in the back with two benches on either side, and a fabric tarp over the top of it.

There's already a handful of geared-up rebels inside, but Dina and I manage to jump the queue when I hear the words 'Ben-Assi,' and presumably the word for 'butcher' bandied around. We climb in and sit next to each other close to the back of the truck alongside maybe 20 or so others.

The mood is feverish; I look around the back of the truck and don't see a single face that isn't beaming delightedly, enthusiastically chanting or singing Aljarrian tunes, or staring intensely forward, trancelike. Someone begins to beat out a drum rhythm with their foot; everyone else soon follows.

And then we're moving; I see bodies shunted backwards as the truck makes a rapid start.

"What can we expect here?" I ask Dina. She's staring out of the back, watching a cloud of dust follow us as we fly through the streets.

"Honestly, I don't know," she shouts, making herself heard over the roaring engine. "I've never been in this situation before. Usually I was posted as a medic, recon or establishing a forward base. Only when you came along did I start living the interesting life."

"We're going to Safiqq," a man sitting opposite us shouts back at us. He's holding an M4 rifle with both hands and has a pattern of camouflage paint dried onto his face, all different shades of tan and beige. He appears to be from the region, but his English is very good. "The government forces on both sides of the town fled, so we're going to take back the town."

Take back the town? That sounds like a battle to me.

"Are we expecting resistance? Are Darida's men still in the town?" I ask the man.

He's wearing a badge sewn into his jacket with a skull and crossbones on it, and under that a bullet-proof vest with ceramic plates stitched inside. He also has a small respirator tucked under his chin, like those used by doctors dealing with infectious diseases. He certainly looks ready for battle.

"I sure hope so!" he says.

I look at Dina, who smirks back at me and begins checking her rifle. She's clearly ready for this; the charge into battle to take back her country. However, I'm a little more worried.

Kris, this is potentially a very dangerous situation, Vega says as the others on the truck begin singing the chorus of some song. *The government forces within this town are cornered, but that doesn't mean they won't fight to the death. Additionally, Darida has shown an appetite to set up traps before.*

I nod to myself, letting Vega know I understand. I see another two trucks following us, so I know we're not exactly low on reinforcements here, but this will be my first taste of actual frontline battle.

It's exciting. And it's terrifying.

CHAPTER 50

We're perhaps an hour into the journey by now. The party-like atmosphere has subsided, instead replaced by a stranger, more contemplative atmosphere. Everyone inside the truck is quiet and focused, with the occasional word shouted loudly in Aljarrian met by the rumbling stamping of boots. Everyone is focused, harnessing a nervous, frantic energy.

The blasts from enemy mortar shells outside are already beginning to blare out; I see a couple of guys jump in their seats upon hearing them.

Another one lands right beside us – the deafening roar of an explosion, followed by the showering of dirt and sand on the fabric canvas covering our truck. We must be close.

Suddenly, I feel skin against the back of my hand held nervously by my side. It's Dina, grabbing my hand without a word. She looks at me and narrows her eyes in a silent display of support.

I have no time to respond; the truck judders to a halt and a chorus of yelling picks up among us. We watch the man with the skull and crossbones badge jump out first and follow him. After Dina jumps, I throw myself out of the back of the lorry, landing on both feet with a jolt that goes all the way up my spine.

I make way for the others to jump out, and when everyone hits the sand we begin to follow them, marching quickly with our rifles drawn. We eventually shelter under a bridge where a river – now dried up – once flowed beneath.

Another team from a different transport truck joins us, and we soon have 40–45 comrades beside us. A tall man wearing wraparound sunglasses and a red bandana begins addressing the crowd. Dina translates again.

"He's saying we wait for the signal from another division, and then we rush the town."

An artillery shell lands just beside the bridge, hitting a couple of us with chunks of dirt and sand. I drop to the floor instinctively, and then look around in alarm; no-one seems to be hurt, thankfully. The man goes on yelling.

"He says they're tired and backed into a corner. We're close to encircling them."

Just as Vega said; they're cornered, encircled, and know their only two options are surrender or fighting their way out. It's going to be a punch-up all right.

I look over to Dina; she's got that fiery, determined look in her eyes again, holding the stock of her rifle with one hand and her locket with the other. I think to ask her to stay behind me – let me soak up the bullets – but it's too late; the bandana man shouts and we all begin to move.

We trudge on, marching at first and quickly accelerating to a jog, following the other 40 or so soldiers in front of us. I hear gunfire ahead and see that the horizon is thick with smoke. There's shouting all around, contributing to a febrile, animalistic atmosphere. It's unlike anything I thought I'd ever experience.

We reach a dusty verge just ahead of the outskirts of the town, and throw our bodies against it, taking over. I can see buildings beyond it – charred, broken walls and collapsed towers and minarets. I also see a couple of relatively intact concrete buildings with glaring, black openings where the windows once stood.

There's a spray of gunfire hitting the verge in front of us, blinding me temporarily with dirt and sand. It's clear enough where it came from.

Muzzle flashes in that building, directly in front of you. They're firing from inside it, Vega says to confirm.

"Enemies in front!" I yell, unsure if anyone can even understand me. Dina yells after me, and word soon filters across the verge that a bunch of us are to provide suppressing fire while a team assaults the buildings ahead.

"Suppressing fire?" I ask Dina, extravagantly flaunting my battlefield inexperience once again.

"Shoot everything you've got in their direction," she yells at me. "Make it impossible for them to aim at our guys."

I take a sharp intake of breath, and after watching and waiting for a group of rebels on my right to begin their assault, I peek over the verge with my rifle and begin firing in the direction of the concrete building, as does Dina and a couple of others beside me.

The sound is deafening; each gunshot is like a hammer blasting off each eardrum. But my shots appear to be hitting home; I see each bullet either hit the building in a cloud of dusty concrete or disappear into the darkness within. Then I see activity – shadows and limbs moving frantically – and I keep firing.

When my clip is empty – 30 bullets sent over the verge and into the enemy's den – I quickly reload, remembering what Dina taught me. But by the time I'm done, our comrades are beside the building, kicking in a door, and preparing to assault.

I see flashes of gunfire within – golden flashes and falling shadows against the walls – and my heart beats a nervous, frantic rhythm. I take another deep intake of breath and look across my right to see Dina and the others get to their feet, preparing to rush in.

This isn't my first gunfight, but it feels the most real somehow. During the drug deal ambush or the encounter outside the schoolhouse or the last gunfight I don't even want to recall, I felt like I was viewing myself from afar; like I wasn't a participant, but a remote viewer. As if I were watching a movie.

Here, with my finger wrapped around the trigger and the dust kicked up from gunshots in my eyes, I feel like I'm at war.

Shaking myself out of my pointless musings, I stand up and run towards town with Dina and the others. We run to cover – the wall of a mechanic's garage, it seems – and Dina discusses with them what comes next.

"We're pushing into town from here," she says to me, translating. "We'll need to provide cover for heavy support."

"Heavy support?" I ask, as another artillery shell explodes nearby provoking a jump from both of us. She motions to the guy behind her, who I see for the first time has a large rocket launcher strapped to his back. Holy cow, how did I miss that?

We file into the mechanic shop through the backdoor – five of us, including heavy support – and clear the building, moving room to room and ensuring no enemies remain within. Then we move to the entrance, overlooking a large public square. I peek between the blinds on a window; it seems quiet enough, but I know that'll soon change.

Another large explosion goes off nearby making the walls rattle, and everything hanging on them – tools such as drills, wrenches, and a painting mask – shake and fall. The sounds of explosions are growing closer and becoming more numerous.

I see the others opening the steel shutters and preparing to move into the square outside. I brace myself – readjusting the grip on my rifle – and stride in front of Dina, provoking a dubious look from her.

After a count of three syllables, which I'm guessing are the first three numbers in the native tongue, we charge across the square. I sprint forward, checking behind to ensure Dina is keeping up, and we crouch against a waist-high wall. I look over to see another squad on our side making the run too. It seems we're making progress…

We jump the wall and pile into the next building – a massive warehouse, full of wooden crates. We begin to clear the building, Dina and I splitting off from the others to look upstairs.

We climb a staircase slowly, aiming our rifles into every shadow every step of the way. Slowly – our footsteps echoing out across the dusty wooden floorboards – we progress through each room. Eventually, we reach a large hall full of old, antiquated printing equipment.

"What is this place?" I ask as we pass the equipment and end up in some sort of locker room. Most of these lockers are neatly closed, unlike the rec center's changing rooms; it makes me think someone was using them recently. Civilians, or worse.

"This was a publishing office," Dina says mournfully. "My mother had a contract with this company."

I give her a look – an earnest expression, hoping to let her know I sympathize – before we press on. We finally come to the last unexplored door up here: it's blue with black grime around the hinges.

Then I hear something and get a strange feeling – the strangest, almost imperceptible sense that there's danger ahead. It was probably the rest of our team on the level below us, but I have a terrible, niggling sense of doubt.

"Ready?" Dina asks, her rifle pointed forward and the stock tight against her shoulder, preparing to open the door. I hesitate, and then I hear something else – a creak of a floorboard or the rattling of a table?

Dive!

Vega yells the word out of nowhere; it dances through my mind like an electric shock. I grab Dina by the shoulders and force us both down to the hard floorboards. She cries out in pain and confusion.

"What the—"

Four bangs – one after the other, each feeling like a punch directly in my chest – and four bullet holes in the blue door with flecks of paint and wood flying into the air in a fine spray of dust.

Dina and I lie on the floor, my arm still draped over her, and we don't make a sound. I breathe out quietly and slowly rise to my feet. Then I take a look at Dina – laying on her back, her rifle beside her – before concentrating on the door.

Behind it I hear movement; someone adjusting their stance or posture. Or maybe just hyping themselves up to step through the door and face their destiny. I tighten my grip on my own rifle, aiming it towards the door as I watch the handle turn.

Another gunshot pierces the air – the whip crack of the shot rippling through me like an electric shock. And then a couple more. I smell gunpowder, and look down to see Dina lying on her back, aiming her rifle; its barrel is smoking. I look into her eyes and see something I've never seen before. She looks afraid.

There's a muffled noise behind the door – the slow, unmistakable crash of a body hitting the floor – and then another eternity of silence.

I lock eyes with Dina again; she blinks and re-asserts her usual expression, looking firmly at the door. I take another step towards it, place my hand on the cold, metal handle, and turn it.

Inside is an empty room; frosted glass windows – half of

them broken – and unremarkable beige tiles cover the floors and ceilings. It's a shower room; there's blood seeping into the drain in the middle of the room and a body lying beside it.

Before I can take a better look at him, Dina rushes beside me. She sees that he's down, and crouches beside him checking for vital signs.

"He's dead," she quickly announces without any emotion.

I think back to Dina's telling me of her first kill; an unarmed man hiding behind a door, if I remember rightly. No wonder she looked afraid; that must have been quite the trip down morbid memory lane.

We walk back downstairs and meet the other three we came in with, but any pleasantries are quickly tossed aside when an explosion blares out upstairs, shaking the walls of the building and showering us in a layer of concrete dust, dirt, and cobwebs. We fall to our knees instinctively; I cover my head.

"The hell was that?"

"Something must have hit the floor above," Dina yells out in reply. "C'mon, let's go."

"Go!? Where!?" I cry, still on my knees, but Dina isn't interested in answering that one. She and the others begin to march to another room. I haul myself to my feet and follow.

I find them in another warehouse, this time empty. One of the others jams a button on a wall, slowly opening a metal shutter to the outside world. There we see an empty street, but the sound of the battle is close by. Bullets seem to split the air, whizzing between positions behind us and positions deeper within the city.

One of our comrades receives a message on his radio. He frantically relays it to the rest of us, sounding a little daunted, and Dina then talks to me.

"We're going out again, they need us."

"Need us?" I ask, wondering why we're so special. Then I

see the rocket launcher again, weighing heavily on that poor man's back, and feel a wave of panic. What kind of monster do we need to take down with that?

They count to three between them and rush out into the street again. I follow, sprinting towards the bullet-hole pocked wall of a large building. When we make it, I see that we're on the left side of a road with numerous abandoned or burned-out cars sat on it. There are rusty blotches on the road; I know immediately they're old blood stains.

On the other side we see another squad – four rebels from our truck, including the man with the skull and crossbones and the impeccable English – ducking behind a jackknifed truck, motioning for us to take a look ahead.

Dina flattens herself against the wall and takes a peek around the corner. When she turns back, I see a bead of sweat drop from the bottom of her nose. All the color has drained from her face.

She says a word in Aljarrian to the others – a single, low syllable, which sounds notably grave. Then she turns to me and says one word: "Armor."

Armor? A tank? I crawl on my hands and knees to the bottom of the wall, where the corner of the building meets the sandy pavement, and look through my rifle sights. Sure enough, there it is: a large, tan-colored tank sitting in the middle of the street, maybe 70 yards ahead of us.

It whirs and grinds and hums a hideous chorus of sounds, the engine chugging along inside it and the caterpillar tracks occasionally revving into motion, jolting it forwards or backwards. Its turret is aimed elsewhere, but that soon changes.

"It's moving!" I shout, watching the turret turn towards our friends on the other side of the road. The long barrel slowly rotates to face in their direction. They begin shouting and the four of them start running, leaving their positions by the truck.

"I think it's gonna fi—"

I don't even finish my sentence before a shell is launched. The shockwave is the first to hit me; a warm blast of energy, feeling like my face was pushed inside a pizza oven. The noise is so loud I barely even register it; a nightmarish crack of a whip, like a volcano blasting its lid.

It starts raining – not water, but small metallic pieces of debris from the truck opposite. I can't even see the other squad now. There could be a billion pieces of them for all I know.

Kris, if you get hit by that it's game over, Vega says. *I surely do not need to tell you that the damage caused by a hit from a tank shell would be catastrophic, and the nanomachine network would be powerless to protect or heal you.*

Well, thanks for that priceless info Vega.

I look across the street as the cloud of dust and smoke subsides and see another large building; thick, stone walls three stories tall. Seems like a former bank or the like. And if I run, I can make it there quicker than that tank barrel can follow me…

"Dina," I say, stating the idea before the words 'suicide mission' can jump into my head. "I'm going to run across the street. I can distract it and make the turret follow me over there. And then your guy can blow it away."

The words spill out of me like I'm quoting some stupid action movie. I can't even believe I'm saying them. Yet here I am, getting to my feet, and psyching myself up to sprint.

She looks at me skeptically, then across the street, and then back at me. If I didn't know better, I think I see the tiniest sly smile at the side of her lips. Like she respects my courage, or maybe just wants to see me and my nanomachines grow a leg back.

"I don't hate the idea," she replies. She turns and speaks to the others, who look at me with a mixture of expressions from grave concern to admiration and respect. "On three?"

I prepare myself, tensing the nanobot-primed muscles in

my thighs and calves. I see the rocket launcher lifted off the man's back and prepared for launch. Among the *pop, pop, pop* of distant gunfire I close my eyes, rub my fingers along my temples, and take a breath.

Then I think I'm ready.

"One, two…" Dina says, as the soldier beside me readies the rocket launcher on his shoulder. She looks me in the eyes with optimism; she believes in me. "…three!"

I begin sprinting, gripping my rifle tightly in my right hand, swinging it forwards and backwards with the motion of my arms. I dodge debris and junk along the road and sidestep the wreckage of the jackknifed truck.

Almost immediately I hear the loud mechanical grinding noise of the turret turning to follow me. The sound fills me with hope and then with dread.

I jump up to the curb and slide past the corner of the bank building, with its large brick walls hopefully protecting me. I can't see or hear any evidence of the other squad; I think they got away in time.

I soon hear another rapid series of sounds; a brief *pop*, the turbulent rush of something sounding like a firework, and then the eardrum-stinging bang of a hard metal shell being cracked open.

I steady myself, then peek out from behind the corner of the bank. There's the tank – still standing in the middle of the road, still juddering and jolting forwards and backwards, spasmodically – but with a molten, white-hot core of fire burning in the middle of it and a spiral of thick black smoke rising into the air.

I see Dina and the others celebrating, and allow myself a moment of joy too, rolling onto my back and pumping my fists in the air. I hear gunfire in the distance still like popcorn popping in the microwave, but even that seems to be dying down.

I sprint back across the street to meet the others, and we

exchange high fives. Then we see the other squad of our comrades further up the block, trailing a group of Darida's men. I look closer, and see the enemy combatants have their hands in the air. They're surrendering.

"I think we did it," Dina remarks with a bright glint in her eye. "I think we broke them."

CHAPTER 51

I'm sitting back in the publishing office warehouse, perched atop a crate with Dina sitting opposite. She's rolling her locket between her fingertips with her lips twitching delicately, like she's trying to say something but can't quite put it into words.

A couple of hours have passed; the sun is beginning its slow descent in the sky and the battle for Safiqq is over. With the loud and obvious destruction of their last bastion of defense – the smoking remains of the 'armor' – the remaining forces defending the town surrendered. We took around 20 prisoners of war and liberated up to 100 civilians.

We won.

"We really did it," Dina says at last. "I've fought this war for four years. Four years of my life, burned to fuel this never-ending brutality. Now I feel like it's almost over."

"Maybe start thinking of going back to college," I tell her, putting my hand out to meet hers and giving it a squeeze. "Maybe we'll all need new jobs soon."

I say the words happily, but they're tinged with uncertainty. I haven't yet considered what happens to me when this war is over. It's not like I get to go home; I'm dead to my homeland. Literally.

"What will you do?" she asks me, echoing my thoughts.

"I don't know. Know of any other wars being fought nearby?" She smiles at my question, amused. "I mean, I did pretty good against that, uhh…"

I pause; all of a sudden, I can't think of the name of it. The huge, twisted, molten pile of scrap metal lying in the middle of the street. The barrel, the turret, why can't I remember what it's called?

"The uhm, you know, the uhm…" I say the first thing that comes to mind. "Lord of war."

Dina laughs, unable to restrain herself. She puts her palm over her mouth, giggling uproariously. "Lord of war!?"

Tank, Vega says, with a barely concealed tone of ridicule.

"Tank!"

Dina laughs some more. This isn't the first time a girl has laughed at me; this may not be the 100th time. In the past I'd want to crawl into the earth and fossilize myself. Now I feel like I want to laugh along.

"I don't know if this army thing is your true calling, Kris."

"Yeah," I say with a grin on my face. "You might be right."

We both flinch when we hear another booming explosion outside. Darida's remaining men have been flinging artillery shots at us from afar since the end of the battle; the flailing attacks of a losing side.

I hop off the crate and walk to a different, darkened corner of the warehouse, away from Dina's hearing range.

"How are we doing, Vega?"

You broke a toenail sliding for the wall. And you very slightly sprained a ligament in your forearm tackling Dina to the ground. Other than that, you're unhurt.

Wow, I managed to fight on the frontline, take back a town, and play a role in destroying a tank and still emerge relatively unscathed.

"Are you impressed?"

Am I impressed that you did not get hit with a tank shell directly to the head? Yes, I suppose I am.

I suppose that's the biggest compliment I'll get from Vega, but I'll take it.

I walk back to Dina, and we agree to head back to the hastily set up FOB – which I'm told stands for Forward Operating Base – inside a former supermarket. We walk side by side up the street and pass the still-smoking wreckage of the 'Lord of War,' not so mighty now.

Suddenly, we hear desperate shouting up ahead. It's not exactly an unusual occurrence, but there's something about the tone and tenor of this shouting that sends shivers down my spine. It sounds like someone drowning, choking, spluttering. But I know that's impossible here in the desert.

Kris, there's a problem, Vega says, making me stop dead in my tracks. *I'm detecting something problematic in the air.*

Something problematic in the air? I grab Dina's arm, pulling her back to me. She spins on her heel, looking at me with annoyance at first, but she quickly seems to realize that I think something's wrong.

"What's the matter?" she says after a few confused moments.

It's a nerve gas, Vega says. *It's odorless and colorless, but it's there and it's deadly. You need to find a gas mask or adequate ventilation far from here immediately.*

"Hold your breath," I tell Dina, knowing that whatever nerve gas will do to her, it definitely won't be good.

"What?" She looks at me in panic; I think she finally believes my intuitions.

"Hold your breath, we're getting out of here!"

I drop my rifle and grab her around her upper body, forcing my right shoulder into her chest and lifting her into an unhappy fireman's carry. She thankfully goes along with it. I turn and begin running, hauling the combined weights of myself and Dina as fast as I can back out of town.

You won't be able to breathe for long; the nanomachines can only go so far to protect you. You'll eventually lose consciousness.

I hear him, but I keep breathing. I can't afford to hold my breath yet; I need to use what strength I have to get Dina to safety.

I keep running – my thighs feeling like leaden weights already – and try to control my breathing. We pass a couple of civilians – a man and a woman – beginning to choke. They put their hands to their throats and cough wildly, gesturing at us to stop and help them. But we don't. I can't.

We pass the tank's wreckage again and see one of our fellow rebels vomiting into a gutter. Another civilian is staggering around as if he's drunk. Another woman is screaming at the top of her lungs. I keep running.

Blurry figures stagger around like zombies; I lock eyes with a woman – her pupils tiny like pinpricks with tears running down her face like raindrops – and begin to feel the panic rising within me. I wish I could help these people, but I have to get Dina to safety.

I'm back at the warehouse when I start feeling dizzy. Cobwebs appear at the sides of my vision, and I feel my face growing red hot, like I'm wearing a veil of fire. I stop for a moment and stagger sideways.

Kris, focus!

Vega's voice drags me back to reality, and I immediately see something in my mind's eye; something I saw earlier. The mechanic's shop: I saw a painting respirator mask fall from the wall…

I begin to hold my breath and start running again, out of the warehouse and across the public square. My legs are giving out on me – I feel like I'm running underwater – but I somehow keep trudging forward. My veins pump magma and my skin burns, but I keep going.

I make it to the shutter and to the mechanic's shop. I throw Dina down onto her feet, and point in the general direction of the wall with the mechanic's tools on it, and drop to my knees.

"There! Mask!"

She runs towards it, but I don't get to see what happens next; the cobwebs at the periphery of my vision take over and I feel myself fall backwards. And I don't stop; I keep falling into the deep, black forever.

I see my cloudy window of vision grow ever smaller as I fall until it's gone completely, and I see nothing.

CHAPTER 52

Kris, you should be able to hear me.

I'm still adrift in the great nothing. I can feel nothing. I can see nothing. But Vega's is still there; a disembodied voice speaking to a disembodied me.

I had to put you in a brief restorative state to protect you from the effects of the nerve gas. I was forced to take direct control of your neuromuscular transmitters and have the nanomachine network manually stimulate your respiratory system. However, all of your biological functions should soon be restored to normal.

I'm a disembodied consciousness, still floating in an endless sea of the blackest water. But slowly I see a window of light opening up. It grows larger and larger until it's all I can see: a blurry field of flickering white.

"Kris?"

I hear a slightly panicked female voice. I don't even recognize it to be Dina's at first.

"I'm okay," I say, keeping my eyes open for the first time. Everything begins to race into focus again; I'm lying on my back, staring up at the ceiling and Dina's face. I move my hand to touch my face to prove to myself that I still can.

"You've been out for a while. I was worried you'd never wake up."

I move my legs, all the way down to my toes, engaging every muscle. Then I slowly sit up; Dina moves out of my way as I do so, clearly surprised I'm able to recover so abruptly. As I watch her move backwards, I see the painting respirator mask on the floor beside her.

And then I think about the gas and the countless people outside choking, spluttering, drowning in it. Terrified, red, watery eyes, begging me to do anything I could to help.

"What happened? With the gas?"

"You passed out for an hour or so; I put on the mask, left you here, and tried to help the others outside, but…"

She pauses, finding herself unable to finish her sentence. I look over her shoulder through the open shutters into the square outside, and see bodies. Lifeless, unmoving bodies, one next to another.

"I don't know what kind of gas it was, but it seems to have dispersed with the wind."

"Darida," I growl, rubbing my brow. My head is banging; someone is aiming a jackhammer directly between the two hemispheres of my brain. A headache that Vega can't prevent. "He'd use poison gas on his own town? His own people?" I ask.

Dina doesn't respond. She just looks at the bodies outside, transfixed. And she's angry. I can almost feel the rage evaporating from every pore in her body.

We're back inside the army truck, flying through the desert night leaving nothing but a cloud of dust and the horrifying memories of Safiqq in our wake.

Dina kneeling in the bed of the truck, bent over a couple of injured people – a civilian and one of our guys. One of them is still coughing and vomiting. The other is unconscious, in respiratory distress according to Dina. There are a handful of other people in the back of the truck with us in various states of consciousness.

We're heading to a field hospital in a town nearby. Maybe these folks have a chance, but the death toll must already be 50 or more. I'm exhausted and find myself surrounded by death.

We rapidly pull into town and the parking lot of a former conference center converted into an unassuming field hospital. There are a gaggle of men and women with white aprons and gas masks waiting for us. I do my part in putting a couple of unconscious bodies onto stretchers, and Dina and I then carry them into the building.

Gray faces; open mouths encrusted with blood and white foam; closed, blotchy swollen eyes. Bodies twisted into horrible postures that make me ache just to look at them.

This doesn't feel like war anymore. I always thought war was supposed to be an honorable thing; people would go and fight and be respected. Nations would rise and fall but people would always come together afterwards. I thought there were lines that wouldn't be crossed.

Or maybe I'm just being hopelessly naïve again.

After we carry all the remaining casualties into the hospital – a huge room once used for conferences, but now split off into rooms and wards by temporary plaster walls and inadequate-looking medical equipment – Dina goes off to give medical aid and I'm left sitting on the curb outside.

"Vega," I say, looking around to ensure I'm alone. It's dark, and the streetlamps here aren't working. Sitting here alone in the pitch black feels appropriate. "What can you tell me about the gas attack?"

I believe it was a close relative of sarin, a deadly nerve agent. It works by interfering with neuromuscular junctions – the points at which your brain interfaces with your muscles. Victims generally die when they can't use their diaphragm or other muscles needed to breathe.

"How would Darida manage to do this?" I ask. I feel like I could do without the step-by-step analysis. I saw enough of that in action. "Like, how would he release the gas?"

It could have been loaded into artillery shells and then fired into the town. Or it could have been part of a trap laid beforehand. Without being there to investigate further, we can't truly know yet. And you should get rid of those clothes, the nerve agent is still present on them.

"Right," I say, getting to my feet. I do as he says, shambling back inside, and after some awkward attempts at communication, have an ashen-faced nurse inside direct me to a room in which I can get changed.

Around 10 minutes later I emerge back into the pitch black wearing set of medical scrubs and a camouflage jacket I found inside. I take up my familiar position sitting on the curb.

Maybe there are things I could be helping with inside, but I don't feel I can endure it yet. Seeing those faces – those twisted, pained, blood-stained faces loaded with breathing apparatus and surrounded by noisy machines – is more than I can currently take.

When I pick my head up from between my knees and open my eyes, I see a procession of headlights in the road ahead. I pick myself up and dust myself off, expecting another couple of truckloads of victims. But, as they draw closer, I see they're not trucks at all, but military Humvees.

I stand by the curb and wait for them, shielding my eyes from the glare of the headlights. Four Humvees pull up, and from the second the driver gets out and opens the rear passenger door. I immediately recognize the small figure climbing out.

"Kris," Cantara says, her expression grave and her eyes full of concern. "I came here as soon as I heard."

I salute her and direct her inside. A convoy of military

men – wearing the usual fatigues and black berets – follow her, including one holding a large video camera and another carrying a boom mic with wires trailing. I guess the information war never ends.

I follow her inside, curious as to her intentions.

Over the next half hour, I watch from afar as she goes from ward to ward with her retinue in tow, speaking with doctors and nurses, and ensuring every minute of it is recorded. She dispenses hugs and hands on shoulders, watching painfully over the beds of the stricken.

Finally, she comes to Dina – who's now clad in medical scrubs with a respirator mask on – and speaks with her. Dina makes pleasantries, but even from behind the mask I can tell she doesn't appreciate the intrusion.

"This is no longer a war against the brave people of Aljarran," Cantara says, turning away from Dina and speaking into the camera in English. "Darida has declared war upon all of humanity. Releasing this nerve agent upon civilians in a desperate attempt to turn the tide of the war is a crime against all of humanity."

She's a great speaker, that's for sure. Her speech is rousing; I feel myself filling with adrenaline again. Then I look around and see bodies lying lifelessly on the beds, attached to breathing apparatus and ghastly machines, and I begin to think that doing this here is slightly tasteless.

"If Darida will gas his own people, there's no telling what he will do next," she continues. "The peaceful, upstanding nations of the world must intervene to end this war and remove Darida from power right now."

She signs off, and some of the doctors and military personnel give her an applause. I look at Dina and see her staring with tired, scornful eyes before turning and attending to a patient once more.

Cantara exchanges a few more words with her subordinates, and I just want to get the hell out of here. The smell of cleaning products is turning my stomach; I want to go outside and sit in the dark again. I turn to leave but feel a hand on the back of my arm.

"It's a terrible business, isn't it?"

Cantara is beside me, holding onto my arm. Her eyes are dry and somber.

"I don't like coming here and interrupting the doctors' and nurses' work, and I don't like using these poor people as props in a propaganda video," she says, surprising me with her honesty. "But the world has to know about this. And as quickly as possible."

I look at her and solemnly nod.

Cantara, the film crew, and most of the military guys say their goodbyes to the rest of the medical staff and quietly head for the exit.

But then I see Dina behind a bed, staring a burning hole in Cantara's back. She looks like she wants to say something – I see her clench her fists and narrow her eyes – but thankfully she thinks better of it and goes back to her duties.

It's a *terrible* business.

CHAPTER 53

I'm back in that art exhibit– the one in the church with the giant sculpture of the deer hanging from the ceiling. It's dark and nearly empty, but there are still people milling around. Faceless ghouls wearing tattered clothing.

I turn to face the exit, and suddenly, somehow find myself back in Safiqq on that street with the blown-out tank. It's dark here too, and I'm up to my neck in putrid, black mud. I'm trying to walk, or run, or swim, or fight my way out of it, but it's enveloping every part of my body. I'm drowning in it.

There's a spotlight on me; shining from high above. I'm up to my neck, coughing and spluttering on the pitch-black mud, but the spotlight shines on, bathing my desperate face in its white glare. I can see myself from above all of a sudden.

I see myself as that photograph of the perfect white gull in the dark, black waters.

Finally, I open my eyes to see that the sun is shining through the window directly onto my closed eyelids. I'm back in room 422 in the military complex in Rachiya, and I'm covered in cold sweat. My legs are aching; I must have been moving them in my sleep.

I managed to hitch a ride back with a couple of staff sergeants, and immediately threw myself into bed here. Dina isn't here; knowing her, she's presumably still working at the field hospital.

I slowly drag myself up and shamble over to the kitchen to make myself something to eat. A half-hour or so later I'm fed, showered, dressed, and ready to confront whatever horrors today has in store for me.

I don't have to wait long.

Major General Rahal knocks on the door and invites me to a debriefing of the previous day's events in the banquet hall. I guess it's cheaper than a movie.

When I make it down there, I see the usual gyrating mass of black beret-clad military guys, speaking, laughing, and occasionally shouting. But today there's a new group: men and women in casual clothing – hoodies, baseball caps, jeans. One of them has a large, garish bulletproof vest with 'PRESS' stitched on it in all-caps.

They're a French news crew. I hear them speaking the language, parts of it I recognize from school. A news crew, here within the headquarters of the rebels, at a military briefing. I could wrack my brain to figure out why that's significant, but I only woke up half an hour ago.

We all take a seat and the Major General begins the briefing. He says, with bombast, that our courageous efforts to retake Safiqq and other territory along the frontline was a triumphant success. The last remaining forces of Darida's government were forced to flee or surrender.

For the first time I see Cantara enter the room; she walks in with a couple of bodyguards and leans against the wall, watching the briefing and exchanging whispers with a general beside her.

Major General Rahal speaks now of the gas attack: he says their initial investigation points to a nerve agent delivered via artillery shelling from afar. He begins listing names – names of those already dead. He reads each out solemnly. Eventually I lose count.

"In total 342 men, women," he hesitates, finding the next part particularly hard to say, "and children. That's 342 men, women, and children dead in this gas attack – 342 men, women, and children murdered by Ahab Ebu Darida."

I can't even believe it. I hadn't explored all of the town, but it seems difficult to believe there could have been so many people there. I feel sick.

I close my eyes and see that same procession of ghostly white faces, choking, drowning on their own blood; white pinprick eyes, drowning in a sea of odorless, colorless poison. I feel a bullet of sheer, cold terror hit me in the chest, and I quickly open my eyes again and return to the briefing.

Maybe I was stuck in my own head for too long there, but the Major General has already moved on. He's speaking now about the international response. According to him, NATO are voting on whether to send military aid to us, the rebels, and whether to institute a no-fly-zone.

Everyone in the room begins to clap – even the French press behind their cameras and dictaphones look pleased. I clap along too, although I'm not exactly sure what this means quite yet.

Now Cantara walks to the podium and begins to speak.

"With help from our friends abroad, we will win this war. The tide is already turning. Darida senses it, which is why he's resorted to cruel and inhumane war crimes. First the destruction of an entire town, and now this. But we will win, and we will set our country free!"

I clap again, trying my best to go along with the room's enthusiasm, but find myself overcome by a sudden feeling of nausea. I rise from my chair and make a rapid exit, running to the nearby toilets.

There, I spend a couple of minutes vomiting up my breakfast into the toilet bowl. Tears fill my eyes and my hands shake.

"Vega," I say, wiping my mouth with the back of my hand. "What happened? Is this the effects of the gas?"

No, there are no residual molecules of the gas remaining in or on your body, and the gas has long since been ejected from your neuromuscular transmitters.

"Well," I reply, climbing from my knees to flush the toilet. "Usually when I eat breakfast, I keep it inside my body."

I'm detecting nothing wrong with you physiologically that would make your stomach expel its contents. It's most likely that the cause of this nausea is psychological in nature.

"Psychological? You mean I'm doing this to myself?"

Your last few days have been horrifying for any human being to comprehend, let alone live through. You've witnessed things that most people only read about in horror stories. It's not surprising that you'd suffer some lingering psychological effects from it all.

I look down at my hands and see they're still shaking. I know it probably isn't standard operating procedure to close your eyes and see the red, watery, desperate eyes of the victims of a war crime staring back at you, but I'm surprised by how quickly this crept up on me.

Or perhaps I've been stuck neck-deep in the black, putrid mud of this war for so long I didn't realize it eating away at me until now.

You should take a break from all of this. We can run through a few exercises to contextualize some of the things you've witnessed and hopefully lessen their impact on you.

I wash my hands and leave the toilet. By the time I get back to the banquet hall, the briefing is over. I make my way back to room 422 and find the door unusually ajar. Strange; is this room service?

I push the door aside to see Dina there, still clad in her medical scrubs, slumped over the table in the center of the room facing away from me; an unkempt mass of black hair, resting uneasily atop an exhausted set of shoulders.

"Howdy," I say to her. She sits bolt upright and turns to look at me; her eyes are bloodshot, but she smiles with a sense of relief that I rarely see from her.

"Kris," she says, her voice ragged. "I worried you'd gone back to Safiqq."

"No," I say, trying hard to resist the same awful memories popping into my mind. "I don't think I'll be going back there in a hurry."

I take my place at the table beside her and listen to her telling me about the horrors she's witnessed. The legions of people strapped to beds with tubes down their throats; the poor men walking around one moment only to drop dead the next; the agonizing screams all night and all day.

It's enough to make me nauseous again, but luckily I already evacuated my stomach.

I tell her about the briefing, about the word of help from abroad, and about the 342 who we're told died.

"You were told 342?" she asks incredulously. "Where did they get that number from?"

"They said that's the current death count –342 men, women, and children."

"We treated 59 at the field hospital," she replies, her tone argumentative. "And the generals told us the death count was 104."

"Oh, that's—"

She interrupts me: "Weird? Strange?" She leans back in her chair, crossing her arms. "Cantara is lying to inflate the numbers, Kris."

I don't reply; I just think about what she said yesterday among the news crews and the doctors and the dying victims. It's a terrible business.

"You think she'd do that?" I finally ask.

Dina looks at me with narrowed, sardonic eyes; I can't tell

if it's because she's tired or if she's looking at me like I'm an idiot.

"I think she'd do much more than that." Dina rubs her forehead, followed by her eyes. She's exhausted, and part of me wonders if she's saying things she shouldn't.

"What do you mean?"

"I've spent all night and all morning tending and speaking to victims. I've heard things…" She pauses, rubs her eyes, and continues. "I've heard things that don't add up."

I lean forward on the table, resting my chin on my outstretched hands.

"You'd think the nerve agent victims would be downwind of the artillery shells that hit the town, but the gas appears to have blanketed the town equally from all four corners in an instant," she says.

"So it was another trap," I point out, remembering the last time Darida tried to blow us all to kingdom come. "It's not as though he doesn't have a taste for this."

"Why were sergeants and officers in our units issued with gas masks and respirators? I don't remember seeing them on many missions before."

I think about that soldier sitting opposite us in the truck as we travelled to Safiqq yesterday. The camouflage paint dried on his face and the respirator hung below his chin.

"I noticed that too. But that's not evidence of any kind of conspiracy."

"You're right," she says, putting her head in her hands. "It isn't evidence of a conspiracy. But I have a feeling that I can't get rid of."

She's shattered; I can see her hands shaking slightly.

"You should get some sleep. You're exhausted."

She looks back up at me with those bloodshot, watery eyes.

"You're right again," she says with a smile. "But I wanted to say one last thing. Thank you, Kris. You saved my life."

She laughs; a deep, pained laugh.

"Again," she adds, bashfully. "Thank you for saving my life for maybe the third time. I think I've lost count. I think I remember telling you that you didn't belong here. That you were a war tourist or something; that you weren't a warrior. I was wrong."

She puts her head back in her hands before rising to her feet and leaving the table. I don't ever remember Dina complimenting me like this before. I feel something warm inside; pride? Or maybe just gratitude, because despite the horrors of this war I still found her.

She goes to one of the three sleeping bags that still occupy the room, spread upon an uncomfortable gym mat.

"Goodnight Kris," she yawns. I bid her good day's sleep and go outside to the balcony.

It's hot out here; the weather feels like it did when I first arrived in the Middle East but I want to take this time to enjoy myself. I watch the birds again and try to remind myself of the simpler things in life.

CHAPTER 54

The early hours. It's still dark outside and I can't sleep.

Those same dreams of drowning in mud; that same nausea; the same horrors replaying in my head.

I spent yesterday milling around the complex, trying to find out as much information about this whole foreign intervention situation as I could. Eventually I managed to find some half-awake, English-speaking lieutenant who gave me the low-down.

Apparently, a bunch of countries – including the United States and most of Europe – voted yesterday to begin a series of air strikes against Darida's forces. First with the destruction of Kolajje, and now the mass murder at Safiqq – the nations of the world are taking notice and have finally decided to do something.

According to the lieutenant, air strikes have already hit targets in the capital – a suspected munitions factory, a barracks, and an officer training school.

The war could be over soon. The rebels will win.

And yet I still can't sleep.

Dina isn't here. I haven't seen her since yesterday; we must have just missed each other. I assume she woke up just after nightfall and went back to the field hospital. Two ships passing in the night.

I get up and go back to the balcony. It's still dark, but I can hear the beginnings of the working day below. Engines roaring to life; shutters opening and closing, the rapid footsteps of delivery staff and other such morning species.

"Vega," I say, considering whether talking to him is the future-tech equivalent of counting sheep. "I don't suppose you have any method of making me sleep, do you?"

I do, but you really don't want me to do that.

"Why not?"

I have numerous ways of inducing a comatose state, including simply switching off connections between your brain and your nervous system, which was how I protected you from the nerve agent. However, I have no way of inducing good, natural sleep in you.

"Hmph," I grunt in dissatisfaction. "Keep talking, you'll send me to sleep in no time."

You should be thinking about what you're going to do when all this is over, Vega says, desperately ignoring the ever-more convincing idea that he could bore me to sleep. *If this war ends soon, what are you going to do? Will you remain here to help the rebuilding?*

"Well, let's be honest, I can't go home any time soon."

I think of Dina. Maybe there's a life for us here. Maybe after this horrible war, she and I can adopt something like a normal existence.

But maybe I'm getting way ahead of myself again.

I see the first rays of sunshine peeking behind the buildings on the horizon; shiny air con units and filthy-looking water towers slowly glowing gold with the morning light. I spend an hour or so watching the sunrise before heading back inside for some breakfast.

When it reaches around 8:00 AM, I go downstairs to see what's happening. The mood has certainly shifted; black beret clad military guys laugh and joke. I see smiles and yellow, tobacco-stained teeth at every junction of every corridor.

I eventually cross paths with Cantara in a newly christened 'media room,' used as a briefing space for the increasing amounts of foreign journalists rocking up here. She's giving an interview in French – I had no idea she even spoke it – looking more energetic and optimistic than ever.

Then she turns her attention to a bunch of English-speaking reporters and begins recounting her journey to this moment.

The daughter of the former ruler, deposed in a military coup and exiled from the country. He died six years ago, and Cantara pursued a degree in pharmacy at a Paris university, as well as forging contacts in the Aljarran underground resistance. Too busy for marriage, too embittered to have children, she sought to bide her time.

And when the civil war kicked off, she returned under a veil of secrecy and began rallying the troops in earnest, building connections with rebel leaders and generals, and giving rousing speeches to the populace.

It's a cute story, but I can't help but wonder just how much is embellished. Dina's eternal cynicism seems to be rubbing off on me.

"Ah, Kris!" she calls across the room as soon as she's finished. "I was hoping to see you."

"Oh yeah?" I answer. I feel apprehensive for what she has in store for me, but I try to appear helpful. "What do you need?"

"Can you meet me in my office at 9:00 this morning?" She smiles graciously. I nod at her and do a salute for the media nearby. She salutes me back.

"I wanted to speak to you about the tragedy at Safiqq and commend you personally for your actions there."

"Oh, sure," I say, surprised that she'd bring it up, and

feeling a certain amount of anxiety upon hearing the name of that town again.

She turns and begins speaking to the English language reporters again, and I make my exit. I get to the door and the air begins to feel unbearably hot and stuffy, like I'm stuck in a sauna or an unpleasantly warm greenhouse. I wipe a layer of newly formed sweat off my forehead and know immediately where I need to go.

I pace to the toilets, making it there just in time before vomiting my entire stomach contents up again. I spend a couple of minutes doubled over the bowl making hellish noises before flushing.

"That's two days in a row," I say to no-one in particular.

You should take some time out, Vega says. *Let the war take its course. It seems it'll all be over soon.*

I go back upstairs to change my shirt and try to steady my nerves before meeting Cantara. I fill my canteen full of water again but see that my hands are still shaking. I don't want to admit it, but perhaps Vega is right; perhaps I'm coming to the end of my psychological tether here.

After some deep breathing exercises Vega guides me through, I'm ready to face Cantara again. I head down to her office, past myriad corridors, and past the burly bodyguard who frisks me for any sharp objects I shouldn't have.

I push past the ornate wooden doors that separate her office from the rest of the former hotel and find it just as small and unimpressive as before: a red room, with wide steel sheets bolted at regular intervals over the walls, and an impractically large, dark wood desk in the center.

There's a mess of papers – even messier than the last time I remember it – and a closed laptop as well. There are document binders – some full, some empty – and that strange snowglobe. And behind it all, Cantara sitting patiently, looking up at me with a smile.

"Kris, thank you for attending."

We exchange pleasantries, and I don't tell her I managed to throw up one of the rations she generously provided me with.

"I wanted to talk to you about your position in our army," she goes on to say. I'm curious – and a little apprehensive – about where this is going. I wasn't even sure I had a proper position in the army.

"Of course," I say, trying to convey a tone of confidence.

"I know you're an informal recruit here. We never set up a true foreign division in the Free Aljarrian Army, but I wanted to give you something for your ceaseless courage."

I see for the first time she's holding something in her hand. She stands up from behind the desk with an energetic jump and approaches me. She walks beside me and pins something to the front of my shirt. When she removes her hands, I see that it's a small bronze medal.

"We unfortunately don't have a formal arrangement of medals. That will have to come after we win the war. But, for now I had someone in town produce this for you."

I pick it up and hold it flat to the light. It's a circular, bronze medal a bit larger than a dime. On it, there's a bunch of Aljarrian script and in the middle a large star.

I can't remember winning a medal ever before in my life, besides the stupid participation trophies that every kid at school would get. Sometimes I didn't even get one of those. I feel proud. Before I know it there's a smile on my face; a smile I can't stop making, even though I still want to appear professional here.

"It won't be long now," she continues, walking back to behind her desk, "maybe one last big push into Darida's territory. We're still making gains every day. And I know you'll be there with us when we retake Haramat."

I nod with that stupid, slack-jawed grin still etched onto my face. One big push to retake the capital. I can do that. And it's not like I'll be able to talk Dina out of it, regardless.

"Darida must pay, you know that," she adds, finally. "The victims of Safiqq must be avenged. We will march on the capital and we will win."

"Thank you," I tell her, holding the sturdy metal of the medal between my fingers. "I wouldn't miss it."

I leave Cantara's office with a renewed sense of vigor and energy for this war. No nausea, no misgivings, no second thoughts. We're going to win the war, and I'll delightedly lead the charge.

Is this my asking price? A bronze medal? I must admit the gesture is priceless to me. The recognition that I'm appreciated here. That I've managed to contribute something; that I'm not just here making everything worse, massaging my own ego and childish desire to be some American superhero.

I came to Aljarran as a dead man, fleeing my own home and unable to go back. I've endured intolerable agony. I've taken numerous bullets; I've been locked up in squalor and drank poison here. I've witnessed horrific war crimes that, when all is said and done, will have damaged me way more than any battle.

And yet, it'll all be worth it if I can *do my part.*

I head back downstairs to try and find Major General Rahal, the only English-speaking general around here who seems to know the latest plans. After a few minutes of doddering around aimlessly, I find him in the media room.

He tells me foreign airstrikes are still ongoing. After they're complete and Darida's defenses of the capital are destroyed, we'll make our march on Haramat. I guess I'm still on standby until then.

"One more thing," he says with one hand stroking his chin. "Have you seen Dina?"

"No. I assume she's gone back to the field hospital. Anything she can do to help, y'know?"

He smiles and goes back to working on a small laptop on

a podium in the corner of the room. I head back upstairs, passing a neat line of black berets as I do so.

I do feel the slightest bit of concern for Dina. I'd always expected her to go back to the hospital, but she could be anywhere. Yesterday she was exhausted, barely sensical, and making outlandish claims about the gas attack. Today, she could be further off the deep end…

I make it back to room 422 and make something else to eat – noodles soaked in boiling water with bread and cheese – hoping this meal stays down.

My eyes are heavy and my stomach growls for lack of food. We're all handling the horrific experiences of this war in different ways.

And I've been so mired in my own darkness, I haven't thought about how Dina is dealing with it all…

CHAPTER 55

I wake up from a mercifully dreamless nap. It must be almost evening by now; the heat is dying down, and the sun isn't quite filling the room with that unbearable, cleansing white light anymore.

I get the feeling I didn't awaken naturally, though. There's a noise from somewhere; a rattling, buzzing sound emanating from one of the corners of this room. I sit and listen to it for a moment, and when it goes away I close my eyes again.

After a couple of moments, it's back.

I drag myself up and begin scouring the place for it. Luckily, I've a keen set of ears, ever listening.

Dina's bag, Vega says, locating the noise in no time. *It's coming from Dina's bag.*

I look around and see it beside her bedroll. A camo backpack she took into Safiqq with her and apparently left behind here yesterday. I hesitate for a moment, and then allow myself to go digging through it, reasoning that the circumstances allow.

I soon find her cellphone, an unremarkable – apart from its pristine, uncracked screen – smartphone. An unrecognized number is calling it, but by the time I hold it steady in my hand the call ends.

I can't remember Dina receiving a call on it before. A friend from the former base camp, maybe? Some distant family member?

The cellphone begins buzzing and rattling around in my palm once again; the same number appears on the screen. The third call in as many minutes. Someone is desperate to get through to her.

I tell myself it's down to concern for her and thumb the 'answer' button glowing on the screen.

"Hello, this is Dina's phone," I professionally answer before screwing my eyes closed in embarrassment. *Dina's phone?* Did I lapse into thinking I was answering the phone at the packaging plant again?

"Kris, it's me."

I know the voice. It's Dina. She's calling her own cellphone; weird.

"Come outside, meet me on Hiyabasa Street, down the block from the base. I've got something for you."

And before I can sneak a question, she hangs up. It does strike me as strange that she's trying to reach me on her own phone, rather than calling Alpha Base directly or even walking up here to tell me personally.

But regardless, I throw on a tan baseball cap and some sunglasses I find lying around and depart, making sure to take her cellphone with me to give it back to her.

I march out of the complex, passing the usual quantity of black berets and other assorted generals and press people. The building is buzzing with activity now; mostly people I've never seen before, all of them clad in the typical military fatigues and all of them marching with the same vigor as I am.

When I get outside it's quieter; just a couple of soldiers on guard beside the door and a heap of cigarette butts. I salute them as I leave – I still never know when or if I'm supposed to do that – and continue down the block, keeping my eye out for Hiyabasa Street.

After walking for some 10 minutes – passing a few groups of jubilant schoolchildren, something I haven't seen here until now – I find it, signposted in the native language, and below that in English.

There's a public park on the left side of the road here. Or, at least, there was; a large crater is its now defining feature, along with the twisted metal of a children's climbing frame. A couple of tents sit beside it, guarded by a pile of tires and other assorted scrap.

I wait around nervously, looking up and down the street. Eventually, I feel another round of buzzing in my pocket – Dina calling her own cellphone again.

"Yep," I answer.

"I see you," she replies. "Walk through the park and look for flat number 43 in the adjacent courtyard."

She hangs up. I look around and see the courtyard she's talking about just beyond the playground and its various deadly attractions. I hop over the yellow, dying grass of the park and through a metal gate.

It appears to be a shared courtyard and parking lot for a bunch of modern-looking apartments. One side of the building is damaged – a flat is charred and burned out, leaving only a wide-open void where the floor-to-ceiling window once stood – but every other apartment seems lived in.

The building itself is four stories high, decorated in yellowing-white plastic cladding that's peeling off in places. There are banners hanging from balconies and green garden plants proudly displayed in windows.

I walk a small distance and see the number 43 etched onto a door in a cursive font. I look up and see Dina at the window a story above me, waving. She's wearing a plain white sweater – not the medical scrubs I'd expect – with her hair down as always. She disappears into the apartment briefly before reemerging at the door.

"What took you so long?" she asks, opening the door and letting me through. She's smiling, happy to see me, and grabs me forcefully in a hug.

"Sorry, I'm not exactly familiar with wartime Rachiya."

She lets me go after a warm embrace, and I follow her up a featureless communal area staircase to the flat above.

"What is this place?" I finally ask as we come to the apartment's front door. She pushes it open to reveal a fairly pretty – if sparsely decorated – little apartment.

"This place belongs to one of my friends from my med-school days. Unlike me, she graduated. She lets me stay here when she's out of town."

"Oh yeah? Where is she?" I ask the question, but as soon as it leaves my lips I feel like I know the answer.

"The field hospital," Dina replies, grimly.

We go to the kitchen – a modern, if small, open plan kitchen sharing the same space with the living room – and stand beside the refrigerator together, which hums pleasingly. I didn't realize how much I'd miss the gentle purring of a refrigerator until now – it reminds me of comfort; normality.

"So, what's this all about?" I ask her, looking into those big, deep brown eyes. She still looks tired but has that spark of determination about her again. "Why meet here? Why not at base?"

"I wanted to thank you, properly I mean," she says, confidently. "I can't give you anything, but I can cook."

Cook? I look back over the kitchen, and see a spice rack with some 20-something spices arranged neatly. Beyond that there are pots and pans hung up on the wall and a large cooking stove. I'm so used to dried noodles and stale bread I barely even remember other culinary treats exist.

"Oh, right," I say, completely caught off-guard. But I'm happy to hear it. "That sounds lovely, really."

There's no dining table here, just a small armchair beside a bookcase, so I stand out of the way of the kitchen and watch Dina from as close as I can get without making myself a hindrance.

She puts on a pan of water to boil and begins seasoning some meat. I see soon enough that it's chicken.

"I'm afraid it's a bit of a mish-mash of things. My friend tried, but good groceries are hard to come by, even for a doctor."

"I've forgotten what good food even tastes like," I say to her, feeling my stomach grumbling already. "I may have so-called super powers, but I haven't eaten a decent meal in weeks. No one ever thought Superman could live on a diet of bread and noodles."

"Oh yeah?" she says with a smile.

"Those terrible MREs we're provided, the bread that tastes like putty, the coffee that tastes like motor oil. I think the first day I came here I ate from the trash."

She giggles, covering her mouth with the back of her hand while laying out a frying pan.

"We had that banquet, before meeting…" she pauses, as though the name is difficult to say somehow. "…Cantara."

"Yeah, well, I suppose I've been trying to forget about all that."

Unsettling memories of eating alongside Mikey pervade my thoughts. I try to move on.

"I contemplated eating a rat once."

She stops giggling, halts everything she's doing, and turns to face me with a horrified look.

"What!?"

"It's a long story," I say, trying to rescue this. "I didn't do it. I found a few candy bars that expired a few years previously instead, and—"

"You should stop talking," she says playfully. I oblige.

I watch as she fries some chicken and puts rice on to boil. The smell is already intoxicating to me. Then she cooks up some sort of sauce in a pan, seasons it all, and consults her watch.

"It shouldn't be long."

It's getting dark already; the sky is a strange mix of orange and pink pastels with a low, flat cloud formation above that looks like thousands of tiny feathers, arranged side by side for as far as I can see.

Dina lights a candle, puts it on a saucer, and places it on the hard wood floor of the living room. Then she finds a couple of cushions and puts one on either side of the candle. The room – bathed in hushed tones of orange and pink from the sky outside – begins to flicker orange. I see our silhouettes dancing against the blank walls.

I sit on one of the cushions as she serves up, and we she's done we begin to quietly tuck in. Two plates of chicken, rice, and spicy sweet sauce are devoured by candlelight. The taste is heavenly; better even than the chef-cooked meal at the banquet hall, the one that I'd apparently tried to forget about.

We share a silence together as we eat; unlike most other occasions I can remember in the past, there's no awkwardness.

"This is great," I finally break the silence to say, wiping my lips with a paper towel. I stab the last morsel of chicken with my fork and put into my mouth and chew.

"Thank you," she says, closing her eyes for half a second too long, before slowly opening them. Something tells me she spent another night and day awake.

"So, you've been at the field hospital?"

She averts her eyes from my own, suspiciously.

"It's another long story."

"So long as you didn't eat a rat."

She smirks, but I can tell there's some element of discord behind her smile.

"I told you I had a bad feeling about recent events," she begins, harkening back to our unsettling and half-conscious conversation the other day. "Everything lately feels like we're, I don't know, caught up in some propaganda war."

She finishes the last part of her meal, which up to now she's been prodding around the plate, contemplatively.

"I think that's fair to say. Did you see the news about foreign intervention? Darida's forces are being pummeled by airstrikes. The capital will soon be defenseless, and then we'll retake it. There's nowhere left for Darida to run."

I realize after saying it I'm beginning to sound like Cantara.

"Yeah, well, I think the gas attack was staged."

"Staged?" I say, parroting her words gravely. "But by who? Cantara?"

"Yes," she says, rubbing her eyes. "War is a hard sell. Who cares about some civil war in a tiny country on the other side of the world? But when the citizens of the world start seeing murdered children and gas attacks across their frontpages, it becomes impossible for these popularity-craving politicians not to act."

It does make sense; I think about that picture of the little girl in the scorched remains of her apartment building. The very first picture that drew my attention to Aljarran. It certainly worked on me.

"The gas attack played into Cantara's hands perfectly," Dina says, "she was able to secure the foreign help she needed. The war is turning. All it cost was the murder of our own countrymen and fighters. And we've had plenty of that recently."

"But where's your evidence?"

"Myself, my friend, and another doctor spoke to one of our comrades who'd traveled with us. He was on death's door, half-conscious, breathing and speaking through a tube, but he insisted he'd traveled with five suspiciously well-packaged steel boxes that were distributed to each end of town. Aid for the civilians, he was told."

"And you think they were the containers for the gas?"

The candle between us sways menacingly. I hadn't noticed, but it's almost completely dark in here now. Dina's face is lit orange and red, like we're telling ghostly stories over a campfire.

"Yes."

I don't know what to say; it still doesn't constitute rock-solid proof – Vega certainly didn't detect any evidence of the nerve agent before the attack. But surely the point of transporting nerve gas safely is that none of it can escape before you've set the trap?

"So what now?" I ask, trying to figure out where she plans to take this. "I mean, we're due to assault the capital in days, if not hours. What can you do about this?"

"There's one last lead I wanted to follow up on. And until then, I don't want to go back to the base."

I knew she'd take this path: the path of most resistance. The dangerous, courageous, or just foolhardy need to pull at loose threads until finally the whole thing unravels on her.

"Dina," I say, between gritted teeth. "Don't put yourself in danger. Let me go instead."

"You don't speak the language here; you don't have knowledge of the country and the city like I do."

"Then we'll go together."

She's unyielding; her expression doesn't change. Steely determination, with her eyes reflecting that flickering single flame between us.

"I want you to go back to the base. Act like nothing is wrong. And when we assault Haramat and finally take down Darida, I'll be fighting right alongside you."

"How long have you been awake?" I ask her. Her eyes are

slow, and she has a dazed look about her sometimes. "What, 24 hours? Maybe 36?"

"I don't remember," she says, sighing and bristling slightly at my choice of question. "I need to do this. I can't rest until I find out one way or another."

I feel like I could spend the entire night trying to change her mind, but it wouldn't make a difference. She's set on this course. The experience of being within that field hospital – fighting a losing battle to save the lives of her compatriots – dictate that she'll do whatever it takes to expose the truth.

God, just thinking of those poor people is almost enough to turn my stomach. The dark in this room is doing me no favors. I feel like I'm back there, trudging through the shadows.

"Anyway," Dina says, thankfully dragging us away from the subject. "You've only been here for what, a couple of weeks?"

I nod; I can't remember how many days exactly, but that feels accurate.

"I was kinda adrift before you arrived," she goes on to say. "I was stuck in a repeating cycle of anger and bitterness. All I could think about was the life that'd been taken from me and the people I'd lost. And then you got here and the war started turning around."

I start grinning. I don't mean to, but it spreads across my face despite the nausea.

"Don't even think about it. The war was beginning to turn before you got here Kris."

She laughs and gets back on track. "I'm still angry and I'm still bitter, but someone like you – with amazing, extraordinary powers or abilities or whatever you want to call them – choosing to use them to come here and fight for good."

She pauses, looking like she might shed a solitary tear. I should know better; she doesn't, and she goes on: "You don't complain, you don't back off, you don't give up, you don't let anyone down. And you're so optimistic. It feels like despite the fact you're mostly robot, you're the most positively human of anyone I've met here."

She puts her hand on top of mine. I smile at her.

"Technically I'm around 1/36th robot by weight, but I appreciate it."

She laughs, staring into me with those deep, brown eyes again. She smiles; her teeth appear a perfect white in the candlelight, with two dimples on either side of her lips.

Right now, in this moment, I feel content. Like I don't need to fight and prove myself anymore.

It feels right.

And then I look over her shoulder and see her medical scrubs folded neatly on a table. I close my eyes to try and dispel the thought, but find myself back in those dark waters; drowning in the bleak, hopeless sea of gas. Black, thick like mud. Suffocating me. Choking me.

I open my eyes and try to concentrate on what Dina has started saying but find that my focus is waning; all I can think about is trying to keep the beautiful dinner Dina cooked in my stomach.

It sounds like she finishes with a question – her tone rises – but I still can't hear her. I swallow very cautiously, take a deep breath, and slowly rise to my feet.

"Sorry, is there a bathroom?"

She points me down the hall and to the right, but I don't go there. Instead, I sneak out of the front door – jamming one of my boots to keep it open so that I don't get locked out – and go out into the courtyard.

There, I find a dark corner, away from prying lamplights and Dina's earshot, and lose my dinner to the tarmac below.

"I've got to stop doing this," I mumble to myself between dry heaves.

You've got to have a break, Vega replies dryly.

After some 15 minutes of standing still or doubling over with my hands on my knees or going in for more heaving and gagging, I think I'm done.

I look around and head back into the apartment building and up the staircase to Dina's friend's flat. I quietly close the apartment door and walk into the living room as though nothing happened.

"Hey, I was just—"

I see Dina lying on the ground on her side, with her head gently resting atop a pillow. Her body rises and falls slowly with her breathing, and her eyes are happily closed. She's asleep.

"Oh man."

I sit beside her, cursing my haunted innards. After a couple of minutes I scoop her up from the floor – putting my arms beneath her upper back and under her legs – and carry her to the single bedroom here, where I carefully place her on the bed. She doesn't stir.

Then I head back to the living room, re-arrange the two pillows, and get comfy on the soft carpeted floor.

And then I blow out the candle.

CHAPTER 56

'm out in the Aljarran desert this time, only I know that I'm dreaming. I'm walking. I have the feeling that I've been walking for hours.

I hear a shell explode way off in the distance behind me. I turn around to find myself in Cantara's office, with the steel sheets bolted onto the walls and the huge, impractical desk. But it's scorching hot in here. There's no ceiling, in fact. The sun beats down on me relentlessly.

I open my eyes and find myself on the floor of Dina's friend's apartment still, with two ruffled pillows arranged haphazardly around my face. The sun is beaming down on me through the window, like I'm an ant under a magnifying glass.

I get up, feeling the side of my face and the texture of the carpet imprinted on it.

"Dina?" I call out but get no response. I check the room I put her in but the bed is empty.

She must have left already.

I look around the room – stealing a couple of things from the refrigerator, apologizing out loud to Dina's faraway friend as I do so – and prepare to leave.

I get as far as the door when I see the post-it note sticking there: *'Didn't want to wake you. I'll call you again soon. Dina'*

I forgot to give her the cellphone back. Never mind, I guess that's how she wants to reach me now. I sneak out of the apartment, ensuring the front door locks behind me, and make the walk back to the base.

There I'm greeted by the usual couple of dour-faced guards and their heap of cigarette butts, but strangely the place seems quieter than usual. The former hotel reception isn't the frantic hive of activity it once was. Instead, a man in a black beret sits sleepily behind the desk, nodding at me as I pass.

Similarly, the banquet hall is quiet – there's a couple of guards as well as a projector screen stuck on the final slide. The corridors are empty; my footsteps echoing as I walk down them. The whole base feels like a felled animal, its arteries and veins drained of blood.

I walk to the media room; similarly quiet, save for a couple of European reporters tapping away on laptops, and Major General Rahal sitting behind a podium, drumming out a message on his cellphone.

"Major General," I say, still unsure how a member of the informal foreign legion is meant to address a military leader here. "Where is everyone?"

"We've established a new forward operating base closer to the capital. Most of the armed services have relocated there, but Cantara is still here."

I smile at him, followed by a slightly awkward salute. I turn to leave, but he speaks again.

"Cantara would like to speak to you."

I feel a slight tenor of nervousness – my heart pumps quicker – at the mention of Cantara wishing to see me. I really shouldn't be worried – yesterday she gave me a medal for God's sake – but Dina's suspicions seem to have made me uneasy.

I head up to room 422 to shower and brush my teeth, then change into a new set of clothes and go back downstairs to see her.

The haunting, compounding hotel corridors – flush with carpets worn thin from overuse and rows upon rows of imposing wooden doors – are empty, with only a couple of bureaucrats in shirts and ties passing me.

When I make it to the office – enduring the customary frisking for weapons by Cantara's guards – and take the final walk through the short corridor to her room, I'm still not entirely sure what to expect. I try to put an unassuming face on, but the tiny, niggling feeling that something isn't right claws away within me.

When I'm told she's ready, I push my way through the door and find her sitting there, small and modest as always, behind her desk, with her face illuminated by the glow of a laptop screen. I salute her; the mere action makes me feel diminished somehow.

"Kris," she says warmly, "I was hoping to speak to you."

"At your service," I reply, putting a smile on my face.

"We're close to finishing this," she begins with a devilish grin. "The general staff have moved to a new forward base in anticipation of our assault on Haramat. One final push is all we need, and Darida's whole house of lies will come tumbling down. We've almost won."

I nod again. I allow myself the faintest bit of pride in sharing that achievement.

"But I have one last task for you."

I wait, as she diverts her eyes from my own, and scans her desk for some papers. She brushes past the snowglobe, almost knocking it to the floor, but manages to steady it and bring it back to the desktop at the last moment.

"We need a recon team to explore Haramat International Airport. It's been partially destroyed by foreign air strikes, and all Darida's men should have been driven away from there, but we need to know for sure. You were part of the most successful recon team we had, so, if you should want it, the job is yours."

One last mission? One final push to the capital? I feel that taste for adventure and excitement – constrained for 24 years, only now unleashed – rising within me again. I can put my so-typically-me feelings of unease to one side for now, I think.

If Darida is to be toppled, and Aljarran freed again, I want to be there, and I'm sure Dina would say the same.

"I'm in," I say, with as much Hollywood bravado as I can muster.

"Good," she says, leaning back in her chair. "Major General Rahal will brief you and the rest of the team in 413. Go as soon as you can."

I salute her one more time and leave the room, with the heavy wooden door slamming shut behind me.

The first thing I do when I'm out of the rabbit's warren of corridors surrounding Cantara's office is pull out Dina's cellphone and text the number she called me on yesterday. I tell her that I'm being assigned a new recon mission and to call me as soon as she can.

One last mission, huh, the all-hearing Vega says. *When it's done, and when this war is over, can you do us both a favor and take some time off? I'm struggling to run your biological processes on two candy bars a day.*

"When we win this war, I'll take you to a nice Italian restaurant, my treat," I mumble into the collar of my jacket as I head down an empty hallway. Vega doesn't reply. I'm only half-joking.

Room 413 is empty, at least for now. A tangled mess of folding chairs, facing in all different directions as though used for some military seminar, and bunch of non-descript, empty folders sit atop podium. There's a photograph on the wall I hadn't noticed before: a black and white image of 100 or so people all lined up like a school picture.

I walk up to look closer and see that it's the former hotel staff – a caption reads 1993 – but something else catches my eye. Someone has used a thin, sharp object to meticulously cross off the faces of around half of the people on it. Mostly the men, but some women too. People dead in the war, I presume.

I avert my attention when I hear footsteps in the hall behind me. All 6'6" of Major General Rahal appears in the doorframe, and behind him is another face I recognize.

"Kris," the Major General says to me, "I've heard you've met Abbas."

"Hello," Abbas says, holding his hand out to shake mine. I think the last time we spoke we'd just escaped being vaporized in Kolajje. I shake his hand.

The pair of us pull some chairs out while Major General Rahal fiddles with the projector. After five or so more minutes, two more men join us: two Aljarrians I don't recognize, named Zahid and Riyad, and Estevez, the Spanish team leader who also accompanied us to Kolajje.

"So, this is all of you," Rahal says, walking to close the door. A team of five; I can deal with that, but Dina's lack of contact is worrying me slightly.

He begins the briefing: Haramat International Airport is the biggest in Aljarran. It was a busy transport hub in the pre-Darida days, and even after he stole power it was an influential airport in this part of the world.

Of course, when the civil war kicked off it was quickly seized by Darida and used as his main military airbase – shipping weapons and munitions all over the country and serving as the base for his range of clapped-out Russian fighter jets and barely flight-capable attack helicopters.

However, with the foreign-led airstrikes now pummeling his territory, Darida's once treasured airport is now a bombed-out wreck. The hangars are destroyed and his fleet of prized aircraft have been blasted off the map.

"Your mission is to travel to Haramat International Airport and report back on the state of it. If there are no enemy forces still stationed there, and if the airstrip is still in a useable condition, it'll be an invaluable location to fly our troops into and stage an assault on Haramat."

The frontline is now almost a thing of the past. Instead, Darida's few remaining men have fortified themselves within the handful of cities they still hold. We can carefully drive the few hours to the area surrounding the airport and then continue on foot, according to the major general.

Estevez is made our leader, and after a few questions from the others we're all free to arm ourselves. The atmosphere is heated. I look around and see a mixture of faces: the jubilant, the focused, the expressionless.

I check Dina's cellphone, but still no reply.

The one face I want to see isn't here.

CHAPTER 57

I can't stop thinking about that photograph of the staff with most faces crossed off ingloriously. If I'm right – that it's some former staff member's informal way of keeping track of the hotel's casualties – all of that could soon be over.

We can take back the airport and we can take back the country.

I'm standing in an armory in a basement underneath the base. I haven't been here before – maybe I lacked the requisite medal – and it's mostly empty now that most people here have moved on, but some of the good stuff remains. Weapons, ammunition, gear, body armor.

There are rows upon rows of steel shelves and hanging racks like you'd see in some post-apocalyptic tailor. The walls are hard, blank concrete, and there's a florescent lighting tube above each rack. And it's cold.

I walk up and down the rows, looking for the rifle I used last time. I can't even remember its name to be honest. After a few minutes of looking I find it, slinging it around my shoulder by a fabric strap. Then I take a new set of military gear – a belt, a Kevlar helmet, and a tactical vest with ballistic plates inside, which Estevez tells me will stop a bullet at the right angle.

There's another large steel door ahead, hastily painted red and looking like the entrance to some great, industrial dry cleaners; I walk up to it, but a black-beret clad soldier stops me, putting his palm to my chest.

"No enter, armory just here," he says in broken English.

I watch as one of the Aljarrian men – Zahid – picks up a large rocket launcher with RPG-7 stamped on the side in crude black ink.

"For a recon mission?" I ask incredulously.

"You never know, it is a military airport," Zahid replies in slightly accented English.

Estevez looks at him and shrugs.

"You're the one carrying it."

We finish arming ourselves, and then pack a few bags full of the usual essentials – water, food, extra ammunition, and a medical kit. I slip Dina's cellphone into my own bag after seeing that she still hasn't replied.

We carry the stuff outside – Zahid hauling his RPG-7 – and pack a five-seat sedan; a remarkably mundane car for a team preparing to strike the first blow to end a war. It's dusty red with a slight dent over the right-hand door, but it seems to run smoothly – the engine hums like a hotel minibar.

Abbas drives and the rest of us pile in, and in no time we're en route to the airport, again feeling like some surreal spring break trip. We're even packing fireworks.

The three Aljarrian guys have a conversation between themselves, which sounds cheerful enough. I turn to Estevez beside me; he's looking straight on, focused or perhaps just trying to keep any sign of nervousness from his face.

"So," I say to him, "you came back."

"Yeah," he says, staring ahead still. Eventually he turns to look me in the eyes. "Couldn't stay away."

"I thought you wanted out after Kolajje."

"Yeah, I did," he says, a note of dejection in his voice. "But then I realized I have nowhere else to be but here."

"What do you mean?"

"There's nothing for me back home but bills, debts, and outstanding warrants." He shifts around sheepishly in his seat, like this is an uncomfortable topic for him. "At least here I can do what I'm good at; do something that gives me purpose."

"I guess we all want to feel like we matter to the world," I reply.

"Mi padre died last week," he says next, using his native Spanish. "I could have flown home for the funeral – I could have made it in time but I didn't."

I think about my own dad for the first time in a while. I can picture him now sitting by the window, smoking his cigarettes, and fearing God. If he died, would I go back for the funeral if I could?

"Besides," he says, snapping me out of that troubling question, "I might soon meet him anyway."

It's some five hours later when we get to the designated place to leave the car. We passed a couple of our own military convoys on the way, plus a few hastily assembled checkpoints.

Every soldier of ours we drove past looked like they're living on no sleep. Tired eyes with buzzing, excitable pupils. It's like a mad all-night rave in which everyone's still waiting for the main event.

We pull up by the side of the road with the tall air traffic control tower of the airport just visible over the horizon. We've got another couple of miles or so to walk, all the while on the lookout for hastily set traps left by the fleeing enemy.

The airport is set some 20 miles away from the city in an

otherwise empty patch of dusty, rocky desert. I hear gunfire far away and the ever-present drumming of artillery, but aside from that the scene is remarkably tranquil.

We begin the walk, doing the usual hop, skip, and jump over treacherous jagged rocks and perilous sands. You don't realize how much you miss dodging trash bags left by the side of the vomit-soaked streets in the city until you're here, navigating this ankle-hating labyrinth.

We walk in single file – me volunteering to go first – towards the tower in the distance. Something about walking silently in hyper-vigilance, wondering if at any moment you might get your legs blown off, makes the time fly. Before I even realize it, we're almost there; I can see the tall chain link fence that separates the airfield from the desert.

"All right," Estevez says. We all gather round. "We approach quickly and with as low a profile as possible. We'll look for a gap in the fence, but if necessary we use wire cutters."

The sky is pink again; a surreal formation of clouds are ahead sitting low in the sky and growing upwards from dark purple bases rising high, like violet mushroom clouds. Even the sand and rocks around us seem to glow pink like we're on another world.

We approach the fence; it's sturdy and some three meters tall. After practically walking on our knuckles alongside it for a few minutes though, we see our opening: a crater where a section of fence once stood, presumably from a misdirected airstrike. We clamber through and climb back out of it, and we're on the airfield.

We run over to the slightly bent and misshapen steel wall of a former hangar blown out of recognition by an airstrike. I can see the air traffic control tower 200 yards or so ahead dominating the landscape, with the airport terminal itself tucked away behind it. Craters litter the airstrip, but any fires have gone out.

Beside the twisted steel, Estevez gathers us in a circle and we talk over the plan.

"We move from hangar to hangar, ensure there's no-one lying in wait for us, and then we can begin to think about clearing the airport building itself."

He peeks out from behind the wall, looks down the airstrip, and begins digging out a diagram with his finger in the sand of the various hangars, buildings, and other features of the airfield. I stop counting when he reaches the 15th.

"This place is huge," Abbas says, with some uneasiness. "I can't believe they sent five of us to recon this whole thing."

"We can do it," Zahid says, wearing his rocket launcher on his back. "We'll stay here all night."

Estevez goes on with the plan, drawing out approaches, peeking around the corner every so often to confirm. I start to drift off, however. Every so often I see a flash of something in the tower. An old computer screen or a flickering bulb, perhaps?

"And, as I can see it, the best—"

Estevez interrupts himself; he flies forward, landing face first on his diagram in the sand. For the very briefest moment, I'm baffled, before the sound hits us: a distant gunshot. A high-pitched bang in the distance, followed by a low, rumbling echo.

"Sniper!" Someone shouts it; I can't tell who but we move.

We run around the side of the hangar wall and behind it, putting half an inch of twisted steel between us and the traffic control tower. There, I take a quick peek out and look at Estevez, whose body is still slumped, motionless, over our best laid plans to explore this place.

"Is he dead?" Abbas asks.

"He isn't moving," I reply. I see a dark red patch in the sand begin to spread out underneath him.

"If the shooter is in the tower, we can't escape," Abbas says, panic evident in his voice. "What the hell do we do?"

The tower covers all exits; it watches over the entire airstrip. It's true, we're pinned down until we can isolate and take out the sniper.

I walk around the back of the destroyed hangar and look out onto the other side of the airstrip, being careful not to show myself to the tower.

There's 20 meters to the next hangar, which appears to be in a much better condition than the one we're cowered beside. There are tall, slightly rusted walls, painted with the number two this time, and a small door slightly ajar.

I quickly pace back to the others.

"We can make it to the next hangar, but it's a sprint – maybe 20 meters. Could be a better shout than staying here."

I look around and see pallid, unsure faces. The excitement of participating in the overthrow of Darida is gone, replaced by a fear for our own mortality. The scene is eerily quiet; no wind and no sound of any distant gunfire. Only the desperate breathing of my comrades.

"We should take cover in the next hangar," Riyad says, taking me up on the offer. "We can make it if we're fast."

The others reluctantly nod their agreement. We all make the short walk across the back of the mangled, twisted metal of hangar one, and prepare for the uncovered, unprotected sprint to the door.

"Okay, on three," I say, feeling that pit of dread in my stomach again. The surge of adrenaline is almost enough to take my breath away. "One, two…"

I see the others clench their hands around their weapons and harden their postures.

"Three!"

I throw myself into a sprint, charging forward and pumping my thighs like pistons, focusing solely on the entrance. In a couple of seconds I make it and burst through the door, which slams into the wall behind it.

I turn on my heel and see the other three breach the doorway, Zahid – hauling his heavy rocket launcher – coming in last. I keep expecting to hear a gunshot, but it never comes. A rush of relief soon grips me and I stagger on the spot; my helmet almost sliding off my head until I steady and tighten it.

"Good job guys," Zahid says, breathing heavily.

The inside of hangar two is dark; it's a huge structure, slightly bent from the explosive force of the impacts around it, but still standing at least. We find ourselves at the back of it beside a set of small, prefab office buildings, like boxes set aside from the building itself. The doors of the hangar are wide open overlooking the entire airfield.

There's no aircraft in here – the main floor of the hangar is instead filled with crates, some tall, some small, some wooden, and some steel. They're arranged haphazardly like a climbing frame; a huge, mismatched monolith of nooks and crevices.

"We can use the crates as cover and attack the tower from there," I tell the others, jabbing my finger at the numerous gaps within the array of boxes.

"Sounds good," Abbas replies, more optimistically than before.

We take one last look around the hangar – aiming our rifles ahead of us – before slowly approaching the fortress of crates, the only sound being our heavy footsteps and the jostling of Zahid's RPG on his back.

But then I hear something else.

A short, high-pitched scrape of a footstep on concrete ahead of us, maybe? It's enough to make me freeze on the spot and hold out an arm to halt Abbas beside me.

In the dim, pink hues of the last remaining dusk light, I see something emerge from behind the crates. At first it looks like a long, thin wire, slowly pointing upwards.

But then I see the man emerging behind it rising to his feet behind a waist-sized box. The wire is a barrel of a rifle, and the rifle is pointed at us. My heart skips a beat and I feel my fingers tighten around the fabric of Abbas' combat vest.

Trap!

"Get back!" I hear myself yell.

I see a handful of muzzle flashes – bright yellow lights popping off ahead of us – accompanied by the thunderous, echoing crackle of gunshots. I turn and sprint back for the space behind the office structure, propelling myself forward frantically. With our booming footsteps, I hear the others do the same.

"YAHH!" I yell out, feeling a sharp stinging sensation in my palm like some exotic Aljarrian species of wasp stuck its stinger right into me. But I don't let it stop me. I make it to the office building, sliding into the shadows behind it, and see Abbas do the same.

Safe from the view of the crates, I look down at my hand. It's a painful crisscross of dark crimson blood, with a large, purple wound in the middle of it, passing through my palm and out of the back.

I look onto the floor of the hangar and see Riyad and Zahid; two lifeless bodies stretched forward and face down with the slight spatter of blood ahead of them and Zahid's RPG still attached to his back. Undignified and unresponsive.

"Oh man, oh man," Abbas repeats to himself, gripping his rifle by the barrel. I find myself taking deep breaths, but try to steel myself, putting the stinging sensation in my left hand out of my mind as best I can, and listen for the inevitable damage report from Vega.

You've had a bullet pass through your hand. It fractured a couple of your metacarpal bones and associated ligaments. You may be weak in that hand.

"How many?" I ask out loud.

Six sources of gunfire within the crates, Vega replies.

"I don't know, oh man," Abbas says, still clutching his rifle ineffectively.

"Abbas!" I yell at him, grabbing him by his combat vest again. His eyes – drowning in panic – begin to focus on my own. "There's one way out of this!"

He's breathing heavily, but I begin to see the sanity creep back into his gaze.

"Okay, all right," he says, finally relinquishing his grip of his rifle's barrel and seizing it by the stock and trigger again. "What do we do?"

I look out beyond the doorway, but realize we'd be sitting ducks for the sniper again. Then I turn my head and stare out across the floor. There's another office building on the other side of the hangar – a small box of a room, but one in which I could seek cover behind. If I can sprint over there, we could attack the crates from two angles.

"I need you to cover me," I tell him, thinking back to my sprint in front of the tank in Safiqq. "I'm gonna make the run to the other office. I need you to fire a whole clip at them and make sure I get there."

"Okay, I can do that."

He readies himself, aiming his rifle while we're both still hidden from view. I quietly ask myself what the hell I'm doing before counting Abbas down from three again.

On the third beat, I begin my sprint, launching forward on the deafening din of gunfire from behind me. It's a 60-yard sprint, but I throw everything I've got at it, gripping my gun and flailing my arms by either side madly.

I'm almost there – 10 yards, five yards…

I feel another pain in my foot – like I stepped on a nail or something. I pick my foot up into the air and fall the remaining few yards into the shadow behind the office block.

A bullet passed through your right foot; it may be lodged in the sole of your boot.

"Yeah," I reply, feeling that stinging, throbbing pain of a bullet wound that I seem to be getting so acquainted with these days. "I can deal with it."

I pick myself up, staying off my stricken foot, and look across the floor at Abbas. He's reloading his rifle, and when he's done he meets my gaze with a nervous but unyielding glare. I grip my own gun, putting the stock to my shoulder, and prepare myself for the fight of my life.

"Okay Vega, let's do this."

I drop to my knees, and then fall on my side, aiming through the iron sight of my rifle at the first guy I can see. He's facing me – his face covered in black camouflage – aiming directly at me. I squeeze the trigger and feel the jolt of the single gunshot, the recoil shaking my body.

To my surprise – and relief – the man slumps down into the box behind him. I see another couple of muzzle flashes beside him – hellish flickers of flame in the purple haze of the hangar – and steady my aim.

I squeeze the trigger again, spraying five or six or seven bullets at the next two guys standing side by side atop another crate. The first falls to the ground in a heap, and the second dances around on the spot, giddily almost. I see two dark patches of blood on his jacket and know then that I got them both.

I take a deep breath of exhilarated relief and feel something in the direct center of my chest – a couple of impacts, hitting me as hard as I've ever been hit in my entire life. Two monstrous punches to my solar plexus. I wheeze and cough and use every joule of my remaining energy to fling myself back into cover.

"God… damn!" I splutter, taking fast, shallow breaths, trying to fill my lungs again.

You just got hit in the chest by the impact of a couple of bullets, Vega informs me as I try to control my diaphragm. *They didn't enter your body; your ballistic armor stopped them.*

"It doesn't feel that way!" I wheeze in reply.

You're far better off with those bullets remaining outside your body, I promise you.

I look back at Abbas to see him firing his rifle again – the flash illuminating his features, contorted in an ugly face of anger and fear.

Regaining my breath at last, I limp back to my feet trying not to put any weight on my right foot. I take another peek around the corner. I see some blood and a couple of bodies but no other soldiers.

"What do you see?" I ask Vega.

There are two soldiers perched either side of a crate by the far right of the hangar.

Sure enough, I can pick out two rifle barrels aiming and firing towards Abbas' position. I focus my gaze and see an arm accompanying one of them. I steady myself, aim, and fire another volley in their direction, flinching slightly at the deafening sound. I'm still not used to it.

I duck back around the corner and begin to shout something to Abbas, but when I see him I stop; my mouth hanging open, forlorn.

He's lying motionless on his back with his rifle thrown some two yards behind him. There's a pool of blood by his head. And he's quiet. The entire hangar is quiet in fact. Death and silence fill the air.

I'm the only one of us left.

I reload my rifle – casting my mind back to Dina's instructions on how to do it – and hear the empty magazine hit the floor with an echoing *clink*. Then I take another look around and hop over to Zahid and Riyad.

"Guys," I say, anticipating no response. They're both lying in the same position they fell, blood growing around them. I look over at Abbas and see the same thing.

I twist my ankle the wrong way, and have to place my foot on the floor eliciting a sudden rush of excruciating pain.

"Arrrrgghh!" I yell; the sound booms throughout the steel walls and ceiling of the hangar. But I'm not just in pain. I'm angry. I'm furious; I can practically hear my blood rushing in my ears.

I think about Estevez and the father whose funeral he never went to because of this stupid war. I think about Abbas and all the lifeless Aljarrian bodies I've seen. I think about Mikey.

I grab the rocket launcher – and the leather strap affixed to it – from Zahid's blood soaked back, and limp purposefully to the crates. It's heavy – there are a couple of extra rockets attached to the strap – but I'm powered by hate and fury now. When I'm there, I find a position where I can see the air traffic control tower in clear sight.

I sling my rifle around my neck, balance the RPG on my shoulder, and take aim – there's a small iron sight on the top, and my finger finds a trigger below – I prepare myself. For the shortest moment, I hear something – a roaring, grinding engine, getting closer – but it's too late for second thoughts.

I squeeze the trigger and hear the immediate high-pitched whistle of the rocket launch. There's no recoil – the whole launcher feels lighter now the rocket has left the barrel – so I can sit and peacefully watch the fireworks with a smile on my face.

Sure enough, the tower erupts in a huge incandescent blast. A cloud of black, choking smoke balloons out of the top of it, like some deadly jellyfish rising into the purple dusk.

"Hah, hahah!" I laugh. My hand throbs with pain, my foot is in agony, my breathing still ragged, but I allow myself to enjoy that one. In fact, I can't resist.

Sitting here among the corpses of my friends and my enemies, I laugh uproariously.

I put one hand back on my rifle, carrying the empty launcher with the other, using it as a crutch against the crates as I hop around them, seeking to get a better look at the airstrip. I navigate my way past and over the boxes as well as the spent munitions and debris on the concrete floor.

But despite the distant roar of the burning tower, I can hear something else, something louder even than that. The grinding, wailing, whirring of a hellish engine. I close my eyes and try and will myself to face what I know is coming.

"You recognize that noise, don't you?" I ask Vega.

Yes, unfortunately.

I glance over a couple of taller crates, seeing it in the lingering purple light: a large, armored tank surging towards me on its tracks, chewing up concrete and debris from the airfield as it moves. The turret is facing slightly to the right – the barrel shorter than the last tank I had to deal with – with a spotlight fixed to it.

You should retreat, Vega says as I sink bank below the crates. *Hide until the crew emerge or it goes to check another location. You have the mobility advantage, despite the state of your foot.*

I sure don't feel like I have the mobility advantage, but I think I could hide within the three-dimensional maze of crates. I shift around in my position and feel the weight of the two extra rockets attached to the launcher's leather strap. I'm still holding an anti-tank weapon here: the Lord of War killer.

I begin untying the rocket from the strap, twisting my mouth shut and humming a tune of agony as I use my left hand as best I can. Finally, I manage to free it and fix it onto the end of the launcher.

I notice you're not retreating Kris.

"What do I do? Hide and leave this thing to blast another squad away?"

I crawl on my knees, holding the RPG on my shoulder, finding a waist-high crate that I can spring out from behind.

I take a deep breath, wipe the tears from my eyes, and try to psyche myself up for this. One rocket, that's all it will take.

"Three, two…"

I spring upwards on my one good foot, holding the RPG steady on my shoulder. I see the purple sky turning to black, and the tank, now just 30 yards or so away from me – a huge armored monster, with steel skin. Its turret is facing me directly. I'm staring into the deep, dark void within its barrel.

The spotlight switches on, blinding me and bathing me in painful white light. Fear grips me; I can't remember the last breath I took. I tense my finger on the trigger...

There's a terrible sound; a deafening whip-crack that seems to sever me from my body. Suddenly, I feel like I'm transported back onto that subway train, staring at Burden and his homemade bombs strapped to his chest. And then I feel myself slipping, falling into dark's embrace.

CHAPTER 58

I feel a hand on my face. It doesn't feel like mine, but I know somehow that it is. I open my eyes and see the familiar, somewhat reassuring sight of the hangar ceiling; rusty, corrugated metal, with blue steel I-beams keeping it all in place. I even see a soccer ball lodged up there.

I can't hear the tank anymore. In fact, I can't hear anything. My eardrums must have been blasted out again. But I'm in pain; every bone in my body feels like a painful, leaden weight. Every muscle feels like stinging, torn hamburger meat.

Only now do I begin to wonder what the hell happened to me. Did the RPG misfire? Did the tank explode and take me with it?

I rub my face again; the feeling is coming back to my fingers. I progress to moving my arm beside me and then wriggle around on my back. Using the side of my right hand, I try to sit up from the floor, bending at the waist.

I see my assault rifle, still held on a strap around me. I see crates, some on fire, some smoking, some blasted into pieces; sharp, splintered wooden debris lies all around. I see the tank, standing there proudly and undaunted; a magnificent beast, its barrel shaking slightly and smoking.

And then I see the state of my legs; they're both gone above the knees, with a pair rusty red stains trailing along the floor ahead of me. My pants are a mess of torn, red fabric, and my boots no longer exist.

I sink back to the ground, letting the back of my head hit the cold concrete. I guess the tank fired before I could.

I close my eyes and bite the collar of my jacket, trying to get a head start on resisting the mind-numbing pain that I know will follow.

Most of the ... will be ... should be able to hear me now.

Vega is back; my eardrums must be repaired.

"Vega," I mumble, my voice straining. "What happened?"

It appears the tank shot a shell into the crates in front of you. The crates exploded and the debris destroyed your legs.

I feel myself begin to lapse out of consciousness; I open my eyes and see that my peripheral vision is disappearing.

Kris, you need to focus – you're still lying on a battlefield here.

"Focus? I've got no legs, what am I supposed to do? Crawl out of here?"

If necessary, yes.

Something feels different. The cacophonous, demon-like roar of the tank's engine seems to have died down since it fired the shot. I hear it replaced by something else – a slower sound, like an idling engine, and voices. Maybe two separate voices, speaking a language I don't understand.

I try to rally every last remaining bit of strength in my devastated body; I fight through the pain and pick myself up on the side of my right hand again, trying to bend at the waist to get a look as I did before.

With a deep, tortured breath, I manage to accomplish the task, and after fighting off another moment of light-headedness I see that there are two soldiers – one climbing out of the tank, one having just done so – looking around the crates.

They're checking on their buddies; the guys who Abbas and I managed to take out.

This is your chance Kris. You still have your rifle.

I look down and see my rifle beside me, still slung around my neck. Part of the wooden stock is scratched and singed, but it looks to be in working order.

I reach over to it with my right hand while planting my left elbow on the ground beside me. Then I get a familiar feeling of the stock and trigger, and slowly, painfully lift the rifle's weight, aiming it one-handed.

I look down the sights – rapidly breathing through the pain – until I'm aiming at the guy jumping out of the tank. Then I hold my breath and squeeze the trigger.

The recoil from the shot knocks me back, but not before I see my target fall over the body of the tank. I pick myself back up again, wheezing and spluttering as I do so, to see the other man racing over to see what happened with his pistol drawn.

One more shot Kris.

I steady my grip on the rifle and aim it in the man's direction. He turns to see me – his face turning from concern, to bafflement, to abject horror when he sees that I'm still fighting, despite my lack of legs. He lifts his pistol, but it's too late for him. I squeeze the trigger and see a small, dark red wound open in his chest.

He falls limply to the ground, and I allow myself the same pleasure – my elbow giving out from underneath me and the back of my head hitting concrete again. I feel the pain beginning to ratchet up – the adrenaline from the firefight already dissipating – and give myself back to the great black void.

I slip away into unconsciousness, leaving the pain, the noise, the death, and the struggle behind.

―――

Kris, it's time to wake up.

Vega's voice is unwelcome. It's the first thing I hear, and with it comes an avalanche of pain; a great, relentless pressure, like my legs are being pressed in a trash compactor, only I know that can't be the case, because I have no legs.

I open my eyes and see that hangar ceiling again and the soccer ball lodged up there. But something is different. There's a new source of light in here. And they're moving. Several halos of white light are flickering around the ceiling and walls like ghosts.

And then I hear voices. Quiet voices, but seemingly growing louder. My finger twitches on my rifle – I'm still holding it close to my body – but I know I don't have the strength to fight off another squad of Darida's goons right now.

I should probably be afraid but I'm not. I close my eyes. I just wish I could drift off again and embrace the nothingness.

"Holy crap," I hear a man exclaim in English. There's another set of voices, and then I hear footsteps. "What a damn mess."

I feel like I recognize the voice. It's European, slightly tired and cynical.

"Oh hey, I think I knew this guy. He's the American kid."

I don't need to open my eyes to know who it is. It's Tomas. He's speaking to a man with an Aljarrian accent. The other man mumbles a couple of things before Tomas replies.

"Kris was his name. I guess I should make sure his body makes it back to the States. Or what's left of it anyway."

I allow myself the smallest of smiles to creep upon my lips, despite the crushing pain.

I hear the other man begin to walk away. Then I open my eyes, and begin writhing around on the spot, planting my left elbow back on the ground, trying to prop myself up.

"Hey man," I say to him, my voice worn but my tone jovial.

"Whoa," he spins around, turning to face me. His long,

blond hair spins with him; he quickly skims it out of his eyes. "You're not dead!"

"Nope," I say with a deep breath. "But I wish I was."

"Your legs!" he shouts, squatting beside me awkwardly, like he wants to administer medical support but has no idea how.

"What legs?"

I smile at him. Rather than smile back, he just looks horrified; his mouth hanging agape. Now I'm enjoying myself.

"We need to get you to a field hospital, man. You look like you've lost a lot of blood."

I lie back again, feeling another wave of pain wash over me.

"Do me a favor, would you?" I see his eyes widen, waiting receptively. "Get me the hell out of here."

CHAPTER 59

We're maybe an hour away from the airport now, and my pain is finally subsiding. My legs have thankfully stopped bleeding – my nanomachines succeeding in clotting the wounds – but I'm still lapsing in and out of consciousness.

Another day, another few pints of blood spilled. But at least I took a bunch of Darida's men with me this time.

"We gotta get you to a doctor man."

"No doctor," I reply, unhappily slurring my words a little. "I don't need a doctor."

Tomas is insistent. He's still laboring under the apprehension that I'm an average guy with an average hatred of hospitals.

I managed to convince him to leave his buddies behind and to drag me away from the hangar on a plastic tarp. From there, he put me in a car he found on the airfield and hot-wired it. Then he drove us away from there and into this stupid argument about doctors.

"Put me in a room somewhere, give me a couple of days and I'll be fine, just watch.

"Fine!?" he yells, incredulously. "I don't think you're gonna be fine, my friend!"

"I'm different. You'll see."

I close my eyes again, and by the time I open them we're parked up outside a gas station that looks to have been long-since abandoned. There's a huge sign out front, bearing the name of the petroleum company who supplies it, as well as a few bullet holes for good measure. The pumps have been torn out of the ground, presumably by people looking for a final few gallons.

The shop portion of the building is composed of broken windows, sagging walls, and empty shelves but I'm not exactly feeling picky about accommodation right now.

Tomas drags me out of the car, and I fall to the floor outside with a painful jolt.

"Jesus, man, careful," I rasp at him. He looks at me like I'm a corpse that re-animated and started yelling at him.

Finally, recruiting the use of the blood-stained plastic tarpaulin again he manages to drag me inside, the broken door of the gas station providing little resistance.

Inside, most of the shelves are empty, aside from a couple containing only the most unappealing-looking items: moldy bread, long-expired vegetables, etc. Broken glass litters the floor and there appears to be no power. All in all, it feels very unlikely I'll bump into a doctor here, so I suppose it has that going for it.

Tomas drags me to the wall before letting go of the tarp and collapsing to his knees to regain his breath.

"This ain't how I imagined my day going, you know," he says.

I get the feeling he'd have left me back in the hangar if I hadn't bailed him out of the jail a few days ago. He's a slippery character, but luckily for me a slippery character is just who I need right now.

"What the hell happened back there?" he asks, breathing

normally again but maintaining the same look of perplexed horror on his face.

"We were sent on a recon mission, but they were waiting for us. My whole squad got wiped out. And then I got into a fight with a tank. The tank won."

He shakes his head incredulously. Then he looks closer at my legs, each a horrible mass of amorphous dark red flesh, glistening in the moonlight.

"You're not bleeding anymore at least. How's that even possible?"

"I told you, I'm not like everyone else."

He shakes his head again, but something tells me he's beginning to believe.

"What were you doing at the airport?" I ask, only now beginning to think of the coincidences that united us again.

"Haramat is falling. Darida's men are retreating and surrendering in massive numbers. It won't be long now until he's hanging from some lamppost somewhere. So, me and a couple of boys I know thought we'd explore the airport, see if we could find anything of value there. You wouldn't believe the kind of things we've found already."

"Looting, huh?" I laugh, feeling some discomfort from my ribs as I do so. "Why am I not surprised?"

"I need to go back there; my friends will be waiting for me." I hold my fist up to him – he looks upon the bullet wound in my hand with surprise and disgust before gently fist-bumping me. "I'll come back in a couple of days to pick you up. You sure you'll be okay here?"

"I already feel better," I reply, looking again at the items left on the otherwise empty shelves.

He gets up to leave but pauses in the doorway – his frame blocking the moonlight, basking me in familiar darkness again.

"What are you?" he finally asks, apprehensively. "Some mutant super soldier? Some CIA lab freak? I mean, I've read some stuff online. Heard about the things happening in Area 51 or whatever, but…"

He trails off, seeing my expression harden and perhaps realizing he sounds as crazy as I do now.

"I'll tell you in a couple of days. It'll all make sense."

And then he turns and leaves. I hear the car door open and the engine start.

"Okay Vega, how do we look?"

You've lost a lot of blood, and a substantial portion of the nanomachine network has been lost or damaged, both by the tank's shell and by the efforts to quell the bleeding. But your condition is stable. If you can avoid any extra excitement, you'll be back on your feet within two to three days.

"Two to three days?!" My voice echoes throughout the gas station; luckily, I hear Tomas' car pulling away outside.

"My arm took, what, 36 hours?"

That was an arm. This is two legs. If you wanted to go back to the airport and recover your limbs I could work on re-attaching them, but failing that you'll have to wait until they're rebuilt cell-by-cell.

I'm imaging myself crawling along the desert sands, hauling two severed legs with me. It probably isn't the solution I'm looking for.

I peel my combat vest off, matted with sweat and flecks of blood, and I note the two very impressive black marks where the bullets hit the ceramic plates.

Then I take the rucksack – crumpled and misshapen out of recognition by me landing and lying on it multiple times – off my back, peeling each strap from my shoulders slowly and painfully. Then I go rummaging through it, looking for Dina's cellphone.

To my relief, it's still in one piece and still switches on, but there's no service out here. I wave it around in the air, nonchalantly wondering if it's just my position on the floor, but it's useless.

I lie on my back and close my eyes. I see Dina's face staring back at me. How long has it been since I spoke to her last? Two days? I wish I could get through to her. I can see her now, rushing to take back the capital and finally get her hands around Darida's neck.

But that's one fight I'll have to sit out.

CHAPTER 60

The last couple of days I've felt like a man abandoned on Mars.

I've been laying here, sleeping or watching the sun move across the sky. Occasionally I've crawled to survey the shelves' offerings, managing to pilfer a couple of well-expired pastries, a bag of chips, and a few candy bars. It isn't exactly the vacation Vega wanted me to take, but it's been slow.

Sporadically I hear a car or two pass outside, or an artillery shell going off somewhere, but mostly this little patch of the desert is entirely empty. The war could be over by now and I'd have no idea.

On the other hand, the nanomachines rebuilding my legs have apparently been busy; two large, fleshy mounds of scar tissue have been growing down from the bottom of my thighs this entire time. New flesh, glistening pink in the sun, is blossoming and bubbling away all the time. It's impressive and utterly horrifying.

The itchiness is driving me out of my mind; the only relief I seem to get from any of this is sleeping, which I've done most hours of the day. Still no cell phone service either; it's killing me that I can't get out of here and see Dina again.

I've just woken up and batting a couple of troublesome flies away from my legs when I hear a car pulling up outside. I drag myself across the floor and seat myself on my ass among the broken glass and candy-bar wrappers. I try to cross my gross, fleshy pink legs beneath me, realizing I've got no great excuse for how they look.

To my relief – and, to be honest, my surprise – I see Tomas by the door. He really came back.

"So you're still here," he says casually, strolling in with a sports bag in one hand. He's halfway through saying something else when he sees the state of my legs.

"Holy hell, what happened to you?"

I look at him, barely able to conceal a grin.

"Sit down, you'll get used to it."

I chuckle to myself, realizing that any other kind of reaction would be pointless. He's staring at them; two new legs, a foot and a half longer than the last time he saw them, with a pair of half-formed ankles and feet below, all still a slimy mess of scar tissue.

He drops the sports bag beside me, and then he drops to the floor alongside it, a picture of disbelief, distrust, and disgust.

I tell him about the body, the nanomachines, the miraculous healing, all the hits. He nods along, wide-eyed with an almost fearful look on his face. I think he deserves an explanation about all of this. And even if he tells anyone else, who's gonna believe some drug trafficker?

"So that's how you managed to break us out of that jail?"

I nod, taking the opportunity to take a look inside this sports bag. There's decent food in here: MREs, coffee, dried meats, even fruit. I eagerly tuck in.

"Well, you finally did it," Tomas says with a 1000-yard

stare locked on his face. "You convinced me to get the hell outta this dead-end country."

"Huh?"

"You're telling me there's technology out there that can make kids like you into super soldiers?"

I narrow my eyes at him.

"No offence," he hastily adds, "but what the hell am I still doing out here, running drugs and looting airports like an average schmuck? If there are secret agencies out there with nano-robot-whatever super soldiers, growing whole new arms to slap me about with, what the hell chance do I got?"

He really should have had that thought after getting his car shot up in a drug-deal gone gnarly, or maybe upon being locked up in some underground torture den, but whatever works for him, I guess.

I finish eating, and – using my new baby feet for the first time – hobble out to the car, leaning on Tomas the entire time. I stumble around gingerly like a newborn foal, but eventually I get there.

"Where are you going?" I ask him.

I catch him looking at my feet again before tearing his gaze away to meet my eyes.

"Rachiya, and then Mehdirran, and then home."

"You got anyone waiting for you at home?"

He shakes his head and turns on the engine.

"Not really. I just know I'm not gonna stay here long enough to get on your bad side."

He looks at me with a playful grin on his face, but I can see there's real fear behind it; there's a smile on his lips, but his eyes don't trust me. It's a sight I never thought I'd see. Someone is *afraid* of me.

We get on the road again; after a few miles, I pull Dina's cellphone out again, turn it on, and see a single bar of service. I wait for a few minutes for any messages to catch up but get nothing. No pleasing message tone, no anticipated buzzing; nothing.

I try to call the last number she called me on, but there's no answer. It rings three times before reaching a generic voicemail service. I clench my fingers around the cellphone in frustration; Tomas evidently sees me.

"What's the matter? No signal?"

"No, it's not that," I reply, trying to keep my composure. "I just expected a text or a call or something."

"Things have been crazy out here," Tomas says, taking a hairpin turn in the road far faster than he should; I dig my fingers into the fabric of my seat to steady myself. "The capital fell yesterday. There's pockets of fighting here and there, but the war is over."

The war is over. I really did sit on my ass – surrounded by trash in the worst R&R spot in the world – and sleep through the glorious triumph of the Aljarrian people. Still, that doesn't explain why Dina hasn't been in touch. I've always thought she'd book us first row tickets to see Darida's fall.

I quickly and worriedly tap out a message – filled with the usual platitudes – and hit send. When it's gone, I can barely even remember what I wrote.

"So, what are you gonna do now?" Tomas asks me, drumming his fingers on the steering wheel. "If you're really not CIA, that is."

Those three letters again. If I ever meet a CIA agent, I'm going to ask them why every foreign freedom fighter thinks I'm one of them.

"I can promise you I'm not CIA." I sit back in my seat, trying to put the cellphone out of my mind. "I need to find a friend of mine. And then? I don't know. Maybe I'll stay behind and help with the rebuild. Maybe I'll move on."

"Help the rebuild huh?"

He sounds dubious. I wait for him to launch into another speech, blaming me for thinking I can solve everything and telling me that we're doomed to make things worse for the Aljarrian people, but that speech never comes.

Four hours later I wake up from another snooze. Tomas has the windows ajar, and there's a cool, desert breeze sweeping into the car. I look down and see that my legs are almost back again: the two mounds of flesh at the bottom of my ankles have sculpted themselves into the heel of my foot and extended outwards to form my feet and toes.

"Not long 'til we get to Rachiya," Tomas says, seeing that I'm awake again.

I check Dina's cellphone again to no avail. Then I start looking around the car again, finding a bottle of energy drink in the glovebox, which I crack open.

"Ya know," I say to Tomas, "you don't happen to have another pair of boots, do you?"

He looks at me before looking again at my feet, and some color seems to drain from his face.

"No," he answers, pointing to his own feet. "These are still the same boots I liberated from that guy in the jail cell."

"Liberated, huh," I laugh to myself, daring to investigate Tomas' strange code of ethics again. "Liberate anything else recently? Money? Drugs?"

He looks at me and shrugs slightly.

He turns another corner, and I'm temporarily blinded by the sun hanging lower in the sky.

"Where do you want dropping off in Rachiya?"

"I guess I'd better go see if there's anyone left in Alpha base."

"Ah, the old hotel?" he asks. I'm surprised he knows about it. I can't recall ever seeing him there or hearing him talk about it before.

"Yeah," I answer, "It was a former hotel, but they turned it into the military complex for the rebellion. Cantara was based there. I guess she'll be moving to the capital now, though."

"Buddy, everyone knows about that hotel."

He says it with a certain sly smile on his face, like there's some great secret he's only just figured out I'm not party to.

"What do you mean?"

"It was part of a massive hotel chain before the war," he says, drumming his fingers on the steering wheel excitedly. "Then, when Cantara rose to power in the rebel leadership, she took it over, 'repatriated it' or whatever. All of the old rebel leadership – the sorts of people she had to step on to assume the throne – were imprisoned there."

"Imprisoned?"

"Imprisoned, tortured, murdered," Tomas adds. "The mayor of this town, a couple of rebel generals, a newsreader or two. Hell, even the fruit dealers who went on strike and kicked this whole civil war off disappeared without trace."

We fly around another corner as he drums his fingers ever more angrily.

"People have a habit of disappearing in this country. Darida did it. Cantara does it. And I bet there's all sorts of filthy, hidden secrets underneath that hotel building."

"I've been underneath it, it's an armory," I reply. "The whole place is a lot more mundane than you think. There are generals, reporters, soldiers. There's Cantara and her office. No fruit dealers, no executions, there's certainly nothing as lurid as a torture chamber."

He turns to look at me with that sly, all-knowing grin again.

"Are you sure?" I don't say anything in reply, but I begin to think of Dina. There's surely no chance, is there?

"You know I've ran with some pretty shady characters, don't you?" he asks me, looking over at me, his eyes full of tenacity. "I knew a guy who they called the 'dentist.' He was only a dentist's assistant before the war, but they managed to promote him to pulling people's teeth out to extract confessions. That was all within the hotel."

I snort in derision.

"He told me they'd keep piles of stolen trinkets down there. Gold teeth, jewelry, whatever they could take from the poor folks who'd get on Cantara's bad side. Man, I wish I could have gotten down there and looked through that stuff for myself."

I don't say anything in reply. I just think about that large, hastily painted red door in the armory underneath the hotel. Maybe my first call should be to pay that place a visit and prove that Tomas doesn't know what the hell he's talking about.

CHAPTER 61

Another hour later and we make it to Rachiya. I can already tell the city is in a strange mood; the usual convoys of military vehicles are gone, and the only people left on the streets are older folks carrying large bags and walking slowly throughout the crater-pocked pavements.

It's quiet here; the whole focus must be on Haramat now. The banners of Cantara's smiling face still hang high, swaying gently with the desert breeze, but I can't sense much excitement or jubilation in the air; everyone is still just dodging the broken slabs in the sidewalk. The war may be won, but the struggle goes on.

"Well, it's the second time we've done this," Tomas says, pulling up a block away from the former hotel. "I'd tell you to look after yourself, but..."

He looks at my feet again, now almost completely grown back, and the tattered, blood-soaked rags of my former pants hanging high over my thighs.

"I'll be fine," I tell him, still trying to mask my unease at everything he told me. "You're getting out of Aljarran?"

"Tonight," he replies. He pauses before speaking again.

"Don't take this the wrong way, man, but I hope I never see you again."

I smile and hold out my hand for him to shake. He takes it, squeezing and shaking it.

"I feel the same way, my drug-running friend."

I get out, feeling the hot asphalt burn the soles of my feet. I instantly arouse the glances of a couple of older people walking by, but they continue on, no doubt conditioned to seeing blood-stained guys in military fatigues by now.

Before I can slam the door shut and wave him away, he says one last thing to me. "Don't let Cantara manipulate you, man," he says dejectedly, brushing a strand of blond hair from his face. "These so-called leaders, they're no good for us. You're worth a 1000 of them."

I nod, trying to parse his meaning. He's not someone I ever held in high regard. A drug runner, a criminal, a thief, but he did keep his word to me.

I watch him speed off, leaving me in a cloud of dust that I wave away. I check Dina's cellphone again, but after seeing nothing I decide to pace back to the hotel and get some answers for myself.

I round the corner of the square and see the customary black beret-clad guard, holding his rifle with one hand and a cigarette with the other. He does a double take upon seeing me – my pants now appearing like fashionably torn, red shorts – and begins speaking on his radio. Luckily, I think he recognizes me from when we left.

"No others," I say to him gravely when I get close, speaking of Estevez, Abbas, Zahid, and Riyad. I don't know if he understands the words, but maybe he can understand the tone.

I walk inside, and the slightly warm, stale air hits me. It's dusty in here now; where there were once 100s of people marching up and down every corridor, there's almost no-one here. Just a girl of maybe 21 behind the front desk, looking me up and down suspiciously.

I point at my legs, and then point downstairs to the armory, as if to tell her I need a change of clothes. She looks baffled – no doubt wondering what the hell happened to the legs of my pants – and nods, and I head downstairs.

It's the same old armory – empty steel shelves and clothes racks. There's a man standing guard – the same guard as last time, I think – beside that ominous, mysterious red door, and a couple of other soldiers pass me as I enter, giving me the same strange looks I'm becoming accustomed to. I hear their footsteps echoing through the staircase as they leave.

I pick out one of three pairs of boots left, as well as some poorly folded pants and a pair of socks and change my clothes within one of the rows of empty shelves. Then I turn my attention to the red door.

You're going to go in there, aren't you?

Vega obviously knows my intent. My eyes lingering on the door and the guard a little too long, I imagine. I kneel to tie my lace and mumble into the collar of my jacket.

"You guessed it."

The complex looks to be running on a skeleton staff, Vega goes on to say. *You might be lucky enough to just have that one man to deal with.*

"Maybe I can talk my way in," I mumble to myself again. Vega doesn't answer that one. He must remember my attempts to sweet-talk the detective back home.

I finish tying my laces and walk slowly over to the guard, who maintains his dutiful stare right past me, holding his rifle with both hands close to his chest.

"Hey, man," I say to him, "what's behind the door there?"

Finally, he averts his gaze from over my shoulder, both of his eyes darting to meet mine without moving his head. He arches his eyebrows before repeating the same broken English mantra as before: "No enter."

"Ahh c'mon man," I say as his grip tightens on his rifle. "I'm curious."

He finally turns his head to face mine before baring his teeth at me and saying a word in his native tongue.

I back away and try to make a face like I'm sorry. I turn on my heel so that I have my back to him, and I see his posture relax out of the corner of my eye.

Then, as quickly and brutally as I can, I spin back around with my elbow, striking him cleanly in the jaw with it. The pain hits me instantly, resonating all the way down to my hand; it feels like I spiked the tip of my elbow on a bowling ball.

The guard, however, isn't troubled by any such feeling of pain or discomfort. He crumples to the floor, immediately unconscious. His chest rises and falls with each breath, but his eyes are closed and his expression is empty; there's nobody home.

Ruthless, but efficient, Vega says in my ear.

"Did I break my goddamn elbow?" I cry, still feeling it throb.

No break or fracture detected. Hitting bone on bone hurts, Kris.

If I'm ever high enough on my own supply to wear my own 'superhero' outfit, I've absolutely got to include gloves and elbow pads.

I step past the downed guard and try to open the door. It has a large, red handle, crudely painted with a single, uneven layer of paint. I push down on it, and feel the entire door shudder with a metallic *clank*.

I push it open; slowly, it obliges, sliding along the concrete floor with a grinding, painful howl. Another blanket of hot, stale hair hits me in the face, but this time worse than before. Damp and acrid, it feels like no natural air ever gets into this place.

I see one long corridor, lit by the very occasional dim twilight of a solitary bulb. There are puddles of water on the floor and strange stains decorating the walls. In contrast to the clinical white florescent light of the armory behind me, someone evidently doesn't care much for shining a light in any of these corners.

To my right are a series of unremarkable doors, all of them closed. To my left is a set of empty lockers like those you'd find at a high school. Probably a remnant of the hotel's past life when it had staff without guns and black berets.

You should do something about him, he might wake up.

I look back and see the unconscious body of the guard. I drag him through the threshold of the door, and then push the door shut behind me. It closes with a pleasing, echoing *clunk*.

I look around and get an idea right away. I pick the guard up, hooking my hands beneath his armpits, and use all my strength to haul him up to my height. Then, I help him into one of the lockers and stash his unconscious frame inside it before closing it. *If it was good for me in high school, it's good enough for you, my friend*, I think.

I walk a couple of steps and open the first door; a blank, characterless brown door with a steel handle. Inside I flip a light on and see a few large, industrial-scale laundry machines, grimy and dusty. Nothing controversial in here it seems.

I'm detecting a large concentration of airborne chemicals here, Vega says. *Hypochlorous acid and chlorine gas are present in the air and on surfaces.*

"That makes sense if it's a former laundry for the hotel, right?"

I move on, exiting that room and exploring the next, behind a similar dull, brown door and featuring the same trio of large, industrial washing machines. There is the unmistakable smell of cleaning products in the air and a large groove in the concrete floor looking like something heavy was slid across it, but aside from that the room appears to be legit.

I walk to the next room, panicking slightly how I'm going to the explain to the folks upstairs why I knocked out a guard and hid him in a locker. When I push the door open and find the light switch, I see this room is different.

There are stacks of cages – two, three, sometimes four high. Some have crumpled or broken bars, some are tarnished with red, rusty stains, and some are otherwise spotless. They look like the sorts of cages people keep dogs in down at the shelter.

"What the hell," I find myself mumbling, as I walk up to one of them. I brush my fingertips along one of the cages – one with the dark red scarring – and wait for Vega to give me his verdict.

Dried human blood.

I stop cold in my tracks and slowly retract my fingers into my palm. Jesus, what if Tomas is right? What if we've been sitting on Cantara's dirty secret this entire time? I look around, and the same whiff of cleaning products hits me. Has someone been trying to clean this place up?

The blood stain is maybe a month old, Vega continues, *given the decomposition, but it's impossible to say with certainty. And there's one more thing: I can detect evidence of two of the chemical pre-cursors to sarin nerve gas.*

"What?"

Vega lists the long, unpronounceable chemical names of two compounds.

The two compounds on their own are harmless, but when mixed they will be the same deadly nerve agent used in Safiqq. It's a high probability someone stored the two compounds here at some point.

"So she was right."

I leave the room, hurriedly pacing to the next. I get to the fourth and final door – another dull, unremarkable door – and hover my palm over the handle, hesitating. There's a thought that scratches away at the back of my mind: the thought that I'll find something terrible. It's a thought that's impossible to ignore but too dreadful to confront.

Finally – on the count of the 10th heart beat I feel palpating through my body – I turn the door handle and step inside. When I find the light switch, I see that it isn't like any of the last three rooms.

There are coffins in here. Wooden coffins, more than six feet long and maybe a foot wide. And there are dozens of the stacked on top of each other or loose on the floor. A couple have the lids slid slightly off and a few have no lids at all.

I expect a more incriminating smell, but the odor in here is the same as elsewhere; the same mind-numbing mixture of cleaning chemicals.

I take a deep breath and approach the coffins, seeing that the ones without lids are empty. I push the lids off the couple that were ajar and see that they're empty too. Empty coffins? What the hell is this all about?

I make my way over to one of the sealed coffins and give it a nudge. It rattles slightly, like a box full of toys. There's something in it, and I don't think it's a body.

It's nailed shut in three places, but after digging my fingers into the soft, unvarnished wood, I manage to prize the lid up and off. I push it to the floor and look inside.

The first thing my eyes are drawn to is the garish yellow case of a cellphone sitting proudly atop the pile. There are dozens of smartphones here – maybe hundreds – all different sizes, shapes, and states of repair. I pick one up and see what appears to be dried, crusty crimson blood on the screen.

Below and between the cellphones lie a sea of smaller items. Tiny silver broaches, sparkling in the light; golden necklaces, tangled up with countless others. There are even what look to be wedding rings; I plunge my hand into the box and find a dusty gold ring engraved with a phrase in Aljarrian.

"This is what Tomas was talking about," I say to myself, dazed.

I push the coffin to the ground; it falls, spilling its contents all over the floor, with beads of silver and white pearls rolling into the dark corners of the room.

I turn my attention to the one underneath, digging my fingertips into the gap between the lid and the frame, and prize it off. Immediately I'm dazzled by the precious metals on show, lit by the dim overhead light. Cigar boxes, bracelets, even a diamond-studded watch are in here.

I dig around inside with my right hand, hurting my fingertips against the various hard, shiny gems and jewelry. I pull out a large, gaudy earring; it's slightly tarnished silver with what look to be diamonds embedded in it. But occasionally a diamond is missing, and what lies in its place is a layer of deep red, dried blood.

I turn around and look to the sealed coffin closest to the door. It's been haphazardly dumped on the floor, set aside from the others. I'm guessing this is the one they sealed last.

I prize it open, and on my knees on the dirty, damp concrete I dig my hand around inside. There's a handheld gaming console and another obnoxiously huge wristwatch, plus a wince-inducing gold tooth, and a white gold engagement ring. I pick up a leather wallet, stitched with the name Masood, and a silver locket with an accompanying dirty silver necklace.

My fingers are drawn to the locket; I carefully pick it out with both hands, feeling a bitter, acidic rage building within me.

My fingertips find the tiny, metal clasp that keeps it shut. I close my eyes and unclasp it.

When I open it, the sum of all my fears is confirmed. It's the sapphire: the one that I created. The one that I gave to Dina.

This is *her* locket. This is *her* sapphire. In a coffin, filled with teeth pulled from people's mouths and jewelry stained with blood.

I think of the last time I saw her – sleeping, innocently and quietly – and find myself squeezing the locket. I ease my grip just as I feel it begin to buckle under the pressure.

"What happened to her?" I ask myself out loud. "What did she do to her?"

Vega is silent. I clench my fist around the locket and shove my fist into the cold concrete floor beside me, pushing myself to my feet.

Every time I close my eyes – every time I blink – I see her face staring back at me. The locket sits burning in my palm, radiating heat and anger throughout my entire body; I find myself charging down the dim, dark corridor, and before I realize it I'm pushing the heavy, painfully wailing red door to one side.

I need answers, and I can only get them from one person: Cantara.

CHAPTER 62

I find myself in the corridor outside of her office and everything around me is a blur. There's a dissonant chorus of shouting from all angles, and a hand clenches itself around my upper right bicep. I step away from it, looking to find out who has the stones to stop me, and see all six feet six inches of Major General Rahal.

"Kris," he says with urgency, "what the hell are you doing?"

I turn around to see another couple of guards wearing black berets and looking at me with urgent, bitter gazes.

"You can't just charge past her security," Rahal clarifies. I feel his grip ease on my bicep and I take a step back, still dazed and led by the adrenaline surging through me. "If you want to see her, you need to ask."

I look behind again and see everyone's expressions soften. One of the guards begins to walk away.

"Sorry," I say sheepishly. I try to regain some of my composure, while still feeling the locket in my palm pulsating with vengeful energy. "I just got back from the airport; our entire team was lost."

Rahal looks concerned; his expression turns from displeasure to unease; whether real or affected, I don't know.

"Yes, I did worry about your mission when we didn't hear back from Estevez."

I think of Dina again and the cellphone she never answered.

"She's clearing up a few loose ends. We're heading to Haramat today; she's going to address the public there."

A few loose ends, huh? I look around me and sit on an empty chair, intending to wait.

"I'll tell her you're here," Rahal then says before looking at me expectantly. "It's been a bitter, bitter conflict, but it's over Kris. The war is won."

I stare up at him, barely concealing the tears in the corners of my eyes, and nod without so much as a smile on my face.

Around 10 minutes go by with me sitting silently and still. I see bodies pass me and hear cheerful-sounding words spoken, but it's all a haze.

Rahal's giant frame appears in my peripheral vison again.

"Okay, Cantara will see you now."

I stand up and pace the remaining steps to the next door, tightening my grip on the locket.

Cantara's office lies beyond this one last corridor. Red walls, with the occasional dull painting, and a large, ornate wooden door lying at the end of it. I charge down it, walking purposefully, my footsteps echoing as I do so.

Kris, be calm, be composed.

Vega's advice rings in my ears, but I don't give him any kind of acknowledgement. I turn the door handle.

"Kris, I was worried about you."

She's sitting behind her desk, as per usual, her tiny figure hidden behind stacks of boxes. The messy files and papers are gone, all presumably packed away in anticipation of her triumphant return to the capital. That snowglobe – the curiously out of place vision of Haramat under snowfall – still remains.

She's wearing a purple suit with a white shirt underneath. She looks dainty, fragile even. I hover by the edge of her desk, trying to conjure up the words I need.

"Are you okay?" she asks, seeing that I'm clearly not. "Sit down."

"The airport," I finally say, my voice struggling to make it out of my throat unbroken. "It was a bloodbath. Estevez, Abbas, all of them, they're gone."

She shakes her head and rubs her forehead with her palm. It's a display of anguish I've seen before and one that I'm sure is well-practiced.

"I'm so sorry. We thought we could trust the intelligence we received, but something obviously went wrong along the way. I'm glad to see you're uninjured though."

Uninjured, huh?

"The Butcher, the gas attack, the airport," I go on to say, each memory stabbing at me like an icepick. "I've survived some catastrophes, haven't I?"

"You have," she replies, either not detecting, or choosing to ignore the irony in my words. "You should be proud. You're a true hero to the people of Aljarran."

"Dina," I reply, almost immediately. Cantara's face contorts into puzzlement. "Dina is a true hero."

"Of course," she replies. "Please pass along my best wishes to her."

She averts his eyes from my own and looks down at something on her desk. I get the feeling she's trying to move me along.

"Thank you for coming to see me Kris and do let me know if there's anything you need."

I stand up, but rather than leaving as she might expect, I lean over the desk, and hover my fist over the paper in front of her before opening my palm and dropping the locket in front of her.

She looks up at me quizzically and calmly, before picking it up between her thumb and forefinger.

"What's this? What am I looking at?"

"I know the truth about the gas attack," I tell her, never breaking eye contact. She puts the locket down and stands up on the other side of the desk before crossing her arms defiantly.

"What are you talking about Kris?"

"Dina knew it from the start. She suspected something didn't fit. She spoke to survivors and other doctors who'd worked on the victims. She'd heard about the suspicious packages driven to Safiqq, and the coordinated release of the gas, quite unlike what you'd expect from a shelling from afar."

"Listen to yourself," she says, breaking eye contact with me. "You think I'd gas my own soldiers? You're delirious."

"I've been downstairs, Cantara," I add, saying her name with all the venom I can muster. "I know you or your worker drones stored the precursor chemicals down there."

She meets my eyes again, and after a couple of fraught moments she seems to take a deep breath.

"Do you know how many of my compatriots have died in this war? How many of my old friends I've buried? By my count, this civil war has cost a million lives. Darida spent a million lives to remain in power."

She leans over the desk slightly, her fingers digging into the surface like a set of sharpened talons.

"You know I used to work here. I was a receptionist at this very hotel; my father got me the job before he became president. My first job at 18 years old."

She tries to laugh, but there's too much sadness on her face to be convincing. She looks up to the ceiling.

"There's a photograph in a briefing room we use around

here. It's a picture of me and my old friends: the entire staff of this hotel some 30 years ago."

I think back to that photograph hanging in the briefing room. It didn't occur to me that a young Cantara would be in it, but then again I wasn't looking for her.

"Every morning when I get a briefing on the citizens dead or missing in action, I listen out for the names of the people I worked with here. And every morning, I mark the faces of my fallen friends. Four years into this terrible war I've lost most of them. Two-thirds, almost. Friends that I'll never see again. That will never come back."

I feel the rage rising within me again. We've all got friends who won't come back.

"It's my duty to end this war, Kris, and I have to make tough decisions. The support we got from abroad was essential. We couldn't have won the war without it."

She takes another sharp intake of breath and looks at me with watery, despondent eyes.

"Yes, I staged the gas attack. If I hadn't, we would have never received the help we needed. I'll go to my grave knowing that."

She admits it, but I'm still not done. I want the whole truth.

"I saw the cages downstairs. I saw the coffins. I saw the valuables you've stolen from the people you disappeared."

I see her claws dig further into the desk.

"You want to know what this is?" I point at the locket. "This is Dina's locket. She'd never part from it."

I put my fists on the table and lean closer to Cantara.

"Where is she?" I ask.

We stare at each other for a few seconds at the most, but it feels like a hateful eternity. Finally, she blinks.

"I don't know," she says. Her voice quakes as she says it. I don't believe her.

"Where is she?" I ask again, my tone harshening, every word spit through my teeth with barely concealed rage.

"I don't know," she repeats, leaning closer to me and meeting my aggression with her own. I look into her eyes – large, deep, brown, and expressive – and they remind me of Dina's for the briefest second.

"But so what?" she finally asks. I feel my right hand grasping something on the desk; smooth, cold, heavy. "I wouldn't let anybody hinder my plans to end this war. If she wanted to do Darida's dirty work, she deserved everything she got!"

I clench my fist around the object in my right hand, and in one furious, thoughtless motion, pick it up and throw it at her. I feel it leave my fingertips and watch it fly with every millimeter of nanobot-assisted precision I have.

It hits her forehead with a thunderous, deathly sound, like the impact of two bowling balls on a fatal collision course.

The sight makes me panic. I barely remember grasping it, and I don't even know what the object was, only that it was hard, heavy, and that it would hurt. I look behind her and see the snowglobe bounce off a wall and fall to the floor. It has small smatterings of blood on its glass surface.

Cantara stands there, silent and motionless, her eyes having drifted off into the space behind me. The room is gripped by a strange, deathly silence. A drop of blood then falls from her hairline. The drop soon becomes a trail; and one of her eyelids begins to twitch.

"Oh God, what did I do?" I mumble to myself. I feel a wave of dread wash over me and my heart beating through my chest. I'm gripped by peculiar temptation to load a reset that doesn't exist.

Cantara falls to the floor, landing on her right side in a clumsy heap. The blood begins to gush from her forehead, soaking the carpet below it.

I clamber across the room and around the desk before

helplessly standing there, unsure what to do next. Her eyes are glazed over; she's drawing no breath.

I drop to my knees beside her and put my fingers on her neck. I keep them there for as long as it takes.

She's dead, Vega confirms. *Massive, sudden catastrophic trauma to the brain I would presume.*

I look at the snowglobe, peacefully nestled in the carpet beside her. There are a few drops of blood on it, and within a snowstorm rages.

I probably don't have to tell you that this represents a problem.

Vega's voice snaps me back to reality. I stand up and look around the room. It's still deathly silent, but it won't stay that way for long. I grab Dina's locket from the desk and slide it into my pocket before seeking advice I should have sought a while back.

"Vega, how do I get out of this?"

The panels on the walls, he replies. I look up to see the shiny, stainless-steel sheets laid intermittently over the walls. *Pry one of them away.*

I do as he says, digging my fingertips between the wall and the panel, tunneling them as far as I can to the crevice before pulling with all the strength I have. I feel the smallest, almost imperceptible movement and redouble my efforts.

Half of the panel pops off with a loud *prang,* bent away from the wall and quivering slightly. I see what it concealed: a window with a black grill separating smaller panels of glass.

I look around for a handle and manage to force it open. I take one last look at this whole, horrific scene before striding out onto the windowsill outside. I'm on the second floor; the sky is darkening and the ground below seems to be a courtyard of some sort within the hotel. There are lamps, benches, and slightly browning grass.

I jump down, landing on the grass with a painful jolt to my ankles. My newly grown bones didn't need that. I manage to haul myself to my feet and limp away down the courtyard, past an ornate archway onto the quiet street beyond.

There's an open window nearby with a radio blasting out some Aljarrian pop song, along with the smell of something being fried, but I'm far from hungry right now. The smell makes me sick to my stomach.

It's only a matter of time until they discover her body, and then another short matter of time until they commence a nationwide manhunt for you. The chaos and jubilation of the country's liberation could delay things somewhat, but you're on a countdown if you want to get out of here alive.

I see a couple of tan-camo-clad military man walking; I straighten my posture and try to look past them, rather than at them, desperate not to arouse their attention. They stroll past me without any sort of acknowledgement. Any news about their leader's unlikely passing surely hasn't reached them yet.

I limp a couple more steps down the street, navigating my way over the cobbles in the pavement. There's a set of car headlights slowly approaching behind me; my shadow dances on the wall in front.

"Hey Kris,"

I feel that shock of panic again: a defibrillating blast directly to my heart. I turn around and see a small two-seater car that's seen far better days. Behind the wheel, with his head partially sticking out of the driver's side window, is a familiar face.

"Oh, Salman, right?"

He smiles, nodding at me. I haven't seen him for a while; before the Butcher, I believe. The car slows to a standstill beside me.

"How are things my man?"

Shall I tell him everything? That I just assassinated the leader of his country?

"Just overthrew a tyrant," I reply, trying to force a smile.

"It feels good, doesn't it?" He laughs; I know he thinks I'm talking about Darida. "Four long years we've waited for this."

I smile again, and then wipe my mouth with the back of my hand, feeling my eyes beginning to well up with tears.

"Everyone's traveling to Haramat to see Cantara's first speech," he says as I limp to his driver side window. "Are you going?"

"I mean, I suppose so, yes."

I hadn't even thought about it until now. If I had my wits about me, I'd be trying to escape the country as quickly as I could. In a matter of hours I'm going to be the most wanted man in the country.

"Get in," he says, disappearing back through the open window and behind the windshield. "I'll give you a lift."

I always expected to see Darida's fall with Dina by my side. I find her locket in my pocket and roll it between my fingertips. I can't be there with you Dina, but I can be there to witness the culmination of everything you fought for.

I walk across to the passenger side and let myself in. Salman smiles at me hospitably before twisting a dial on the radio and beginning the drive.

I'll worry about escaping the country later. All I know is that escaping Rachiya feels like the right thing to do now, and hopefully among all the frantic chaos of a newly liberated city I can slip away unnoticed.

I sit back in my seat, staring out of the window as we drive.

Maybe there's a chance she's still out there somewhere. She lost her locket in the hotel, and it was thrown carelessly into one of those coffins.

But deep down, I know that isn't true.

I know she's gone. I'll never see her again.

This desert, this country, this war, I feel like it's taken everything from me.

Dina's words, true for her then and true for me now.

CHAPTER 63

Poor Salman. The man has had to sit there, trying to engage me in small talk the entire journey. Eventually, it seems he gave up and we travel in silence.

I've been clutching Dina's locket, staring out at the dark wastes of Aljarran, trying to process exactly what has just happened.

The innocent, war-wearied people of Aljarran just deposed their mass-murdering tyrannical leader. They'll likely never learn that the heir-apparent was another mass-murdering tyrant; only that she was killed in cold blood by a foreign intruder. What happens now?

I think of all the times I trusted Cantara. I let her put my life on the line, as well as the lives of my friends. Then I think of all the times Dina told me not to trust her. She was right, I was wrong.

Suddenly, I can't get the bullet that killed my mother out of my mind. Another deadly weapon flying through time and space on a course that would change my world forever.

Will Aljarran be better off without Cantara? I sure hope so.

Will I be able to escape Aljarran? Is there even any point?

"We're almost here," Salman says. I bolt upright in my

seat, back to the here and now. I hear car horns in the distance – a melody of creatively pitched honks and pips, the soundtrack to the wildest street party imaginable.

The city is dark, its buildings illuminated by streetlamps and fires. We pass a group of men and women dancing in the street – Salman swerves to avoid hitting them. I see a teenager scaling a lamppost, some 20-feet high in the air, trying to tear down a banner bearing Darida's grinning face.

There's a great orange glow in the distance behind the towers and domes of Haramat's center. It grows and shrinks rhythmically. At first I think it's just light pollution from the vibrant celebrations, but the closer we get, the more I see it for what it really is: fire, and a huge one at that.

Salman begins chanting something from his open window; a group of men on the pavement follow. I see a procession of desperate-looking people in tattered clothing to my left, with their hands out, beseeching the line of cars for aid. Refugees, I presume. I have to shake my head despondently at them and they soon move on.

A man walks up to Salman's window as we're stuck in traffic; they begin speaking in their native tongue before he walks away. I feel a needle of worry, wondering if the news about Cantara is here yet.

"So, they're burning the palace," Salman says. I look over at him to see he has a sly, satisfied smile on his face. "Darida built it when he took power. The people hated it."

I look again at the orange haze on the horizon; a vibrant, vengeful halo around the city of Haramat. It's like the entire city has been turned into a crucible upon which every last memory of Darida's regime will be burned.

We pull up to a hill overlooking the burning palace. There's a bronze statue of Darida here, wearing military regalia – tall, proud, and ostentatious – but a bunch of rebel soldiers, plus a dozen or so citizens, have already slung ropes around it, ready to pull it down.

We watch as they tie the ropes to the bumper of a truck, and after a couple of abortive attempts they manage to get enough traction to send the thing toppling to the ground. It falls face-first, sending splinters of bronze in every direction.

A rapturous cheer erupts from the gathered crowd. I permit myself a small smile; Dina would have loved this scene. I'm at least glad I could have witnessed it.

Something small and feather-light lands in my hair. I brush it out and take a look at my hand afterwards. It's a tiny, white snowflake like piece of ash, I think.

I peer over the column where the statue once stood and see the fires burning downhill: Darida's opulent palace up in roaring flames. I feel a gust of wind and another sprinkling of ash from the fires. Snow in Haramat, just as the snowglobe predicted.

"Hey, look," I say to Salman, but see that he's gone. I look back at the car, and then take the short walk to the statue lying in ruins, but he's still nowhere to be found.

I suppose I should get around to disappearing too. I turn around and make a bee-line for an alleyway between two apartment buildings, full of open windows and loud music from within. I only get a couple of steps before I hear someone call my name.

"Kris!" I turn around; it's Salman. He's standing in a secluded corner of the square far from the crowd with a cellphone to his ear. "Over here!"

I slowly walk over to him as the crowd gathers on the hillside to watch the palace aflame. I see them with their backs to us, dancing jubilantly in the falling ash.

"Hey, I was thinking I might get out of here," I tell him as I draw near. "I'm not really a party kinda guy."

"Oh, sure," he says, putting the cellphone down. "Just one thing before you go."

I feel the presence of someone behind; the faintest change of air pressure around me or maybe just the trillion nanomachines in my body telling me something isn't right. I begin to turn my head but feel a burst of sudden pain that contorts every muscle in my body and puts me straight onto the floor.

I hear a yell, a high-pitched scream that leave my lips, but I don't realize until it's over that it's mine. When I open my eyes again, I see Salman and another man standing over me with the unknown man holding something malevolent-looking weapon.

I stare at Salman with desperate pleading eyes, but see no mercy in his or his friend's.

He thrusts the weapon into my crumpled body, eliciting another few moments of agonizing pain as every muscle in my body constricts and tightens. I see the blue flickers of electricity out of the corner of my eye as I thrash around in the dirt. Clearly a weapon my futuristic suit of armor can't protect against: an electric stun gun.

"Hey, you've got the wrong—"

I don't even finish my sentence before Salman sticks a giant piece of tape over my mouth. I then watch as a black bag is placed over my head, and I'm plunged into darkness.

I feel them slip a pair of tight steel handcuffs on me, and painfully pick me up by my two cuffed wrists, feeling like they could dislocate my shoulders.

They walk me forward, and I hear a vehicle's engine idling and the unmistakable sound of a sliding van door. I know they want to put me in that van, and I know I have to do everything I can to resist them.

I hold my breath before attempting to mount my escape. I backheel the shin of the guy behind me on my right; he yelps in pain. I try to break their hold on my wrist, gyrating myself forward clumsily, but I soon find myself riding the lightning again.

I scream and arch my back, finding myself on the floor once more. They painfully pick me up to my feet – hands grasping my wrists and wrenching them up again – and into the back of the van I go. I graze my fingertips and scrape my nails on its hard wood flooring, but it's no use. The door slides shut.

Well, this is a predicament, Vega says dryly. I make a muffled, grunting noise through the tape on my mouth. *Hold the chain that connects the handcuffs with both hands; the nanomachines on your fingertips will work to degrade the steel.*

I hear the van's engine roar to life, and almost instantly I'm jostled to the back of the van by its rapid getaway. I find a more comfortable position, sitting with my back to the cold metal frame of the van, and do as Vega says, grasping the chain between my fingertips tightly.

It should take 30 minutes or less, depending on the quality of the handcuffs.

My life potentially hinges on whether Cantara's army sourced poor-quality handcuffs. How did it come to this?

The world feels a lot smaller right now; all I can hear is the van screeching around corners and accelerating down roads. All I can feel is the steel chain heating up between my fingers. And I can't see a thing.

They haven't killed me yet, which must count for something. Maybe I'm due a pre-execution dressing down from the generals or some farcical trial for the public? Either way, their delay is my opportunity.

I can't let it end this way; I can't become another body in one of Aljarran's mass graves. I may be legally dead already, but as soon as this van comes to a stop I'm fighting with every sinew, drop of blood, and nanomachine that I have.

I'm waiting – tears in my eyes, the taste of blood in my mouth – for no longer than 10 minutes before I hear the van pull onto a gravel driveway and come to a stop shortly afterwards. I test the sturdiness of the chain, but every link appears to be intact still.

With a loud, invasive racket, the van door slides open. I sit motionless, waiting to feel hands on me. The van's suspensions sink as another set of feet climb aboard, but I feel nothing yet.

After a few moments of holding my breath in anticipation, the black bag is whisked off my head. The lights are blinding, but I quickly adjust to the scene.

The van is parked within a large, empty warehouse, and there are four people in front of me, one of them hopping out of the van with the bag in his hand, and one of them pointing a handgun in my direction. Salman is the other, watching me with pensive, suspicious eyes.

All of them, aside from Salman, have smart, tucked-in white shirts, along with an assortment of colorful ties. Not what I expected from the late Cantara's hit squad for sure.

A man in the middle with short, neat black hair and glasses smiles at me. He's white, and his tie is decorated with a motif of the stars and stripes. He has a pistol in his hand.

"So," he says, in a decidedly US accent. "You're the American raising hell in Aljarran, huh?"

I sit motionless; the gun is pointed way too closely at my face to commence any song and dance right now.

The American straightens his tie.

"I'm special agent Thomas," he announces, before saying those same three letters that have followed me everywhere during my adventures in Aljarran…

"CIA."

AFTERWORD

To be continued in The Gift book two: DRONE.

After the cataclysmic end to his time as a freedom fighter, Kris finds himself captured and blindfolded in the back of a van. He comes to believe this may be it – his end is near - only to unbelievably discover that his kidnappers are fellow Americans.

It's soon revealed that the CIA has monitored him for a while, and after quickly learning of his misdeeds in Aljarran, they decide to capture him before the nation's warring factions can, and throw him in a black site prison. They know nothing of his secret powers, but find him intriguing nonetheless…

Kris soon learns that they wish to make him an offer. They tell him they'll release him on one condition: that he assassinates a disloyal former agent, rumored to be a big player in the drug trade in South America. However, with the ghosts of Aljarran still haunting him, can Kris become the CIA's monster for hire?

Thank you for reading; please leave me a review if you have the time, and follow me on Facebook to hear the latest news about the sequel.

Printed in Great Britain
by Amazon